W9-CAR-787

Praise for
GENNITA
LOW

"Few authors can hit the ground running and immediately prove they are genre forces to be reckoned with—Low is one of those special few. Her hard-edged, gritty and romantic books are genuine thrill rides."
—*Romantic Times BOOKreviews* on *The Hunter* (4½ stars, Top Pick)

"*[The Hunter]* is a book I highly recommend to anyone who wants a sexy, thrilling adventure with just the right touch of romance mixed in!"
—*The Romance Reader's Connection*

"An intense novel…great romantic suspense with military flavor."
—*Romance Junkies* on *The Protector*

"Gennita Low delivers a gritty, powerhouse novel of suspense and intrigue…a roller-coaster ride of nonstop action."
—Merline Lovelace, *USA TODAY* bestselling author, on *The Protector*

"Intriguing, intelligent and emotional…to the top of the keeper shelf for this one!"
—*The Romance Reader's Connection* on *Facing Fear*

"A true masterpiece."
—*The Road to Romance* on *Into Danger*

GENNITA LOW

VIRTUALLY HIS

MIRA®

ISBN-13: 978-0-7783-2448-5
ISBN-10:   0-7783-2448-6

VIRTUALLY HIS

www.MIRABooks.com

Printed in U.S.A.

To Mother and Father
To Magic girl—Mom misses you every day
To Ranger Buddy, virtually bigger than life
To Stash, virtually mine

ACKNOWLEDGMENTS

My special thanks to Maria Hammon and Dee Clingman, who patiently read and reread my chapters. I'm sorry I kept the secret identity of the commando from you two! You are gems. *Terima kasih!*

Hugs and love to my agent, Elizabeth Trupin-Pulli, who always believes in me.

Thank you to my wonderful editor, Tracy Farrell, who shares in my vision of Super Soldier Spy.

Thank you also to these special groups of romance readers:

1) TDD Delphites, especially Karen King, J.P., Mirmie Caraway, Katherine Lazo, Cherry Bo Berry Adair, Kylie "Susan" Brant, Sherrilyn Kenyon, Sandy "Sadista" Still, who have been my lifeline and support all these years

2) RBL Romantica Romance readers, especially Leiha Ha and Jaycee, whose love for the romance genre is legendary

3) GLow World Yahoo Readers Group, always there to answer my questions.

All of you have a special place in my heart.

Author's Note

In 1975, research into remote viewing was initiated at the request of the Central Intelligence Agency (CIA) under a program called SCANATE (Scan By Coordinates). In 1978, after a series of successful tests, the Army Intelligence and Security Command (INSCOM) initiated a project called GRILLFLAME utilizing military personnel to perform as remote viewers. These projects morphed into STARBURST, and then STARGATE. In 1995, information about these activities was finally released by the CIA and the American Institutes for Research (AIR) prior to the projects' termination.

According to current release of information, there are no further remote-viewing experimentations in the military or CIA.

Other resources of interest from the Internet:

www.oddcast.com/home/index.php?id=141

Memo

CC: Intelligence Security Command (INSCOM), Task Force Unit Chief for Operation; Los Alamos Task Force Unit Chief Scientist for Operation <redacted>; CIA Remote Viewing Sector Task Force Unit Chief for Operation SuperVision (SV); Defense Intelligence Agency (DIA) Asymmetrical Strategic Counterintelligence Warfare Task Force Unit Chief for Operation <redacted>;Armed Forces Medical Intelligence Center (AFMIC) Task Force Unit Chief Bio-Scientist for Operation Bio-Bot; COS COMMAND <redacted>

The new century calls for new measures of defense and Intel gathering. By the President's orders under the Homeland Security Act, all the operations above will be combined under one new operation to create a new weapon.

In the last decade, COS COMMAND's V-Program has proven very successful in our infiltration and search/destroy operations. Our COS commando unit remains one of our elite teams.

Welcome to our new and improved: **The Supersoldier-Spy.**

The resources from tests from all departments listed above will be shared to create a total soldier-spy of body, mind and spirit. His body will be trained by the best in our defense branches—military and covert warfare. He will be chosen from the fittest among his peers within the groups known for their fighting spirit and skills.

Out of these, he must also fit the CIA phase requirement. Once we find this soldier, his mind will be put through the supercovert remote viewing (RV) program, a system that will teach him to see with an inner vision. He is expected to use this skill to overcome barriers that our chain of command might create.

The spirit of our superwarrior will be naturally strong and fearless, with these essentials enhanced by a top-secret biochemical serum, created and tested by our Intel scientists. Our different versions have shown that the use of it curbs emotions, especially in times of stress, thus enhancing willpower, clarity and determination during the mission. He will need less sleep, and feel less pain when injured.

This serum will be the unknown factor. It has been tried under varying conditions, never with a soldier capable of remote-viewing. Our goal is to use both to our advantage.

The test-candidate will be difficult to find, but the

V-Project, with our nine commandos, has proven that we can achieve a higher level in our warrior training.

This supersoldier-spy will be our new covert weapon. Who will be the first candidate?

Prologue

Good morning. After introductions and theory yesterday, I thought we'd meet in the most important place in your life for the next few months.

This is the CVR room. You'll notice that it's all gray. The color is like white noise to remote viewers, blocking out distractions and mental interference. Yes, Miss Roston, that means psychic interference as well as sophisticated spy detection devices. No, it isn't one hundred percent foolproof.

You'll each have a monitor, and both of you will be assigned a unit number. I've been told some of you will have a co-monitor who will remain anonymous for the time being. Your main monitor will guide you through your remote viewing experiences. Your secondary monitor will observe and check your progress through each level.

Remote Viewing Training Session Three

Each time you practice this relaxation technique, we'll extend the theta waves so you'll go deeper. Yes, Miss Roston, it's similar to a hypnosis state. It's more like self-hypnosis so no, we aren't manipulating your actions. Miss Roston, you should address your cynical concerns to your monitors.

Remote Viewing Training Session Five

There are secrets to remote viewing. Your reaction and problem solving will be evaluated by your monitors. To pass your tests, here are a few simple things to remember. One, you have to learn to relax quickly, even if you're a type A personality. Even if you've been out in a hot and sweaty traffic jam, once you enter this room, you should learn to put all that behind you without any trouble. The key is to think of watching a flower bloom, and become that flower.

Two, you have to think outside the norm. Your day-to-day solutions won't work in remote viewing. The key is in trusting that you can locate a target from ideas, concepts and feelings. The key is in becoming an observer instead of a participant, and processing what you feel and think.

Three, you have to be able to reduce outside physical and sensory interference. Things are hooked up to you sometimes. You are constantly monitored. The key is in the ability to ignore your physical body and absorb what your mind sees as your reality. That way, you won't need to walk miles around this room simply because you happen to be doing that in a remote viewing session.

I think those three points are the most important, although there are always more secrets. Yes, Miss Roston, we do have a secret handshake. That's between you and your monitor.

Remote Viewing Training Session Seven

Remember, you are sensing your targets, more than seeing them. At first, anyway. For example, coming out from a dark cave into sudden sunshine won't be an immediate knowledge. You'll just suddenly sense brightness, and then you'll sense coming out of some space. It is up to you to turn around and look behind you and make the deduction of where you are, i.e. coming out of a cave. This is what your monitor's duty to you is—as an anchor and a guide. He can't see what you see but the more you trust him to guide you, the more he'll see through your eyes.

Yes, Miss Roston, we do use experienced remote viewers as monitors, too. The problem is, the monitor who is very talented becomes so involved with the target that he or she involuntarily starts remote viewing as well. Then you're left on your own. Yes, it'd be nice if there was a way we could communicate what we see, but that's still not possible yet. That's why your drawings are important. I'm aware your artwork is terrible, Miss Roston.

Remote Viewing Training Session Eight

Bilocation is your phantom body, so to speak. When you first bilocate, you'll feel like you're falling at a rapid pace. Or a stumbling sensation, as if you'd spent the previous night drinking too much.

Concentrate on your senses. We'll teach you how to isolate one at a time so you don't get confused. Inexperienced beginners have a difficult time adjusting and figuring out where they are. For example, we'd send them to Mount Fuji and even after several promptings to describe their sensations, they couldn't deduce that they were on a snowy mountain.

You're correct, Miss Roston, in focusing on the cold first, since that's the obvious first sensation, to discover the source. That's a good start.

Are we ready? Please sign the Human Use Agreement Form in front of you. Please read the part stating that you understand that you're participating in an experimental program using humans, and that you'll not hold the federal government responsible for any damage that might occur.

Remote Viewing Training Session Nine

This first exercise has to do with diversion from fixation on one's body. Look into the mirror and study the reflection, including yourself. The object is to trigger the mind into "observation mode." You're essentially looking at a 2-D visual reflection of a multidimensional environment, thus making it easier for your mind to digest and process the needed information.

No, Miss Roston, I'm not saying you can't trust your senses. That's another exercise. Remote viewing is all about point of view, just like witnesses to an accident. We'll work on point of view first. In other words, the "observation mode" enables you to filter out overwhelming sensations and interruptive perception. Now, each of you report to your monitor what you observed in the mirror.

Remote Viewing Training Session Ten

I'll pound this into you all at every stage of our lessons. In remote viewing, the most important element is non-contamination of the remote viewer. Our Intel must be as objective as possible. That's why we use multiple remote viewers who do not work together because we want to analyze and compare all the Intel given by them and not be worried about possible corruption.

Who decides the physical target? Someone not directly associated with the remote viewing process. He decides the target pool and has no contact with any of the remote viewing process. To preclude contamination and possible sensory leakage, a middle person is usually used between the person who runs the pool and the viewer.

There are various ways to reach a target. The novice remote viewer acts on the information in an isolated envelope, sometimes with coordinates. You'll find that, as you progress, you won't need that anymore. Sometimes an Outbounder, a physical presence at the target, is all you need. This is usually for very complicated targets.

Contamination of data happens easily. A monitor who asks too many questions or pushes a remote viewer too quickly can destroy a whole operation. No, Miss Roston, we don't send remote viewers to the physical site after the collection of Intel. One, you'll be too out of it, physically and mentally. Two, you aren't trained to handle certain aspects of that Intel. Oh, yes, I do know what you all are being trained to do. It remains to be seen whether you can do it, doesn't it?

Remote Viewing Training Session Eleven

I realize you're experienced in combat training, so your belief system has been honed to rely on what is around you in the physical world, and the rules and restrictions around that. In remote viewing, there are no particular rules and restrictions. You can say that your conscious mind is delving into your unconscious mind for information and at each level, you're tapping deeper. You're "out there" in the ether, but you're actually also relying on "in here," whatever your belief system is— in the brain, in the mind, in your soul, in your head.

The level each of you can achieve depends on your belief system and your ability to get past what might be uncomfortable for you. Some of you won't be able to do it and there's nothing wrong with that. Forcing yourself won't help at all; in fact, it will just make things worse. I've seen this happen in trainees too eager to please.

Now, the first simple step in talking about the unconscious mind is, perhaps, agreeing that there is a subconscious state of mind. Show of hands? For example, we've all done lucid dreaming at one point or another in our lives, finding ourselves in a dream and being aware of it, yes?

We have attempted to get the individual mind to do this at will, but so far, we haven't had much success. Usually, the moment the individual realizes he's dreaming, he wakes up, and loses control of whatever situation he's been in.

Yes, Miss Roston, I would call lucid dreaming a sort of simple remote viewing, like a question-and-answer session between conscious and unconscious states. How interesting that you think it's more than that. Maybe you're in the wrong experiment.

Remote Viewing Training Session Thirteen

Please read the 1990 Report given by Science Applications International Corporation (SAIC). The organization sent an agency to test out a task for a certain remote viewing program. The task was specifically this: could an agent in the field be tracked through remote viewing, and was it possible to target what that agent might be doing? You will find the agency's conclusions at the end of the report. I'll give you a hint, Miss Roston. We received a special funding bonus in 1991.

Remote Viewing Training Session Fourteen

This partial quote hangs on the wall of The Monroe Institute in Virginia where we're going for a visit this afternoon:

"I am more than my physical body. Because I am more than physical matter, I can perceive that which is greater than the physical world. Therefore, in these exercises, I deeply desire to Expand, to Experience; to Know, to Understand; to Control, to Use such greater energies and energy system as may be beneficial and constructive to me and those who follow me."

You'll learn today that there are many different techniques in achieving remote viewing and that there are other agencies besides ours who are actively working on their own programs. Yes, Miss Roston, we share some of our findings with them. Yes, Miss Roston, some being the *relevant* word here.

Remote Viewing Training Session Fifteen

We like to reword some popular sayings here. Today's phrase is: Can't see the trees for the forest. In remote viewing, you depend on your senses, but overstimulation can cause the viewer to lose sight of the target tree. That's why we allow no stimulants in your system as your mind and body learn to let go. An experienced remote viewer can bilocate with stimulants present in his or her system, but always remember, something new will always affect the senses, i.e. the forest. To counter that, you, as a remote viewer, have to learn to control your emotional environment. There are different exercises you can learn to overcome the times that you feel yourself losing control and getting lost in the "forest." I've read your file, Miss Roston. We'll start with something simple for you; no coffee for a few weeks. I see nothing humorous regarding your comments, but yes, sex provides chemical stimulants in your brain, too.

Remote Viewing Training Session Seventeen

In remote viewing, we train you to consciously move your brain into theta waves. Most of you are familiar with terms such as "higher state of consciousness" or "altered state." You'll have to work through your belief system to achieve this goal.

Once you've crossed this hurdle, you'll find it easier to go into RV mode. An experienced remote viewer can remote view without outside manipulation at all.

In summary, there are four brain wave states that range from the high-amplitude, low-frequency delta to the low-amplitude, high-frequency beta. These brain wave states are common to the human species. Men, women and children of all ages experience the same characteristic brain waves. They are consistent across cultures and country boundaries.

Yes, Miss Roston, you can synchronize brain waves during sleep. It has been done successfully to induce group meditative states. No, remote viewing is strictly done alone, so we won't be going out and having "fun together." Sorry to disappoint you.

One

Did he really want this assignment? He was used to being asked to seduce, but never one of their own, and agreeing to do so would mean getting closer than a regular monitor and trainer. His fingers tapped on the well-used dictionary on the small table next to him. The word for the day was *quintessence*.

How appropriate.

Here at COMCEN, the quintessential element uniting all its operatives was danger. He'd perhaps been here too long, because now they wanted him to train the newcomer. *Not just any newcomer.*

If situations were assigned as some form of karma, there was no question that danger was his. He thrived on it, not out of necessity, but because it was what was natural to him. Danger called to him and he'd always answered.

And by design, if there was karma, then it always came to him in the form of dangerous women. Poetic justice, he supposed. Everyone had a weakness. He was one of the fortunate few who knew exactly what his weakness was. He again looked at the woman on the screen.

There was something enticing about a dangerous woman. He should know. He'd been married to one. He understood his inclination for them very well. They had the aura of toughness that he admired—and enjoyed stripping down. Their strength, intimidating to some men, was both sexy and challenging at the same time. It added an extra kick, knowing that the woman he was bedding might kill him in bed. It must be that poetic justice thing again, the secret wish to die while fucking around with danger.

His lips curled mockingly at the thought as he continued studying the screen in front of him. How could a woman everyone called Hell be anything but dangerous in and out of bed?

And he knew instinctively that sooner or later, he would be inside her. His eyes followed her movements, catlike and sure, as she went through her morning exercises. Even in a controlled environment, there was something untamed in the way she threw herself into the training. Wildcat. If they even made it into bed.

From the beginning, his reaction to her had been visceral. Any normal male's would have been. After all, he'd watched her in training for months, watched her eat, sleep, drink, watched her take her clothes off whenever she went swimming in the pool. She didn't like to swim with any clothes on, and he'd enjoyed those sessions, knowing that it was partly voyeuristic, partly because he knew she knew someone was watching her. Mostly, it was because of all the candidates, *she* had won. A woman who'd beaten out a bunch of men in mental and physical war games. He already knew that all the male operatives at COMCEN were curious about her.

She'd started her nude swimming innocently enough, and he'd enjoyed the undisguised pleasure of a woman comfortable with her body. He hadn't forgotten that first time. Her hands carelessly unzipping her pants. Her long, long legs kicking them aside. And she'd looked at the warm water and a small smile had spread out, a glimmer of sheer abandon that had pulled at something inside him.

It'd caught him by surprise, that emotional tug. He wasn't usually so easily moved. He'd had to stop himself from leaning forward, closer, as he continued taking in the sight of her slipping off her underwear.

He recalled that moment even now. She was impatient, as if she couldn't wait to be free of the restrictions of clothing. He was equally impatient, too, in that male sort of way that was also restricted by clothing.

Her lightly-tanned body was surprisingly feminine for someone who'd gone through so much training. He'd caught a few seconds of soft feminine curves before she'd dove into the water. She'd surfaced with a small sigh of delight, sweeping her hair out of her face. Pure unadulterated delight. And that smile…he'd dreamed of that smile that night. He'd known it wouldn't be there as soon as she figured out that there were always cameras at COMCEN.

The day had come. He'd felt the difference immediately. It was in the way she stripped her clothes, in the furtive motion of her eyes trying to find the camera eye. The interesting thing was, it hadn't stopped her from continuing to swim naked. She did another unexpectedly interesting thing. She hadn't gone to Kirkland, her medical advisor, or her any of her trainers. Instead, she'd asked the interactive supercomputer at COMCEN. He'd listened in to the conversation with interest.

"Hey, Eight Ball, am I being watched at this moment?" she'd asked aloud. "Besides by you, I mean."

"Yes, Hell."

"By how many people?"

He'd authorized certain information to be released. "One, Hell," the computer had replied.

"Man or woman?"

"Man."

"Is he my trainer, the one who's been watching my workout every day?"

That question had amused him. He should've known she wouldn't have bought into Kirkland's explanation about it being standard procedure since she was now going into a new phase. She was smart enough to figure out that they had tapes and records of all her training since day one, so her asking now was for someone's benefit. His.

"Sort of."

"What do you mean, sort of? What kind of computer are you anyway? Computers don't say sort of, don't you know that? It's either positive or negative."

But Eight Ball, short for "Magic Eight Ball," a prediction-through-computation program, was a different kind of computer. His programmer wasn't averse to adding odd little programs that gave his creation a unique personality. The result was a computer that frequently mixed up its language usage between that of a surfer and a robot.

"It's neither positive nor negative as of now, Hell. So…sort of, dude."

"Where's the camera?"

"I have not been authorized to tell you, dude. Do you have the password for information access?"

"For a computer that's supposed to be way cool, you suck, Eight Ball."

He'd laughed at her reaction. But since that day, that smile had disappeared. He'd kind of missed it, except that it was now replaced by a different kind of smile. A knowing, dangerous curve of those shapely lips, as if she were challenging him to show himself. She was, after all, a GEM operative; like all the female operatives in her elite independent agency, she knew how to get a man's attention, even if she couldn't see it.

If it was male reaction she was going after, he had plenty on his end. A naked dangerous woman like her didn't get angry. She got even. Even though she couldn't see it for herself, there was now a mockery in her eyes and her smile that told him she knew. Any normal man watching her slow taunting movements would combust from the heat.

But normal wasn't a word usually associated with him. Ice water flowed in his veins. Women had accused him of having a lump of ice for a heart. He had wondered, sometimes, if maybe he'd forgotten what love was. So before they'd even met, they now played a game.

He kept watching, assessing how he could push this woman out of her comfort zone. She kept fighting him with a nonchalance that was targeted to make him feel male discomfort.

It had been a long time since he'd reacted to someone so strongly and thoroughly.

Not that he didn't like women. Just mostly the dangerous kind. He sat very still as he watched the woman wrap her lithe body around the dangling chain, her hands looking small in contrast to the thick links. She pulled, testing it, her head cocked slightly as she looked up at her target.

Elena Rostova, GEM operative, now working for COS Command. Although others called her Hell, and she preferred to be called Helen, Elena suited her. There was something about her....

It must be that challenge thing again. His instinct told him that the lady had something to hide. But then, didn't every operative? He had quite a few secrets himself, things that he preferred not to share with anyone. He respected an operative who kept certain things to himself because one who blindly followed orders and told every single detail exactly as it happened, like the perfect little soldier, could be very dangerous to him and his team.

His eyes narrowed slightly. Therein lay the problem, didn't it? He watched Elena's graceful body as she attacked her routine. The perfect soldier-spy. Every agency had been looking for one, training dozens and experimenting on countless others to find the perfect combination of traits. Someone high up on the covert chain had managed to convince different agencies to train special candidates, even as they sweetened the deal by giving them extra funds for which to compete. It didn't matter. There were limited bodies to get to the finish line.

"Quintessence," he murmured. He liked opening the dictionary randomly every morning to pick out the word for the day. Uncanny, how it fit. COMCEN wanted a supersoldier-*spy*, contracting the best available inde-operative from their new partner, GEM. Elena Rostova was very good at many other things besides soldiering. Supersoldier-spy. The quintessential dangerous woman.

And she was his. At least, he amended, for a while. Then, like all of them, she would go and do her job. Because she wasn't just going to be a supersoldier.

In the end, COMCEN's candidate had won the big prize, and to all intents and purposes, Elena Rostova was his to mold. She didn't know that yet, of course. She'd been given the usual need-to-know-only information and she had apparently followed her contract to a T, so far. Well-paid for it, too, and now, very, very well trained. But a woman didn't give up two years of her life just to train herself for an experiment. No, she definitely had something else she was keeping to herself. Knowing that pushed away some of his reservations a little. He didn't want to be part of a program where the candidate was just an obedient contract employee out to make money.

She was an attractive woman—some might say exotic—with a natural strength and grace that showed in the way she used her body. From the different tests given, she'd shown that she wasn't afraid of taking risks, almost foolhardy sometimes, but her report cards from various trainers before him sang nothing but praises. And these were from men he knew were very difficult to train under.

Having seen her on tape and close-up, he had no doubts about her extraordinary skills. Once he agreed to include himself as part of this experiment, they would find out for sure how good she was because he would be there to watch her. Not just physically, but mentally.

That was why he'd been watching her. Wanting a dangerous woman was one thing; agreeing to do dangerous things with her was another. And this coming experiment would mean he'd be a lot closer to this woman than he'd ever been with any other.

And watching her had become…a habit. The physical package alone would tempt a man, but he'd found himself wanting access to her mind, to know her as intimately as he knew how she liked to nudge one of her hands between her legs when she slept.

He'd seen her in action with other trainers; he knew her capabilities. Yet, there were moments when she'd let down her guard, when she'd thought no one was watching. He'd seen that look in her eyes, and had wondered what'd put it there.

And COMCEN—damn its knowing think tanks, always measuring and calculating—was waiting patiently, letting him walk into this himself. They hadn't had him all these years without knowing a little about how his mind worked.

He watched as she climbed at a slow and controlled pace that showed the physical fitness some of the best from Special Forces had honed into her. The length of the chain extended for nearly thirty meters from ceiling to floor and she was halfway there already. He glanced at the stopwatch on top of the screen. She must be going for a personal record today.

He'd never seen a woman with such an intense need to succeed. There was something personal in this contract for her and it was the driving force that had motivated her from day one.

So there was a woman inside that trained body, even though she had kept it well-hidden for these two years. Smart, very smart. And his intrigue grew.

He tapped on the communication pad next to his hand. "Put Elena through Test Alpha."

"Helen, darling. She prefers to be called Helen." The low, distinctive voice belonging to GEM's chief came through the intercom. "And if she passes?"

His gaze left the screen for a second. He hadn't expected T. to be on the other end. These days she very seldom showed up at COMCEN. They must really want him to sign on to the experiment to bring her in. "Then I'm one step closer to being convinced to be *Elena's* monitor," he said, his attention returning to the subject matter.

"She's passed every test so far," T. noted, her amusement at his soft emphasis apparent.

"So what's a few more?" he asked. *Elena Ekaterina Rostova* definitely sounded more dangerous than Helen Roston.

"They think you have apprehension."

"Yes, do calm my fears, T.," he said dryly. "I'm quaking in my shoes."

T.'s laughter was husky. "Darling, that'd be the day. I'll initiate Test Alpha tomorrow."

"No," he said. "Now."

"She's already overexerted."

"Exactly how I want her." He was going to do a lot more than overexert her. And because he knew it would heighten his own sense of awareness, he didn't want to allow her to take her usual naked swim. It would fuel his part in Test Alpha. "Now, T."

"Anything to make you happy, darling. That was what they said to me."

"Go mess with someone else's mind. We'll talk later," he said, and tapped the button to turn the intercom off.

Elena continued her climb to the top, the gleam of perspiration coating her smooth tanned flesh, then gave an exultant hoot of satisfaction as she hauled herself onto the small ledge at the top. Hands on hips, she looked down from her height, her face glowing with the intensity born from adrenaline and exhaustion.

And that was why there was little room to fail. Her fierce competitiveness wouldn't allow it. Besides, he had no intention of losing this wildcat.

A small, mocking smile played on his lips. Funny. That almost sounded like he was making it personal himself.

Hers had never been the easy way. Helen Roston was of the opinion that if she had to make a lot of money quickly by selling her body, she might as well do it training to be the world's next mega-soldier-whatever. Which was about the hardest possible way to make a living but—she grinned wryly—at least her body would look good if she died from overtraining.

Her body being the operative concept here. After all, there was no guarantee that she would come out of this alive. Oh well, Enrique had always accused her of having a death wish. Hellacious, he'd called her choice of living on the streets alone. He was learning English because the American dollar was strong and American tourists were easy victims. So "Hell" she had been called ever since. Russians loved nicknames, and it wasn't long before everyone on the street knew her by that name.

She hadn't been able to resist the contract, though. After reading the questionnaire, she'd seriously considered it for a month before she'd shrugged and answered "yes" to all the questions and then made an appointment to see the director. What harm was there to enhance one's special abilities? Blame it on her being an orphan. There were always those constant niggling questions at the back of her mind about her background. Once and for all, she would be able to find out exactly how *special* she was. No more questions. Or unanswered dreams.

A lot of money would get her out of GEM quicker and she could... She shrugged. She hadn't quite decided what she could do yet. But once she bought out her contract with them, she would feel a whole lot better.

Not that they were difficult to work for. Far from it. GEM had given her a life an orphan girl from the Russian ghetto could only dream about, had given her the means to be *somebody*, but she didn't want to spend twenty, thirty years of her life playing spy games, or being a contracted liaison between agencies, or running different lives under different aliases. There had to be more to life than that.

She wasn't made to live within a group anyway.

Even when she was a wild child on the street, she'd refused to run with the gangs. She preferred to take care of herself, thank you very much. She wasn't going to succumb to any of those boys asking for the usual nasty payments, so she had to learn to fight hard and run harder, because she didn't always win.

Ha, if they could see me now. Helen grinned at the ridiculousness of the old Broadway song running in her head. What she was being asked to do was show business of a sort, wasn't it? So the song was appropriate.

Everyone wanted to see her, actually. It had been almost two years of training and now everyone wanted to see what she had become.

She wiped the perspiration off with a towel. What had she become? She asked herself that question quite a bit and had no real answer. She'd come close to a personal revelation the other night. She'd woken up in the middle of one of her too-darn-vivid dreams, sat up, and declared quietly to no one in particular, "I'm very close to *being.*"

It was one of those profound moments one couldn't quite grasp, especially when one jolted up in bed suddenly. But Helen knew it meant something. She always had that voice-in-the-head thing that came out of nowhere, when something important was coming.

That was one of the reasons why she had been chosen for this project, of course. Having what they called psi—or strong intuitive abilities—was a definite plus. She didn't care what they called it. Voice in the head. Psychic blah-blah. Intuition. That voice had saved her life a few times. She had explained to the CIA department that she wasn't one of those people who communicated with some other presence or had any kind of power to; she just sometimes heard a warning or made a really good guess. Whatever. The CIA white coats seemed to have accepted her half-truth. She hadn't told them about her dreams, but then, they hadn't asked. Never tell them everything, that was her motto.

She was looking forward to her dip in the pool, more so than usual. That climb up the chain had tested her endurance and her muscles were pleasantly aching. A quick relaxing swim would make sure she didn't cramp up later.

"Agent Roston, go to Chamber Two."

Helen frowned at the electronic voice instructing her from the intercom. She walked over and activated the speaker. "Why?" Her training had stayed on the same schedule these last few months. "What's there?"

"I'm just delivering the orders, Hell. Get your pretty ass over there."

Helen chuckled. It was funny to hear a computer using her nickname with such familiarity. "If you weren't a computer, Eight Ball, I'd find you and kick yours."

Eight Ball was COMCEN's computer. His programmer had given his mother program its own choice for personality and gender in certain communications feedback. For some weird reason, the computer had taken up a surfer's easy laid-back drawl, although it tended to trip itself up while trying out surfer lingo. Eight Ball, she suspected, was another open-ended experiment on the loose in this place.

"If I had an ass, Fly Boy would say 'go for it, dude!'" The computer mimicked the commando's voice to perfection. "Chamber Two in twelve minutes, over and out."

Helen frowned again. She didn't have much time. She'd just have to go wearing her sweaty leotard and tights. At a sprint.

She dropped the towel, punched the buttons on the panel, and slipped out of the training area while the door was still sliding open. No time for the elevator. Chamber Two was three flights up. Trust them to pick a place that required climbing up instead of running down.

She pushed the door to the stairwell and starting running two and three steps at a time. She paused at the landing, taking a quick moment to flick her bangs away from her eyes.

"Test," that voice in her head warned.

Her awareness immediately turned rapier-sharp. She pushed open the exit door that led into the corridors. She didn't sense any danger around the corner. She didn't think they were planning to kill her, not after investing all that time and money, but she couldn't ignore that warning in her head either.

"Test." The repetition was even more urgent now.

"They do that all the time, so what's so different about this test?" she muttered. Realization came like sudden daylight. *They* weren't testing her this time. *Someone* was. Maybe it was *him*.

The corridor was dead silent and she knocked on Chamber Two. An envelope was stuck on it, with her name, Elena Rostova, written in bold font, along with *Do Not Open*. She raised her brows. Very few people used her real name. She peeled it off the metal. The door swished open. There was no light coming from within.

"Games, games, games," Helen murmured and stepped inside. The door behind her sealed shut and it was pitch-black in the room. Every one of her senses reached out into the darkness.

"Walk ten paces forward," a voice said from all around her.

Sen-surround sound. "Do I get to turn and shoot?" Helen joked. Excitement roiled in the pit of her stomach. It had to be *him* talking to her.

"No. Ten paces forward, Elena."

She obeyed, counting aloud. It was unbelievably dark in there. She stopped when she encountered something with her feet. A thickly-padded mat. She stepped onto it and finished her count. "Now what?" she asked when she was done.

"Open the envelope."

She carefully did so. "This isn't easy in the dark, you know," she complained. "There's nothing inside."

"You're expecting a note. Never assume anything in here."

She wished she could see the person talking to her. The voice was a projected echo, deliberately masking any recognizable tone. She slipped her finger into the envelope and felt something.

"It's small. Roundish. Too small to be a button," she said.

"It's a pill. Take it."

Her mouth fell open. "You're kidding me, right?"

"It won't kill you."

She could have sworn she detected mockery, even with that amplified resonance. She looked around in the darkness. Not that she could see anything. "Look, this is getting irritating. Why am I in the dark and why must I take a drug?"

"It's part of your training."

"Usually, I'm given a set of instructions and my instructor tells me what's going to happen," she said. But she'd known this new instructor wasn't going to be anything usual. He'd been watching her nonstop since her arrival. She'd felt him. He was everywhere. Funny thing was, she'd been more intrigued by the game than outraged at the lack of privacy.

"I see. Tell me, when you're playing operative in the real world, do you have someone telling you what's going to happen next?"

Helen narrowed her eyes, feeling just a twinge of impatience rising. "Training, I said." She pivoted around. "I'm not taking any drugs unless it's the serum that's specified in the contract. This pill isn't it, is it?"

"You won't know till you try it. And in case you're wondering, yes, I'm your instructor and yes, this is a training session. Take the pill, Elena. As specified in your contract, you'll let your instructor direct you as he or she sees fit."

"Within reason," Helen argued. She'd added that part to the clause herself. "Tell me. If I take this, what's going to happen to me? Besides not dying, I mean."

"First you will fall unconscious."

Her whole body went taut. "What? No f—"

"Then you'll wake up in fifteen minutes. You'll find that you can't move your body. Certain parts of you will feel nothing. You'll stay paralyzed for the duration of the session."

In the two years of her training, even through medical tests, no one had given her any drugs to render her unconscious. She'd been extra careful to establish a mental block when working with the CIA; she didn't trust them or their tendency to hypnotize certain subjects.

She rolled the pill between her thumb and forefinger. Why now? What did he want to do to her?

"Fighting what you can see is easy, Elena. It's fighting what you can't see that will be your ultimate challenge. Remember what's coming up. A dose of the serum is just like fighting what you can't see, isn't it?" A tiny pause. "I can't force you to take the pill, but you'll be putting potentially more harmful drugs into your system. This one, I can guarantee you, is a common drug that I know to have very few side effects."

Helen laughed incredulously. "I'm supposed to take your word for it," she remarked.

Silence.

Whoever her instructor was, he was waiting.

She rolled the pill again, her thoughts going a hundred miles an hour. Test, that stupid voice in her head had said. He was testing her for something entirely different from her previous trainers. She chewed on her lower lip for a second, then, before she changed her mind, she popped it into her mouth and swallowed.

"Count from ten backwards when I tell you to."

Helen noted that he didn't seem to have any problems seeing her in this darkness. Special glasses with image-intensifier? But if so, he still wouldn't be able to tell whether she had taken the pill. Her eyes searched the darkness. Where was he?

After a few minutes, he ordered, "Start counting."

She turned around as she counted. "Ten, nine, eight…" There was just nothing to see, not even a hint of light anywhere. "Seven, six…" She had to stop moving. Could darkness spin? It felt like the darkness was swirling all around her. "Five, four…" She couldn't feel her feet. "Shit…" She fell forward. So that was what the mattress was for, was her last thought.

Her eyes flew open. It was still that darkness but she felt strange. She tried moving but she couldn't feel her body and she couldn't see. She didn't like this one bit. No reason to panic yet. He told her that she wasn't going to be able to move, but she could feel a warm body against her. A very warm male body.

"What's happening?" she asked. At least she could talk. "I feel funny."

No answer. She could feel her vision swaying, like something was moving really fast around her. It suddenly occurred to her that she was being carried. And that she was upside down because her hair kept getting in her mouth when she tried to talk.

"Where are you taking me?" she asked, spitting her hair out. "Answer me, dammit."

Whoever it was seemed to be going faster and faster, until she grew dizzy. He couldn't possibly go that long. Where the hell was she? No longer in the room, for sure, but why couldn't she see anything? She could make out shadows now—light and dark shades of blackness. There were strange smells, like foliage and the outdoors, then the scent of clean laundry, then of burning wood, then of salty air. She frowned, totally confused, because she couldn't see any forest or fire or anything that could give her any clues to her location.

She felt that floating sensation again and from the change of shadows, she could tell that her body was sliding off his as he swung her around. She stared up, trying to see who this stranger was, but it was that odd shadowy shape again.

He should be panting from that long run but she couldn't hear him breathe at all. Suddenly, he jerked around and there were armed men all around him.

She could only watch in horror as they shot him and his body slid away from her view. She couldn't help him! She gritted her teeth and tried to move but it was no use. She was totally at their mercy.

They surrounded her. She could hear them now— male grunts and cursing. She gulped in air as they pulled at her body. She could feel them pulling her legs apart....

She bit down on her lower lip. She wouldn't scream. She wouldn't panic. She was going to find a way out of this. If she could only see—

The noise around her was jumbled, as if she was standing in a very crowded room. She breathed in as someone started a fight and everyone around her, including her attackers, became involved. The shadows made everything even more confusing since she couldn't tell who was hitting whom. But she smelt the blood, heard screams of pain, saw bodies falling around her.

And there was nothing she could do.

There're too many bodies. Just too many people. Those screams.

"Shut up!" she yelled out.

All of a sudden, there was silence. A lone figure climbed on top of her. It was him. She recognized the shape of his body. For some reason she recognized his scent.

"I thought you died," she whispered. *Where did everyone go? And why couldn't she feel the danger?*

She felt his hands on her useless body, felt his hands on her thighs as he slowly parted her numb legs.

Helen squeezed her eyes shut. She must be mistaken. She'd thought—wait, maybe something happened in the dark room and someone took her while she was unconscious. Maybe her kidnapper was a hostile, too.

She let out a hiss of outrage as his hands intimately slid up her inner thigh, then up her rib cage, across her breasts. She was going to kill him when this drug wore off. She was going to tear his hands off first. A thumb caressed her lower lip for a second.

He kissed her on the mouth, his lips moving over hers lazily, as if he had all the time he wanted. She gave an outraged gurgle at the back of her throat when he nudged her lips apart and swept his tongue inside, engaging her in intimate play. She could feel his tongue exploring hers, not like a rapist, but like a lover, coaxing and playful. Blinding fury welled up as she tried her damnedest to turn her head but it was useless. Her mouth was his toy, muffling her curses.

It was the longest kiss she'd ever shared and it was *sharing.* There wasn't much she could do when she still couldn't shake her head free and her mouth was open for him to taste. Their tongues tangled silkily, seductively, as he controlled the pace, opening her wider, till she found herself growing breathless from trying to speak and move at the same time.

He likes your mouth.

Oh great. Now her warning voice was also analyzing kissing techniques. And why was her heart beating so erratically? She was shocked to find that her eyes had closed… She forced them open, blinking rapidly. She was *not* getting turned on by this man. No matter how good his kissing technique was!

He finally released her and she heard herself gasping for breath. His shadow moved over her, his hand deliberately cupping her breast.

"I'll kill you if you touch me," Helen managed to say through what felt like swollen lips.

She heard the front zipper sliding. She felt the coolness of the air on her bare flesh. He pulled the front halves of her shirt apart and she could feel his knuckles grazing her naked breasts. Her heart galloped like she was having a heart attack.

Wait a minute, wait a minute! Something's not right. I was wearing a leotard with no front zipper. I was wearing a bra.

Test. Suddenly everything fell together like a well-designed puzzle.

Test. No sense of danger. The drug. All the different smells and sounds. Nothing solid…just tactile. They weren't testing her physically. Everything was a mental test.

"This isn't real," she declared firmly and loudly. "I was wearing a bra in a tight leotard with no zipper. I'm not half-naked. Game over! Now let me see you, you fucking bastard!"

The next time she was faced with a tiny pill, she was ready.

"You know what to do with it."

Helen shook her head. "I'm not taking it."

"Why not?" His voice, even electronically enhanced, was soft, persuasive. "Are you afraid?"

"Of course not." She wasn't. She just didn't like the feeling of being helpless. "I already know what you're trying to achieve. You want me totally in your control. You want me afraid, or are trying to make me afraid. Am I right or wrong?"

"Somewhat, Elena. If I ask you to take off your clothes now, would you?"

She cocked her head in the dark. "No."

"Why not? It's totally dark in the CAVE and I promise it won't hurt."

"Look, I know what you're trying to do," Helen said, exasperated now. "It isn't working. You're trying to find chinks in my psyche and I've been trained to resist. You aren't going to win."

"But why are you resisting your trainer? Wouldn't it be simpler to go along with it, knowing what I'm going to do, and then following through with today's training lesson? Why the need to tell me that you aren't going to lose? Or, are you just afraid, Elena, that you will lose?"

Oh, he was good. Whoever her new trainer was, he definitely wasn't just some Special Forces guy or CIA shrink trying to beat her into shape mentally or physically. This man was trying to figure her out by pushing her sexual buttons. The thing was, she couldn't figure out why he was doing it…yet. It'd only been a couple of weeks, but already he'd challenged her more than any of her other trainers, both physically and mentally.

"Okay, fine." She popped the pill into her mouth,

crushed it between her teeth because she was that pissed off. She wanted to taste its bitterness. "I'm not going to be very happy if you start taking my clothes off again when I wake up. I'm tired of it. That's a warning."

"Then I'll make sure they're already off before you wake up."

"You..." She didn't even have time to finish cursing him, falling forward as the world spun into darkness.

When Helen came to, she didn't say anything, using the time to figure out what he was trying to do. Again, she couldn't see the person carrying her. This time, she was in his arms, the way a man carried a lover, and he was walking slowly. She heard the lapping of water. Splashing at his feet. He kept walking.

She knew it was useless but she still tried to move. She really, really hated this feeling. She felt the water touching her bare buttocks. She gasped—both from the cold water and her outrage that she was indeed "naked"—as he took both of them deeper into the water.

"I'm so going to kill you," she said between her teeth. "I told you not..."

She gasped again as he let go of her. She sank, water getting into her mouth. She couldn't move; she was going to drown.

This isn't real. This isn't real! You got to keep your head! She realized now that he'd purposely done the one thing he knew would distract her—making her think he undressed her. She needed to remember that virtual reality was all in the mind. He was pushing her to accept this, getting her ready for the next phase.

Willing her panic and anger away, Helen relaxed, allowing her body to float. He was her trainer; he wasn't going to let her drown. Just as she reasoned this to herself, she felt his arms gather around her, pulling her upward to the surface. Her face burst through the water and she took deep breaths of air into her lungs as she felt him lifting her higher, till her chin rested on his shoulder. She coughed, very aware of his arms around her nude body.

"Total immersive virtual reality between two people is going to be different from going solo, Elena," he said softly in her ear. "I give you the reality that you have to accept in your mind. Just as I have to accept what you see when you remote view because if my mind rejects it, then this experiment will fail. You have to get very comfortable with whatever reality I provide here, just as I have to do the same with the reality you say you see when you remote view. Am I making sense to you?"

"Yes." But that didn't mean she had to like it.

"The nudity is just a little quarrel between us. I know you don't feel comfortable when you aren't in control, I totally understand that, and that's why you are naked now, in the water, in my control because you have to get comfortable with this notion."

"Only in virtual reality," she assured him sharply.

"That's fine."

They were still in the water. She shivered. How deep was the water? *Not real, Helen, it's not real.* She breathed slowly, steadily. Fine, she got the lesson, so she would shut up and just let the drug do its thing until she was able to move again.

His hand came behind her neck, gently turning her head up. Looking at his shadowy form was the most frustrating thing after the fact that she was in someone's control.

"Do you know what made you even madder than being stripped naked by someone?"

"I'm not stripped naked. It's all in my head," she said, and tried to smile nonchalantly, "so I'm not mad at all since none of this is real."

"Then you aren't allowed to lose your temper if I kiss you again," he whispered, his head coming down on hers.

And there was nothing she could do as she floated in his arms, nothing at all, as the hand behind her neck firmly forced her head back. He explored her mouth intimately, his tongue tangling with hers.

He was enjoying this too much, she thought dazedly, even as she fought against her own response. He liked being in control of her and the more she fought him, the more ways he would find to get at her. It was all standard operating procedure in the book of mind manipulation. But, besides what he was claiming to be doing, what else was he trying to manipulate her to do?

Later, back in the changing room, she stared at her lips, which looked redder than normal. He was diabolical. He hadn't undressed her. It had been all in her mind because he'd *made* her think he was going to do it while she was out. Again, playing with her fears.

She traced the outline of her lips with her fingers. Sensitive. As if she had been kissed thoroughly.

"But it's not real," she whispered to her reflection.

Two

Internal focus wasn't Helen's strongest point. She much preferred action; thinking too much only muddled up one's life. However, these new games were designed to make her work mentally as well as physically, and she couldn't help but feel a little pissed off. She hated being manipulated and these days, *someone* was doing a whole lot of manipulating of her mind and body.

Helen scowled, then quickly schooled her features. The last time she had betrayed herself like that, *someone* had pushed her through a series of exercises that he knew she would dislike, even though she now knew how everything worked, that nothing was actually real.

She looked around the room. She had learned much about it in the last couple of months. The CAVE Ultimate—Cave Automatic Virtual Environment—was a ten-by-ten-by-ten room that was the newest in virtual reality immersion. Since its invention at the University of Illinois in Chicago, certain government agencies had further developed and enhanced the unique features of this new technology.

One of the unique features of the CAVE was that it allowed multiple participants to experience the illusion that was virtual reality, with one participant controlling the environment. That first experience from two months ago—that had all been done with her alone in this room, with her invisible instructor in charge somewhere in the COMCEN complex. She now knew that he was in a similar CAVE somewhere, wearing the same type of special bodysuit that she was wearing but with the controls all on his side.

That part of it was tough for her. She hadn't liked what had happened that first time, even though she now knew they were testing her. No, *he* was testing her. She'd had this feeling all along that that dream-world into which she'd been thrown was entirely his creation.

He'd had her put in darkness so she would feel unbalanced. That had solved the problem about the special glasses, too. If she had been able to see, she would have seen the VR goggles that covered half her face floating a few inches above. He had given her that stupid paralytic drug so that she couldn't feel the rotating mechanical VR chair on which they'd placed her. All those feelings of being carried, being upside down, and the dizzying rush of movement were created by that equipment.

Even after watching it in action without her on it, she was still amazed at how everything coordinated with those goggles. Wireless tracker-tabs that looked like sticky markers were placed on certain points on a person's body, and these tabs corresponded to the chair, letting it know exactly how to move the person. That was how she was manipulated physically. It was inter-active virtual reality at its finest.

This was probably the most expensive playroom she'd ever had the privilege to romp in. Not bad for a dirty Russian orphan who only wanted a new Barbie doll, eh?

Helen grinned at the thought. Oh well, let him be dia-bolical. She was tired of controlling her emotions when he was around.

He was silent today. Not a word. It made her want to rile him to get some reaction, but that would only betray her irritation. Today they'd used the wireless trackers and a new pair of gloves. She'd stood on a glo-rified treadmill that created the illusion of motion while she got used to "spatial control of nonspace," as her sci-entist-tutor Dr. Cunningham had explained to her.

She was being prepared for the final frontier, so to speak. TIVRRV, appropriately pronounced *TERROR,* stood for Total Immersion Virtual Reality Remote Viewing, the top-secret project that required body and brain immersion and stimulation. Anyone who volun-teered for this crazy experiment ought to be terrified.

He was so damn quiet—why didn't he say some-thing? Or was that the new test?

"You know, I've never had my brain waves syn-chronized with a man's before," she drawled, touching the lever to the right of the chair. The goggles raised slowly above her head. She peered up into them. Noth-ing, of course. "What exactly does that do, in your words? These scientists haven't been able to explain it to me satisfactorily enough. I can't get excited at terms like Immersive Visualization and Interactive Mind Flow."

She waited for ten seconds. The remote viewing training had been the toughest of everything she had been through, for her, because it was all about letting go mentally. But this new trainer, with his secretive ways, was taking it even further. He was ruthless with his need to control her and he didn't care if he made her furious while doing it. In fact, she was sure he was somewhat amused by her rage. She was waiting for the day she'd see him in the flesh; she was going to wallop him.

When she'd told him that, he'd replied, in that odd quiet way that always made her nerves sing, "I look forward to it." And then he'd kissed her.

Who was he? What was he? She wanted to know everything about him like she was sure he did about her. Not everything, she corrected fiercely. He couldn't read her mind. If he could, he'd know just what she'd thought of him after what he'd put her through the first time in the CAVE. And all the torture she was going to put him through. It still pissed her off to think that somehow he managed to turn her on with his kisses. She had been celibate way too long.

After two months, he still managed to rattle her when he ordered her to walk into a dark room. Not fear. Anticipation. His body felt so real and hard when she was crushed against him. He'd slowly tip her head back and then bend his down toward hers, taking his time, until every nerve in her body screamed silently for that kiss. He was toying with her. Bastard.

"Hello?" she called out softly. Fine. She didn't want to be polite anymore. The memory of those first sessions with him still ticked her off. "Just so you know, I didn't think that last kiss was that fucking great interactively. Next time, don't freeze my body up and I might show you exactly how to kiss a woman, asshole."

She turned at the sound of a cough. It was Derek the boy wonder computer wiz. A very embarrassed computer wiz, his face flushed as he looked at everywhere but her.

"Ahem, umm, Miss Roston, can you follow me to the programming room?"

Helen cocked her head. "Cutting short my training today?"

Derek shook his head. "Actually, we're ready to go to Test Bravo. We've finished the program that will enable you to choose an avatar for yourself as well as your monitor. Now we'll test it after we've connected the brain wave simulation program."

More techie terms to learn. Test Bravo. That meant she'd passed Test Alpha. "Okay, let's go," she said, then stopped short. "Wait a minute…did you say for my monitor? Is that the same as my trainer?"

"Yes, ma'am. It's the same person."

"And we're creating an avatar for him?" She understood the term. "I know an avatar is a representation of a user in a shared virtual reality. It's usually some form of animated entity in web forums or web interactive games, right?"

"Our new program goes beyond that," Derek said, with a proud smile. "You'll be amazed at our human simulation software and advanced digital mapping. Everything looks and acts superreal. In any case, you have total control, ma'am."

Helen smiled widely. "Is that right?" she drawled,

and looking up at the goggles, she gleefully rubbed her hands. Test Bravo sounded more fun already.

"You mean I can program the avatar to look like some Greek god if I want to?"

Helen sat back in the chair, crossed her ankles and clasped her hands behind her neck. She laughed, her amusement ringing out in the small room, as she rocked her chair gently. She narrowed her eyes speculatively as she stared at the computer screen, then turned to Derek, who was standing in front of it.

"Yes, ma'am," he answered, trying to keep his face straight. "Greek god or any deity you have in mind. Your monitor said you choose how you want to see him."

Helen laughed again. This might be the easiest part of her training. A virtual reality simulator with her own self-designed trainer. After a grueling year of hand-to-hand combat training with handpicked military personnel, she liked the idea of being the one in control again. It wasn't quite so much fun when a bunch of men were ordering her around and she had to undergo strenuous testing all the time. Not to mention the medics and scientists standing around, constantly poking and prodding her.

"Well, then…let's modify this hideous male you've designed for me, sweetie."

The programmer's face flushed pink at her teasing. Clearly he wasn't used to someone like Helen Roston. He slid a quick glance at her long Lycra-clad legs. "What's wrong with the model? I thought most women like their men tall, dark and handsome."

Helen arched a brow in mockery. "Excuse me, but are you telling me I'm like most women?"

"She isn't. She's one hot babe who will kill you in a hundred different ways," a voice mocked back from behind them.

Helen didn't turn around. "Ha, said the guy with the killer looks." Flyboy was one of the most handsome men Helen had ever laid eyes on. An awful flirt, too. "How come you didn't use Flyboy as a model, Derek? I heard he did a VR program for some big project to attract government funding."

Flyboy came up behind her and Helen felt his hands on the back of her chair. "Sweetheart, why would you need a VR version when you have the real thing right here?"

Helen looked up and grinned. "You know, I can get Derek to make my VR trainer look like you and then I can do all those unmentionable things that you keep promising me."

Flyboy grinned back and winked. Derek coughed. "I could," he said in a careful voice, "but really, I think it best if your trainer-avatar is someone you imagine, Miss Roston. It is simulated training, but there's a real person whose brain waves will be connected to yours, and, it's not a great idea psychologically to bond with a real person who isn't real…I mean, you know what I mean…."

His voice trailed off and he shrugged. He opened his mouth to continue but Helen waved him off. "Understood," she told him and shrugged at Flyboy. "See? Can't have you as my dream guy either. There's too much brain wave—" She waved her hand dramatically and added, in a mock British accent, "Brain wave immersion, creating cerebral confusion between reality and illusion."

Even Derek couldn't help chuckling at the wry

mimicry of the professorial tone of Dr. Hollingsworth, the scientist in charge of Mind Viewer, the thought immersion program. Helen had had to sit through a few of his lectures as he explained what she meant to the program and how the experiments were supposed to work. That was when she'd first met Flyboy. Since he had been in a simulation program recently, he'd joined her a couple of times so he could also answer her questions. She was glad. She understood Flyboy's easy layman's description better than Dr. Hollingsworth's technical language.

Besides, Flyboy was the only one of the infamous nine commandos who had taken the time to get to know her. He had introduced her to other operatives, widening her circle of new friends.

Helen liked him. She hoped the rest of the commandos would accept her as easily as he did.

"I'm heartbroken," Flyboy said, giving her ponytail a swift tug. "You'll just have to go out with me and I can make your dreams come true, Hell."

"Yeah, yeah, okay, let's get this started." Helen straightened in her chair and sucked on her forefinger. "First, forget those bulging muscles. I mean, you made him look like some romance model, like what's-his-name..."

"Fabio," Derek supplied helpfully.

"Now how is it you come up with his name immediately?" Flyboy countered.

Derek whipped out a paperback. His face was flushed again. "I took this off my sister's bookshelf. He is Fabio, isn't he? I thought I did a pretty good job with the digital imaging. I did add some changes, of course."

"You did use Fabio as a model!" Helen stared at the

book cover in amazement. It portrayed a half-naked man with long hair, his muscles impossibly ripped. She looked at the other model on the computer screen. Yup, the likeness was there. Same longish hair and muscle tone. She thought of what had happened to her during that first run-through of CAVE Ultimate. Revenge was going to be so sweet. A wicked grin broke free. "Well, let's see the goods, Derek. Take his pants off."

"What?"

"Sheesh, if you're going to design my trainer's avatar and he's to be specifically to my taste, shouldn't I get to order all the details?"

There was a short silence. Flyboy burst into laughter. He pulled a nearby chair between Helen and Derek. "I want to see this. Let's check out the junk on Miss Roston's made-to-order trainer, Derek."

"I…"

Helen patted the man on the back. He had the look of someone facing torture. "Come on, I promise it'll be over soon. Let's start easy. Peel off his pants. And I want him blond, please."

"What happened to tall, dark and handsome? Or is it because I'm blond?" Flyboy asked.

"Oh, shut up, you. He's my Greek god, and I want him blond, and much sleeker, with chocolate eyes."

"Hey, I have blue eyes!"

"Make his eyes chocolate, Derek."

"Yes, ma'am." But he was clearly reluctant to give up his "creation."

"Leaner, not so muscular."

"Yes, ma'am."

"I know you meant well, Derek, adding that fur, but

really, not so much chest hair, please." She suspected that Derek grew up playing too much interactive Dungeons and Dragons on the Internet. The avatar he created was the classic "I kill for food and magic" stereotype she'd seen advertised in game store windows.

"What, you're going to bury your face in his chest? These are going to be some VR training sessions! Are you sure the powers-that-be want that?" Flyboy asked, laughing.

Helen turned to Derek. "Didn't they order you to tailor the thing to my taste?" she asked.

"Yes, ma'am. The idea for this phase of your training is to simulate the missions before you get your dosage. You need your trainer to talk you through as your body reacts to the drugs and the doctors thought it best to give you a measure of control of his avatar."

"Uh-huh. Hear that mumbo-jumbo, Flyboy? That means I get to make the guy as sexy as I like, and I demand a blond Greek god with chocolate eyes. For a start." Helen cracked her knuckles. They were going to play with her mind, anyway, so why not have some fun with it? It was strange, but meeting her so far invisible trainer added a level of excitement that she couldn't explain. It wasn't going to be a real meeting, but better than that shadow he'd been using in the CAVE. "Let's start from the top."

"He looks a lot better than the model Derek cooked up for your avatar," T. observed. She leaned over to take a better look, then laughed. "Oh my God, she's having fun, isn't she? That's Helen for you."

"Is she ready?" the man questioned.

"Oh yes, as ready as a test supersoldier superspy can be," T. said, half-seriously. "She's been trained by Special Ops. She passed several of the CIA remote viewing tests with flying colors. She's achieved 72.5 percent accuracy. She's one of my best operatives and she's not called Hell for nothing, you know."

"Yes, but she isn't the best." He turned to look at T. "You are."

T. fluffed her hair. "Darling, how do you do that? Praise and accusation at the same time. I couldn't take two years off for that kind of training, you know that. It'd ruin my nails. I picked the best operative we had. She's single, unattached, and very ambitious. She wants to do this."

It wasn't a good enough explanation for him. He wanted to know the real reasons. "She's single and un-attached—you're sure of that." It wasn't a question. He didn't want any third-party complications when he was just beginning this phase of their relationship.

"That's what she says and she's been training very hard all this time. I haven't seen any romantic affilia-tions except for some go-nowhere dates. I trust my op-eratives, and when Helen said she would do it, she meant it. That girl is very talented—I'm lucky the CIA didn't snatch her from me."

"She's too independent. CIA doesn't like that."

T. shrugged. "That's what GEM is. We're all inde-pendent and if they don't like it, why do they keep con-tracting us? Are you going to have a problem? This is going to be just as tough for you. Your brain waves being linked to hers during experimentation. Those sci-entists called it mind-bonding, darling and…" She cocked a brow. "We know how your mind is."

He smiled for the first time, a small quirk of his lips. He canted a brow in answer. "What, you don't have confidence in your top operative playing mind games with me? And it's Mind Setter, T."

The two phases to the Mind Viewer program were named Mind Setter and Mind Former. The first phase set the brain immersion in motion, linking him to Helen by synchronizing their brain waves during sleep, then after a period, during tests. They'd started this phase a couple of months ago.

"Darling, I prefer my term. What's happening is more intimate than mind-setting, or whatever Dr. Hollingsworth calls it." T. crossed her arms. "Remember, Helen isn't just trained in NOPAIN now. She has all these things being experimented within her mind. Who knows what she would do to you?" A challenging gleam entered her golden eyes. "Bet she'll fight you all the way. GEM operatives have great resistance."

Yes. A dangerous woman. The man returned his gaze back to the screen. "Not if I look like that. She can't do anything to me with that image in her head."

T. looked at the new image of the avatar. "Superspy. Remote viewing-trained. Combat-ready. And once she takes the drugs, she should be a supersoldier—fearless, with little capacity for emotion, and less need for sleep. You'll probably be the only one holding on to her mind. Be gentle with her, hmm?"

"I thought you said she would give *me* trouble?"

"I just don't know about the drugs. You never know with drugs. You, better than most, understand how that is. They've done things to you in your program. That's why you're a perfect balance. Guide her through her first mission and get her back safely."

"I've no intention of failing, T.," he said softly. It wasn't the guidance part of Mind Setter that would be the problem between him and Elena Rostova. It was getting her ready for him.

"Okay, I put on these goggles and then he's just going to be there?" Helen loosened her ponytail. She weighed the goggles in her hand. Lightweight plastic, malleable in feel. "We can talk and everything? Do we need to go to the CAVE to test this?"

Dr. Kirkland, Dr. Hollingsworth's second-in-command, shook his head and pointed to the virtual reality chair and equipment at the far corner of the room.

"Not today. This is just a run-through and we thought we'd try out the new VR Portal. We're going to monitor your heart rate and vital statistics. You can talk while we get both your brain waves in sync."

"Wait, he's here somewhere? We aren't using a simulated program?" Helen looked up at the doctor sharply. "Where?"

"He's in a similar test room, Miss Roston," Dr. Kirkland said as he nodded to his assistant. "This is just a test to see whether the communication comes through."

"But it's virtual reality." Helen pretended to frown. She understood what was going to happen but it didn't hurt to hear the doctor's version of the truth.

"The simulated reality is virtual but your trainer is real. You already know that. He has to be, or you won't be able to get real instructions when you're in your remote viewing state."

"Oh, I know I don't see *him*—it'll be my blond god but still, do I have to call him something?"

"Miss Roston, we'll get to that as soon as we start this program. Right now we don't even know whether you two are in sync."

Helen grinned. "Doctor, I'm in control of this hottie in my head. How in sync do I need him to be?" Flyboy chuckled as the doctor tried to remain serious. She turned to Derek. "You make sure he's still naked. I want to see the goods before I agree to have you guys mess my mind up with drugs."

The reference to the more serious aspect of the experiment brought a quick nervous nod from the young programmer. Helen gave him a soothing smile. Ironic, really. She was the one who might go psychotic and she had to comfort the poor guy. She looked at the goggles in her hand. This was it, the final phase before…

She could feel her heart beating faster and she glanced up to see the doctor looking at her closely. Like she was some mouse in his lab, she bet. Oh well. She had agreed to this. She took in a deep breath. Fear, especially of the unknown, was normal.

A beep distracted her. Flyboy reached for his back pocket. He gave a sigh. "Damn. I have to go, babe." He stood up. "Call you later? Drinks? Massage?"

Helen wrinkled her nose. "I have to go to philosophy class. Want to come along?"

Flyboy shuddered. "You're kidding me."

Her smile was devilish. "Come along and find out," she invited.

Flyboy shuddered again. "You win, Hell." The beeper went off a second time. "Got to go. Later."

Helen nodded to Dr. Kirkland and held out her arm. She remained quiet as he read her statistics to his assistant. The goggles sat in her lap, their gleaming surface reflecting parts of her face. Such a little thing with such power. She had done VR before but this was going to be different. This time, unlike the CAVE, someone was going to be in her head. Remote viewing was weird enough. This was going to be one step more into her strange new role of supergirl.

Fifteen minutes later, she was strapped into the sensor jacket, sitting on the VR chair. Derek looked at her expectantly. Dr. Kirkland adjusted the headgear.

"Ready when you are, Miss Roston."

Helen nodded. "Ditto."

She knew what to expect. At first it would be dark, like a movie theatre. Without the sensor jacket, she could see a whole movie on a huge screen all in her head. Then, when they turned on the switch or whatever they called it, she would experience virtual reality in a training facility, all her movements guided by the sensors. It wouldn't be the same without the CAVE's special sen-surround elements, though.

She'd been thinking a lot about this. The training in the CAVE was for him to test how her mind worked. That was why he kept pushing her buttons. That was why he was always in control. This time, in the Portal, it would be different; she would be controlling the missions with her remote viewing. It seemed that her secret trainer was preparing himself to deal with *her*.

One more difference than the CAVE. He'd be closer now, too. He'd be in my mind. Anticipation squeezed the pit of her stomach.

She glanced around in the darkness. A few seconds went by. "I don't see anything," she said out loud.

"Hang on one more minute, Miss Roston," Derek said in her right earpiece. "Still trying to get the signals right."

Helen rolled her eyes behind the goggles. Idiots. They were going to fry her brain cells before she got to see her yummy dream guy.

Fried brain cells for a naked man in your head. Who's the idiot?

Helen jerked in her straps. Whoa. It was still dark, but that was definitely not her voice. There was no shadowy figure, though. She coughed. "I think I hear something," she said out loud. "Derek?"

"Okay. That's good. Keep trying."

"Keep trying? Keep trying what? You're the one who's supposed to know what's happening!"

Silence. Helen waited for a moment, then sighed. Obviously the doctor had told Derek to shut up. She peered into the darkness. Okay, this was getting ridiculous. Should she say hello out loud? Uh-uh. No way were they going to witness her making a fool of herself talking to nobody. She was going to think this conversation, see whether that worked. As in remote viewing with her guide during the CIA training sessions, she moved her lips and spoke silently. It usually took several minutes before the internal conversation became "normal" enough where she wouldn't be aware of the need not to talk out loud.

"Yoohoo!" she called, in her head. *"Yoohoo, naked guy, wherever you are!"*

Silence.

Helen made a face. *"Dammit, I know that you can hear me!"*

"Thought you wanted to see me."

Great. She hated smart-asses.

"Thought you liked my ass. You requested nice and tight, buns of steel, if I remember correctly."

Helen sat there, stunned for a second. Whoa. Wait a minute. He could read her thoughts. She had thought…

"You had thought to have a conversation with me, which is how it'll seem to be once they get all those electrodes to work correctly…."

"Can you read every thought?" she asked fiercely, realization rapidly dawning on her. Damn. The brain wave synchronization. Of course he would be reading her thoughts. She was thinking this reality. The talking was virtual.

"I'm your monitor, so in virtual reality land, I monitor your thoughts. I'm sure I'll get to know you better as we continue this."

"Wait a minute!" A sudden burst of light caused Helen to blink, her eyes trying to focus. There was a strange humming in the back of her head, or maybe not, because it went away as soon as she tried to concentrate on it. Movement to her right. She turned.

Oh, my. Naked guy at three o'clock. He was exactly as she'd told Derek she wanted her trainer to look. She found that she could walk toward him as he stood there in all his glory. She gulped as she circled the magnificent man, checking out the details. He looked so real! This virtual reality program they were using was simply amazing.

Facing her trainer, she gave him her trademark devilish grin. *"Oh, yeah!"* she whooped.

"I gather you like me naked."

His voice had a sexy Southern drawl, just as she'd requested. Helen grinned again. *"This is too cool for words,"* she told him, smirking wickedly. *"It's good to finally see you. Don't you like being naked?"*

He looked down at himself and a glimmer of a smile touched his beautiful lips. *"It's your program for now."*

"Yeah, yeah, I know. Once they get it all ready, I'm supposed to get all serious. But right now, you're mine, mine, mine!" Helen badly wanted to touch him, but something stopped her from reaching out. She liked the idea of finally having him at a disadvantage. Cocking her head, she drawled, *"But they didn't say I couldn't have you naked all the time, even if you're training me."*

"Won't it be boring? Looking at this body all the time?" There was unmistakable laughter in that voice.

"Hey, I made you, so how could I get bored of you so soon?" crooned Helen. She was getting more intrigued by the real man behind this. What other things could he teach her, besides the stuff they'd been doing in the CAVE? And what was his role?

"More than you think."

She blinked in surprise again. She had to learn how to control her thoughts in here.

"You're quick. See, the first lesson's almost over."

He reached out and touched her face. She felt his fingers caress the spot just below her earlobe. It felt real, just like in the CAVE.

Which reminded her—she smacked his hand away. *"I want to know something. I—"* Looking at him, she found she couldn't talk seriously to a man standing so nonchalantly naked in front of her. She swallowed, trying to recapture her irritation. *"I want to know something about that first night."*

"What would you like to know?" He didn't seem puzzled about which night.

"What if I hadn't guessed that it was some kind of virtual reality program? Would you have...continued?"

"Taking your clothes off, you mean? Touching you?"

He was blunt. Helen hadn't wanted to say those words. She shrugged. She still hadn't reconciled with the knowledge that she'd been turned on by that phantom kiss. *"Yes,"* she said.

"Yes."

She glared at him. *"Even if I'd said no?"*

"You hadn't," he pointed out. *"If you remember, you said you'd kill me, but not once did you say 'stop' or 'no.' So yes, I'd have continued."*

He was right. She'd been furious—both at her response to his kiss and then at his intimate touching. *"Would you if I had?"* she insisted.

"Yes. It was a test, Elena. Either you pass or fail it."

He lifted his hand and caressed the side of her face again. A shiver ran down her spine.

"What name should I call you?" Could one sound breathless in one's mind? His fingers tickled sensuously. She could feel a frisson of awareness sliding like silk against her skin. She'd gotten used to him touching her. She should be mad as hell at what he'd put her through, but now wasn't the time to challenge his way of introducing himself. After all, Dr. Kirkland was trying to get the goggles to work right. She was sure she'd foul up their equipment testing if she started kicking Naked Guy's ass.

"You choose." There was mockery now in that voice, too, as if he'd read her mind again.

"No, you choose." She wanted to see how clever he was.

He leaned closer and she swore she could smell cologne on the man. This was freaking unbelievable. His breath even tickled her ear. *"Hades,"* he whispered. *"And you'll come when I call."*

He snapped his fingers. There was that humming again and the lighting in the room dimmed.

"Miss Roston? We're done for now. Please stand by while we take each sensor off."

Hey, wait a minute! Where did he go? It was over? Helen looked around as the place returned to darkness. She hadn't even checked him out thoroughly yet! *"Hey, you!"*

Of course he didn't answer. It was strange as she sat there, seeing nothing, trying to grasp the memory of what just happened. Damn. It left her feeling bereft. Hades. Hell and Hades. Damn smart-ass.

The goggles came off and she blinked again, her eyesight focusing back on Derek the programmer. He looked extremely pleased, as if something grand had happened. Oh yeah, of course. They had managed to sync brain waves today. Yippeedo.

"How was the avatar, Miss Roston? Everything like you ordered?" he asked.

Helen sniffed. She didn't like the way it had ended. She was the one in charge still, wasn't she? He was still her naked guy.

She shook her head as they freed her from the straps and sensors and whatnots. She swerved the seat toward the computer. Mr. Hades was going to get a big surprise.

"Not quite," she said and tossed Derek a wicked look. "I found him lacking in the size department. I want to make some parts bigger."

She had been watching Derek earlier and with her photographic memory, she repeated a sequence of typing on the keyboard. Then she played with the mouse and watched the cursor on the screen follow her movements.

She hated to admit it. Those times in the CAVE, when he'd chosen to put her in roles where she felt dominated, pushing at all her hot buttons, testing her emotions as if he wanted to learn how to switch her on and off, had sometimes left her feeling vulnerable. She didn't like that at all, and the bastard knew it. She knew he was testing her mental strength, to see how far she would allow him to go.

She wrinkled her nose. She was going to push some buttons herself. Her forefinger tapped on one of the keys several times. And a few more. She laughed in naughty satisfaction. Revenge was satisfyingly sweet.

"Hell, yeah!"

Three

Philosophy class was an odd course for them to inflict on her. After all, thinking too deeply would affect action. Analysis paralysis, that was one of her Special Ops. trainer's favorite sayings.

"You start thinking about how dark it is in there, you've already lost half the battle, Roston," he'd said, during one session when she had to belly-crawl into a pitch-black tunnel. "There's active anticipation of danger and there's passive anticipation. The second type will get you killed."

But they insisted on philosophy classes at the Center. Helen hadn't thought she would enjoy them. She wasn't particularly interested in logic and reasoning; she reasonably explained to the tutor that if she had any logical brain cells at all, she wouldn't have signed up for this experiment in the first place. Everyone had laughed at the workshop.

However, the sessions weren't entirely useless. There was a method to their madness, she supposed. Command Center definitely had a different approach. Analysis, Helen found, was used to paralyze latent emotions, such as fear and anger.

She understood that fear could be a major stumbling block in the coming experiment. It could defeat her. It was important therefore that she learn to shape her fears into something tangible so she could overcome them.

Helen was getting so damn good at pretending, it should scare her. But it didn't, really. Fear, as they had told her from the beginning, would eventually be under her control.

She applied fresh lipstick in the restroom, and made a face. She'd learned at GEM that reality had many faces. Often, what one saw in front of oneself was just part of the truth. What mattered most was the hidden agenda.

She knew from day one that she was different. She'd sensed the danger behind the reality around the friendly strangers who'd approached her, but food was a powerful tempter to a hungry kid. She had options—accept the food and go with those nice GEM agents or remain alone. Hunger could conquer anything, even fear. And something about the whole thing gnawed at her, so she'd followed them. And here she was.

Unanswered questions. Looking for the unvarnished truth. That was her driving force in life.

Pulling her loose hair into a ponytail, she fluffed the bangs away from her forehead. Her hand wandered on its own to the spot below her earlobe. How did he know she liked to be touched there?

That irritated her. She didn't mind being psychoanalyzed by their team of head doctors; she was trained in NOPAIN—nonphysical persuasion and innovative negotiation—and she could easily evade questions she didn't want to answer. She had even grown comfortable with them staring at her through their microeyes; it was in her contract. She had known when she'd agreed to this experiment that her life wasn't going to be hers again. What was it Enrique always told her? *Ya gotta let the big boys think they're bigger and stronger before you can whoop their ass,* Elena. She smiled at the memory of the older punk boy who was her sometime companion. At fifteen, Enrique—a name he'd chosen for himself—was more grown-up than most kids his age. Street wisdom still made a lot of sense in her world.

Her smile turned into a frown. She hadn't counted on someone knowing little things like her erogenous zones, though. Again she wondered about this trainer behind the avatar. Was he anything like her creation? Did he remote view, too? And if so, how far along was he? Her training hadn't taken her into some of the higher levels she'd read about—the government was too eager to try her out.

Helen looked at her reflection. She had to admit that letting her create her trainer's avatar was insidiously clever. Psychologically, she would immediately have an innate response to him already. Maybe it was one of their tricks, to make her assume that it was a man—

Nah. Hades sounded too much like a man. A woman wouldn't have said those last lines. She closed her eyes, recalled the scene in her mind with the quick vividness that was now so familiar…

Her instincts rose like a radar. Her eyes flew open.

"You know, I thought I smelled your perfume," she remarked calmly.

"Liar. I don't have any on today." T. appeared from one of the stalls.

"Oh? Are you testing me, too?" Helen turned to give her full attention to her operations chief. "Or are you here to tell me who my trainer is?"

T. shrugged. "I don't know everything."

"Who's the liar now?" There was no one higher in her agency here—she had the security clearance.

T. shrugged again, then turned to the mirror. "They're very secretive here at the Center. Surely you've noticed that? I rarely get to talk with anyone other than the commandos I work with, and I've been here almost two and a half years."

"This partnership GEM has with them—is it that great?"

Ever since the news had gone through the grapevine that their contract agency was now working with COS Command, there was rampant gossip that the "partnership" would become a merger, and that GEM's independence could be history. So far, Helen hadn't seen any difference in the way her agency worked, but then she had been deep in training and hadn't had the time to really pay close attention.

Helen studied the tall blond woman who was her operations chief and mentor. Even after all these years, it was still tough to read T.'s emotions. T. was a chameleon, able to project whatever was needed for the situation, and when she was in her element, even Helen's intuition couldn't gauge her chief's real feelings about anything.

But Helen trusted T.'s judgment more than anyone else's. It was T. who told her she had a special gift, who had always encouraged her to use her special instincts during dangerous situations. It was T. who told her that she had far to go in GEM.

"It's been highly beneficial," T. told her. She smiled. "I just love the way we both seem to have our meaningful conversations in the ladies' room."

Helen wrinkled her nose and thumbed at the exit. "Out there is the macho man's world. This Center is full of them. You know it, and I know it. Some of them are sexy as get-out but I don't trust any of them."

T.'s smile widened. Her brows arched meaningfully. "Not even your hot trainer?"

Helen let out a sigh. "Why are you trying to use NOPAIN on me? Just ask your damn questions outright, T."

"Darling, you've been delightfully evading and dodging those head doctors all these months. Why can't I try my hand on you?"

"Because you're on my side." Helen cocked her head. "I hope?"

"Yet you don't want to tell me everything. I'm still your operations chief, Hell, even though you've been out of touch lately, what with secretive CIA RV training and disappearing for weeks without debriefing." T. played with the many rings on her fingers. "They're playing with your mind, and as a friend, I'm concerned that you might forget this is a contract, not a permanent thing."

"Ha! How could I forget right now I'm the CIA's and various government agencies' favorite toy? I'm the most watched woman in the spy world now, barring a few hundred posters of calendar babes. I've been monitored, recorded, prodded and probed. They had me hooked up to devices that measure my pulse and pretty much every body function they could think of. I'm sure they've tried every available way to look into my mind while doing those experiments in remote viewing. T., darling, I'm the last person to forget what I've become."

"Which is?"

Helen frowned. Damn. T. got her there. She hated it when T. won in NOPAIN. She shrugged, trying to evade. "I don't quite know yet. After all, they pulled me out of training as soon as I finished Phase Two, and I'm still miffed about that! I was getting to be quite good at their stupid little tests. Why did they interrupt my remote-view training?"

T. continued turning one of her rings. Her amber-gold eyes were thoughtful as she studied Helen. "Maybe they were trying to keep within the time limit of the contract. Or maybe they didn't want to lose you. You do know the high cost of the advance stages of the CIA program."

T. didn't mean in financial terms. She had been frank about the real dangers when the contract was offered but Helen had been intrigued. Getting a bird's eye view of so many agencies was an operative's fantasy. "Yeah," she said, with another shrug. "The casualties end up in some mental ward and they didn't want to risk me. Not too soon anyway."

T. nodded. "You've been doing excellently. They're eager to start with what you can do now. They told me those flashes you have are longer now."

Helen turned back to the mirror. "I'm not supposed to elaborate too much about the project to anyone."

"Darling, your state secrets are safe with you. When

I want an update, the info I seek is your welfare. However…" T. paused, her eyes narrowing. "I can see I can't depend on you for that."

Helen met T.'s eyes in the mirror. Her reflex had been to be defensive because she had to be alert all the time and she knew she'd been doing the same with T. She allowed a part of herself to relax. "I can't explain what's happening to me, T.," she said quietly. "It's exciting and scary."

"And it's going to get more so, with this new phase. Remote viewing plus virtual reality is going to play with your mind even more. That's why they decided that you needed to be connected with a real mind outside. This virtual reality trainer—he's your anchor, Hell. You can trust him. You have to allow yourself to depend on him sometimes."

Helen smiled and turned back around. It was now her turn to trap her operations chief. "Thought you said you didn't know him?"

T. smiled back and took a few steps closer. "I didn't say that," she mocked. "I said I didn't know everything. I could be talking to him through VR, too, you know. You have him looking like some blond beefcake. I myself prefer James Dean. Bad boys are more my style."

Damn. Thought she had her. "What? You wouldn't make him blond like your dear Alex Diamond? What will he say to that?"

The GEM grapevine was rife with gossip of what was happening between their operations chief and one of COS Center's top commandos. Romance was the word being bandied around. A GEM sister had wittily called it Operation Covert Combustion, and it wasn't too far from the truth, since T. appeared to be playing a game of total ignorance of a certain commando's presence at the Center. Helen cocked an enquiring brow.

T.'s face was unrevealing, her gaze shuttered. "I'm sure he gets his fantasies taken care of, darling."

Helen laughed. She bet. T. was also the master of disguises, a woman of a hundred faces. She could see how she confused her men, even Alex Diamond. She sobered. "I can tell you one thing, chief. Once you're immersed in this program, you find that there aren't any fantasies left in your life. Or maybe it's one big fantasy now. Take your pick."

She knew T. needed to know this. It was the operations chief's job to make sure her operatives stayed as safe as possible. Any contract taken up by GEM had dangerous elements and right now, Helen's was probably way up there on the list. She wanted to keep her chief in the loop as much as she could.

"Tell me how so?"

"Part of remote viewing is projecting imagery. Part of it is fortune telling. After a while you aren't sure whether you're doing that all the time unless you're very strong mentally." She gave T. a level look. "And I'm very strong. I'm going to get stronger. That's what all these psychoanalysis and philosophy classes are for, to help me stay grounded."

T. took one of her rings off and handed it to her. Surprised, Helen turned her palm out. "What's that for?" T.'s rings weren't just rings.

"Keep it on. It might be useful later."

"You're not going to tell me, are you?"

"Nope. Trust goes along with it."

"Ah." More NOPAIN. Helen watched as T. slipped the ring on for her. "This would mean something entirely different if you had a dick, T."

T.'s laughter echoed in the tiled room. She stepped back. "Soon you'll have to convince a bunch of suits with a demonstration. Are you ready?"

Back to business. Helen played with her new ring. "Yes."

"By the way, you're spending the night here at the Center."

"Damn, why?" She was already spending too many nights here lately. She loved being surrounded by lots of color, but colors created natural mental blocks for some reason. "I don't like their sparse comfort."

"It makes sense to. You'll have another VR session before the show. Center wants to make sure everything goes smoothly. That means the more they monitor your brain waves while you sleep, the better."

They had been doing that the last few months. Helen spent a few nights there every week, sleeping on some kind of bed with enough straps and electronic gear on it to qualify it for an S and M contraption.

"Today's test run went well—you two connected. You don't know how much this operation depended on that outcome. Believe me, darling, there were quite a few high fives today. They had actually expected more problems, but from what you described and what they could tell, the synchronization was delayed because of lack of sensory data. Once you've gotten used to sharing brain waves, communication will be better. He wants to do it one more time before your big show and tell."

Helen hid her surprise. T. loved ending their meetings

with unexpected news. Provoking emotional reaction was her hobby. "So soon? He misses me already, huh?" She couldn't help smiling, though, at the memory of what she had added to the avatar. "May I ask why?"

"He wants to talk to you about the coming test."

"Really? How interesting. He's concerned about my well-being, too," Helen said dryly.

T. waved her ringed hand, signaling the end of the meeting, and headed for the exit. "Oh, by the way, he told me to ask you to think about Greek gods and their stories. He said you'd understand. Ciao, Hell."

Helen frowned at that last comment. That VR trainer obviously loved to play games, just like T. Greek gods. Well, he was probably listening in when she was talking to Derek about her ideal man looking like a Greek god—a blond Greek god with chocolate eyes was what she had ordered. Now it made even more sense why he had picked the name Hades, the Greek god of the Underworld. Recalling that he'd known her nickname, she growled under her breath. She should have named him herself. She could see that he was going to be a challenge. A mischievous smile formed on her lips as she opened the door and sauntered out. A big challenge.

In a secret test facility, Virginia

"Okay, Agent 15, here's your chance. Your operational status is green. Bilocate to target and tell us what you see."

"Why is he shaking?"

Stop shaking. Concentrate, or you'll lose their interest. Deep breath, deep breath...Zoom.

Dark. Dark. Tell them what you see.... "I see it now! Classified meeting. Nine men. Four in uniform, one with enough medals to add several pounds to his weight. Three in civilian suits and ties. Two in lab jackets. They are sitting in a half circle around a conference table, facing a media screen. Conversation is quiet, tense, with some of them shaking hands. Do you want me to go closer and get the conversation?"

"Jesus, I hate how we need to guide them through every step. Don't they know that by asking them to look at the specific location, they're supposed to get information? That means see and listen in, Agent 15, do you hear me? We want to know the person in charge of the new candidate."

I hear you, fuckers. You're my monitors and I'm remote viewing for you. What the hell do you want?

Zoom.

Random words. Relax. "Okay, I'm going to concentrate on their conversation now. I'll tell you what I hear when I surface."

Give them what they want. Come on, Andrew, you can do this. Concentrate on the one with all the medals. Yes, yes, the words are audible now....

The Pentagon

"They don't have time to send talking heads to negotiate or discuss anything, Colonel. They functioned as a center for covert subversive training and activities, and the less said about what goes on in there, the better. It isn't in the business to explain itself to anyone, even to the President's most trusted men. Because of that, it's a good neutral place to test our candidate."

"Such as the multilateral test that's coming up." The colonel frowned, disapproval on his face.

"Yes. The best candidate just happens to be one of their own, so they're sure to want a lot of control over the tests. COS Center's operative won, so they get to set the rules. Some of them, anyway. This is a historic moment, though, don't you agree? Nine government branches, active and covert, working together for national security?"

The colonel snorted and muttered something rude in connection with Homeland Security under his breath. Audio feed from the speaker interrupted the conversation and the scrambled signal on the video screen cleared. Everyone's attention turned to the image addressing them.

"We've reviewed each of your task forces' lab and training reports. You were sent a copy of each, and we have agreed that the Center's test offer is by far the superior candidate of the program. So everyone here is on the same page, we're going to quickly go through the subject's profile in the file in front of you. The first page is the medical report from the D.I.A. scientists. The subject's mental and physical health is stable at ninety percent. Her psychological evaluations prove a strong psyche and system of belief. Her decision-making tests are in the top percentile. The stress chart shows excellent capability in multitasking. Positives—good attentiveness, quick grasp of situations, fearlessness, has been pretrained outside. Negatives—a tendency to independence and secrecy.

"Second are the combined reports from the Special Forces trainers from Year One. Physical endurance is above normal and completion of the one-year training with Special Forces was above average. Subject passed basic and advanced tests.

"Third is acknowledgment from the CIA task force in charge of Project Inner Space from Year Two. Their report is classified Red. Acknowledgment that subject finished Phase Two of Project Inner Space and showed no signs of mental stress or behavioral changes.

"Four is FBI background reports. Subject, as are most operatives in this contract agency, is an orphan. No family history available. No attempt taken to look for natural mother and father. Contract agency will not release information. We see this as a nonissue.

"Here is what the Center will provide at the next stage. We'll combine—"

Secret test facility, Virginia

No! Zoom!
No, no, please, no! Zoom!
"Dark, dark...oh, no...I can't hear anything any more, sir. I tried to focus on the screen, to see who's talking and...it just turned dark. I hear nothing now." *Blast of power. Really, really powerful energy.* "I heard him but I couldn't see...him."

"Dammit, Agent 15! Zoom in. It's important to identify him."

They don't understand. Too strong. "I tried... Can't see any more."

"Do it again, Agent. Zoom in. This is an order."

"Tried." *Zoom. Dark, totally dark.* "Tired. Mental block."

"You'll try again or there won't be another dose, do you understand?"

"Please. I need…something…. Everything's dark."

"If it's a mental block, you know you'd have felt it. Did you see any striking colors? Was there anything different?"

"No." *Don't want to tell them yet about that odd feeling. Too hard to describe. They'll start asking harder questions.*

"Maybe he's really used up for us. We should just get rid of him."

"No, too risky for now. We have some information at least. The new toy is ready for some tests. We just have to find out more."

"We're already familiar with all those phases. Hell, we've done a majority of them. What is the Center doing that we haven't tried?"

"Let's make him look again. Maybe he'll get something new. Agent 15, do you hear me? We need you to go back in after you write up what you saw."

"Write? Are you nuts? Look at the drool on the bastard. He's all washed up. There's no control over him, even after giving him the remote coordinates. We need another one soon."

"It isn't like we don't have a bunch of potentials in this facility but we have to do this slowly. They're garbage but their minds aren't."

Say something or they'll put you in that dark place again. No more dosage. No more happiness…say something quick! "Please! Please, please, I need it. Pain. Headache. Please." *Bands of steel tightening.* "I need some rest to write the report. I promise…once…head-

ache gone…I'll look again. I'll find out everything….
Please."

"Give him another dose. We don't have time for you
to rest, 15. We know you like floating out there, messing
with God knows what—"

Another dose? They're giving me another dose so
quickly? "Oh yes, I can do this with another dose. I'm
ready, of course I'm ready." *I'll stay away from the force*
this time. I'll focus in on that voice and find out for them….

Zoom. Zoom. Oh, this is fine. Look at all the pretty
lights moving so quickly. I don't even have to adjust
anything and I can still get them in focus! So cool. I
don't even need to hear the monitor's voice anymore.
No need to stay grounded anymore. What the hell for?
I can stay out here and play with the lights….

COS COMMAND CENTER (COMCEN)

Kevin Kirkland liked standing where he was, listening
in to the conversation that few were privileged to hear. Part
of the reason came from knowing that no one from the
Pentagon, except the other man in the room, knew that he
was here. It put him in a trusted position, and he knew the
man talking right now didn't trust many people. Strangely
enough, that was the topic of conversation at the moment.

"If you want her to trust me, then you'll have to let
me handle this my way. Her agency is now merged with
mine, and I have more knowledge of GEM operation
procedures than anyone in this room."

The man's voice was quiet and firm, with an underlying steeliness. From his angle, Kirkland had an excellent view of the wide screen. Four of the men were in

uniform. The other five were heads of departments connected to high levels of national security. Their attention ranged from direct interest to skepticism.

"This is a Classified Flux type project. We've always monitored every operational target," one of the men in uniform said. "This will be the first time we're using an ordinary outside operative and giving her free rein to achieve a mission. You're the monitor for us. Letting you handle this your way, as you put it, can put every mission in jeopardy."

"The COS Center is possibly *all* Classified Flux, and we aren't monitored in the way the military has to be, sir. I'm part of the V-Program, also a Classified Red project, and the success rate in our missions depended on our autonomy and secrecy. As for Miss Roston, I doubt anyone else would call her an ordinary operative, sir."

"Aside from her being a woman, she's still a contract agent, nothing we could count on," one of the men pointed out.

"She's from GEM and the operatives from there are highly regarded by every covert agency, national and foreign. COS Center has been working with them the last few years and our partnership has been very successful.

"Part of it is due to our training, but most of it is because of the ability of each operative to make quick decisions during his or her mission. In Miss Roston's case, it becomes complicated with every agency—CIA, DIA, NSA, INSCOM just to name a few—having trained her and wanting to claim her as their own, *if the experiment is a success*. There is a danger of information dissemination, of too many cooks spoiling the broth. She's GEM and therefore, she's mine. This project belongs to COS."

There was shocked silence as the men digested the speech.

"You're saying that you want to make all the major decisions of every operational target, that we're to listen to you?" The incredulity in the man's voice echoed the stares of the others around the table.

"Yes. Have a good day, gentlemen."

The man cut off the satellite feed and turned away from the screen. He punched the intercom on his desk. "Tell Derek to get the room ready."

Now that the camera was off, Kirkland came forward. He'd listened in often enough to know exactly when to interrupt. He watched as his test patient unbuttoned his shirt with one hand while offering his other arm.

After a few minutes, Kirkland rubbed alcohol and drew blood, then checked his stats. He labeled the tubes, putting them away in a small case. "Same questions— no nicotine, alcohol or caffeine the past twelve hours?"

"No."

"How's the stress level today?"

"I haven't killed anyone today."

"At least you're retaining your sense of humor after pissing off some of the most powerful men in our country."

"It's relaxing. You ought to try it sometime, Kirkland."

"To each his own. Of course, I feel quite powerful now knowing that I have more information on what COS Center has been doing with Miss Roston." The doctor smiled at the direct stare of the man in the chair.

"Yes, I understand. That also means I'm potentially in more danger than most people."

"Yes."

"Don't you worry they'll axe you?"

"No."

"Why, if I may ask?"

A glimmer of humor appeared in the other man's eyes. "They don't like working with each other, Kirkland. They hate having things out of their hands. Yet someone more powerful than they are is ordering them to continue this research, year after year. Why?"

Kirkland cleared his throat. The answer was pretty obvious. Everyone wanted their own COS success story. "Because covert and subversive training work?"

The man straightened his elbow and Kirkland placed the Band-Aid over his vein. "The success rate tells the story. And as long as it remains so, they won't question how we run things here. We pick and choose what we do, and we give them the results."

"It was nice to see you defending Miss Roston, especially with their remarks about her being a woman. After working with her these past few months, I find her more than just the test subject those people view her."

"Really?"

"Don't you like her? You've talked to her, seen her up close."

There was a pause. The man stood up and buttoned his open shirt. "She does have a sense of humor."

"Especially the way she made you up as in the VR program."

"Is this relevant for your evaluation?"

"No. But I'm curious about your reaction, that's all. How does it feel to be seen as something you aren't?"

The usually serious face of the project monitor cracked a slight smile. "I'm not the one who needs psych evaluation, Doc. She is. I've been through enough tests in this lifetime to know what you're up to."

The doctor sighed. Closing the file, he tucked it under his arm. "I suppose that's why you're the best for this phase. You have the experience to guide her, especially if the serum doesn't go well with her system."

"The test dose will tell."

"The previous tests with soldiers gave the exact results we wanted, although we don't know the long-term effects. It'll be doubly important with Miss Roston, who has been subjected to so many programs. She should be a mess, but she's remarkably stable."

"Yes, Kirkland, I can tell you like her. I'll take care to keep her safe."

Kirkland cleared his throat. He hadn't wanted to appear too concerned for Miss Roston, but he'd gotten to like the young woman.

The intercom buzzed. "Derek's ready, sir."

"Is she asleep?"

"Yes."

Dr. Kirkland picked up his case. "Shall we go?"

"Wait."

The man turned on his monitor and flipped channels. Helen Roston's room at the Center was all gray, just as her test required it to be. But the woman in there wasn't gray. Even from where Kirkland stood, she emanated a vibrancy all her own. The way she slept, on the right side of the bed, blankets kicked off. The way her features were perfectly composed, a small smile still playing on her lips. The way she was dressed, in a small shirt and underwear. Gray, of course. The way one long naked leg was tucked under the other. Helen Roston obviously didn't mind being monitored half-naked. Just like him—Kirkland returned his gaze to his patient.

"If I weren't a doctor, I would feel this is an invasion of privacy," Kirkland said.

"She signed the agreement. She knows we'll be watching her when she undergoes sleep training here."

"She thinks scientists and doctors are. Not you."

The man glanced at Dr. Kirkland, a brow raised. "She's a smart woman, Doc. She's GEM. She has more training than you'll ever know." He returned his gaze to the sleeping woman. "She knows I've been watching her."

"She's even more remarkable then. But that's good. She needs to trust you, or this isn't going to work."

The other man didn't say anything as he continued looking at the screen. Kirkland didn't interrupt any more, quietly waiting. He was used to the man staring at the test subject. It was the same intense stare every time, as if he was memorizing every detail of the sleeping woman. Kirkland wasn't a psychologist; he wasn't going to make any professional conclusion about that. As a scientist, he found this whole thing quite bizarre, but all experiments at the Center were bizarre.

The man next to him was probably one of the Center's most successful experiments and at times, Kevin Kirkland wasn't even sure he was human. His abilities were legendary. Kirkland glanced at the screen, then back at the man. What a pair. Helen stirred, stretched, and then turned the other way, tucking one hand between the bed and one leg.

"I'm ready."

The elevator took them to a sealed chamber. It was gray, just like the other room. The man stripped without preliminaries and climbed onto the special bed. Kirkland adjusted the straps and the headrest that was similar to the one Helen Roston had in her room.

"You can skip the subliminal message tape."

Dr. Kirkland paused, trying to hide his surprise. "There is no—"

"Doc. I know when my mind is being fucked with."

How? Another mystery about the man. "I had orders."

"I'm not angry. Just skip the subliminal loop. I'm as honest and loyal to the government as I'm ever going to get. You can choose to tell them that or not."

"I'll have to tell them that if I change any order of the test."

The man reached out, caught hold of Dr. Kirkland's wrist. "I'm no longer a test. She is."

"You're part of it," Kirkland reminded calmly. He sighed. "I won't put on the subliminal text."

The man released him and settled back comfortably. "Is she on theta wave yet?"

The doctor read the panel on the brain entrainment machine. The tonal frequencies were specifically designed to merge the brain waves of both right and left sides of the hemisphere. "No. Beta."

The man closed his eyes. "Don't get on theta till she's in REM state."

"Why do you want her to be dreaming when we hit theta?"

"Just do it, Doc."

Kirkland nodded and dimmed the lights. His other orders had been to follow the man's intuition when it came to the tests. This sounded like one of them.

"Good night."

"Good night, Doc."

Kirkland punched the code to lock the chamber and took the elevator to the next level. Derek turned around, the audible tones from the two machines in the background.

"We aren't using the subliminal tape for Chamber B tonight, Derek. And we're going to wait till Miss Roston hits REM before theta stage."

"Why, Dr. Kirkland? Are we now monitoring her dreams?"

"No, we have enough on our plate with this operation. We don't need that." Yet. He didn't know. "Adjust the template."

The monitors only showed the brain waves and breathing patterns of the subjects. The panel registered the vitals and different changes through the sleep session. There was privacy for Miss Roston, even if she didn't know it. As for the other…that display was top-secret and even Derek didn't have the clearance to know his identity.

"Alpha wave," announced Derek.

That man could fall asleep at will. Even after three months of watching it happen, Kirkland was amazed at the man's total control. He checked Helen Roston's monitor. She had started Rapid Eye Movement, usually the period when dreams happened.

"Slow down to theta, Derek."

The doctor opened his case and pulled out the files to make his notations. There was nothing unusual at the slowed-down readings. Over the intercom Helen Roston let out a soft snore and a tiny purr.

Four

She dove in after him. He was like some magical sea creature—beautifully formed, sleek and powerful, and very, very fast. She wanted to get close and see all of him. Circling around in the dark waters, she lost sight of him between the rocks and shadows. She couldn't hold her breath any longer and struggled upwards. She'd swum too deep. She would never make it to the surface. A powerful arm curved around her waist. She turned. She couldn't see but she knew it was him. She put her arms around him, holding tight as he seemed to shoot through the water like a rocket. Somehow, she'd known he would be there to get her out.

The first thing Helen heard was the tick-tock of the clock. She opened her eyes slowly. It didn't surprise her anymore, waking up and hearing things louder than they should be. All her senses, especially her hearing, were usually magnified when her mind was in between sleeping and waking. Sometimes she fancied she heard conversations but that could be just part of her dreams.

She stretched out her arms over her head and gave a yawn. Dreams. She had always had vivid dreams; it was something she didn't tell anyone, not since she had been in the second foster home with a strict ultrareligious family. She cracked her knuckles as she continued staring at the clock, watching the second hand slowly moving around.

Strange. She couldn't clearly remember last night's dreams as usual. Frowning, she focused inward. She'd been dreaming but it didn't feel right, as if she had been observing from the outside. She concentrated harder. She remembered the sounds of the ocean and someone swimming. Watching, she'd held her breath, waiting for the person to surface, but she hadn't been able to keep up. She'd given in, and sucked in big gasps of breaths.

That was all. How odd. She'd never had a swimming dream before, especially in the ocean; she didn't like open seas. And that feeling of disengagement…she tried to find a description…like…hmmm, like she didn't belong.

Helen laughed and rubbed a hand over her eyes. God, she would go insane if she did this to herself every day. It was probably them fucking with her mind. That had to be it. She knew what was going on while she was sleeping. She had signed an agreement allowing them to hook her up to their machines while they experimented with her. It was called Human Use Agreement and reading it had made her laugh. This must be one of their experiments. No doubt they would ask her whether she had been dreaming later.

Her eyes drifted to the camera on the wall. They had told her there were no microeyes, just that thing on the wall, and if she needed to, she could switch it off. She had grinned at the facilities director who told her that, and had innocently asked whether they were telling her she had the privacy to masturbate if she felt like it. The poor woman's face had lit up like a bad rash. Dr. Kirkland had choked.

Helen didn't know what had prompted her to embarrass the poor woman like that. It was just a defensive mechanism, the knowledge that there was to be no privacy making her feel even more outrageous. Subtlety had never been her strong suit, after all.

The red blinking light on the camera signified that it was on, that someone was watching right now. "Good morning," she called out conversationally, giving the camera a little wave. With her arms above her head, and her bare tummy showing, she must look provocative. She wondered whether it was Derek or Dr. Kirkland watching her at this hour. Poor guys didn't get any sleep. "You know, it's awfully nice of you to let me know when you're watching. The Center is more considerate than the CIA quarters. They wanted to see everything most of the time. I found six microeyes hidden in places where they weren't supposed to be, naughty bad CIA boys."

She scooted up, flinging untidy tresses from her face. "You could send in some breakfast. That would be ever so nice. I mean, even lab rats get fed." She tilted her head to one side, gave the camera a wink. "How about it, Doc?"

She gave a sigh and rolled off the bed. She hadn't made any close friends here at the Center. Dr. Kirkland was nice but one couldn't get too close to a man who took notes on everything one did. So she amused herself by talking like an idiot just to throw them off.

Training like this was tough on the mind. There was

no one to whom she could confide most of the time because everyone was scrutinizing her, reporting on her activities and her thoughts. She'd grown used to being flippant about everything, even when she was in pain. She grimaced. No doubt that, too, got reported.

Whatever. She must have been doing the right things because she'd passed every phase of their tests. She was almost "operational," as they called it—validated to work on real targets. The coming final test was it. There wasn't any fear of failure in her mind at all. She was anxious to get going.

There was a small buzz as someone outside keyed in the security code to her chamber. The door swished open and the facilities director appeared with a tray in her hands. Helen blinked in surprise. Oh wow. They had sent her breakfast.

"Good morning." As usual, the woman didn't have any expression on her face at all as she set down the tray on a nearby table. She was dressed in gray, just like the surroundings. Helen wondered whether she had orders to do that. "They told me you asked for breakfast."

"Oh, umm, yeah, but now I feel terrible because they made you bring it." Helen studied the woman for a second, still wondering the exact duties of a facilities director.

The woman placed an envelope beside the tray. "Here are your instructions today. There's plenty of time for breakfast."

"Thank you. Tell Dr. Kirkland thanks for getting me this, too," Helen said, sitting down.

The woman paused at the door. "It wasn't Dr. Kirkland who ordered your breakfast, Miss Roston."

Nice exit line. Helen was now totally convinced they

were messing with her. Oh well. She wasn't going to bite anything but her breakfast. Too early in the day to play mind games. Strawberries and pears. Yummy. Either a lucky guess or somebody knew her favorite fruits. Of course they knew. She sniffed at the shake. It smelled of banana. There wasn't any coffee, of course, although she would love a cup to start the day.

She took a tentative gulp of her shake. It didn't taste bad; there was more to it than milk and banana ice cream, though. She took another swallow, trying to figure out the tart aftertaste.

She picked up the envelope and slit it open with the knife. Settling back in her chair, one leg carelessly over the other, she began to read the instructions for the day. She laughed.

The first line was: "It's protein powder and some vitamins in the shake. Drink it up."

Picking up the glass, she gave the blinking camera a mocking toast. They had a sense of humor around here. She resumed reading.

"Morning schedule. VR session. Lunch Break. Psychoanalysis session. Break. Pretest prep. Questions and Answers. Break. Use this time to mentally prepare yourself. Please have a good snack before your big session. Time of meeting will be given during Q and A. Good luck."

It sounded like a school schedule and the beginning of the old TV show *Mission Impossible* all mixed together. Of course, now that she had brought it up, the stupid TV tune was going to play in her head all day.

Humming the ditty, Helen finished her breakfast. Today was the big day. She was the star of the show so she had better look good. She knew from scuttlebutt that some of the agencies were against the choice of a contract agent as the test candidate, and she was determined to prove them wrong. She loved challenges.

By the time she stepped out of the elevator, she had half an hour to spare before her VR session. The Center had twelve levels, as far as she'd been able to count. She was allowed access to only six of them. It had taken a while to find her way around the place because the inside didn't look anything like the building outside. Its interior was like an octopus, with different tentacles winging out. She had yet to find time to explore them all.

Turning the corner, she bumped into Flyboy. He must have just finished training. Shirtless, with a towel hanging from his shoulders, he looked tan and luscious.

"Hey there, gorgeous!" He whistled as he leaned a brown and muscular shoulder against the wall.

That line should have been hers. The man was one beautiful specimen. He had the body of a gymnast, trim and well-balanced. Six feet of male musculature. Being a pilot, he wasn't built like a fighter, but nothing about him was soft. Was there any part of him that was imperfect? She eyed the silver chain dangling just above his impressive chest, her gaze trailing down the well-defined washboard abs to the stringed sweatpants riding low on his slim hips. Her eyes slid back up to meet his. His sexy blue ones gleamed back invitingly.

"You look like a walking soap commercial," Helen drawled. The man knew his effect on women and didn't try to hide it. She sniffed. "Unfortunately, you stink."

"I'm on the way to doing that commercial right now. Want to join in?" His voice was sensuous, caressing.

Helen shook her head in amusement. Ah well... proposition in the morning. Good omen for the day. "Another time, sweetheart. I have VR this morning. You didn't get to see me yesterday. You said you wanted to compare notes. You have...oh, half an hour...if you're still interested."

Flyboy straightened and pulled on the ends of the towel. "Can't. How about lunch?"

Helen grinned. "Is it a business lunch?"

"Absolutely. What we do is our business, baby."

She laughed. Subtle he was not. "Don't you have something important to do, like fly your commandos out to some dangerous place to save the world?"

"Nope, bad guys must be taking a day off," he quipped.

Flyboy was one of the nine commandos of the V-Program, some top covert group with whom T. worked. Helen didn't know too much about them but the few she'd met the past few months convinced her that they weren't your normal commandos. For one thing, they were all damnably attractive, as if sex was part of their armor. For another, her operations chief's name was linked in gossip with one of them.

That in itself was a revelation. T. was...T. Helen had seen firsthand how men were around T., no matter what disguise she happened to be in. Any man who had managed to hold the top GEM operative had Helen's respect and admiration. For sure, he wouldn't be a normal kind of guy.

Speaking of the devil, Alex Diamond came around the corner. Like Flyboy, he was stripped to the waist, towel over one shoulder, sweatpants wet from exertion. Helen ran her tongue over her teeth.

Wow. She had to check out one of these morning training sessions one of these days. Alex Diamond was at least half a dozen years older than Flyboy but his physique certainly didn't show it. Lean and hard, his arms were roped with muscles. He looked extremely fit, like an extreme-sports athlete. Dangerous. Yeah. The man had that aura in waves.

Flyboy leaned and whispered into her ear. "Hey, remember me?"

Helen slanted him a teasing grin. "A girl's got to enjoy the view God gives her. Good morning," she called out a greeting. "Crowded corridor."

Diamond, as always, just nodded. She couldn't remember speaking more than a few sentences with the man. Strong, silent types always were a challenge to her.

A door opened. Helen's smile widened. Oh, the fun was about to begin.

"Morning, T.," she chirped.

Flyboy chuckled, folded his arms and relaxed against the wall again. Alex stopped, his light blue eyes meeting her chief's. Helen pursed her lips. *Operation Covert Combustion.*

It was like watching two blond lions about to do some X-rated stuff on *Animal Planet*. Neither T. nor Alex said anything as they stood there. Their eyes, though, were doing a hell of a lot of communicating.

"Well, I've got to go, chief," Helen said, shifting her weight from one foot to the other.

"Meet for lunch?" T. asked, not looking her way.

She shook her head. "I have other plans." And deliberately stepped on Flyboy's toes. He didn't react at all.

"I'll call you," T. said.

"Yeah. Come on, Flyboy, we're late," Helen said, heading off. She would have liked to stay and watch. Flyboy followed her as she turned the corner.

"Man of few words," Helen commented. "You're heading in the wrong direction."

"I came with you to get an apology." Flyboy wiggled his foot at her meaningfully. She looked back at him innocently. "Diamond has a way with words, believe me. And, with women, too. I saw how you were looking at him."

"You think T. and he are going to make a soap commercial of their own?" Helen asked. When he shrugged, she gave him a friendly shove. "Oh, he's taken, Flyboy. Can't you see the sparks flying in the air back there?" She patted him on the jaw, privately amused to see a touch of jealousy in his eyes. "You, on the other hand, are still an available hottie."

Nothing like a compliment to soothe the savage beast. Flyboy grinned. "And don't you forget it, sweetheart. Shall we meet later then, or was that just a ruse to get out of meeting your O.C.?"

She gave him another innocent look. "Don't know what you're talking about. We'll meet downstairs near those ghastly house plants, okay?"

Flyboy laughed. "The ghastly house plants. Yeah, that's about the right description for those damn ferns. Okay, but I'll be ten minutes or so late."

"Now how would you know I'll be waiting for ten minutes?"

He winked. "I'm a COS commando. I know everything."

Yeah, and a half-naked man calling at her hormones

to boot. She wished she had time to stay right there and chat, but duty called. She ran an appreciative eye over that gorgeous body once more and gave Flyboy a mocking salute before sauntering off.

Helen didn't doubt that he had women calling him at every hour. She wondered whether every one of the gorgeous nine from the V-Program was like that. Arrogant and too sure of themselves. She had to ask T. about them one of these days. What the hell was V-Program, anyway?

"Morning, Dr. Kirkland. Are you ready to suck more blood out of me?" Of all the scientists and medics who handled her, she liked Kevin Kirkland the best. For one thing, he had a sense of humor. For another, he didn't treat her like a lab rat all the time. Sometimes, she even thought he actually worried about her well-being.

"Morning, Miss Roston. How was your sleep?"

Medic Room 3 should have been renamed Special Room for Helen Roston. As far as she knew, she was the only patient who went in and out of the place. Every instrument in the room was part of the Helen Roston S and M toys, as she called them—from the head-scan machine in the corner to the oscillators on the tables that monitored her. And to the left was the VR room. Most women had jewelry and shoes. She had tubes and electrodes.

"Normal," Helen replied.

"Any interruptions?"

She sat down on the familiar leather sofa. "Nope." She looked around casually. "You'll have to take me to the viewing room one of these days."

"Viewing room?"

"The one where you watch me sleep."

There was a pause. "We don't watch you, Miss Roston. All we do is monitor your brain waves and stats."

Interesting. He was the second person—if you could call Eight Ball a person—confirming that someone else was watching her. Helen crossed her legs. "What, don't you want to study my sleeping positions as well?" she asked lightly. "Might as well. You all seem to know just about everything else."

Dr. Kirkland smiled as he pulled on plastic gloves. "How do you feel about tonight's test? Do you feel ready? Anything bothering you?"

Putting an arm over her forehead, Helen stretched out in a classic psychiatric patient pose. "I don't know, Doc. Sometimes my left foot seems to want to go one way and my right foot, the other. And I get totally confused whether it's because one of my stepfathers hit me on that foot once. The left one, I mean. And being he's a male authority figure, Freud would say that I have a problem with—"

"All right, Miss Roston, it's good to see that you're mentally alert." Dr. Kirkland shook his head. "I don't know why I bother asking questions of either of you. Evasion, evasion, evasion. How's a doctor supposed to make charts? Let's begin then."

Either of them, huh? She was getting some good information this morning. Helen sat back up, offering her arm for the usual procedures. She looked at the door leading into the VR room. She had a few questions for her trainer, too.

She found out that they called the new VR chair the Portal. She watched Derek and some technicians playing around with it, using the goggles, head-scan gear and the special gloves on themselves, as they adjusted and fine-tuned the machine with its straps and electrodes. The experimental gears and switches excited geeks like them. She could tell from their little whoops now and then that they were having the time of their lives.

She shook her head, but was glad that she'd been allowed to watch them at work. She was going to find out as much as she could about the experiment and all the equipment, but being explained to and having it done to her were two entirely different things. Yeah, yeah, synchronized brain waves. A communications link that utilized her "talent." But the reality—or the experience when it happened—was a jolt to any normal human being.

"We're activating the Portal, Miss Roston."

Derek's voice jerked Helen back from her reverie. She was so used to people doing stuff to her body that she could drift off without even feeling needles. She took a deep breath.

"Give me a sec." She wanted to be in total control this time. Someone else in her head. Get used to that, Helen. She released her breath, then mockingly drawled, "A girl's got to get ready when she meets a Greek god, you know." She flexed her fingers. *I want to get him closer.* She smiled, and instructed softly, "Okay, proceed, Derek."

The darkness didn't last as long this time. There was a quick prickle of awareness as something was turned on, then there he was, larger than life, in front of her.

Helen couldn't help smiling. Well, what was there

not to smile about, when she had created this beautiful creature herself? Her eyes went lower and her smile turned into a wide grin. Who said a girl couldn't have her cake and eat it, too?

No need for greetings. *"How do you like your changes?"* she asked impishly.

"I suppose any man would thank you for extra blessings," he replied dryly.

She waved her arms out experimentally. The sense of space was so real, even though her mind was telling her she was really in VR mode.

"So, are you ever going to tell me what we do during these sessions? Besides me admiring your beauty, of course." She had read the contract and the stages of experiments but this was the vaguest part. What exactly was this man to her? *"How many times do we meet?"*

"Look at it as a getting-to-know-you kind of thing," he replied. Was that a hint of mockery? *"And we meet as often as we can."*

Helen sauntered closer, tilting her head to the side a little as she looked up at him. *"So this is like questions and answers?"*

"Something like it. For now."

It was unnerving how the avatar just stood there unmoving. *"Can you make yourself appear with clothes?"* she asked.

"No, you have total control over what I look like, Helen."

"Oh. Am I embarrassing you?"

"But you wanted to."

"That's not so!" Well, a little, but it was just her need to assert control.

"Yes, control is very important to you, and I don't blame you at all. Your life isn't your own these days."

"How do you read my mind? And how come I can't read yours?" She wrinkled her nose. *"Those brain wave sync tests, right? Somehow you can read my thoughts."*

He shook his head. *"No,"* he assured her quietly. *"Those tests aren't advanced enough to read subjects' minds, Helen. Let's just say that I find this situation quite unique myself. The VR is supposed to let me see what your mind is projecting when you're in session, but my sensory perception is also picking up things I shouldn't— sometimes your thoughts, sometimes your feelings."*

She didn't think she liked that at all.

"I don't blame you."

"Oh, stop. You're going to make me nervous about my own thoughts."

"No, you have to learn to get used to me, Elena."

She stepped closer. It was strange how he sometimes switched to calling her Elena. It made their conversation even more intimate, somehow. *"Why?"* she asked. His eyes drew her to him, dark chocolate, and so secretive.

Again he shook his head. *"If I tell you, you'll just anticipate and then fight it. It's in your nature. I can feel it. You hate being told what to do and how to behave."*

Helen didn't want him to tell her what she was like. *She* was the one trying to find out what he was like, dammit. *"T. told me to think of Greek myths. Hades kidnapped poor Persephone into the Underworld. She must've told you they call me Hell-on-Wheels. Is that why you chose that name?"*

"Apt, don't you think? Although I much prefer Elena."

The way he said her name made her think of doing things with a man—naughty, private things. She quickly pushed the thoughts away.

Hades reached out and waved his hand. The perception of white light disappeared and Helen found herself in a desertlike place, a blazing sun above her. He waved again, and like magic, the sudden ovenlike heat was gone, and they were standing near the edge of a building, a long way above a snarl of traffic. She could feel the wind beating on her body and she reached out to grab his arm to steady herself. It felt hard and muscular.

"Fine, you have programmed controls at your end to play with the scenery," she yelled above the wind. *"So you're Hades giving me a tour. What's that got to do with your being able to read my thoughts and feelings?"*

Hades turned suddenly, his eyes sharp and assessing. *"Give and take, Helen. That's the foundation to a good relationship. What's your remote view trigger code?"*

Five

Her RV trigger. That was an essential key to her remote viewing. Any viewer had a code or a series of images to keep his or her hold on reality. Remote viewing was free-form…dangerous; without an experienced human monitor or a trigger code, the viewer could be lost in the ether. Mind…reality…ended up somewhere in the twilight zone.

A gust pushed Helen forward, closer to the edge of the building, and she tightened her hold on his arm. She willed herself to ignore the drop below. *"No,"* she said. *"Nice trick, but my mind can withstand trick questions."*

The wind stopped just like that. They remained standing at the edge of the tall building. *"I know. GEM's NOPAIN's a wonderful tool,"* Hades said, *"but that wasn't a trick question."*

Very few people outside the most covert ops could casually bring up NOPAIN in conversation. Most operatives asked its meaning or its usage. Obviously, Hades already knew, and seemed to be trained in a form of it. The KGB and CIA each had their versions of NOPAIN. So, was her trainer once from the CIA? That was highly possible since COS Command recruited all its operatives from the different branches of covert government. Something else to file away.

"What do you call that wind?" Helen demanded. She didn't like the fact that he still hadn't moved an inch. *"A finger itch at your end? You're constantly trying to scare me. I haven't forgotten our first meeting, you know."*

Or forgiven. But *forgiven* was an intimate word, pushing a training incident into the realm of the personal. She'd told herself that she wouldn't make anything during her training personal, even down to the times when she knew they weren't supposed to be watching her. She was going to be exactly what they were training her to be—a supersoldier-spy. But there were times, what Hades did with her in the CAVE, that almost crossed the line. She had a feeling that the person behind her avatar did that a lot.

A ghost of a smile appeared on his lips. *"A test."*

"Of?" It irked her that he didn't address her comment about how he'd introduced himself.

"Your reflexes. You didn't show much surprise at the sudden temperature changes. And you also aren't afraid of heights. That's good to know."

Helen stared hard at him, then laughed. *"Reacting to temperature changes? Excuse me,"* she pointed out in between chuckles, *"but I'm not the one naked here. You...ummm...didn't react much to extreme heat and height, either. That's good to know."*

She was still holding on to his arm. When the wind

was gusting hard, his solidity was very reassuring. An image of an anchor materialized in her mind.

"That's good to know."

Helen glared at the man beside her. She was getting terribly tired of his reading her thoughts. What she needed was…pure adrenaline. Without allowing herself to deliberate, she tugged at Hades' arm and stepped off the building. It was a heart-stopping moment. His eyes met hers for that split second just before the free fall. He twisted his body and held her in his arms. There was no surprise in his gaze. Or fear. Whoooooosh.

Rush of air. Heart pounding. Her eyes closed as her head spun. In the back of her mind, the good Helen was already scolding her stupidity. *Helen, you dumb-ass, you can die from this, you know? VR is simulation of reality! A fall can result in fatality.* And the wicked Helen, despite knowing how bad her decision was, still grinned back.

By logic, a falling body from atop a high-rise tumbled down. *She wasn't tumbling; she was floating.* Panic should make her claw the air. Scream. Kick out. *She was enveloped in warmth and there was no fear.*

The spinning stopped. Helen opened her eyes. And saw nothing because she was buried in somebody's chest. She heard the pounding of his heart. He was warm; he even had a scent. She turned her head. The scenery around them had returned to the white nothingness.

"Don't move," Hades instructed softly.

She had a feeling that if she disobeyed this time, she would regret it. *"Don't make a habit of ordering me around,"* she said, and was a bit annoyed at the huskiness of her voice. Dammit, did his arms around her have to feel so real?

He didn't answer. There was a short silence as they sort of floated. Helen didn't mind. Now that her body had caught up with her head, she felt a bit weak-kneed and breathless. Her arms, she discovered, were between their bodies and if she moved her right hand just a bit lower…

"That was a good test of me, but wrong time," he told her, his voice vibrating in her ear.

"Why?" She forced the former suggestion from her mind.

"Because you alarmed poor Derek and Dr. Kirkland. The spike in your stats was unexpected and I didn't tell them we were doing anything too dangerous today."

Today. Something else to mull over later. Hades must have some kind of communicating device with Dr. Kirkland and Derek. *"So am I suffering cardiac arrest in real life?"* She felt pretty calm about that. Besides, she was busy trying to stop her right hand from checking out something more interesting.

"No. You didn't go splat. I turned that reality off. That's the easy part. Stopping your mind from thinking that you're falling to your death, however, is an entirely different thing."

She slowly slid her head up to look into his face. His skin was smooth against hers and she ignored the urge to lick it to see whether he had a taste, too. He looked incredible up close, chiseled cheekbones and perfect lips. His eyes were half-open, sensual. And all those lovely blond locks cried out for her hands to run through them. This was a great way to have a heart attack.

There were more horrible ways to die, she supposed. Perhaps having a logical and calm conversation about simulated reality would settle her mind.

"What kind of incredible tech machine is the Portal, anyway? You can't push a button and create a new reality? A net to scoop us up? A shorter jump?"

"You wanted to test me," he pointed out, one golden brow lifted in mockery. *"No more thoughts. Just reflex...you wanted to see what I would do in a situation where you put yourself at risk."*

"So you just let us fall?" she countered, imitating his mockery by lifting her own brow. She was going to ignore the little dig about putting herself at risk.

"No, Elena," he replied softly. *"Think of how you felt right after the falling sensation."*

She stared thoughtfully at him. *"The adrenaline was there. My body believed I was falling. But my mind told me I was floating."* She frowned. *"No, you told me I was floating. My head was spinning like crazy. You told me to close my eyes. I didn't react like someone falling off a high-rise and I should have. I don't have that much control over my body. Somehow, you made me feel...safe."*

He was silent again as she continued staring at him, absorbing her own analysis. The realization that she had been undergoing training all along was...a bit galling.

"And now," he said, and she swore she felt something in his mind, like a switch, *"we fall—"*

Helen gasped as the sudden speed of falling came back. There was no more floating sensation, just a chaotic jumble of emotions as she tumbled. All she could do was grab hold of Hades tightly, focusing on him. The fall felt like forever and she rebelled at the thought that he was forcing the trust issue on her. She held on tighter anyway.

She let out an "ooooommmff" as she landed unceremoniously on something soft. And Hades was all hard and masculine on top of her.

"—*onto a bed of feathers,*" he finished and for the first time, smiled.

If she hadn't felt so pissed off at having been tested and tricked again, Helen would have taken the time to admire that glorious mouth. "*You could have done that the first time,*" she accused, trying to gather her scattered breath and wits together.

"*What would that do?*"

She didn't have an answer. Well, she did, but it had nothing to do with feeling safe.

"*Would your mind have accepted the sudden change?*" Hades continued. "*You aren't that used to VR games yet, my sweet Elena.*"

The endearment rolled off his tongue like hot honey. Helen was suddenly very aware of the softness of the bed below her. And the hardness of the body on hers. He was telling her that he was the expert in virtual reality and this game was under his control.

She met his dark gaze defiantly. "*Okay, I got the lesson. I'm to depend on you to keep me safe. Now let's change scenery.*"

Oh, man. She was beginning to think creating her dream man was really a bad idea. Well, not bad, not with that slow smile he was giving her. But definitely not to her advantage. It suddenly dawned on her that he was quite comfortable using her creation to manipulate her.

"*Who said the lesson is over?*" he asked in a low voice.

A naked man. Correction, a very hot-looking naked man. In bed with her. This was one lesson Helen didn't need to understand. *"Look, Hades,"* she began, batting her eyes innocently at him as she pushed at his chest, *"I really think you're really sexy but it's too soon in our relationship to really do anything about it. You have to give me time to get to know you better."*

His amusement crinkled the corner of his eyes. *"Which brings us back to the beginning. What's your RV trigger, Elena?"*

Her eyes rounded. *"Oho, seduction now, Hades? Surely your knowledge of all things NOPAIN tells you about that, too? It didn't work the first time."*

"That wasn't seduction. We're done with the nonpersuasive portion; we're now into the innovative negotiation part." He shifted, putting more weight on her. *"Didn't Hades do that with Persephone?"*

He was trying NOPAIN on her? Hell narrowed her eyes. *"I'm not negotiating anything with you. For one thing, I'm not your captive."*

"But think of the rest of the myth, Elena. It fits, doesn't it?"

Helen was familiar with the story. In Greek mythology, Hades kidnapped Persephone and took her to the Underworld as his bride. While her mother, Demeter, the earth goddess, looked for her daughter, she ignored her duties and everything started to die. Hades made a bargain with Zeus. He would allow his bride to visit her mother every six months but she must return to the Underworld to stay with him for the remaining six. And that was how the world had its seasons. When Persephone came home, Mother Earth was happy and everything flourished; when she was in the Underworld, everything went into hibernation or died.

"In other words, if I don't negotiate with you, the real world is going to dry out and die without me? Haha, Hades, you're putting too much importance in my role. And umm, do you mind getting up? It's very hard to have a conversation with a naked man lying on top of you."

Now why did she have to pun about the hard part? He mocked her with that smile again and still didn't move. She was going to lose her temper soon. Great, next she would be fighting and wrestling with a hard naked man. This wasn't quite how she thought she would experience VR. Well, not right now, anyway.

"We don't have much time, Elena. The coming test depends solely on your success, and your success is my interest, my job. Without the trigger, I can't help you if you should have any problems." His head dropped lower. His breath warmed her cheek. *"Without the trigger, I can't talk to you when you're remote viewing."*

Helen refused to move her head those few inches to the left. He didn't seem to even realize that he was lying naked on a woman. That was because he wasn't really some Greek god hottie, you idiot. He wasn't real, and so her state of turned-on-ness wasn't either. *"You're in my head talking to me now so why not when I'm remote viewing?"*

His hand cupped her jaw, tilting her face toward his. *"The theory is that you would be in an alternate state of mind. The function of this virtual reality training is to get your mind used to having me in it while thinking and knowing everything is virtual. But even with that, my participation isn't guaranteed because I don't have your talent. When you're remote viewing, it's basically a personal VR experience. You're alone, seeing and ac-*

cessing information with your senses. But with TIVRRV, we're going beyond that in this experiment. We've prepared every way we could—brain wave synchronization, mental prep, physical compatibility. I'll be there with you, seeing what you see, and with your remote trigger, I can…" he leaned even closer, his lips inches from hers *"…communicate with you, be your second pair of eyes, and pull you out if there are any problems."*

Helen looked into those dark eyes and instantly regretted it. The man was pure temptation. She had been craving chocolate for days and those sinful chocolate eyes were going to be her downfall. She grasped for a lifeline. *"Theory,"* she said, and there was that stupid husky frog in her throat again. *"That doesn't sound promising."*

Her senses vibrated with need as his lips came even closer. She struggled to pay attention to his words, not to the heat rising between her legs.

"Every theory has a promise," he whispered. *"Theoretically, I'm not real, you thought so yourself, but…"*

She swallowed the rest of his words as he kissed her. Gently, as if he wasn't sure whether she was real himself. Tenderly, as if she was really Persephone being seduced. Her lips parted involuntarily and she felt his tongue delve in, slow and deliberate in its search for hers. Oh. My. God. The man could kiss. Or it could. Her virtual-made man. Whatever.

Stop thinking. Close your eyes.

She closed her eyes. *That was him ordering you to close your eyes, Helen.*

His tongue tangled sensuously with hers. She responded hungrily. This was something dark and forbidden, something that had been missing in her life for two years. Temptation to give in to feelings beckoned like some siren.

Open your legs wider.

Her limbs slid open without a second thought. *Helen Roston! You're not going to f—* Every protest melted instantaneously as his heat dug heavily against hers. It didn't help that *she* had enhanced that part of him a bit bigger than normal.

She had read all about teledildonics, a program used by people addicted to virtual-reality sex. She hadn't thought much about that use of the technology. Her focus was on the self and how she was going to get used to a simulated environment. She'd never thought about sharing it with someone else. In her head. In a sexual manner. It hadn't occurred to her that a program could be so seductive and sexy, that she would enjoy a kiss with something that wasn't real.

"I can feel your wetness. Is that real enough?" Hades lifted his lips from hers, gently giving her swollen ones one last kiss. *"You see? Everything, in theory, has lots of promises."*

Helen ran her tongue over her upper lip. Two could play at this game. She reached down and did what she had been thinking of doing the last ten minutes. He was hot and…very aroused. *"Can you feel that with your sensors?"* She gave him a squeeze. *"How does it feel to have something done to you and it's not really happening?"*

"But it is happening. I can feel your hand, just as you felt my kiss." His eyelids lowered. *"With your trigger, it'll be similar when you remote view."*

The man was unbelievable. Theoretically, he was having the experience of being pleasured by a woman's hand, yet she wouldn't have known that if she weren't the one doing the pleasuring. Maybe it had been so long, she was losing her touch? She reached down with the other hand.

He grew larger in her grasp. She stared smugly into his eyes and even though they remained unreadable, she sensed steely determination in him. They were testing each other, and neither he nor she was going to give in. She had the upper hand. How far would he go?

As far as I want to take it. She was beginning to recognize that mocking tone.

You're so damn good at reading my mind, find out the trigger code yourself!

Instead, he moved suggestively, pressing his thighs intimately against her, flexing himself in a way that didn't require any mind reading on her part. *"I could try, but I prefer your free will, Elena. Makes things easier. Your willingness to stay here. To work with me. Depends on your free. Will."*

He kept his sentences in time with short thrusts of his hips. Helen sniffed, wanting to laugh. He wasn't as controlled as he looked. *Giving you my secret means free will? Come on, Hades. It gives you control. I might only have been through Phase Two of RV training but even they had given me warning about mental manipulators.*

You're betraying yourself, sweetheart. That's Three.

Helen smiled. He'd betrayed himself, too. He knew more about remote viewing than he had let on, and he didn't deny that he was a mental manipulator. Keep filing, Helen, keep filing. *"Ooops,"* she said aloud.

Hades smiled back, unperturbed by her testing him. *"Give and take,"* he reminded her. *"So now I know you're a little more advanced than they've trained you. Good."*

"Why, good?"

"Never let everyone know you have something extra up your sleeve, Elena."

"And everyone includes you, right? But you plan to know everything." Whereas she knew nothing about him. It irritated her.

"Not everything." His voice now had that lazy edge of a man enjoying himself, and why not, he was grinding against her hand and body even as he was having this conversation, punctuating each short sentence in the most sexual way. *"Boring. I like to string it out. Next session. If you pass the test. Tonight."*

Oh, she would. She wasn't going to come so far and not go that final... She stopped herself just in time. She peered up at him suspiciously. She'd almost given herself away.

I saw something.

Shit! She released him, disgusted with herself. She hadn't bargained for this kind of access into her mind. She would complain to T....

"No one knows how far we can go with this. They want their supersoldier-spy. They didn't ask how or what COMCEN's going to do to achieve this."

So T. didn't know either. Like she'd said earlier, she was a lab rat around here. *"Is this why we're doing everything virtual? So you can see what you can do? You think you can remote view through me?"*

"Theoretically. I already told you I don't have your talent."

She had many questions, but chose not to form them. Not yet. Something very important was being revealed to her and she meant to get him to talk. *"Scientists have theories, Hades. And theories are a bunch of formulae and words. We are neither."*

"We are the drivers behind these theories right now. Why did they stop at Phase Two with you? They didn't want to waste time and money, just in case you fail."

"Become a mental case, you mean."

"I'm not going to let that happen."

Sure, sure. A virtual dream man was going to take care of her. The irony was totally befitting the situation. *"Why not?"* she challenged. *"Are you going to change into a white knight and come to my rescue?"*

His gaze was enigmatic and she pushed against him. *"Why not?"* she repeated.

"Give me the trigger and I'll tell you."

She could lie, but he would know. Why would they go to all this trouble to put their new toy in jeopardy? She couldn't read the man but she could trust her instinct. It had always been a sixth sense for her. Right now it told her that there was more to this experiment than everyone was letting on, that there were layers of mysteries to this man. But her intuition was also telling her that he hadn't planned any harm against her.

He didn't even seem to be breathing as he waited for her decision. But he was still hard and hot as he lay on top of her.

Helen closed her eyes and passed him a mental picture.

She didn't give him everything. If he were so damn good, let him figure it out when he watched her later.

His lips came down on her mouth again, and without thought, eyes still closed, she opened hers. He rewarded her with a drugging kiss, the kind that promised hot sweaty sex, with a big satisfying orgasm. But she was a GEM operative and no amount of innovative persuasion was going to divert her attention.

Why not? She persisted. *Why am I so important? Come back and I'll tell you.*

Her eyes flashed open even as everything became a bright white light. Dammit. He tricked her after all. *You coward!* Her yell reverberated in her head like an echo.

"Miss Roston?" Derek's voice came on in her left ear. "Your trainer has signaled that the session is over. He said you might need a few minutes to wind down."

Wind down? She wasn't the one walking around with a big stiffy! Arrgghhh. She was going to kill that man.

"Let me take some of the electrodes and thingies off myself. Guide my hands." Helen was determined to find out as much about the Portal as she could now that she knew it could do more than virtual reality.

She felt Derek undoing a few straps. He moved her right hand slowly so she could feel each different node in the band. "Press here for release," he instructed. "Just feel the back of your neck. I'll show you how to unhook it after it's off."

"Okay."

Helen blinked when the goggles were removed, then cracked her neck. "How long was I in there?" The chair was very comfortable but the body wasn't made to be still for long periods of time. A thought struck her. She hoped she had been still! "Ummm…did I move a lot?"

"Not much. Your body was responding to the wavelengths very well. Your stats showed lots of mental activity going on, though. Want to look at the charts when they are printed out?"

"Yeah. Can I also have a copy of that program that created the avatar?" She was glad the mental activity stayed mental. She didn't want to think what her body looked like writhing about. Not to mention her hands exploring some big parts. Sheesh. She needed some time to think this out. No doubt T. would be amused at the idea of having wild monkey sex in virtual reality, but Helen would prefer to keep that private.

She got out of the Portal, brushing down her pants. Oh-oh.

"I need a quick bathroom break, Doc. Can the post-checkup wait?"

Dr. Kirkland was copying things from his notes. "Of course, Miss Roston. Go ahead." He checked his watch. "Everything is on schedule, don't worry."

Helen nodded. Halfway out the door, she turned back. "He had us falling off a building, Doc. I don't know about his, but tell him that's not good for my health." Ha. Let him take the blame.

Dr. Kirkland looked up from his files. "I wondered what all those spikes in the readings were about. He did pause to come out of sync for a few minutes to instruct us not to panic. I guess that was the point when all your vitals were a bit erratic."

Derek snorted. "The term 'gone haywire' describes it better," he said, pushing his glasses back up.

That must have been when Hades had ordered her to stay quiet while her face was buried in his chest. She remembered feeling strange, as if her body and mind were separated. Then all the blood had seemed to rush into her head. So he *could* communicate with Dr. Kirkland and Derek, and was giving them a rundown of the situation while he was holding her.

"You mean, if I had an unexplained seizure, you would be pulling me out of the chair?"

She meant that as her usual way of teasing, but Dr. Kirkland's expression was solemn. "Your life is in my hands, Miss Roston. I take that very seriously. This isn't just your monitor room; it's your connection back to us. I'll bring you right back here if something goes wrong." He smiled, softening the gravity of his words. "But I also know you'd probably be all right as long as he's around."

He being Hades, of course. People sure had a lot of faith in the guy. It was her life they were playing with and everyone was talking as if he had any say about how the experiment was going to go. One would think he was in charge of the program or something. T. Kirkland. Hmmm. "Better start calling me Helen, Doc, if you're going to get all serious about me."

She caught him smiling again at her parting shot as she headed out the door. The restroom was empty. Good. She checked her reflection. She looked normal, although her usually hazel eyes had a tinge of green in them. That happened whenever she was emotionally charged. Okay, aroused. She made a face at the mirror, then moved quickly into one of the stalls. She pulled her pants down.

Aroused. She came in here because…she didn't even need to check…her panties were wet. She touched herself and fell back against the commode with a small gasp. Her sensitivity was like an electric current. She moved her middle finger and shuddered at the extreme pleasure that shot up from point of contact to somewhere behind her eyes.

"Sweet holy hot tamale," Helen muttered. She slid her finger again and bit down on her lower lip. "This is not good."

She pulled at the toilet paper a few feet away. This wasn't good at all. She was all hot and bothered by some image in her head. Worse. She was about to have the best orgasm she'd had in…months… Shit, she couldn't remember when she was this urgently close to coming without a man around.

She blew her nose into the paper. Well, this was getting more and more interesting. Or fucked up. Or both. Should she report her condition to Dr. Kirkland and T.? Or should she keep this quiet? The doctor was recording her brain waves and vitals to help keep her alive, but umm…she didn't think she wanted to explain why she was simulating sex with her trainer. As for T., nothing would surprise T., but she would use the information for more of her mind games later. Of that, Helen had no doubt.

Well, she wasn't going to have someone coming in here and catching her moaning by herself. Hades said they were the drivers behind the theories, so she was going to wait and see what he would do. If he reported what happened, then she was bound to get questions from either Dr. Kirkland or T.

Washing her hands, Helen looked at her reflection again. Her eyes still had those green glints, dammit. She curled the loose tendrils of her hair behind her ears. She would not allow herself to be manipulated by someone unseen. She was a GEM operative first and this was just another contract. GEM operatives always got the better of their men.

Arousal during a job was nothing new to him. He'd seduced women while interrogating them. If need be, he'd used sex to manipulate and retrieve information.

"I'm fine. I don't need any help," he said and clicked off the intercom.

He got up and walked through the private entrance into his quarters, unzipping his VR avatar suit as he stepped into the shower area. He stepped out of the garment, slung it on a nearby rack, and closed the shower door. He turned on the water, leaving it on cold.

He looked down. His hand reached for his flesh, his eyes closing involuntarily. Anticipation was a strange aphrodisiac. She'd aroused him more than any other woman had been able to in a long time, and this time hadn't even been real. Nonetheless, her hands and her lips had the same effect of her actually physically being with him. Her having made a certain part of him bigger hadn't helped, since he felt the heaviness of his erection even more during the session. The unfamiliarity of it had actually made him harder, tempted him to go a little further.

He wasn't averse to crossing the line. God knew he'd done that more times than he could count, but in all those times, he'd been in total control, even in the middle of sex. He opened his eyes, ignoring the sharp stab of cold liquid needles on his head and shoulders. He thought of how wet she'd felt. Real or not, he'd felt her response through the feedback oscillator. His lips twisted wryly. The experiment—a virtual reflection of her virtual reality experience being fed back to him— was going to be more successful than they'd thought. He had felt her very close to coming without having touched her. What would it be like when their minds became even more in sync with remote viewing?

The cold water didn't appear to affect his current condition. Kirkland would be coming over here soon. He squeezed a small amount of liquid soap in his hand. Reached down. Closed his eyes. And thought of the feel of her hand around him.

Six

"**I** want you to find out the identity of our target. Here are the coordinates. Find out exactly what they're doing. Remember how it felt to lose to that woman. We aren't going to let some other candidate win, are we? Think of it. You can beat her. This is your chance."

Zoom.

Dark. Dark.

"This is where I am. The room inside the monitor room. Right turn. Electronic panel. Going to open…"

"We're not interested in the panel, Agent. Go through into that room on the right. What's in there?"

Zoom. Focus.

"I…the door is gray and made of…"

"Agent 22! Just walk through it."

"I…can't."

"What does he mean, he can't?"

"I don't know. He's never said that before. Listen, Agent 22, go through the door and tell us what's in that room. This is an order."

Zoom. Close-up. Make door open. Make door disappear.

"I...can't. Can't go through. Feels like thick liquid. Like drowning. No, there is some electrical current. I feel energy. No, waves, like..."

"Shut him up. Those drugs are really fucking him up more and more. He's useless."

"Agent 22, this is your monitor. I'm your guide. You can trust me, remember? You can go through anything. You're the camera. Tell us what you see. Zoom in."

"Can't...see. Feel lots of pressure. Like waterfall. Like electric current. Like big waves moving and rolling together."

"He isn't even making sense. The others never had this problem. Waterfall, big waves?"

"Let me try another way. Agent 22, listen to me. Why can't you go through?"

Zoom. Pan back.

"This is what I see. Someone walks into the room. A doctor. He opens a drawer and pulls out some files. He walks back toward the entrance. The phone rings. He pauses, then returns to the desk and picks up the phone.

"He says, 'Yes, I'm alone. I punched in the secured line. I'll bring them to you and we can go over them.' The doctor then hangs up. He has the file..."

"Oh, shut him down. We want to get into the room, not follow this doctor."

"No, it's okay. We'll see where the doctor's going,

find out more about this project. Follow him, Agent. Where's he now?"

Zoom. Cut.

"Entering another level. Gray carpet. Looking up. Different...I can't see well."

"Follow him, Agent. I'm here with you. Don't be afraid."

"The passage is light, then dim, then almost shadowy. Like a tunnel with strange walls. The doctor knocks on a door. The pounding's so loud! He palms the scanner and the door slides open. The doctor steps into the—oh, my God—"

"Shit! He's screaming like he's in pain! Why's he covering his eyes?"

"Agent, what's wrong?"

Dark. Dark. "Can't see, can't see! Loud! Mental block. Can't see! Headache. Get me out, get me out!"

"That's the second time his stupid headaches have interrupted the sessions. I say let's use someone new."

"Please, please, I need another dose." *Dark. Gone.* "It hurts! The air is like water. The energy is beating on my head."

"You're right. The drug has eaten his brain or something. Look at his vitals. He's having difficulty breathing."

"I say let him suffocate. It would be natural causes, right?"

"No. They'll discover the serum in his system. We don't want anyone to be suspicious about any of the patients here. Let's snap him out of it. Agent, can you hear me?"

Dark. Dark. Very, very dark.

COS COMMAND CENTER

Kirkland put down the files he had brought along on the huge desk that dominated the room. The private living quarters suited the owner—stark, simple, and work-oriented. He couldn't find a single thing there that betrayed anything about the man who was casually putting on some clothes in front of him. Like the desk, his presence dominated the room. He wondered whether the man had any other life outside here.

"Here they are. Nothing unusual. I assume the session went very well? She mentioned you both were falling from a great height. Did you plan that?" Dr. Kirkland sat down.

He watched the man throw the wet towel into a bin nearby, then walk with that unhurried air he always had toward the small kitchen.

"No, it was unplanned," he said as he poured a drink from the refrigerator.

Kirkland nodded at the silent offer of a glass. "Was it a test of her reflexes? Or how she was adjusting to VR?"

The Portal was the newest tech advancement for VR and with its brain wave synchronicity mode, he was concerned about the complex issues behind the program. As a doctor, he was excited to see two candidates so suited for the new program. He had been a junior aide during the first experiments in the V-Program years ago, and now he was part of the main research team of V2, as COMCEN had secretly renamed this program.

"Yes."

"They like to file every finding and effect about Miss Roston ASAP," Kirkland said.

"Later, Doc. Tonight."

Kirkland usually advised against that, but he was talking to a man who could recall a memory of a map of a hostile camp down to the color of the coffee cup in the hand of the man he had assassinated from six years ago. He would never forget the amazing show of the man's computation abilities during the initial stages of finding and approving the trainer role for V2.

"Will you be at the Q and A session?" Finishing the cold protein juice, Kirkland got up to put the glass in the kitchen sink.

"Probably, if I'm back. I'll want to listen in on the tape if I'm late."

Kirkland noted the new shoes the man was putting on and wondered what assignment he was going into. "I'm sure Miss Roston will be asking a bunch of questions. She's the one taking all the risks, after all. She's been very cooperative, though. Her psych profile said she wasn't a team player but I find that to be untrue."

"Are you sure, Doc?"

Dr. Kirkland caught the amusement that flitted momentarily across the man's face. "She has always answered every question, even the ones that were private. She hasn't objected to the lack of privacy and has forgone many things without complaint. It's not every day we find a woman like that," he pointed out, and hastily added, "or a man."

The amusement was now evident in the man's voice. "I know you like her, Kirkland, no need to get so defensive. GEM operatives are very professional. The few I've seen and worked with have always been exceptional when it came to adapting to extreme environments. Hell's exceptionally good at her job." The lips quirked. "She also has an exceptional way with men, as you noticed."

So it was Hell, the nickname her friends used. That was quick progress. It was very good that the two of them were getting along.

"Yes, it'll probably help speed our synchronization," the man agreed.

Kirkland rubbed his nose, trying to hide his surprise. How did he always read his mind at the oddest moment? It was unsettling, even after all these years. "Yes, of course."

"You're probably going to stay up all night wondering which came first, the synchronization of brain waves or the ease with which we're relating to each other."

Kirkland silently agreed, although the chicken or egg question wouldn't worry the people who were going to watch the test tonight. Some of them hated what they mocked as 'woo-woo' stuff. But with nine department heads sitting in—some of whom were already miffed that their candidates didn't get them the crown—this was a very important project for them. And it all rested on one woman's shoulders right now. He wondered whether she understood the importance.

He looked at the worn book opened on the kitchen table, glancing down at the page quickly. "E, huh? What's today's word?" He'd recently become aware of the other man's strange habit of thumbing through the dictionary. "Is it a difficult one?"

"Exceptionally hard." There was that small quirk of lips again, as if something was privately amusing him.

Oh...exceptional. Kirkland looked down at the page again. "Constituting, or occurring as, an exception; not ordinary or average," he read out loud, "needing special attention or presenting a special problem." He glanced up and quizzically asked, "Which meaning?"

The quirk became even more mocking. "Both."

He was missing a joke here somewhere; he was sure of it, but then he was slow to catch them. Following the man out, Kirkland watched him pick a set of keys from a panel that had dozens of sets hanging there. "You're dividing your time with too many operations," he observed. "Consolidate and give someone else more responsibilities."

"We all have to do our assignments, Doc, but Miss Roston will get my top priority, don't worry. Now I have to get going." He pocketed the keys. "Is that what you wanted to hear?"

Kirkland sighed. Mind games, that was what they were all trained for. He was just a poor scientist trying to get some results in a controlled environment. Needless to say, COMCEN wasn't a good place for scientists.

"You're fifteen minutes late," Helen announced as Flyboy hurried down the stairway to her, his long limbs in crisp white pants.

"You're a tough woman," he said when he reached her at the bottom. "I told you I'd be ten minutes later than you, and that makes me five minutes late."

"What were you doing, beautifying that perfect coif?" she mocked.

Flyboy laughed, his teeth perfectly straight and white,

of course. He looked boyish in his cream T-shirt and pants, his hair flicked back carelessly. He tapped on his watch.

"How much time do we have before I have to get you back here?"

"We're eating outside the Center?"

"What, you want to be cooped up in here all day? Want to come or not?"

"Yeah." A breath of fresh air from everything would be welcome. "Where are we going? Not too fancy a place, I hope?"

Flyboy's grin was devilish. "That's for another date. Got to slowly work you up to fancy. Then you'll appreciate me more and more."

"Ah," Helen said with a nod. They walked past security, then through the double doors. "It's cheap hamburger and fries then."

The weather was balmy outside, just turning a bit cool, especially in the shade. Flyboy put on his sunglasses as he pointed to the vehicle parked not too far away.

"My, my, Center must pay their commandos very, very well," she murmured. This was an expensively-packaged European car, with the extra knobs and whistles under the hood, the kind one admired in a magazine with no hope of purchasing. She paused a few paces away to admire it. "Six hundred horsepower. Double overhead cams. Sixteen valves, supercharged. Top speed 180 miles an hour. Zero to sixty in five point five secs. Back to dead stop thirteen point five secs."

Flyboy gave her a bemused look. "Not quite the typical girl talker, are you? Next you'll tell me you're a race freak."

Helen stole a quick glance at Flyboy but he was just looking at her with open admiration. Strange coincidence that she had just passed on a certain image to Hades, and here was a race car. Still, they couldn't have possibly produced the exact image in that quick a time.

"I like cars," she said in an easy voice. "You must be superrich to own this one, sweetheart."

"I like speed." Flyboy grinned as he flipped the car keys into the air. "And I test drive vehicles for anyone who is kind enough to lend me fast things."

T. had told her about Flyboy's love of anything that flew. He was the youngest of the original COS commandos, enthusiastic and eager.

"Is that how you do everything? In hot pursuit?" she teased.

Flyboy laid an arm over her shoulders and hugged her close to him. Lowering his voice, he said, "It can be hot, but it doesn't have to be fast all the time, babe."

Helen laughed, shaking her head. He was incorrigible.

"Look who's going out," Flyboy added.

Helen turned and watched as Alex Diamond approached, motorcycle helmet tucked under his arm. He looked just as lethal in a leather jacket.

"We're bumping into each other a lot today," Helen remarked. "You lunching, too?"

Alex studied them for a moment. "I didn't think you were allowed to eat anything other than the crap they feed you in there," he said, not even pausing as he walked by. Clearly, he didn't expect a conversation.

Meaning alcohol, caffeine, ibuprofen... Helen went through a mental list of all the no-nos she had to observe. She shrugged. What was new about her boring life? She caught sight of the motorcycle parked nearby. Nice machine.

"At least I can still speed, right?" she called. That was probably the longest sentence the man had ever said to her.

Diamond turned. "Good luck, Helen," he said quietly.

"Thanks." Helen frowned as she looked at his back.

"What is it?" Flyboy rubbed her shoulder.

"Nothing." Except Alex Diamond's stance, the way he stood so still, reminded her of... She shook her head mentally. "Just one of those passing thoughts. Now, let's see you test drive this baby, Flyboy."

He unlocked the car and bowed extravagantly as she got in. "Zero to sixty in five point five secs, sweetheart. We're going maximum horsepower."

Helen batted her eyes. "Oh, my. The things you do to a girl's heart rate."

Helen liked to analyze a man by the car he drove. This expensive vehicle might not be Flyboy's but he looked very comfortable in it. His hands ran around the steering wheel as if he were giving it a caress. He made some quick adjustments, then turned to make sure she had her seat belt on. He winked as he leaned over, pulling on the strap.

"Just double-checking out of habit," he said.

She had a feeling that he did a lot of double-checking. In his job, the tiniest mistake could be fatal. The way he moved around, looking in control, he seemed to be about to take the car for a spin in the heavens. Like any sportster, the interior was more like the inside of an aircraft, with just enough legroom and head space, and the instrument panel lit up by all kinds of dials.

"What's the fastest speed you've driven in a car?" she asked, curious.

"Two hundred, two hundred and twenty." That was traveling the length of a football field a second. "Scared?"

She arched a brow at him. He grinned. The car started with a smooth growl, like a wild animal ready to take off. Flyboy gave her a grin and an A-OK signal. "You ready?" he yelled above the engine.

"Show me what you got," she challenged back.

Minutes later, they were flying down the scenic route. Not that there was much of that to see, Helen mused, as everything zipped by at an alarming blur. She glanced at the man beside her, his attention totally focused on the road. He changed gears and accelerated smoothly, one hand on the wheel and the other still on the stick shift. She watched the speedometer going up into the red zone.

She liked fast cars, always had. And she was totally fascinated at the ease with which Flyboy was handling the vehicle. Minimum movement, as if the car was an extension of his body. Just a totally relaxed man, enjoying something that would have most people at the edge of their seats. He made her forget how noisy these cars were. There was joy radiating from him that would make a woman jealous.

She didn't interrupt his pleasure, preferring to let him take her wherever he wanted. This was probably a side of him that he seldom shared, when he dropped that heartthrob image and became pure pilot. Here, that teasing streak had taken on a quiet intensity that she had never seen in him before.

When he finally slowed down, the car purring to a more manageable speed, he turned and flashed her a smile sexy enough to curl her toes. The man was definitely turned on by speed.

"Thanks," he said, simply.

She understood. They had a love for living on the edge and not caring about the consequences. "Was it good for you, too?" she teased.

He laughed, a carefree sound, as if this was the best ride of his life. "Ah, Helen, Helen. What you do to a guy."

"Tell me what you think of this car."

He took the turn off the scenic route, back to normal highway traffic. "It corners extremely well. I barely needed to move the steering wheel. That's what makes a great car, in my opinion, the cornering speed."

"It's a good driver that makes the cornering speed," Helen pointed out.

He glanced at her briefly. "How did you get to like racing? You're obviously familiar with cars. I know you've driven very fast before because you didn't even hold on to anything just now. Either that, or you're an adrenaline junkie."

Helen laughed. "Or both," she suggested, as a slight evasion. "Speed is fun, and being the one in control of it is an indescribable feeling—like being at one with the world."

"As close to Zen as one can get," agreed Flyboy. "How experienced are you behind the wheel?"

"Not as experienced as you think. I don't have the resources that you have."

"So, who owned the few cars you did drive?"

She studied her nails. "Boyfriends."

"Whoa. Wealthy boyfriends. I'm not in your league, Miss Roston."

"Yeah, I'm a picky girl," Helen mocked, "but you got one thing going for you, babe."

His laughing eyes met hers. "What's that? Fantastic sex?"

Oh, he would be fantastic in bed. All he had to do was lounge there and be devoured, but of course he knew that already. "Nope." She leaned closer conspiratorially. "Being a pilot, you have other bigger things for me to ride in."

They both laughed. One thing fun about flirting with Flyboy. He didn't take himself too seriously. That was very important in Helen's playbook, especially in a good-looking guy.

Lunch gave a good opportunity to ask some questions outside the Center. Helen was never sure who was listening in at that place. She'd watched T. carefully scan the ladies' room, where they usually met, with one of her special rings. Granted, her operations chief was a very careful woman by nature, but if even she was paranoid about her workplace, then Helen figured she had better be, too.

Flyboy and she had a mutual passion—racing—and she understood his love for speed very well. He actually described it better than she could, probably because he had traveled at faster speeds than she would ever have the chance to try.

"Euphoria, or close to it. You're flowing and floating, even though you know you aren't, and you have total control of the craft. You can go upside down or nose-dive, and still feel perfectly at ease. There's no conscious effort, yet…" He trailed off, studying her. "Not boring you, I hope."

"No, no, not at all. It's the feeling of fearlessness. Or lack of fear. It's just you and…well, if it's driving, you and the road and total focus."

He seemed surprised and pleased at her words, as if he hadn't expected her to understand. But Helen had enough information to know that despite his flirtatious demeanor, Flyboy wasn't all heartbreaker; he could fly some of the most sensitive aircrafts in the world. Besides that, he was a COS commando, a man who had undergone extreme experiments and training, just as she had.

"Yes," he agreed. "And trust, total trust in yourself and the vehicle."

Which brought up the subject of *her* vehicle, the Portal. Of the people she had been introduced to these past few months, Flyboy was the most approachable. Because he had used VR for his work, their conversation naturally turned to aspects of her training.

"Yes, I want to try out the Portal." He answered her questions in between bites of hamburger. "It's modeled after the one I'm famous for, you know."

"What do you mean?"

"They were creating a new simulation program to train aviators. I was the Flybot," he said, then threw back his head and laughed at his own pun.

"I've seen that film package with a simulated you," Helen admitted. "Very patriotic, very nice…you looked marvelous."

Flyboy shrugged. "That one was a funding package for Congress. I haven't seen that version, actually. Part of my work was to help improve sim-flight training and that was my main interest. The other thing was more…" He shrugged again, his blue eyes scornful, as he searched for the right word. "For show."

Helen tapped his hand playfully with a straw. "Hey, you never know, your sacrifice probably brought some funding into the research for the Portal. And my training, too!"

He smiled. "Well, put in that way, I suppose being treated like a piece of marketing meat is okay."

"I hope I don't treat you that way."

Flyboy cocked his head. "No," he said softly. "You don't."

Helen chewed on one end of the straw. "You know, you really do have the nicest blue eyes, not a tinge of gray in them at all. And when you smile, all a girl can think about is…meat."

She burst out laughing, unable to continue her teasing. Flyboy joined her.

"You're a scamp, that's what you are," he told her, leaning over to tweak her nose. "You almost had me there. How they mistake you for a serious dedicated operative is a mystery."

She shrugged. Life couldn't be all business all the time. "Are you going to be there tonight? I heard a couple of the commandos are interested in checking out X."

They had agreed to refer to the serum as X in public. The serum was, of course, the drug to be tried out on her later. Helen Roston, female supersoldier-spy. Say that fast three times. She grinned at the thought. After a year of training, she was well past the apprehensive state and into the macabre. That was, as any seasoned operative knew, as ready as one could possibly get before restless anxiety settled in.

"I think I'll be there, barring some commitments. But I know Armando Chang will, for sure. He'll be there to answer your questions."

"Armando. I don't think I've met him."

"No, he hasn't been around lately, but of all of us, he's the one you should talk to."

"Oh." She made a mental note about Armando Chang. "Tell me what you know anyway."

"You mean, other than the chemical reports you've read? I don't know how the new stuff will be different personally."

"No, how did the original version work on you?" Helen had read enough to understand the effects on a human body. They were words. She was interested in the experience. "What did it do to you?"

Flyboy sat back, studying her as he weighed his words. Interesting that he would need to do that, since he had answered all her previous questions quickly. Maybe he thought she wasn't ready to hear whatever it was he had to say. Again, interesting.

"Armando should be answering this because he took the new stuff," he began, "but I'll try to give you just my take on it. Our dosages were small. It didn't work on a few of us. For me, I felt very alert, which is great for flying. As far as I could tell, everything functioned normally except that everything was also noticeably easier to do."

More questions floated through Helen's mind. Armando Chang had tried the new stuff? Could he remote view? "What do you mean?"

"The most difficult tasks were..." Flyboy pointed to his dessert "...a piece of cake. I was very goal-oriented, but then, I am a pretty focused person when I'm working, anyway."

She had noticed that. "Yes, flying aircraft needs that. I imagine X makes an ordinary person extremely attentive to details," Helen said thoughtfully.

Flyboy took her hand in his. "It's a drug. Always remember that. No matter how you feel, just keep that in mind, that it's the drugs. You said you see the Portal as your vehicle, and yeah, in a way you have to trust it to help you do your job. But you have to trust X, too, and that's tougher than you think."

She had already thought about that. Drugs, after all, invaded a body, took control of some aspects of it. To allow them to work, she had to trust them. Same as she had to trust Hades. Who in his right mind would? Yet, millions of people took drugs day in and day out, without thought, with total trust.

"Why did you let them inject the stuff in you, anyway?" she asked, curious now that she had some answers. "Did you have a choice?"

His smile was flippant. "I'm a COS commando," he stated simply. "We're different."

"And that means you aren't ever going to tell me."

"You'll understand more about it soon, so why go into details?"

"Does that mean you know more about my program than I do?" She arched her brows. He was still holding her hand, his thumb massaging the fleshy part under hers.

"They call you V2. What does that tell you?"

Quite a bit, Helen admitted. Quite a bit.

Seven

The meeting was supposed to be informally formal, one of those terms at Center that Helen hadn't quite figured out yet. She took it to mean that they didn't have a dress code. Whatever. Q and A meant mean exactly that, no matter how they did it. Those attending had to do with her training in one form or another here, and this was the first time Helen would get to see them together. Flyboy had told her at lunch that Center was a very tight-knit community, especially within its special programs. The Q and A sessions before any mission cleared the air.

Most of all, she wanted to meet Armando Chang. T. had told her that Center was keeping an eye on him. The newest COS commando, he had used the new version of the serum the most, and of them all, according to T., he was the most affected.

"He has changed, Hell," she had said during one of their private briefings. "Not just the way he acts, but the way he talks, too. I've met him before he was part of the program, so I can tell the difference. But the change is slow enough that Center can't actually pinpoint it to the drugs themselves, you know? He's still effective, he's somehow worked his change into an asset for the operations."

"How so? How did the drugs change him?"

"You watch him at Q and A. We'll talk more later. He's a matter of concern for GEM because we certainly don't want to put you in any danger of losing your mind, darling."

Helen's eyes widened. "You care, you really care!"

"I don't let any of my agents take unnecessary risks," said T. "Even you, although I've always encouraged you to take chances more than the others."

That had been a revelation. She hadn't known T. had such confidence in her. "I know I've sometimes gone against your orders. I don't know why you put up with me."

"You work with what you have. And who said you hadn't done exactly what I wanted you to do?"

Helen had made a face. That was so T.

"How am I doing so far with this contract?"

"Everything showed that you're the perfect candidate, Hell. They were looking for someone who had what they called 'visions' with proven results. GEM can vouch for your record. Of course, they could pull any number of government-tested psychics for that but they also wanted a highly-trained operative who could do covert work. Your training with them gave them an idea what kind of skills you have and calmed the fears of those against hiring a contract agent for something so special."

"There was only one snag, right?"

They both had laughed because it had been very apparent the last year and a half that some of the more traditional departments were very miffed that the best candidate for supersoldier-spy was a woman. The sole exception had been the group of individuals from the remote viewing program. Their training had opened a brand-new world inside of Hell, one that had taught her how special she really was. She knew she had surprised many of them with her rapid progress; they had remarked that very few had gone through each level of training that quickly.

Helen unzipped her jacket, popped a fresh piece of gum in her mouth, and entered the conference room. It was thoughtful of them to let her ask some questions before injecting her with their experimental drug, but part of her didn't really trust that this was only to "clear the air." Perhaps this was a test, too, to see how she handled anxiety and fear.

Her long months of training was basically a walk through fire. Each government department had a piece of her, had molded her for its purpose. Each of the programs in which she had undergone training had tested her in its insidious little ways. The worst was the CIA bunch; they had tried their damnedest to make her paranoid. But that was good. It trained her to always keep an eye on everyone and everything around her.

She walked past all the eyes watching. She was used to all that staring by now. It was amusing, really. She actually had had her fill of macho men; living in close quarters with two different special operations forces had made her very comfortable with having them as companions. Or enemies. Not everyone believed in using female contract agents.

She wasn't quite the object of lust for many of these men, so there went her ego down the drain. Yet she represented something more, even might have struck a note of fear in a couple of them, and so there her ego soared again. Boy, it was tough to be a woman.

Normally, she would turn and give everyone a chirpy greeting but she didn't feel like it today. After all, this was serious stuff. Later tonight, she was going to prove how all these months' work and COS Center's new training had molded her into their objective. It was time to put her game face on.

So, Helen my dear, how does it feel to be a weapon? She sat down, crossed her legs daintily, crossed her arms, and blew a bubble. It felt pretty damn cool to have everyone wondering. At the moment, she felt like the strongest woman on earth, which was very strange. She should be feeling vulnerable and tense…shouldn't she? Yet, she couldn't deny the excitement surging inside.

She was just tired of waiting. A body could only train so much. A mind could only absorb so much. Her well of patience was almost dry. She missed the real stuff, where the real danger was. She missed speed. This afternoon with Flyboy punctuated how out of touch she was with what she really, really loved, and that was living on the edge. No amount of training under simulated conditions would take the place of real fear. No amount of testing could take away the real unknown.

The serum was the unknown here. She was ready for the next phase.

"Miss Roston." Dr. Kirkland joined her at the table. "Helen."

He smiled. "Helen. Do you need any introductions with anyone in the room? I think almost everyone is here."

Helen looked around. She recognized most of them. "Who are those two talking to T.?"

"Dr. Marilyn Vaughn and Dr. Vasilia Kasparov. They will answer any questions you might have about the serum."

Marilyn Vaughn didn't look like a scientist, or Helen's image of one, anyway. She was dressed in a black frumpy housewife-looking dress, with bright red flower-print. Her hair was combed into a Victorian-style chignon. From where Helen sat, she looked more motherly than scientist. On the other hand, Dr. Kasparov looked exactly right, with a shock of white hair and sharp, intelligent features. Helen remembered reading that he had defected from the former Soviet Union.

"Were they part of the team with the original serum?"

"Marilyn was, but Dr. Kasparov joined a bit later."

"Who else isn't here, then?"

Dr. Kirkland looked around and checked his watch. "Armando should be here any moment now. He's always the last to arrive. There he is…good God."

Helen turned to the door. She bit her lip in amusement. They weren't kidding when they said the meeting was informal. The man they were talking about had everyone's attention now.

Armando Chang didn't look like a scientist, commando, or any special operative she'd ever seen. He had on a black cloak, the kind that flowed to the ground. His hair was long and a diamond stud glinted from his ear. His mixed heritage—high intelligent forehead, widow's peak, slanted catlike brooding eyes over high cheekbones—gave him a very exotic air.

Every pair of eyes looked in his direction. The atmosphere in the room had gone considerably more apprehensive. Apparently, Armando Chang made everyone a bit nervous.

"You look like a damn vampire," someone said.

Helen had to agree. The cloak covered him from neck to foot, and with that hair and those eyes...all he needed were red lips and fangs. He caught her looking at him and acknowledged her with something like a smile, but not quite. No fangs...yet. Helen raised her brows in greeting. With the cloak hiding his body, arms and legs, he definitely looked unworldly. Except that he had stubble. Vampires—not in any books or movies she'd ever read—rarely had five o'clock shadows.

"It's cold out," he said, as if that explained away the cloak, and with a swift motion, he had the front of it parted and it fell off his shoulders dramatically.

All Helen knew about Armando Chang was that he was the weapons expert of the V-Program commandos. But as she very well knew, words did not make a person. The man sauntering toward Dr. Kirkland and her, cloak draped over one arm now, walked with the air of a bad boy. Files with asterisks and notes didn't tell her that. It was the all-black getup, the black biker T-shirt with the picture of a skull on the front, the worn and rumpled black jeans with the silver belt, legs tucked into black leather boots. Uncombed and unshaven, Armando Chang looked as if he had come to work after having tumbled some biker chick and had just thrown on the clothes by his bed. With T.'s words in mind, she wondered again how the serum had affected him.

"We meet at last," he stated, his arresting eyes sweeping over her from the top of her head to her feet. "You don't look anything like the picture in your file."

"Nor do you," countered Helen, not bothering to stand up. The one she saw showed him with a short haircut, combed to the side. Same arrogant look in those dark eyes, though, as if he thought he'd better things to do than to be there.

Or, right now, here, at the meeting. There was an air of impatience about him, even though he was standing still and acting strangely.

Acting. Her senses whispered as his gaze met hers.

He had the American accent down pat, but the file had told her he wasn't an American. Right now, his voice held a tinge of mockery, as he subjected her to a head-to-toe inspection. "You were all glammed up in the file. Different color hair. In fact, I didn't even think you could possibly be able to train with Special Forces, not with those pretty pink nails."

"And you look like you've seen wilder days since your picture was taken, Mr. Chang," she said coolly.

"T. has been a great teacher. I'm sure you're just as good with deception." He dropped the cloak on a nearby seat. "Hi there, Doc Kirkland. Didn't mean to ignore ya."

Dr. Kirkland gave a faint smile. "That cloak must be part of your new act."

"Yes, I have a show later."

Helen frowned. Act? That word had just crossed her mind moments before.

"Armando, darling." T. appeared. "Helen, you haven't met Armando yet. You have to see one of his shows in town one of these nights."

"Sorry, lost me there…shows?" Maybe Bad Boy Armando played in a band.

"Armando is studying to be a part-time magician. He travels all over the world with his bag of tricks…useful for Center, of course. He's building quite a reputation."

"T., love, it's illusionist." Armando looked around. "Is Diamond around?"

"No, he isn't."

Armando smiled. "Good," he said, and brought T.'s hand to his lips, his dark secretive eyes gleaming. "I have you all to myself at last…although it's much more fun with him scowling at me across the room."

T. laughed. "Don't let this devil persuade you to assist him in his tricks, Hell. He has a way of making you disappear for hours."

T. had her ways of warning her operatives. Helen didn't need it, though. She could tell Armando Chang was a troublemaker. "Did you get into trouble?" she asked lightly.

Armando looked down at Helen. "T. always gets out of trouble. Would you like to magically disappear?"

Helen cocked her head. She should stand up. The man was issuing some kind of challenge, although she wasn't sure what it was yet. "I didn't mean T.," she said softly. "I meant you. Did you get into trouble?"

Armando's eyes didn't leave hers as he pulled out the

chair next to hers. "Assist me in my next illusion and you'll find out."

Helen shook her head. "I have other important things on my plate."

"Ah, yes, you are the new anointed one, the ace up the sleeve, the fat in the fire." His mockery was spoken in that same low tone, so that only their circle heard them.

Helen broke eye contact and turned to her operations chief, giving her an inquiring look. "Don't tell me—he's the poet of the V-group. You know, there's always one in a story—the cynic with the acid tongue who throws out ambiguous lines."

T. gave her one of her amused looks. Her amber eyes darted back to the man sitting next to Helen and they narrowed fractionally. "We'll have to discuss Armando's talents later, Hell. I think the session is about to start."

Everyone had slowly moved to take a seat around the table. The two doctors sat directly across from Helen. A big screen lit up behind them with the dissected image of the human brain.

Armando leaned closer and whispered, "Here's the scientific part."

Helen whispered back, "All illusion, just like your area of expertise."

"Flyboy did mention your wonderful wit," he said with amusement, then relaxed indolently back into his seat as Dr. Vaughn tapped on the mike clipped on her collar.

After the initial welcome and introductions, both scientists gave a brief presentation, using the brain chart on the screen to explain what the serum did, some of which Helen already understood. Most of the first questions by those present concentrated on the general medical aspects of synthetic biochemistry. Everyone participated with answers and suggestions, bringing up operational procedures for clarification, showing that this was the usual practice for them. Perhaps, she mused, this wasn't a test of her, after all.

She noted that Armando Chang didn't ask any questions or offer any suggestions. Unlike the others, he hadn't taken any notes. In fact, looking down at his lap, she noticed he was rolling two balls in his right hand.

"SYMBIOS research uses controlled substances to create the necessary chemical that will bind with opiate receptors at different sites of the central nervous system—the brain, the brain stem and spinal cord—thus altering both perception of and emotional response to pain through an unknown mechanism."

"Why unknown?" Helen asked. Out of the corner of her eye, she now counted three balls rolling around in Armando's hand.

"We don't really understand exactly how the drugs work, Miss Roston, even though they do work," Dr. Vaughn replied.

"It's very normal," Dr. Kasparov said, in a heavy accent. "We still don't comprehend much about the human brain, how even something like an over-the-counter drug inhibits or blocks certain brain responses. It's often explained as 'through an unknown mechanism.'"

That was very reassuring, Helen thought. But she had to agree on one point—the brain was the power behind all mysteries. How else would one explain away a phenomena such as remote viewing? "What can I look forward to once it's in me?"

"It increases your pain threshold by producing analgesia that blocks your pain receptors. It's anti-anxiety. It acts on the limbic system, thalamus and hypothalamus of the CNS to produce hypnotic effects. It also blocks serotonin and motor neurons," Dr. Kasparov explained.

Did they talk like that when they were in bed with their lovers? "In other words, I feel less pain, less fear, and need less sleep," Helen stated. She checked Armando's hands again. They were empty. She glanced up quickly. His eyes mocked her silently.

"Hypothetically, yes."

Oh, great, it was back to theorizing again. "Do you have a success rate?" she asked. Remote viewing had success percentages depending on how advanced the viewer was.

"We have had certain success with SYMBIOS 1. I must also add that I have had the opportunity, while under two other agencies, to study their chemical work. They're working on different recipes and producing different results with synthetic serums."

"This is SYMBIOS 2, Helen," T. said. "Everything depends on your chemical and biological reaction to it. Dr. Vaughn and Dr. Kasparov have double-checked your charts."

When they were discussing whether to take on the contract, Helen had gone through all the precautionary medical tests to make sure she didn't have any unexpected allergies. GEM had outlined all the possible scenarios that could happen to her should the drug fail.

Another intuitive flash zinged through her mind. She glanced around the table and caught many pairs of eyes covertly watching Armando Chang as Dr. Kasparov gave another dry summary of the medical dangers that could affect her mind. If he was aware of the attention, he didn't show it. He was staring at the pad on the table for his notes. Helen looked at it and was startled to find some sort of sketch on it. How the hell—she hadn't seen his hands on the table. Okay, time to end this.

"My question, then, is what happened when the V-Program commandos took SYMBIOS 1? And I understand Agent Chang is going to explain about SYMBIOS 2." Helen swirled her chair to face Armando Chang. She chewed on her gum and snapped it noisily. "End of science part."

He rubbed the stubble on his jaw as he studied her. He then nodded. "And now we talk of the magic part. What it did. Specifically, to me."

He stood up and walked deliberately around the table to stand in front of the video screen. He turned and somehow managed to fit the profile of his face in front of a section of the brain on the screen, giving a very absurd and yet, telling, image. Helen looked at everyone carefully. They seemed to be holding their collective breath as if they were waiting for an explosion. After a moment, Armando turned and pointed to several places on the dissected image of the brain.

"Abracadabra. Just words. They tell you it's going to affect this and that, here and there." He tapped his forehead. "Magic. Illusion. You see and feel its effect, yet you keep telling yourself there's a trick in the whole thing."

Armando opened his hand and a small fiery ball

appeared to glow in his palms. He blew on it and it went out immediately. He stared at his empty palm fiercely for a few seconds. Someone coughed nervously. Helen was beginning to see what T. was talking about.

"I don't think Miss Roston wants to see any illusions right now, Armando," Dr. Vaughn said. "We know you've had some trouble with SYMBIOS 1 and then we switched to SYMBIOS 2, but as long as you don't go into Psych to deal with it, we can't help you."

She hadn't imagined it, after all, Helen thought. There was some kind of tension in the room, hidden behind the relaxed discussion, and the man causing the uneasiness was Armando Chang. Even T. was watching him very carefully.

"I've been to Psych," Armando said. His wry grimace was dismissive. "A waste of time. First they play with your brain, then they play with your thoughts. Besides, I passed all their tests, minus a few headaches. I apologize, I forgot to behave. Miss Roston, ask your questions. Although I'm relatively new among my peers, I assure you I know what I'm talking about, or they wouldn't have wanted me here. The two words to fear—synthesize and assimilate. However, now that I've met you…I don't think you can be frightened away that easily, can you?"

"No. Is that what they fear you would do?" Helen asked.

"They fear I would make you disappear." His face unexpectedly broke out into a smile of pure amusement, transforming the cynical bad boy expression for one unguarded moment. It was gone before Helen could release the surprised intake of breath in her lungs. He put his hands on the table and leaned forward. "Quickly, quickly, before *I* disappear."

The man was walking a fine edge, although Helen had yet to figure out what the two points of that edge were. He was obviously ordered to show up here. His reluctance was very subtle, but she felt it. T. had a lot of explaining to do.

"What did both the serums do for you? Specifically SYMBIOS 2." Since she would have that injected into her....

"For me?" Armando straightened up, steepling his hands under his chin. His eyes were hooded. "Well, for me, once I had the misfortune of being in the way of a bullet which left me with a severely bleeding leg. I didn't feel the pain I should have. Instead I was able to carry on with the mission without limping, or if I did limp, I didn't notice. I should add that the operation included a five-mile hike.

"Then there was the time when I was caught between two warring hostile parties fighting over a shipment of illegal arms. My job was to destroy the shipment, but you can imagine the fireworks flying around me while this was happening. For me, that moment to make the decision as to what my next step was..."

Armando closed his eyes. With his hands still clasped together under his chin, he looked as if he was praying. "It was perfect. Like executing a perfect three and a half somersault dive." He opened his eyes and gazed directly at Helen. "Like making everyone believe you sawed a girl in half. Like making a perfect two-hundred-miles-per-hour pass of a rival race car for the checkered flag. It's a high that's quite memorable. I'm sure it will do similar things for you."

Helen didn't blink. Yet another racing reference for the day. She chewed her bubble gum thoughtfully, ignoring the avid attention that was on her now. "I read the possible adverse reactions—headaches, dry mouth, disorientation. Did you suffer from these side effects?"

"There are always side effects to drugs." He lowered his hands.

"I know that. But did you have any that you would like to share with me?" She lowered her voice a notch, arching one brow mockingly, as she touched his notepad lightly, suggestively.

Standing there in his black T-shirt and jeans, thumbs through the loops of his belt, he didn't seem so strange. It was only when he moved, or when he spoke, that somehow jarred with that bad boy image. It gave Helen the odd feeling that his mind wasn't totally there.

Armando looked at her hand lying on his notepad. "The effects vary. *Alice in Wonderland* had Alice taking pills. The first time, she went very small. Later, the magic pill made her huge. Yet she was never fearful of her situation or was aware of how disorienting her sudden change in size was. I think she was on the SYMBIOS potion myself, but saying it was magic simplified the procedure."

Helen relaxed in her chair. "Thank you. Your answers helped tremendously."

"That's all? Dismissed already by the High Priestess? The mantle has been passed on, just like that?" Armando mocked. "Don't you want to know more? There's always more."

She shrugged. If she wanted direct answers, she had to find another way to get to Mr. Chang. He wasn't going to share in front of an audience. "You'll be around for questions later, right?"

"Affirmative. Later can be better."

"Thank you, then." She gave the group a smile in an attempt to break up the awkward silence. She had a feeling they were playing audience, keeping quiet as they watched the two of them. She caught T.'s eye an instant longer before moving on. "Is it my place to just get to the operation specifics themselves so we could end this meeting earlier? I need some time to myself. Can I talk to someone to move the Psych session?"

Helen had too many questions to feel like being questioned herself. Everyone seconded her motion.

"Okay, can I ask who the operations chief is for this particular mission? In fact, no one has told me who's in charge of the future operations," Helen said.

"I'm operations chief for the test session." It was Drew De Clerq. A quiet man, he was in charge of assigning new operatives to their different branches within COMCEN, and as such was one of the first people with whom Helen became acquainted when she first arrived.

"We'll wait till after this operation to decide the future OC," T. chipped in. "Right now, we don't even know whether there is a future one."

"Don't you think I can do this?" Helen asked.

T. shook her head. "I know you can, but it's up to those department heads to sign off on the project. The contract with GEM is very specific. Training through the various departments, followed by a test session." She paused. "You have two choices. To be successful and make them think they can duplicate the whole process with someone they want. Or, to be impressively successful and make them want to continue to use you. As you can see, some of these men's future jobs depend on you."

Helen grinned at them. "Be nice to me and I'll think about it."

They laughed at her joke. Someone mentioned that with the thousands of dollars invested in her already, the chances of them not continuing if the test session proved successful was low. Besides, they still didn't have their new VR machine.

"Don't be too sure," Armando said quietly. "They're all watching your every move. They want to duplicate the process and be in charge of their own candidate. And why not? Every department had their own covert group, so why should they depend on one outside their domain, especially one as independent as Center? We'd gone through this with the V-Program."

"So you think they're working on a VR portal themselves?" De Clerq asked.

"You tell me. The other labs had tested the Solarbot program using similar simulation systems. Flyboy was the model for the Sim-Flight-Control Systems in Florida a while ago," Armando pointed out. "We watched them. Don't you think they're watching us?"

"Then what's the point of using COMCEN? Especially if every agency isn't cooperating fully," Helen asked. The man might act eccentric but his mind was sharp as a tack. She still wasn't sure what the whole story behind him was, but she intended to find out. Another thing on her list, she thought wryly.

Armando scratched his stubble lightly as he regarded her with those intense dark eyes. "The possibilities are endless. Why don't you remote view and find out yourself?"

The mockery was intentional. He seemed bent on trying to set her off. Helen refused to take the bait.

"That kind of remote viewing has a price," she said. "It'll take more than one remote viewer to go through so many departments, anyway."

She didn't add that officially, she hadn't gone past Phase Two of the CIA program. There were things that she still hadn't learned.

"Imagine that. A coven of remote viewers," Armando said in that low voice, "sitting around creating reality. No wonder these departments might want you to fail."

"They already have them in the CIA," T. pointed out.

"Of course," Armando acknowledged, lazily clasping his fingers on the table. "Underground programs such as mind control and psychic research are held in such high regard by the brass."

"They had wanted their own V-commandos," De Clerq said. "It makes sense that they would want their own V2 version."

"COMCEN has never shared their secrets with them, and I wouldn't use the V2 term to their faces, if I were you. Might make them even more anxious," Armando said. He turned to Helen. "Magicians never share their trade secrets, you know."

Helen shrugged. "They all have a little piece of me. I'm sure they aren't sharing what they taught me with everyone either." Her lips twisted. They were talking about her as if she was some machine that could be copied. "You think they would ever duplicate another me, if they fight over one candidate so much?"

"We'll worry about that when the time comes," De Clerq spoke up. "Right now, it's you and Dr. Kirkland in the front line. I'll coordinate the details. Our liaison will call Center as soon as they've set the coordinates and when the envelope is secured so no one can tamper with it. Then you and Dr. Kirkland will handle the remote viewing part of the operation."

Helen nodded. Every contract agent understood how government departments never seemed to share relevant information, even when they were supposed to be working together. It had happened to GEM several times while they were on an operation—different government departments at odds with each other and putting lives at risks. COMCEN, with the help of an influential admiral, had set up a liaison system a few years ago to avoid any more blunders.

"I don't know how long it's going to take me for the remote session. Sometimes it can go for hours."

"The med team will wait," Dr. Kirkland said.

"Good remote viewers are usually useless after their sessions," Dr. Kasparov said. "Are you sure you can handle the serum so soon after your session?"

Helen shrugged. "That's the test, isn't it? They want to see how all this comes together in one mission." She wasn't totally sure what would happen herself. That feeling of weakness after a tough session was a problem but her many months of training was meant to overcome this exhaustion. "The drug is supposed to make me feel less tired, right? That's part of it."

"Yes, but certain CIA records revealed their tests

had been a bust," De Clerq said. "What happened to the test subjects, Dr. Kirkland?"

"The CIA have their own version of the serum. What interested me most was the difference in dosage and timing they use on the subjects. They still haven't shown all their classified records to our side. It's highly probable that the subjects have been released from the program, but we don't really know."

"I wonder whether they suffer from any ill effects," Armando interrupted offhandedly. "They could have taken a Tiny Alice pill and might be walking around looking at a huge, frightening world."

There was a pause as those in attendance shifted in their seats uncomfortably. Helen supposed everyone was probably wondering whether that was what was happening to Armando Chang. She couldn't quite put a finger on it yet, but she had a feeling she would be learning a lot more about the unfathomable commando in the near future.

"We're taking every precaution to make this as safe as possible," Dr. Vaughn assured from the other side of the table. "Our V-program works. V2 will be just as successful."

"V2. SYMBIOS 2. I'm beginning to get an inferiority complex," Helen drawled. Her joke succeeded in distracting the group as they became more focused on each step of the mission.

By the end of the hour, everyone was satisfied they had all the details of the operation. Most of it would have to wait till after Helen's session. That was Dr. Kirkland's project, the integration of VR and remote viewing. The challenge was to race against time and skepticism. Helen appreciated that no one at the meeting had voiced any disbelief about remote viewing. She had faced some tough grilling at some of the other departments. But that was why GEM had approved its partnership with COS Command Center. Covert and subversive operations covered everything and anything.

There was a hint of anticipation in the air at the end of the meeting. That no one there knew the specified location, and that the success of the operation depended on someone they hadn't worked with was a challenge. To follow her guesswork and believe her orders after that was an even bigger challenge because this would involve using operations high-tech transportation and manpower. The coordinates of the location had been sealed in an envelope, its location a secret until the end of the operation. Everything depended on the candidate. If Helen Roston failed, hundreds of thousands of dollars would go down the drain.

Helen was well aware of this, yet felt strangely relaxed. As she shook hands with her operation coworkers, Armando Chang spoke softly in her ear.

"Great show. Wrong question, though, Helen."

She turned, surprised. She hadn't seen him making his way to her. These commandos could move fast. "What's the wrong question?"

"It's what the drugs do to you, not for you." His dark eyes glittered secretively. "But the crown is now yours, and what treasure there is."

"Illusion is part of a GEM operative's skills." She picked up his cloak and passed it to him. "You aren't scaring me with that insane act, Chang."

A corner of his lips lifted derisively. "Damn. Call me

later and we can meet, and I can correct this problem. Fear is…oh, I forget. You won't be feeling that." He barked out a short laugh. "But you might still need me for other things. Remember—assimilation and synthesis. Only I'll understand what you'll be going through… if you're really as good as they say, Hell."

"Oh, I'm good. You should watch me disappear sometime," she quipped.

Armando gave her an amused smile. "I'm not crazy, I'm just a little impaired," he sang softly before turning away.

Helen stared at his departing back before glancing down at the tiny electronic communication card he had slipped into her hand. She pivoted and came up against T.

"We need to talk," T. said.

"You don't say," Helen drawled. A thought had flashed in her mind when Armando sang that lyric. Might her monitor be one of these COS commandos?

Eight

He watched T. turning her favorite ring round and round as she sat there quietly watching the wound in his left arm being stitched by a medic. Dry blood caked parts of his chest.

Another exceptionally dangerous woman. He smiled at her, tilting his head to one side enquiringly. Flirting with T. was hazardous, but he enjoyed it. Both as a man and as an opponent.

"She had questions about Armando's act," T. said, getting up.

"She thinks it's an act, then?" He'd been watching the young man since he became the newest member of the commandos. An asset with baggage. But who wasn't? "You brought him here, T.," he added, reminding her with gentle mockery.

The medic cut the thread. T. pulled the wet towel from the medical tray, walked over and handed it to him. "Hell is a trained mind probe."

He noticed that she'd ignored his dig about Armando. "Better than you?" he asked, ignoring the offered towel.

She accepted his silent challenge, her amber-gold eyes gleaming with humor. She came closer. Her strokes were slow and sure as she wiped off the dried blood. "She's more intuitive than me," she said, "and she follows her instincts very naturally when she starts a session. She gets the information she needs more quickly than most."

"Do you think she will probe Armando for answers?"

T. arched her eyebrows delicately. "Is your blood red?" She paused in the middle of wiping. "You have to stop it."

He smiled again, amused. "How, with a spell? Perhaps Armando can take care of himself. Tess, things aren't always what they seem, you know that."

"Yes, but his act's making some people nervous, darling. I find it amusing but the more extreme it becomes, the more likely it'll put people in dangerous situations."

She laid the soiled towel on the side of the tray and picked up a clean dry one, handing it to him. He took it this time, and waved away the offer of a Band-Aid from the medic. "We'll have to be extra careful, then," he said. He turned to the medic and added, "Thank you. I can take care of everything else."

He knew T. was waiting for them to be alone. As usual, she took her time getting to her point, priming her target with suggestions. She didn't need to do that with him but she did, anyway, and they both enjoyed the exercise. It was a game, one that most people wouldn't take up. One slip, and the loser gave away a lot of secrets. And when it came to T. and him, the stakes in secrets were high. But their enjoyment was private and mutual. And a secret between them.

"Armando isn't really needed in the operations."

"All the commandos are needed sooner or later, T."

"Hell's getting mixed messages about the serum. It might not be good for the situation."

"I'm satisfied with the situation."

T. walked over to a dresser, opened a drawer and pulled out a folded shirt. She flapped it open, then put it against her body. "You just like to play with everyone's mind, that's your problem."

Here it comes. "And you don't?" His lips curled up in mockery.

T. laughed. "Darling, we're two of a kind but I sometimes wonder whether that's good for the operations."

He strode toward her. "You fit in here, Tess." He ran a finger lightly on the shirt hanging loosely against her. "You know I wanted you…for this experiment."

"Don't flirt, darling…you're afraid of Hell," T. said, realization dawning in her voice. "What did you two do during the VR session, hmmm? Besides learning how to communicate?"

"Just like when you're in the CAVE with me," he replied smoothly. So this was what T. was after. Hell was keeping things close to her chest. "Learning to communicate."

T. laughed again. "I cannot see what an imaginary figure programmed to look like a blond Greek god with a rather large protrusion could be communicating about with one of my best operatives." She dropped the shirt. He caught it. Her eyes narrowed slightly as she added,

"I know you. You can't resist a complex woman with secrets. That's always been your weakness. You've always flirted with me, and you're totally without rules in the CAVE, even with me, but the challenge here's different, isn't it? Hell's giving you a run for your money, isn't she?"

He, too, could evade when he chose. "You don't have to look so smug about it, Tess. No one can give me a runaround like you do with all your different personas, you know that. You've practiced all of them on me, so I know how potent you are in real life."

He slipped on the shirt, buttoning it with one hand. T. took a step closer. He didn't mind her testing him so deliberately. After all, he'd done the same when he'd first met her. Looking for that kink in a dangerous woman was his thing. And he now knew what T.'s was. He'd never use it against her. Unless necessary.

Of course she was aware of having been exposed. And like a woman, she was determined to find his Achilles' heel. The tension between them brought into sharp focus how much he wanted Helen. With T., it was just a matter of male fun and female ego; with Helen, the temptation to go deeper was a constant ache. And this was just in virtual reality. In the flesh…he had an idea he would give in to temptation very quickly.

"A mysterious and elusive man, uncatchable like a shadow," T. said, the tone of her voice soft and sexy, the one she probably used when she was going in for the kill. "Only a shadow tends to lurk close by. You play with the light and dark until one's never sure whether you're really truly here."

He chose to attack first. He lifted a lock of her hair

and twined it around his finger. He tugged at it. "Tess, Tasha, Talia...who can compete with you?"

"You can't distract me, my evasion expert. I know exactly what you're doing, countering my probing. Tell me what you're doing with Helen, darling." She arched a teasing eyebrow. "And don't try to make me jealous. That thing she had enlarged on your anatomy was impressive-looking."

He tugged harder at the tendril around his finger, bringing her face closer. "What is it you want to know?"

"Her performance."

"She hasn't done anything yet."

"Is she adapting well?"

"She knows her mind better than you."

"Can she handle the serum?"

"We'll know very soon, won't we?"

"Does she get along with you enough to trust you?"

"That remains to be seen."

T. affected a frown. "Hmm. It sounds like you two are getting along famously."

"How so?"

She ran a light fingernail down the row of buttons on his shirt. "She doesn't like to talk about herself. Likewise with you. So, with the unexpected twist that your brain wave happens to be compatible with hers...I can imagine the big surprise you two are going to get soon."

Her answer raised his interest a notch. "And what's that?" he asked, eyeing her slender fingers teasing his shirtfront.

She smiled. "Darling, you'll know very soon, won't you?" She stepped back, her small teeth biting her lower lip.

He released her hair. As usual, it was fun while it lasted. "Don't probe my mind and I won't probe yours." He smiled back at her. They'd both gotten a bit of information about their object of interest. He'd have to read up on the brain wave synchronicity.

"Darling, sometimes you're much too tempting."

Helen thought about the Portal as she bobbed lazily in the pool. This was it. Time for action. She had worked her butt off all these months for this moment. This would be the first time to share her experience with someone…if it worked. She frowned. She didn't even know the man who was her monitor, and already he was sitting heavily in her mind.

What would he think of her if he "saw" the things she did? And what exactly was he there for besides to act as an anchor? There had to be more but Helen couldn't come up with an answer yet. There hadn't been enough time to probe his mind. She sensed another agenda, and yeah, it tasted of danger.

He had tested her and freely admitted that there was more to the contract. And what did he mean when he said he needed the trigger code in case things went wrong? How could he interfere with a remote viewer when he wasn't one?

So many questions, and all about one man, some of which had nothing to do with this contract. They had more to do with her feminine curiosity. He had spiked her interest, this voice in her mind.

It wasn't even his real voice—she had chosen the Southern twang—yet there was an underlying seduction in it that was all his. She shook her head. She was a

GEM operative, trained in mind control and covert tactics. She had to ignore the temptation and the challenge this self-created avatar presented and try to understand the man behind it. The idea of someone watching her doing her job in detail was unnerving. Trust. Could she really trust this man?

A noise disturbed her reverie. She looked up. It was one of *them*. The big silent guy, she called him, because he was big and he hadn't spoken a word to her ever.

He was built like an ancient warrior, sculpted muscles with a strange pattern tattooed on his chest and back. He had long, black hair and the blackest pair of eyes she'd ever seen. In fact, he looked so exotic that she always half expected him to walk in wearing some kind of armor—chain mail would look perfect on him—with some big sharp weapon by his side. And he enjoyed getting into the pool and racing her, even though he never said it. They'd just race silently, every time. She'd never been able to beat him. She told herself that it was because he always came in after she'd done some strenuous swimming. One day…one day, she would win.

Today wasn't the day. She had to take it easy. Instead, she lazily swam up and down her lane, ignoring him. But she could feel him swimming alongside, keeping the same slow pace, feel his dark glance on her. Normally, that would challenge her into trying to make him talk to her, but today, it felt strangely comfortable, like he was there to just keep an eye on her.

Keep an eye on her. She snuck a glance at him. His expression didn't reveal anything.

What if—she looked at the man again—her monitor

had dark eyes and dark, dark hair? What if that was why the big guy didn't speak to her? Maybe he was afraid she would catch some familiar phrasing coming out of that incredibly sensuous mouth.

As if he had an idea where her thoughts were leading, the corner of that very same mouth lifted slightly. And still he continued to swim silently alongside of her.

After another few laps, Helen got out, leaving him in the pool without a backward glance. When she had time, she was so going to sit down and read every one of these commandos' files. It didn't take her long to get dressed and she decided she'd head on over to the VR room to look at the Portal before anyone else got there.

"Are you okay?"

Helen looked up. Flyboy stood a few feet away, a watchful expression in his eyes. She had a feeling those eyes didn't miss much either. Why were these guys "bumping" into her left and right? Either they were keeping an eye on her out of curiosity, or someone was ordering them to.

"Affirmative," she replied, turning the corner. He followed her. "Just preparing mentally. You weren't at the Q and A. Busy?"

"Sorry. Had some errands. But I'll be here to watch you at work." His smile was boyish. The serious look disappeared like magic. "Forgive me?"

Helen arched a brow. "For what? You didn't do anything wrong."

"For not warning you about Armando." He shrugged. "He can be a bit overwhelming."

"Do you trust him?"

Flyboy regarded her solemnly. "He's my teammate."

"But he's the newest member of your team, right? So, how do you know exactly when you can trust him?"

"One quickly learns to trust while working together in dangerous situations. It's teamwork, Hell. If I don't trust him, the concept doesn't work."

Therein lay the problem. As contract agents, GEM operatives didn't operate in groups. "But a team still has to mesh," she pointed out.

"Granted, but we're talking about the V-Program here. Not to be all bigheaded about it, but it's a chosen few." He cocked his head. "We weren't thrown together by coincidence or contractual obligations. Are you having trust issues? With the team?"

"No, not with the team," Helen murmured. She hadn't even thought of the team, since she hadn't actually worked with them. As far as she was concerned, she was on her own, remote viewing, and then the team would come in afterwards.

She and Hades, she amended, but in virtual reality, wasn't that like being on her own?

"Does Armando tell you what's happening to him?" She made a face at his pause. "Come on, the others might not see through his act but I do. The question is, is it just him or the serum?"

Flyboy turned and stepped in front of Helen. His blue eyes appeared darker today, more intense. She could sense his hesitancy, he was keeping something from her. "I don't know," he told her. "You might have to find out for us. Armando is sure to talk to you more after you've used the serum, to compare notes, if nothing else."

Helen tilted her her head sideways, narrowing her

eyes. "Hey, that's extra work. Nothing in my contract about probing one of the famed commandos' minds." She was going to do it but not to Armando Chang. "If he's a problem, why is he still on active mode?"

"Our commander hasn't deactivated him."

"Well, then it's between him and your commander, right?" She leaned back, tossing her hair carelessly. "All these commandos running around in active mode...my imagination's working overtime."

Flyboy's eyes twinkled. "Sweetheart, I've just seen your reworked program avatar. Believe me, your imagination *is* the one running rampant."

Helen made a moue. "Damn, isn't there such a thing as privacy? How's a girl going to have some fun around here?"

He shook a long index finger at her. "There is very little privacy at Center. Only in special quarters." He smiled at her again, this time wolfishly. "Want to check them out?"

She made a show of cracking her knuckles. "Well, after a shot of that serum, I should have the courage to venture into the sacred sanctum of the commandos. Do you all live here? Borrrrring."

"Not all the time. Only when we have a job to do."

"All right. Give me the directions and I might give you a ring at your quarters."

Flyboy waggled his eyebrows. "Can I trust you not to sabotage the place?"

Funny. She was just thinking about trust. These commandos were too damn perceptive. She really needed to find out more about them.

Later, after Flyboy left, Helen thoughtfully fingered the communication card Armando Chang had slipped into her hand at the meeting earlier. Now she knew how to find him when she needed him.

In a secret test facility, Virginia

"This is a very easy exercise, Agent 51. You should breeze right through this."

Of course he would. He was one of the chosen few. "I feel great. Thank you, thank you, thank you! I can do this. Trust me, I'll find out what's in that envelope in no time." What he needed was a cigarette but he knew better than to say that out loud.

"We want you to feel comfortable. How are you feeling?"

"Like nothing I can describe. I've missed this so much. Thank you for getting me out of the psych evaluation. It's been months! I told them all I needed was another shot, just a little higher dosage, and I'll be fine. They won't listen. They think I've gone crazy." He wiped his hands on his pants, trying not to fidget. He needed these two men to believe that he was truly okay.

"Well, we don't think you're crazy, but we need your help. If you can go through the tests, we'll recruit you into a special operations program."

"We're going to do this with the drug, right? Just like the program I was in, right? I have to have a shot of it." *Please.* He needed to taste the power again. Remote viewing without it wasn't the same.

"Of course. We plan to keep using it."

"Okay, cool. There shouldn't be a problem then." He smiled in relief. He could do anything with a dose in his system. "I'll do whatever's asked of me."

"We're a bit concerned about your failure with the last tests before they sent you to psych. This higher dosage might have more painful aftereffects."

Higher dosage? He looked around the room eagerly, restlessly. "I told them the headaches were nothing! They went away, didn't they? And they're just headaches, you know. Everyone gets migraines now and then. Migraines…my family gets them constantly. So, I'm convinced the headaches have nothing—nothing— to do with the drug. I feel great now! Don't my stats check out? Look, I'll do anything you ask!"

"Yes, your stats are fine. We're ready when you are, then."

"Yes, yes, let's get on with this. Simple, very simple, finding out what's in that envelope. Any remote viewer can do it. First thing we learn." But with the drug, oh man, the things he could do when it was flowing in him. After those first few times with it, normal RV was like cheap bland coffee. No, no, nothing was the same without it. The pain afterwards was a small price. "I'm ready to bilocate."

"Sign this first, Agent 51. It's just a simple Human Use Agreement form. Standard procedure, as you know. Then we'll move on to the room."

"Oh sure, of course." He would get a cigarette somehow. Calm himself down. A higher dosage. His stomach churned in anticipation. He would have it very soon.

"Helen, we've modified a new button and placed it near the wrist control pad, away from everything. If at any moment you feel you're losing control, or you somehow lose connection with Hades, or you feel caught up or lost, press this button."

She didn't bother to ask what would happen if she did that. Things were going to be iffy, as it was.

"Okay, Doc. Let's roll."

Dr. Kirkland took off his stethoscope. "Do you have any questions? You haven't asked many since the beginning. All right, then. We'll see whether those breathing exercises and sleeping coordination will get the two of you to work in sync."

Helen didn't ask many questions because GEM training used similar methods, but she wasn't going to reveal that. Hemi-Sync audio technology was part of NOPAIN training in gathering Intel from reluctant targets. It was one reason why she advanced so rapidly during the remote viewing part of her training; she was able to focus and project using tools of her trade.

"I'll get the target, don't worry. Will Hades know where it is?" She would rather he didn't. That would contaminate any test. Remote viewers and their monitors usually worked blind. Afterwards, the real information on the target would be given to them.

Dr. Kirkland smiled. "No, the target information is in a specially sealed envelope."

Ah, they were starting with remote viewing standard operating procedure. This would be the easy part, then. "Well, that's simple to find out. Let's hope being in VR won't make any difference. If I give you the wrong coordinates, we would be at the wrong venue, and my remote session would be of no use at all."

"Don't worry, Helen. Your monitor is very good at what he does."

Which was…? One day she would demand a resume.

Minutes later, Helen looked out expectantly into the white space. He appeared suddenly, a dark silhouette against the light. Still naked, of course. Obstinate man. But oh, so gorgeous. Her heart still skipped a beat, when she should be used to that incredible form by now. He halted not too far from her, standing like some regal warrior. She fancied she could hear some distant war drumbeat. She grinned. Next time, she would get him a loincloth.

She was pretty sure if he wanted, he could program some clothing at his end. His skill at NOPAIN was intriguing. By giving her control of his outer form, he was hiding his own agenda. She intended to find out what that was.

Hades watched her with an expression all his own, though, one she was beginning to recognize. It fascinated her that his personality was so strong it came through the visual effects of a program.

She flashed another quick smile. "Was that you swimming just now?" Not that she expected him to tell her the truth.

"No. Ready?" he asked.

"Shouldn't I be the one who says that?" she countered. Remote viewing was her domain here, after all. *"Or have you done this before?"*

"I'm familiar with the subject of remote viewing, but I've never shared my mind with anyone else." He drew nearer, his eyes a melting trust-me-brown.

Helen snorted rudely. *"Nor have I."* And those chocolate-brown eyes were tempting her to share more than her mind. *"But then, transcending time and space to gather Intel isn't something I share with anyone on a regular basis."*

He didn't say anything, just held out a hand, and repeated, "Ready?"

"Yes." She took the few steps to reach him and slowly put her hand in his. Her gaze was steady. *"Everything I'm going to do is classified under the…"*

He shook his head, silencing her. *"I know the whole code by heart. This is an underground project, Elena. You don't have to quote the rules of engagement to me. There aren't any. You and I are doing something they can only imagine, and if we succeed, only we'll know what rules have been broken."*

"Boy, the man can talk serious lingo," Helen drawled. But she could feel her own excitement rising at his words. *"So we're going to break rules, huh? I like that in a man."*

His grasp tightened, just enough to make her gaze at him questioningly. He looked into her eyes intently. This time, he chose to communicate with his mind. *They don't trust what remote viewers see, Elena, you know that. It's sneaking a peek at one point in time and experiments have shown that different viewers see different things and their reports won't help a covert operation.*

Helen shook her head. *That's when they experiment with viewing the future, Hades.*

That's Phase Three.

She winked at him. *Something they haven't trained me in, remember? It's a tough phase, they said, lots of casualties. I take that to mean that they had many failures in getting their predictions right.*

It could also mean another thing.

It was becoming more and more natural to communicate without speaking. *What?*

It could mean many have tried and died, Elena.

That jerked her out of silent mode. *"How? They would just be remote viewing."* She frowned, going back to thinking. *Predicting the future wrong won't kill you, you know.*

He turned. She had to follow his direction since his hand was still holding hers. *One intrigue at a time. In today's session, you're going to show me how you work your trigger code. Then we'll locate the target in the envelope.*

So how come you're leading? Helen mocked, although she didn't resist. She wanted to continue their conversation. He was always leaving her with questions. He stayed silent, the quirk of his mouth mocking her back. If she had the time, she would play with this man.

There'll be plenty of time for that, I promise, sweet Elena.

Before she could come back with a smart-aleck answer, Hades changed the scenery. She looked around, trying not to show her surprise. The place was an exact replica of the windowless remote viewing room at the CIA facility, from the all-gray soft canvas fabric to the all-gray round knobs on the drawers. Every detail was the way she remembered.

"How do you know what those rooms look like?"

"Photographs."

"Oh sure, the CIA takes photographs of their secret rooms so you can reproduce and study them." She tried to shake his hand off. *"Don't lie to me."*

"I'm not," he denied. *"We've been monitoring their program for some time."*

"Why create this in virtual reality then?" Why did they take the trouble to recreate a remote viewing room from another training facility?

She stared at his hand pointedly now but instead of releasing her, he brought it to his lips and kissed her fingertips. *"I thought it might be easier for you if we use familiar surroundings."* He licked the sensitive pad of her thumb. *"You can explain your SOP and tell me what to do in case something goes wrong and you get lost in the ether."*

He knew about the risks of getting lost in the ether then. Helen tried to focus on this as the rest of her body was busy reacting to his tongue. Why was he doing this?

He sank his teeth gently into the fleshy area and she almost moaned aloud. She refused to let him distract her. *"I sit in the chair, turn on the biomachine, concentrate till the brain waves go theta, and then go into an altered state."* Telling him the standard operating procedure brought back some focus.

"Then what does your supervisor do?"

He certainly didn't do *that* to her hand. *"Like everyone else—monitors me, makes sure the vitals don't go crazy."* Her voice sounded husky to her ears. *"Sometimes beginners can't control their imagination. When they 'go' underwater, some would literally choke from holding their breath. It takes time to get used to mind-traveling."*

"Is that what you call it?" he said against her palm, seemingly able to hold a serious conversation and at the same time, explore erogenous zones on her hand that she never knew she had. Currents of delight zinged up her arm as he nibbled on a sensitive spot close to her wrist. *"Does it ever get that real for you?"*

"*It feels real...like this,*" she whispered. The man had a seriously sensuous tongue. How was it possible? It was so real in her mind that she wanted to pull his head down to hers so she could taste that tongue. Was his mind so locked with hers that everything he did affected her so realistically?

Helen moved her palm, delighting in the feel of his face as he stroked like a cat against her hand before turning his attention back to nibbling her, his teeth pulling on her flesh in a slow tantalizing manner before releasing it to kiss it better. She swayed closer. "*And why are you trying to turn me on when there is a job to do?*"

"*I like touching you,*" he whispered back.

He was keeping something from her. "*So many lies, and I'm supposed to trust you?*"

"*I'm not lying.*" He put her hand on his chest, near his heart. "*Scout's honor.*"

Helen laughed. She had created a monster. "*I think you're supposed to cross your heart with your hand.*" But she liked touching him, too. A naughty thought crossed her mind. "*You're big for a Scout.*"

His eyes smiled back at her. "*You know what they say about big Scouts.*"

Helen deliberately slid her hand down his chest. "*What?*"

He didn't stop her hand. "*Big...hearts.*"

"*I can see that.*" She grinned. "*You sure feel ready now.*"

"*Then lead the way, sweet Elena.*"

She had never started a remote session this way before, but then, her monitor had never been quite this sexy or this bold. She turned toward the virtual-made room.

"How long before they get impatient?"

"We aren't given any time limit for the first time. Our liaison said most of them are just mildly curious about this part. They're more interested in the use of the serum later."

"I assume those are the military types." Of course they would be more interested in something that would transform their military personnel into better fighters.

Hades helped her strap into the RV chair. It felt strange, even though she'd been preparing for this, that she was actually going to try to remote view in virtual reality. She had to admit that the familiarity of the virtually-created surroundings was helping a lot to lessen her anxiety.

She studied him as he seemed to know what went where. Although this wasn't the real man, she could sense his knowledge; there was no hesitance in the way he worked the different instruments.

"Tell me what I need to know," he said, when he was done.

"You said you're familiar with remote viewing, so you know that locating an object is a myth, right? The usual target in an RV session is a location and the viewers check in on the scene at that specific moment in time."

It was widely misunderstood that one could find an object or person, like a missing child, for example. Remote viewing was more a scan of the landscape during a point in time. What the viewer saw could then be readjusted to another point before or after the target. The beginners were given coordinates on which to focus, but the more advanced viewer needed only an agreed-upon thought. Hence, the envelope tonight. It didn't matter whether there was anything sealed inside, as long as the target was universally agreed upon. It was important that Hades understood this concept before they started.

Hades nodded. *"Time and specific events, especially one that left few clues, are hard to pinpoint."*

"And that's why no matter how accurate the viewer is, the army will never send any personnel in to verify. The chances of them going into a trap or that the event is bogus are too high." Helen paused, startled. *"Son of a bitch. That's what you're here for, isn't it? You're someone in whom they have a lot of trust. Sure you don't have the ability to remote view on your own, but you can come along in my head and verify, and they'll believe you more than a regular monitor. Why didn't you tell me before?"*

As always, his expression didn't let on about how right her guesswork was.

"When were you going to tell me?" she insisted.

"When there is something to verify," he said. *"I have nothing to tell you or anyone else at the moment. I've explained it to them, that seeing a target is easy for a remote viewer. Accessing it at the point in time mentally, then physically, is difficult."*

Helen's eyes narrowed a fraction. How did he do that, simplify a complicated concept with a sentence? She was also beginning to learn to read between the lines when it came to Hades' imparting information. *"I sight the target. I describe the location as best I can. Then..."* She chewed on her lip, eyes widening. *"Then your experience will help in deciphering the true location and we work in tandem in locating the item in time and event."*

This was something phenomenal, something remote viewers could never do alone. She was learning more about Hades: he was someone with enough covert experience to be able to recognize important targets, maybe even had experience going there in real time. That would simplify locating, for example, a military compound. Describing one usually didn't help, since most military compounds looked about the same, but when there was someone who knew exactly what to look for to double-check the location...

His lips curved knowingly, as if he were catching some of her racing thoughts. She was eager to test her theory, to see whether this was going to work. She settled back into the chair. Let's see how much he understands the ins and outs of actual remote viewing.

"You already know I have a trigger code. An experienced viewer can access my travels with me that way. My monitor was more like a guide. I could hear her no matter where I was. It's almost like virtual reality, but she couldn't read my thoughts or see what I was looking at. During each session, she told me when to break off and monitored my return."

He nodded. *"She locked on to your location through your trigger code."*

Helen tried not to show her surprise. There was that simplifying skill again. *"That's one way to describe it. She could observe and make reports on my progress that way. But I also learned that I could shield myself from her."* She challenged him with narrowed eyes. *"And I'm not telling you how I did that."*

He nodded again. *"Fair enough. What's next?"*

"When the right moment comes, and don't even ask me how to explain it, I bilocate. That's the term they use. I'm physically here but I've traveled there." She made a face. *"Not that it can't get more bizarre than what we're attempting to do today—being physically in one place, virtually remote viewing in virtual reality, and mind-traveling to a third location."*

"We can call it trilocation," he suggested in an amused voice.

"Tell me, what do you expect to learn from this? What makes you any different from an ordinary monitor?" She gave him a telling look when he arched a mocking brow at her. *"Besides the fabulous body I gave you, all right?"*

"We can get into that later, Elena."

She sighed. *"You're not good at answering questions, are you?"* He had evaded every one that would have given her a hint about the Center's final agenda.

He caressed the side of her face. *"It's easier my way, trust me."*

There went those words again. *Trust me.* So far he had done nothing to earn her trust. Sure, he was something else to behold. And probably had the smarts of a scientist. But for all she knew, he might just be some young Derek-type nerd asked to manipulate her.

You don't believe that.

This time she glared. *Stop it. You're probably a fat geek, and gay.*

He laughed. *And what's wrong with that? You created me to look like this.*

She hadn't heard him laugh before. She liked the

sound of it. *Don't tempt me. I'll turn you into a hairy Big Foot and give you lice.*

You won't enjoy lice on you when I kiss you.

Did he have a comeback for everything? Helen watched as he punched in the buttons to activate the biofeedback machine. All of this was virtual reality, but doing the same things that would happen in preparing for a real remote viewing session readied both their minds and added even more focus. Actually, she no longer needed to use a biofeedback machine when she worked by herself these days, but she was taking someone along this time, and since he'd been coordinating his brain waves with hers, their going "under" together added another layer to the "mind illusion." A brain wave synchronization within a brain wave synchronization. She was getting a headache trying to analyze what was happening. A headache within a headache. Ow.

His hand came behind her neck suddenly and jerked her forward. He planted a brief hard kiss on her lips, driving away all thought and analysis. Which was what he wanted, the jerk. She frowned. He had on that expression again. Cool, with that hint of something else, in his eyes. *What was he thinking? Planning?*

He didn't let her go, although it couldn't have been comfortable to be bending over her like that. His hand felt hot. Her head fell back as they stared at each other, and as the minutes went by, she heard their breathing becoming more even, the beta wavelength humming in the background.

"*You have it on at your end, too, don't you?*" she whispered. "*You're in sync with me out there and in here.*"

"*Yes.*"

She could feel their chests expanding as they took in their breaths. The hard imprint of his body. The soft air of his expelled breath. As she focused inward, she could hear…

Is it my imagination or can I hear both our heartbeats?

His hand gave a light squeeze. *It's all in the mind. Believe it and you'll see it.*

It's supposed to be the other way round. See it and you'll believe it. She was strangely excited and restless as she tried to figure out what was happening in this strange environment. For some reason, it was hard to concentrate.

He stepped closer, inserting his leg between hers, forcing her thighs open. *Your mind's too busy analyzing what's happening.*

With her head against his chest, his heartbeat thumped louder. A lot louder than normal, as if she heard him through a microphone in her head. *Why was it she could hear his heart beating?* His hand slid under the front waistband of her pants and inside her panties. Without preliminaries, he cupped her intimately.

Helen jerked. All thought flew out of her head at his sudden invasion. Shocking heat. And total internal focus. Strapped in the chair, her face hidden against his chest, her feet parted, he had total access. And he was taking advantage of that fact, ruthlessly stopping her questioning mind. Her breathing involuntarily grew heavier. He slid one finger inside her.

She pulled at the straps that were attached to her right hand. It was all in the head, anyway. She wasn't held down by him or anything. His finger glided upwards.

Pleasure shot through her system. The sound waves from the machine mingled with her heartbeat. His heartbeat. His finger glided downwards. She forgot about fighting.

She should...kick...his... Her mind clouded as a slow heavy pleasure bloomed. His finger explored lazily, its slow movement shifting all her focus to her senses and the sensations he was causing. He pressed his body harder against her face, or maybe it was the other way round, she couldn't tell. It didn't matter; it just gave him better access to everything. Her body was his to control. Her eyes closed of their own volition. Sound waves and heartbeats mingled and merged, until she couldn't differentiate his from hers. She opened her mouth and tasted his bare flesh. She forgot about questions and analysis.

He knew exactly how she wanted him to move. It was as if he was reading her mind, giving her what she wanted, and then doing exactly...the...opposite. She strained against his touch. She locked on to the sound waves; she could hear the tones changing to theta wavelength. Within seconds, she would feel weightless—no arms, no legs—that floating sensation of bilocation. Hades' touch slowed, too, fragmenting her sense of self even more as her senses stretched outward while he brought her up and held her there. She couldn't think anymore. Almost...almost...

"Not yet, sweet Elena. Checkered flag," he whispered in her ear.

Her trigger code. Her mind was his, too. Bastard. She growled softly as her mind obeyed. She let go, tumbling into the ether like she'd never done before, her whole being singing with pleasure. She was so going to kick his ass.

Nine

There were two kinds of remote viewing. The most basic was coordinated RV, one in which beginners were disciplined. There was a viewer chair and the target was given in coordinates, and the beginner would then draw his or her impressions in an ideogram. This beginning phase gave the monitor a chance to see how the remote viewer was improving; as he or she took more control of "seeing," the ideograms would change from basic cartoonish lines to detailed artwork.

During her training with the CIA, Helen had surprised her monitor at how quickly she had been able to view with remarkable detail. She had graduated into Phase Two at record speed.

Part of Phase Two was ERV, extended remote viewing. No viewer chair was needed. No ideograms were drawn afterwards. The viewer was encouraged to stay out in the ether longer. Helen preferred this. It was more free-form and with her in control behind the wheel, she could set a certain number of laps in order to time herself.

The use of the trigger helped the remote viewer to focus. They could be a camera or a computer, or whatever they desired, as long as they were very good with their choice. For Helen, cameras were too slow and wouldn't work well in certain areas. She wasn't that great with a computer. She hated VCRs, could never record right.

A race car was perfect. She could choose her speed, lap as fast as she wanted, or slow down to quietly take in the scenery. And she was very familiar with a car. Hell-On-Wheels, her fellow operatives fondly called her now and then.

All beginning remote viewers needed guidance. It was a safety rope, in case they got lost out in the ether. With T. watching, Hell had allowed a trigger code to be embedded in her subconscious as a way for the monitor to interrupt a session or to call off a target search.

She'd remove it soon, she vowed, as she opened her eyes and looked around the cockpit of her race car. She looked out of the windshield and a checkered flag waved at her mockingly.

How dare he? She wanted a fight and there was no one around to hit. She was so pissed off she could spit nails.

Are you ready for the coordinates?

"*I don't need any stinking coordinates,*" she yelled.

She had remote viewed enough times to be able to get to the target by just focusing on the envelope. The coordinates were meaningless anyway; it could be empty for all remote viewers cared. It was the universal agreement of the target point that the envelope represented. But she was too pissed off to explain that detail to her monitor right now. Damn him, damn him. She was still aching for his touch.

Later.

"*Fuck you,*" she told him off.

Later.

"*Don't ever do that again,*" she said fiercely.

You weren't focusing on getting us into sync. I was just getting your attention back on the job.

"*Getting my attention back...*" Helen growled in frustration. "*There's the issue of privacy here. I didn't agree to any sexual harassment in my contract.*"

Correction. In the physical realm.

Helen gripped the steering wheel. "*Don't play words with me. You know what I mean, Hades! I won't let you do this to me.*"

Do what?

She bit down on her lower lip. What could she say that wouldn't put her at a disadvantage? Don't turn her on again. Don't make me feel this sexually excited again. A thought occurred.

"*Tell me your hand isn't still in my pants,*" she said.

Not physically.

She had a nasty suspicion that he was truly enjoying his control of her mind and body. "*Hades,*" she warned, "*if you don't stop this right now, I'm going to cut off and return back to VR and then I'm going to find you and kick your little avatar ass.*"

Not while we're in VR, Elena. You can come back but you'll be back with Kirkland and T. because that's where your physical body is. You can only come back to me if I let you.

There was a ruthless edge to his voice that she'd never heard before. Helen sat up straighter, frowning as she tried to understand him.

"What do you mean?" she asked.

Think about it. A remote viewer just returns to her physical body. Look at the VR sessions as extended remote viewing, only synchronized. I control you here— your body, your mind. You're my virtual Elena. And you need to trust me.

"Trusting has nothing to do with what you just did!"

I'll work on it. Next time I'll have you in a more comfortable position.

"What!" He was mocking her! Helen couldn't remember a recent time when she felt this frustrated and aggravated by a male answer. She considered the satisfaction of taking time to pound the dashboard in front of her to bits. She was practically rendered speechless. A wave of pleasure almost shot her out of her seat. His hand was still... *"Hades!"*

I need you to focus on the envelope now, Elena. Take that spin to our target.

"If I do it, will you take your hand away?" she demanded fiercely, still shaking inside.

It seems to be the only way to keep both our minds connected while you're out there. The more you're aware of me, the more I'm aware of what you're seeing, believe it or not. If my hand is making you conscious of me all the time, good.

By not mentally preparing her for the sensual assault, he'd attached himself to her psyche, so that she remained aware of him, even in her phantom body. One couldn't just get that close to achieving orgasm without an overwhelming sense of need for more. And the yearning for more of Hades' touch acted as a mental link. He was totally evil.

He had planned this all along. That was why he'd kept emphasizing trust being the issue. His use of NOPAIN was admirable, if she was in any mood to admire. He had tied her in so many knots, there wasn't any room to maneuver. She *would not* admit that the thought of the location of his hand was bothering her. It wasn't real anyway. It was all VR.

Exactly. Now for this time, let me read the coordinates, so I can go with you without...umm...giving you fits. Or would you prefer I...

Of course even that trailed-off suggestion was meant to zoom in her focus on him and his hand again, enforcing that mental link.

But you're so wet already.

His murmur was like potent wine in her mind. *"Read the damn coordinates,"* Helen spat out.

She turned the key in the ignition. She would not think about his hand. She stared out at the checkered flag as she listened to his voice. She would get there and get the job done. She would *not* think about that hand.

I'm losing your thoughts. Come back to me.

Hades' soft command broke through Helen's concentration. She had been focusing on the tiny screen, trying to get closer to figure out what the electronic key was for. She had been too far away to see what was being typed. Dammit. There must be a way.

Not yet. Just a few...minutes...

Elena, come back to me.

It occurred to her that she hadn't thought about Hades' hand ever since she figured out the electronic key was the target. She'd felt danger and had sidled closer. There was danger in that room. Dangerous people. And that key was dangerous, too.

With her switching her focus and acting on a whim instead of describing to her monitor, she'd managed to block Hades. Somewhat, she amended. After all, just the sound of his voice immediately brought back the awareness of him. All he needed was the power of suggestion, the bastard.

"I was checking on what they're doing with the key," she said.

No need. I've a feeling we'll know about that when we come out of VR. The task was to verify the target and give a specific location.

She had perused the place for a clue to the target's coordinates. Finding location was very, very tough in remote viewing. If she were to look for a trailer park, there were thousands of them in the United States. Here, the clues had been the computer and the transactions those people were making. They were in German, with the Frankfurt address right on the top of the screen.

"Let me reverify the location to make sure," she said. *"I don't want to rely on a computer screen."*

Agreed. But you must work in tandem with me. I'm seeing the same things you are, sometimes disjointedly because I'm not actually sure which way you're turning. I have no control over this, since you're in charge.

"Hey, this is the first time I like the idea of you in my mind," Helen said. *"I'm still trying to wrap my mind around your being able to see through my eyes, period. I mean, you aren't a remote viewer, so you can't be here here."*

Exactly. Brain sync. I'm your VR here and you're my

VR there. That's why I need you to tell me where you're turning. Remember that it's your point of view I'm looking from. The snatches of thought are a plus that no one had considered possible, though.

His explanation was, as usual, uniquely simple.

"*Tell me more about the snatches of thought,*" she asked, curious.

Let's verify location now.

He also had a bad habit of changing the subject when she started to ask too many questions.

She looked around her once again. "*I'll go through the door and quickly check out the layout of this building to see where we are. Then I'll go move upwards and confirm that we're near or in Frankfurt.*"

No need, on the second part. I've been inside this building before. I need you to confirm a few specific things. Find the main floor. There are two bronze horses in the main area, their front legs in the air. There's a plaque on the pedestal which should say Deutsche International.

"*Okay, that makes things easier.*"

She looked at the people in the room one last time then went through the door. There was a long passageway, with only three doors, and then an elevator that had no buttons on the outside. There was a slot for an electronic pass.

"*Going through,*" she told Hades.

Her phantom body easily passed through the door. The elevator stall was still there, waiting for occupants to enter.

"*There's only one button.*" She closed her eyes, ran her hand over it. "*This whole place feels very protected—I mean, very monitored. There are many people in this building, all above us. It feels strange, as if most of them don't know of this place we're in. Yet, those who*

*know, I feel danger, that they have a different agenda
from those who don't. I also feel nothing below us."*

Her eyes flew open. *"Hades,"* she continued, *"we're
underground."*

*I'm experiencing some of your feelings. Are you sure
about the location?*

*"Remote viewing is all about the senses. I've to learn
to trust what mine tell me. We're deep below the earth.
By expanding my consciousness outwards, I can smell
it. Can you where you are?"*

*Only when you give me the feedback, Elena. I'm not
the one remote viewing.*

Sarcastic SOB. She closed her eyes again. *"I'm
changing the universal target of the key to the lobby of
this building,"* she informed him.

She was getting the hang of TIVRRV—this total immersion virtual reality remote viewing. She was back
in the race car, the surroundings "dissolved," and there
was the hum of white noise and car engine.

Out of the car and into the targeted reality.

*"Yes, I'm looking at the pedestal with the two bronze
horses. We're exactly where we think we are. And we
now have the added bonus of knowing that room is
underground."*

Good work, Elena. Checkered flag. Now.

She could choose to ignore his command, but the per-
sistent image of a checkered flag was irritating and also
served as a reminder that she wasn't doing this on her own.

Helen reluctantly disengaged from the scene. On a
regular RV session, she'd have taken off on her own to
investigate more. Obviously, her present monitor was
in disagreement over the importance of that key.

"That key—it holds danger," she told him. That was the best she could explain about her uneasiness.

I feel your sense of it. I also feel your need to stay and find out more, but we don't have the time, Elena. We'll be there in physical reality soon enough and we'll find out then. We'll discuss this when you return here. Checkered flag.

She was surprised at the strength of the mental pull of his order. She'd never felt this strong an urge to end her session when her other monitor directed her. That was why many remote viewers kept their trigger codes a secret.

She closed her eyes and she was back in the cockpit of her race car again. Another thought occurred. Return where? *"Wait, how do we make sure I return to the VR and not my physical body?"* She'd never done it this way before, going back from bilocation—trilocation—into VR.

I've thought about it. We have to use our own special trigger code.

She frowned. *"What do you mean?"*

Remember, our brain waves are in sync when we're in our VR session. You don't have a subconscious trigger because you're already in subconscious.

"It's going to make me dizzy trying to understand what's going on," Helen said in a wry voice. She was beginning to get the idea that Hades had thought about everything long before any questions were even formed in her conscious mind, much less subconscious. Not that she was going to admit that to him. *"Tell me what I need to do, Hades."*

Not do. Feel.

Oh no. She shook her head, as if trying to shake away the suspicion that had suddenly emerged from her subconscious.

Yes. Trust, remember?

Part of her was horrified by this man's ruthlessness. Part of her was fascinated by his cunning. She'd never seen any other operative use NOPAIN as well as T. And against her. Who the hell was this man?

No, not think either. Feel. What were we doing before you bilocated? You have the hand of a naked man between your legs.

Helen shook her head hard. She knew what he was doing. He was making her see herself in VR. Whether he was doing it to her, or not, was irrelevant, because the idea that he had control over her body was enough. He'd cultivated a trigger in her subconscious without her being aware of it. The bastard…the…

You still feel very wet, Elena. Can you feel me touching you? You like it slow, don't you?

"Stop it," Helen whispered. She couldn't possibly get excited at the thought of him doing this to her. How was it that he could turn her on just with words?

If I make you anticipate this every time we end—

She was helpless against his manipulation. Imagining what he was doing to her was sucking her into his game. Yet, she couldn't help herself. She was back in that chair in VR. She could taste his flesh as she strained against his hand. Needing him to go faster…

Then you'll link back here to me in VR. At least, that's what my theory is.

Theory? She was part of a theory. She choked half in exasperation and half in need.

Engine off. Her eyes flew open. She was back in the VR.

Hades was holding her, his brown eyes so close she could see the black rings around his irises. She blinked, trying to adjust to the sudden return.

He straightened. *"Are you all right?"*

His hands— she glanced down at them, then looked up heatedly at him. Did he—

His expression was unreadable as he studied her.

"It was all in my head, wasn't it?" she asked. *"The second time, I mean."*

"All this is all in our heads, Elena," he replied gently.

Frustration rose. She had a hundred questions and knew there wasn't any time right now. *"How is it possible you can make me feel like that?"*

With words. From someone whose face she didn't even know. Somehow he'd made himself her fantasy. No, wait, she had started it by making him a fantasy. Fuck.

"We can analyze this later when we get back."

He was so cool about it, as if seducing women was second nature to him. And she was suddenly angry.

"You're damn right we're going to have some discussion when we get back," she told him shortly. *"Stay out of my pants from now on."*

"It's too late for that."

She undid the straps. *"We'll see about that,"* she muttered. He was right, of course it was too late. If she was successful with this test of her abilities, she would be remote viewing through VR again and he'd already proven that he could bring her back here with him. She should be disgusted. Furious.

Her knees buckled and he gathered her close to

support her weight. She laid her head against his chest and was surprised to hear a heartbeat. This program was too damn real.

"We don't have much time," he said. *"We need to conserve your energy for what's to come. Take a deep breath. Let what happened between us go for now. Exhale. That's right. We'll talk about it later, I promise, but we've got to finish this operation."*

He sounded incredibly gentle. How dare he comfort her after what he'd done? Yet Helen couldn't summon up any anger. She released another breath. Having a tantrum in VR wasn't going to accomplish anything. She needed time to think. Later. When her brain waves were just hers again, dammit.

Secret test facility, Virginia

Liquid sunshine. That was what it felt like to him. Everything in the room looked brighter and cleaner. He felt warm and safe; the stifling fear that had followed him around was a shadow of itself. And that little sneak of cigarette helped calm the excitement. He needed to show them what he could do so they would keep him.

"Ready, Agent 51?"

Agent 51. It'd been a while since they'd activated him this way. He'd tried to tell the doctors in the beginning that it was Five-One and not Fifty-One, but no one here paid attention to him. Until now.

He nodded eagerly. "Yes, where's my monitor?"

"I'll be your monitor today. Go strap yourself in."

He approached the work station with the RV chair. "It's been a while," he murmured. "Let's see. This strap goes to my pulse. This one wraps around my chest. Okay, ready."

He looked expectantly as his monitor placed a sealed envelope on the podium next to the RV chair. "Use this as your target. It contains the coordinates telling where they're sending the other remote viewer. It's imperative we find out what the target is."

This should be a piece of cake. He had done this during training for the special programs even before they had introduced him to the marvels of the drug. He was going into this without a practice run but he was determined to get the results they wanted. That envelope was just for his focal point, though. There was really nothing inside. He needed a bit more information.

"First, if it's possible, I'd like to have the location of the original envelope so I can make a mental link that both the envelope here and the one there have the same information."

"That won't be a problem, 51. Anything else?"

"Can I have a map and a globe in front of me please? In case I need to focus on those." Pinpointing location was very, very iffy in remote viewing. "I…ah…hope you realize that if the target in that envelope doesn't specify location, it's going to take some guesswork."

"Yes, of course. The other side will have the same problem, too, so we start out with even odds." His monitor looked at the camera and nodded, obviously asking for delivery of the requested items. "How are you feeling?"

"Extremely confident," he told him, smiling. "Like a superhero again."

"Very good. That's what we want to hear. Nothing bothering you?"

"Nothing, nothing." No headache yet. He mentally crossed his fingers. The cigarettes would hold off headaches for a while. He checked the different on and off switches as he waited for the globe and map, trying his best not to look nervous to the man watching him. He could sense his suspicion; the serum always gave him that power. He knew the other man was looking for signs that he would fail.

"Here's the information you requested, Agent 51. Remember, we want Intel on what the target is, as well as location. I'll run you through the surroundings for clues, but focus on the target, no matter what."

He nodded. He was eager to get out there. When everything was the way he wanted, he sat back and switched on the tape that carried the tonal frequencies. Soon he was aware of nothing but his mind. Trigger code…

Switch to Channel Three. Set programming time. Set channel.

Timer on. Record.

"I feel the coordinates," he announced.

"Go there, Agent 51," he heard his monitor say.

This was it. This was the best part about the drug. He could do anything. *Fast forward. God, I love this rush! Fast forward! Fast forward!*

A building. It feels cold. Coordinates pinpoint a room in the top floor. I'm going up.

"Is there a room number, Agent 51? Is it a hotel?"

Not a hotel. Not office space. Some important building. Room B for Boy. This is the place. Going right through. Four people.

"Listen in."

It sounds foreign. I hear German words. Let me look around, make sure. There are books in German on the shelves. There are account sheets.

"Is that the target?"

No, the target feels small, much smaller. Feels like a bank in here. Shall I leave to search the building for more clues?

"No, not yet. Work this target. They wanted this room for a specific reason. What's important here? What information are they after? Look at the four people in the room."

Three men, one woman. Definitely not shooting the breeze here, whatever they're saying. German isn't one of my languages, I'm afraid.

"That's unfortunate."

Damn. He had better find out more or they wouldn't use him again. Of course. He could gauge their emotions. *Pause. Slow frame...* He carefully examined the whole scene in slow motion, looking at the figures from different angles. One of the men passed something surreptitiously to the woman while the other two were looking at some information on the laptop. He replayed the scene again.

He felt the love between them, catching a fleeting image of their naked bodies entwined on a bed. Ah, lovers. He felt their shared passion and had the sudden urge to peek into their memories. It had been so long...he needed a quick fix.

"What do you see happening?"

Damn. He couldn't take the chance. Needed to perform. Reluctantly, he pulled his focus away from the energy emanating from the two lovers and returned to the present.

There's a key given to the woman. She puts it in her pocket. The other two hadn't noticed. I'm looking at the laptop screen. It looks like these other two are transferring funds from one account to another. Now they are done. They shake hands. Now the third man, the one who passed the key to the woman, is handing over another key to one of them. This one's an electronic key.

"Good work, Agent 51. Now, figure out which one is the key we want."

He barely hesitated. Of course it had to be the electronic key. But why did the man give his lover that key? He wanted so badly to find out. Perhaps they were cheating on their spouses and so had to meet secretly; if so, that key would have so much emotion attached to it. Wouldn't it be cool if he could—

"Agent 51, is there a problem?"

Dammit! He forced his attention back to the job at hand. He mustn't get tempted so easily or he'd lose the privileges again.

The electronic key's the target. I'm very sure of this. It looks like some kind of master lock to a computer or perhaps a computer program. Not sure. But that's what the other remote viewer's after.

"We need to zero in on the location. Look around you. Pick up clues, find out names, if possible."

He dare not repeat that he didn't understand German. *I'm working on it. Going to move around the room, maybe go out of the building to get a feel. Is that okay?*

"Yes, but hurry up. We don't have time."

He'd never worked against the clock before. Remote

viewing took time, especially when it came to verifying location. Somehow, he didn't think his monitor would take kindly to that observation.

Got it. We're at the Deutsche International headquarters in Frankfurt, Germany. I read the address label on the envelope lying on the table. Wait...

Fast forward...

They've activated some kind of device with the electronic key. It looks like some kind of password decoder. Let me go closer to look at what they're doing.

"Disengage and return, 51. We have what we need."

"Yes, sir."

He looked longingly at the woman. She had memories he wanted. Quickly, quickly...*fast forward.* He plunged into her energy for a moment. An image of a memory. She was squatting between her lover's parted legs. Her mouth was filled with the taste of him...oh yeah, suck it, milk it, baby. *Record.*

Her tongue lapped the crown of the penis, then her mouth came down over it. Oh yeah, this was a good memory. She gave a fine blow job, from the look of it. Take it all in, baby, yeah, like that. Oh, yeah, he was almost there. Look at him straining his big dick into your sweet mouth...

"Agent 51, disengage and return."

Stop. Rewind. Change channels.

Shifting forward to disguise his erection, he worked the crick of his neck, feeling the beginning throb of the headache. His heart was beating very loudly in his head. He hoped they didn't see what he had done that last second in the ether. Sometimes, a good monitor would note the spikes in the pulse readings and ask questions.

"I did great, didn't I?" he said, smiling weakly. "Saw what you wanted...now what?"

"We're giving you another dose and then we're flying to Frankfurt."

Another dose! He'd never taken two dosages in a session before. "We're going to get the key, aren't we?" he asked. "I can't speak German."

"We won't be holding any conversation. We just want the key." His monitor looked at the camera and spoke into the intercom. "Did you get everything?"

"Yes," the person from the other side replied. "I just received a call that the other remote viewer had the location, too. It's going be a race."

"That could work in our favor," his monitor said. "We can see this new toy for ourselves, maybe even acquire her."

"Yes, good idea."

"And if we can get the key before they do, we'll kill two birds with one stone. Wouldn't that be a good way to end COMCEN's little project?"

"I'm calling in the ride. Get ready."

The man on the VR chair frowned as he listened in on the conversation. There was more to this session than competing with another remote viewer. He watched as his monitor prepared another shot. Another dose... He thought of the woman and her memory with her man. He smiled in anticipation. There was going to be some free time on the plane.

"Can I go to the restroom after the shot?"

"You have fifteen minutes. If no one's here, just wait. We're going to be making some calls to verify procedures."

"Yes, of course."

Oh, that was plenty of time. He needed to jerk off. Then he would do it again on the plane somehow. He couldn't wait to replay the images he'd captured from the ether. Usually he'd be wiped out, but with a second dose, he was ready to go off and play again. That woman...he needed to find that woman in the building.

Ten

Helen sighed. So many questions, not enough time. *"When I get out of remote viewing, there's a period which we call downtime. Sometimes it takes hours to get back to normal. I feel weak now in virtual reality, so I can imagine how bad I am when I get out of here."*

"Yes." Hades massaged her neck. *"SYMBIOS 2 will take care of that."*

"Have you tried it before?"

"A version of it. It affects different people differently, but it cuts down on pain and exhaustion. Different versions of it have been field-tested on the military."

She noted that he didn't really answer her question. Of course, it would be inside her soon enough for her to know how it affected her. What, me worry? Her lips twisted mockingly. Too late for that.

"How will I communicate with you while on mission?" she asked.

"I'm your monitor at VR, not in field operations,"

he replied. *"You'll just have to make do without me this one time."*

Helen looked up sharply. *"How will I know you won't be there?"*

His gaze was amused. *"You won't."*

"I'm figuring out how this is supposed to work, you know." She cocked her head. *"As I've told you, locating anything in RV is very tough. A trailer park looks like a million other trailer parks after all, and a building vault like the one we've been in looks like any other, too. It takes time to be specific. I'd have had to really explore around to find clues and even then, I wouldn't be too sure if I had gone off somewhere else in the ether. Yet, with you present in my mind, we have a twofold perception, me on my senses and you on the big picture. How am I doing so far?"*

"That's what any RV monitor does," he pointed out.

"No, there's a difference. You can actually sense my thoughts and feelings, so you have an advantage over a normal monitor, who would have had to really push me to find some kind of recognizable symbol. A monitor just asks questions to guide me to sense different targets, and from there, we draw our conclusions from my descriptions. Yet, you knew exactly how to confirm the location. You told me to go to the lobby, remember?" Helen tapped him on the chest. *"You said you've been inside Deutsche International before. Your knowledge saves a lot of time and makes our target more precise. I might be the star of this show, Mr. Hades, but I have a feeling you're the vehicle driving the whole getup."*

The slow smile he gave her gave Helen a hint of the real personality behind her avatar. It was not just a smile of amusement but of acknowledgment of her conclusions. Deep in her gut, she knew that she was right.

This was no simple trainer. This was a man who had a whole lot of experience with certain targets, who had probably walked among these same targets so he would be able to recognize many of the places and people by sight or sound.

Hades wasn't only her guide or monitor, but also her partner. He was, in fact, here to make sure she didn't fail: he was her data bank of knowledge when it came to the places and experiences. Her awareness of him vibrated even as she spoke, as if the words and thoughts helped her feel out the real entity behind the avatar.

There wasn't a doubt about the warning ringing through her being either. Never mind that he was giving her a killer massage, the slow kneading of his hands making her remember how good he was with them. She stopped herself from thinking about *that,* scowling at him as she watched the sensual tug of his lips widening. She was dealing with a very dangerous man. And he was enjoying himself way too much.

"How's that for insight?" she pressed on.

"You're close," he said simply.

"Okay, I see we have lots of talking in the future," she continued, *"with me asking the questions and you answering them."*

Are you sure you want to talk all the time? You're very stream-of-consciousness, you know, with your thoughts jumping from passwords to speeding to…pleasure.

Helen pulled at his hands and took a step back. *"I bet if I could sense your mind, I'd feel all kinds of sexual deviant stuff."*

His brown eyes lit up with mischief. "Yes."

She sighed. *"And this mind reading only stays between us if you satisfy me with your answers."*

Satisfaction guaranteed. Good luck on your mission.

She could even *hear* the wickedness in his voice. She felt the familiar buzzing behind the back of her neck and bright light filled her sight. Hades had ended the session.

She began to feel the others helping to take off the components attached to her body. Her body felt a bit numb, as if she had been running very hard. Remote downtime could take hours, sometimes days, depending on how long the viewer stayed out in the ether.

"How long was I in there?" Helen asked, leaning back in the seat. She needed a minute…maybe two.

"Three hours." Dr. Kirkland was busy checking her stats. "How do you feel?"

"That's it?" Surprise mingled with disbelief. "I feel like an elephant had walked all over me. Usually that means I've been out for at least six hours."

Dr. Kirkland smiled at her attempt at humor. "I'm not surprised. Projected studies point to the fact that Total Immersion Virtual Reality Remote Viewing will put a lot of stress on the mind and body."

TIVRRV had just been a term in Helen's head as she had gone through the stages of training. But now that she'd undergone the first experience of combining all those stages, she was suddenly aware of the significance of what she'd achieved.

Stress indeed. Not to mention having someone else talking in her head and other things she would rather not tell these scientists. She couldn't focus properly as she tried to recall every detail. "This is good, right?" she asked, rubbing her neck absentmindedly, remembering a warm, sure hand. "Then we'll know for sure whether the next phase actually works."

The next phase was SYMBIOS 2, the drug that would cure all fatigue generated by remote viewing, thus enabling her to complete the mission. This was the tricky part. She was in charge because only she knew what she had seen. A whole group of operatives now depended on her version of what truth was, and if the operation failed, it meant she'd failed.

The world of remote viewing was a strange one. Helen knew that many incidents had been summarized and filed away—world events and secrets—that the government hadn't taken on because no one department was willing to send out a team on the word of a viewer. Millions of dollars could go down the tube. Lives could be lost. No one was willing to jeopardize their teams just to prove one person's vision.

But a remote viewer, trained to spy and trained to go where no one had dared—that was the grand experiment. And Helen was it.

"We don't have much time," the assistant said to Dr. Kirkland.

"We'll give her a few minutes."

Helen shook off the fatigue, sitting straighter. "Get De Clerq."

She stood up slowly and felt as if she was carrying fifty more pounds on her. Whoa. This was totally different from all the other sessions. She scowled at Derek when he proffered a hand. No. She would walk out of here without any help.

Gingerly, she took a few steps, willing her leaden feet to move normally. She found it easier to walk if she stared at each foot, moving one in front of the other as if she were robot-controlled.

"Sweetheart, at this rate we'll never get started." It was Flyboy at the doorway. "You're going to need my help."

Helen scowled. "No, thanks."

He came forward just as she stumbled and scooped her into his arms with one easy swing. "Pride goes before a fall, haven't you heard?"

"And what will it look like if you carry me into that meeting with all the brass looking on? Sure, that'd have their confidence in the mission soaring, wouldn't it?"

Flyboy continued walking. "You're right. But you can't walk in like you're Tim Conway impersonating an eighty-year-old either."

Helen frowned. "Tim who?"

"You know, Carol Burnett's sidekick from her show. The one that shuffles his feet when he impersonated..." Flyboy shook his head. "Never mind. It's not funny when I have to explain his act."

"You watched *The Carol Burnett Show?*" Helen asked incredulously.

"With my mom," he told her, smiling down at her. "Here we are."

Helen turned her head, startled that she'd forgotten that she'd been arguing about walking on her volition. Flyboy had taken her to the restroom.

"This will give you a few minutes while I go get a wheelchair," he said, setting her back on her feet.

"A wheelchair isn't going to give a good impression

either," she pointed out. She fought for balance. Dammit, she was having a lot of difficulty trying to coordinate her movements.

"Not if we have all the medical stuff attached to it as if we're readying you for the drug. We'll make it look okay." Flyboy tilted her chin. His blue eyes were serious, searching hers. "Hey, the most important thing's you being okay. Can you do this?"

Helen nodded. "You don't think I'm going to back out at this stage, do you?"

"No, you don't seem the type, although I question your sanity."

"Didn't I hear you say you put that stuff in you, too?" she asked, arching a brow. "Oh wait, you're playing protective male about it being okay for you to do it but not me?"

His thumb teased the bottom of her lip. "You'll know when I play protective male," he told her.

She smiled at him. He really was so cute for being so concerned about her. "Does Tim Conway do his act in a wheelchair?"

Flyboy dimpled back at her. "When this mission is over, I'll invite you over to see some great Carol Burnett classics. You'll understand what I mean. Now go get refreshed. I'll be back in a few minutes."

"All right."

Helen walked slowly into the restroom. He was right. She needed to refresh herself and get herself ready for the next phase. Her mind was still on Hades, wondering what he was doing now, wondering whether he was as numb as she was, even though she was the one doing all the work.

Her body still tingled when she thought about him. Her mind felt strangely fragmented, something she'd never experienced after an RV session. She still couldn't quite believe what had happened in virtual reality. For two months, he'd prepared her in the CAVE, mentally pushing her boundaries and testing her, and she'd never once suspected he'd been readying her for that moment when he'd used her body's reaction to him as a trigger. After all, it was all virtual reality in her mind.

A dangerous man. She was going to find out who he was, somehow, some way.

Helen looked around quickly as Flyboy wheeled her into the conference room with Dr. Kirkland and Derek behind, holding on to tubes and IVs attached to the chair. Her group was there, along with T. Watching from above, not unlike one of those surgery rooms, was another group of mostly men, some in uniform, with rows and rows of medals for decoration. Presumably, those were the designated representatives from the different agencies such as DOD, Army Intel, and NSA who had sent in their candidates. She could feel their skepticism and curiosity as Flyboy and she approached her group.

Helen decided to go straight to business. "How do we start?" she asked.

De Clerq nodded, then looked up into the gallery. "You can send in your man with the envelope." He turned to Helen. "They have complete control of the envelope to ensure noncontamination. It contains the specific target they had set for you. We'd agreed that once you've written down what you deem is the target, then we'll open and read the contents of the envelope. If your answer is the same as the information in there, then they'll let us handle the rest of the operation our way."

"You mean I get to play *Jeopardy?*" Helen asked dryly. "Write my answer and hope the question in the envelope corresponds?"

De Clerq smiled. "Something like that."

"Do they have any say over the operation?" She eyed the group above them again. They were listening in, of course. "Or are they just my cheering and adoring fans?"

Flyboy pulled out a chair and sat down. "As you can all see, our girl's sense of humor is still intact."

"May I ask why she can't walk?" a voice said over the intercom. They looked up and a tall man signaled that it was him asking the question. "I've seen remote viewers going through downtime and they fared better than Miss Roston."

"Our program is more intensive," Dr. Kirkland replied. "The effects of biotechnology are unpredictable and since I'm monitoring Miss Roston's vitals and reactions, I wanted her to stay as still as possible after her session so I can get a clearer chart of her physical condition before and after drug administration."

Oooh, good cover. Helen managed not to grin at Flyboy who winked. She was going to behave. After all, she was on contract and worth…oh…millions to these people.

"I see," the voice said. "Then let's proceed."

Someone else entered the room. Helen assumed it was the person with the envelope.

"Miss Roston, ready?" De Clerq asked.

"Sure," Helen said. She picked up the pen by her pad. Make it simple or go into details? She decided simple.

The brass just wanted confirmation that she was for real. She handed over the piece of paper to the nearest person to pass, and added, "This is the target, along with location. If you want to know more, just ask questions."

"Thank you," De Clerq said. He took the piece of paper and read it out loud. "The target is an electronic key card that appears to be used to find passwords. It is currently in the possession of two people. The key is now at a building called Deutsche International. Your turn, Mr. Su."

The man tore open the envelope in his hand and read, "The stolen data transfer key, SEED. Where are the thieves, Jack and Julie Cummings? Here are the photos of the two of them."

Helen looked at them. They were the couple she saw in the RV session. Yeah, the names resonated. So, they stole the key. That explained the electronic bank transaction before the key was handed over to the other men.

"I would say that's as close to a hundred percent accuracy as one could get, sirs," De Clerq said.

"We still don't have possession of the key to prove that her information is correct. How long will part two of this operation take? How will she know what it looks like?"

"It starts as soon as Miss Roston is ready. A plane is on standby for Germany and you'll be informed when the operation is completed," De Clerq said.

"And if Miss Roston fails to return with the key?" another voice added.

Helen looked up, trying to guess who the speaker was. It was tough since they all appeared to have a microphone button by their seats. "I know where it is." She addressed all of them, since she couldn't identify the person. "If it's still in that building and I can get access to that room, I'll get the key. I know what it looks like. It's getting to it that will be the problem."

"So how do you propose to get it? We can't have our people storming a building overseas," a high-ranking official pointed out. "That's the problem with these experiments. We can't risk lives and reputation for something that depends on one person's say-so, especially when the information isn't gotten through accountable means. This looking around in some kind of altered state smacks of bad science fiction, if you ask me."

This must be one of the men who had decided not to do anything about the Intel the CIA remote-viewing program had provided the military. Generals and commanders didn't want to be held responsible in case the information turned out to be nothing. After reading the documents to which she'd been given access, Helen had understood. Who would want to explain through the chain of command that they were sending out troops and million-dollar equipment because of something a remote viewer said?

"I'm not here to argue with you, sir," she said quietly. "The government funded this project to train me, so take your beef to the president. And right now, it appears to be my life and reputation that's on the line."

She could hear several people clearing their throats and coughing, as if they were amused with her candidness. She mentally shrugged. She was a civilian; she didn't have to kowtow to these men in their shiny buttons and talk to them as if they were emperors. Sure, they were probably very powerful people but she'd learned from experience that powerful people were often the blindest. Flyboy was looking down at his briefing papers and she couldn't see his face.

She'd bet every dime in her bank account that he was hiding a grin.

"We've discussed this already, Jim," one of the men above them interjected smoothly, "so your point's been taken into consideration. Considering that this is a test, I think it's going marvelously. Miss Roston's answers satisfy me and I think we should let CCC proceed with their usual protocol in running an operation. It's out of our hands now till it's over. Then we'll evaluate from there. Besides, we all sent out our candidates into the training program and CCC's won. Unless, of course, you have a complaint against the very training program on which we, including yourself, have voted for and approved, Jim?"

"Of course not, Tom," the other man said.

"Then let them do their job. Mr. De Clerq, you can proceed. Please call our respective offices when your operation is completed. I've already informed mine to take your call no matter what time it comes in."

"Thank you, Admiral Madison," De Clerq said.

"Good luck, Miss Roston."

Helen looked at the man addressing her. He sounded much nicer than the other brassheads. Tall, maybe fifty-something-ish, he looked trim and dashing, unlike the usual bulky-looking guys in uniform.

"Thank you, sir," she said. Wow, killer smile. She smiled back.

As she watched them file out from the viewing room above, an electronic curtain moved silently across the glass, shutting out the view like a window. She counted about a dozen people up there.

"Good job, Hell," Flyboy said. "Good comeback to the snooty head of the department, too."

Helen grinned at him. "I didn't hear you helping me out. You were too busy swallowing your tongue." She turned to T. "You were pretty damn quiet, too, Miss Montgomery."

"Why bring attention to me?" T. countered. "Look at it from their perspective. Some of them are already miffed that their department didn't get the project and funds. And some of them are military men who aren't used to women talking back at them, let alone a contract agent beating out whom they consider their best candidates. How are you feeling?"

Helen rolled her neck. "Better. I'm good to go."

Dr. Kirkland opened his medical case. "Next time, we'll inject the serum before the RV session," he said, "so we can compare the difference in stats and vitals."

"Okay," Helen said. She watched the needle in the IV being inserted into her vein. She took a deep breath. "How long?"

"It's straight into the bloodstream, so it's going to be really fast. You've gone through the med courses to prepare you on what to expect."

"What likely to expect," Helen corrected. "You guys have added several other ingredients to the first serum. Do you think the other departments have been fiddling with their recipes too?"

"Scientists don't fiddle, Miss Roston," Dr. Kirkland admonished.

Helen laughed because he was doing exactly that right now, fiddling with tubes and needles as Derek wrote things in his notepad. "Whoa!" she said loudly.

"What is it?" Dr. Kirkland asked sharply.

Helen smiled at all the people around the table. They were looking at her intently. "Just kidding," she replied serenely. "Just wanted to see how important I am to everyone."

Flyboy chuckled. "Try standing," he said.

Helen nodded as she watched the last of the liquid disappear into her. It was inside her. She didn't feel any different. Everyone watched as she stood up slowly. She walked away from the chair. The exhaustion was gone. But she still didn't feel any different.

"Rock and roll," she declared, giving De Clerq the thumbs-up.

He wondered whether she was feeling the same sensation that he was—he couldn't really describe it. Like loss. Or missing a part of himself.

Good to have Madison on their side. T. was right. That joint venture with the admiral's SEAL team, giving him information on the drug lords and operatives who had caused the deaths of his men, had been a good move.

He liked Madison, anyway, a no-nonsense man under whom he'd have served willingly, had he stayed in Special Forces. A man of his word was hard to find these days.

He studied Helen for a few moments, his gaze lingering on her face, trying to read her mind. It was strange now, not being connected to her. He was growing used to checking on her emotions and her thoughts.

The emotions were easy to gauge because he felt

it and knew it was her reaction. The thoughts were harder because he had to learn to separate his own from hers. It was easier in the beginning. Her thoughts were focused on his avatar body; images of his nakedness slipped into his mind and he knew that was how she saw him in VR. But it was different in remote viewing. Something had happened in the course of his putting a sexual imprint in her psyche while that brain oscillator had adjusted their brain waves to theta.

He had expected the remote viewing experience to be similar to what they had been doing but instead, her bilocation had been fully projected into his mind, as if she was the virtual reality room and he was experiencing what she was doing there. He hadn't needed to ask her any questions at all; he could see and feel what she was seeing and doing. The only thing he couldn't control was movement. It was a strangely…disembodied experience. With full sensory capabilities.

He was excited by the experience. He'd never thought any new thing at COMCEN could excite him that much. But then, this involved Helen and anything she did excited him. He had thought to be inside her soon, but this was really *inside* her. And he had been there to feel her response to him.

Did she know what he had done? She had to. She was a GEM operative and a remote viewing one. She'd understood the implications of sexual mind imprintment. She probably didn't have the time to analyze it all yet but he had no doubt she would be even angrier once she did. He looked forward to their next session.

He had an inkling what that serum would do. He wasn't suffering from RV downtime or he'd take it himself and do the operation without her needing to have that shit inside her. The thought startled him.

He had never stopped any operative—male or female—from doing what they were trained to do before. In his world, every operative was needed for whatever capacity they were trained. Sometimes, it had meant sacrifice. Often, there was compromise. He had done both.

Helen was perfectly capable at getting this operation done, with or without him. He'd watched her train for this moment and after getting some of her thoughts, he knew she was more than ready, mentally or physically. It was the drug that worried him and with Helen, he was determined not to sacrifice or compromise.

"Operation instructions," he said softly. "Number One, Number Four, Number Seven, Number Nine. Number One will start with initiating a dummy account. Number Five will obviously be transport. Number Four take care of weapons. Stand by for further instructions from Number Nine."

Eleven

Helen shook her head when Alex Diamond offered her a bottle of water. She wasn't thirsty.

"Drink," he ordered.

"Later," she said. She examined the dress she had been given. She frowned when the bottle was shoved under her nose. "What is it with you and water?"

"You have that serum in you. The first time, you forget to eat or drink."

She looked up and found herself staring into his light blue eyes. "I don't know what you're talking about," she said. "I'm feeling neither hungry nor thirsty."

"When did you last eat or drink?"

The thought hadn't occurred to her. "A while," she admitted. "Is it the drug doing this?"

Alex Diamond took her hand and put the bottled water in it. "It takes a few times to remember that what you aren't feeling is still there," he said before he walked off down the aisle of the plane.

Helen stared after him thoughtfully as she unscrewed the cap from the drink bottle. She took a long swig.

It takes a few times to remember that what you aren't feeling is still there. Interesting turn of phrase. And he was correct. Mentally counting, she should be hungry by now. It'd been a long day. Yet she wasn't feeling any need for food or drink at all.

They had told her the effects of the serum but telling her wasn't the same as experiencing it for herself. She had thought, for some reason, that she would feel like a superwoman or something, able to do anything. A high or a rush, maybe.

Nothing. She felt perfectly normal. Yet, she'd forgotten to eat and drink. Of course the drug would be insidious, you idiot. It was a painkiller. Like a giant dose of Advil or something. Like he said—she glanced down the aisle again—she had to pay attention to what she would usually be feeling. She finished her drink as she continued watching him move around the spacious plane.

Number One, that was what they called him during operations. Alex Diamond looked the part of the initiator. She thought of what little she knew about him through files. T. wasn't too forthcoming with the information for some reason. Helen smiled wryly.

Alex Diamond, late thirties, one of the original commandos. One of the five in that incident that had killed two of her GEM sisters, one of whom happened to be his wife. The only one who had ever walked out of a COS operation and had to be lured back into the fold. In a way, Alex Diamond had initiated the beginnings of the merger between COMCEN and GEM.

Initially, the big blast had been thought to have killed all of the operatives. GEM was just a contract agency for COMCEN then, but without Diamond and the others at the helm, COMCEN was forced to change.

Helen wondered how they convinced him to come back. Alex Diamond didn't seem the type that could be easily threatened or tempted. She had an idea T. had something to do with it. Anyway, he was back as Number One, and she was to work with him today. She glanced at her watch. Frankfurt's time difference was six hours.

"Should I sleep, too?" she asked as he came back toward her.

It was disconcerting the way his gaze seemed penetrating and yet, uninterested, at the same time. "You won't be able to the first time," he said. "Your body's confused, even though you feel fine."

"Is that how the serum affected you?"

"SYMBIOS 1. I've heard your version is an improvement," he said, his expression hardening slightly as he added, "as Armando would no doubt testify."

Was that a warning? "They told me the thing about both serums is that they have different effects per individual. I'm just collecting data from all of you who've tried it," Helen said. "It'll help me."

"Help you?"

He was looking at her as if she'd grown two heads. "I'm the test subject, remember?" she reminded him. "Everything you can tell me about how the serum affected you will help me adjust."

Standing so close and being near him longer than the few times they had been together, Helen was able to study him better. He had the long lean body of an athlete. She'd read that he liked to do extreme sports, those daredevil acts that tested strength, endurance, as well as stupidity, and she wondered whether maybe that could be one of the serum's effects. His sun-blond hair and tan certainly testified to an outdoor lifestyle. And there was something untamed about the man, in spite of the crisp and expensive snow-white shirt and tailored pants he favored, as if he held himself tightly inside. It gave him that elusive aura that made a man so damn intriguing.

"None of us have tried it long term or in high dosage," he finally said, "except, perhaps, Armando. You'd best talk to him instead."

"You're not going to tell me about your experience with it," she pushed.

He sat down directly across from her. There was that look in his eyes again, the one that was both penetrating and dismissive. "No."

"Why not?"

"You have a drug in you, Helen," he said quietly. "At this moment, it's running through your bloodstream, taking over your system. You're going to get your answers soon enough, don't you think?"

He had a point, but she had her own reasons. She was looking to find out more about the COS commandos. "So let's go over the details of when we reach our target again instead," Helen said, with a shrug. "I don't think you're interested in playing a card game or something."

"Which part are you confused about? The part where you dress up and stand quietly by me? Or the part where you go off on your own?" he asked.

Helen smiled. She was beginning to enjoy trying to

find a way to rile Mr. Number One. "The part in between. You know, when T. makes an appearance as her
U.N. self. Do you think she would be able to pull off
the distraction? It might look suspicious."

She watched with interest for Alex's reaction. None.
The man was a cool customer.

"She's the U.N. liaison. Lobbyists walk in and out
of that institution every day. Why would a think tank
like Deutsche International be suspicious? They would
welcome any inside information that might further
their agenda."

In her contracted stints with international think tanks,
mostly under the guise of interpreter-eavesdropper,
Helen had learned that deals were often made under the
guise of funded projects. But there was something new
going on here.

"Why do you think Deutsche International would
want to buy a stolen electronic key? I know it has something to do with passwords. What exactly is it?" She felt
as if she had been plunged into the middle of something
bigger than a stolen key, but the briefing on the plane
had only focused on this coming operation, the retrieval, and nothing else. She wanted more back story.
"I know now that the institute isn't just a regular think
tank but a front, a dummy corporation. Care to en-
lighten me further?"

"No," he said.

Helen cocked her head to one side. "Not a very sharing person, are you? Are you so short of words with T.,
I wonder?"

For the first time, she saw a glimmer of a smile
tugging at the corner of his lips. He didn't bother to

answer her dig. Instead he stretched out his long limbs, leaned back, and closed his eyes.

Helen stared at him, for a moment considering kicking his shoes and scuffing that nice expensive leather. She knew what he was doing—punishing her probing. He'd known she wasn't going to be able to fall asleep. She supposed she could get up and walk to the other end of the plane to bother the other two operatives at their little compartments. She didn't even know those two, since no one bothered with introductions.

She had met Flyboy, who was in front. Alex here. Armando Chang who wasn't here. And Big Swimmer Guy, whoever he was. She had never worked with these guys before and yet, here she was, expected to perform as part of their team. Was it part of the test? Whose?

It was becoming clear that she wasn't just being tested by all the departments who were involved in this experiment. She was also being tested by people at COMCEN itself, not to mention her secret monitor. And probably most of these commandos knew about it, hence their leaving her alone. She had worked on teams before. There was always a team protocol, some kind of set rules to follow. She hadn't been told of any. It was as if she was expected to just figure it out on her own, while these guys went about with their operation.

She blinked. Right. She was expected to get the key all on her own after the team had created the distraction.

She reached for the folder by her seat. They had gone over the known layout of the building itself. COMCEN had obviously had dealings with this Deutsche International before. Since it was a front,

COMCEN had probably infiltrated it with some operatives.

As for T., her presence was no surprise to Helen. Alex was right: as a U.N. negotiator and lobbyist, T. would be familiar with the think tank itself. These corporations and institutes tended to work as advisors for different countries and had lobbyists of their own within the U.N.

It would be late afternoon by the time they walked into Deutsche International. By that time, T. would have made arrangements to meet with some of the officials there. The aim was to keep things chaotic with the arriving lobbyists and officials along with their respective entourages.

Add unexpectedness into the mix. Alex Diamond—correction, Alexander Barinsky, Alex's current alias—would make an appearance, too. It was not usually easy to interrupt a top executive's day, especially when he or she had to meet with U.N. officials. Alexander Barinsky's presence, however, would cause a stir; some of the aides were bound to recognize him.

Although a think tank was an independent entity in itself, using different and often unorthodox sources for its research and funding, it was highly unusual for a well-known international weapons dealer to walk in on an official meet. They mixed and wheeled and dealed at private parties, not in public places. Thus, Barinsky's sudden arrival would be a problem for the institute.

But that could be easily diverted with a few big security dudes blocking their entrance, so what was Alex using as bait to get the attention of the right people at Deutsche International? No one had told her that either.

She should feel frustrated. Or, pissed-off at the lack of information.

Helen looked at the blueprint on her lap. She felt mildly...something... She couldn't define the emotion. Like an itch that wasn't quite there.

The blueprint showed only what they knew, so there wasn't any way to find out how to get to those floors underground. There was an elevator—that much she knew. She traced them in the drawing with her forefinger. Which one?

In her mind, she recreated the elevator she'd seen during RV. The wood paneling. The one button. *This elevator only goes up or down from one location.* She chased the image as it faded away. She needed more information.

Staring deeper into the blueprint, she rebuilt the whole elevator again, adding dimensions, adding a richer color—dark oak paneling, two-tone carpet, brass-looking lever on one side of a panel—and following instinct, added the feeling of weight under her feet, the way an elevator would jerk when it moved. The droning of the plane engine sounded like the hum of an elevator. Her finger traveled on its own, moving across the paper. Her eyes closed.

"What do you see, 51?"

"The key's still there," he told them obediently. There was something wrong with the feel of the location, though, but he dared not tell them that. Locating objects had always been iffy anyway. He had time to get to the right place while they waited here.

He felt so good. He had never felt like this in all his

experience with the drug. Doubling the dosage doubled everything. He could target what he wanted faster. He could see the glow. Here was one.

He slipped into the energy of the woman passing him. Oh yeah. There was sex today. He delved deeper, looking for feedback. But the memories were running like slides—too fast—and he hadn't found a way to slow it down yet. Those marvelous feelings he craved rushed through him like one of those European bullet trains. Too fast! No time to enjoy her!

Next.

Next!

"What do you see, 51?"

"The key's still there," he told them again, mentally checking quickly. Of course it was still there; they were decoding something, weren't they? Who cared? He needed—wait, wait, wait. Deep breath. He had to work with these guys here or he would get into trouble. "Many people in this building. It's confusing my senses a bit. Can I ask how we're going to get to the key in this crowd?"

"He's got a point," the other man said. "Why are there so many damn people going there?"

"Make a couple of calls and find out," his monitor said. "Agent 51, if the key changes location, let me know."

"Of course," he said. That was easy enough. It only took quick mental feedback to establish that. He didn't particularly care what it was being used for, not right now anyway. So many people. He must find a way to slow this down.

He felt the woman from that first session, the one with the secret lover. Secret lovers were always fun. They tried out exciting stuff, no quickies in the morning, none of the boring husband-wife roll in and out. He liked what he had seen in her. Where was she?

Change channel. Not this room. *Change channel.* Not this room. *Change channel...*she was here, talking to her man. He jumped eagerly into her energy. Oh, wow. She was talking sexy to her lover.

Her whole energy was beautiful; she was so damned turned on. Talk more, baby, keep talking. Too fast—the images were too fast—but the feeling. Oh, man, the feeling. He mentally turned the volume louder and added her heartbeat and breathing into the cadences, letting her breathy words slide through his being like warm honey.

It didn't matter that he couldn't hear what she was saying exactly. He felt all her sexual need in that voice. Oh, God, she was a hot bitch for sure. Her whole energy was filling up with such exquisite demand for sex. He caught a quick image of her standing naked in front of a mirror, parting her legs. He wanted that memory, he wanted—shit! What could he do to stop this speeding?

He wrapped himself inside her glow, smelling her scent, wanting her. Maybe the drug would taper off just a bit and then he would be here, ready to record.

"He really seems out of it," he heard a voice say in the distance.

"They always seem a bit more into their remote viewing with a higher dosage. He's been answering me, so he's okay. Now, let's deal with this problem with the people. How are we going to get around the presence of so many VIPs?"

"The other side's going to have the same problem, too. We'll take care of them after they retrieve the component. Just make sure our guy here keeps tabs on the key. Let them do the work. We'll know when the key is moved, right?"

"Agent 51, are you still with the key?"

They were so stupid. He realized that now. They had never remote viewed and so would never understand the beauty of it. He didn't need to be with the key.

"It's where it was when I first saw it," he replied honestly. "They have found three of the six codes in the password, I think."

"Good."

Oh, better than good, baby. He was doing better than good. He wondered whether his hard-on in his physical body was obvious to his monitor because he could feel its churning urgency where he was. He needed to do something about that soon.

"Helen, can you hear me?"

Helen blinked. Alex's face was near hers, his eyes watchful. "Yeah, what?"

"I thought you fell asleep but your hand was moving. You didn't answer me the first few times I called your name."

"Oh." Helen looked down on her lap. Her finger was pointing off the blueprint. "You said my hand was moving?"

"Yes. Rather, your finger was moving, as if it was drawing. I didn't want to interrupt but you started jabbing your finger into your thigh really hard and I wasn't sure whether you weren't hurting yourself."

Helen frowned. "Huh." She turned her finger over and studied the tip of her finger. "And I didn't wake up even though I was jabbing myself?"

"Obviously not." Satisfied that she was okay, Alex straightened back into his seat. "What was that all about?"

"I'm not sure," Helen said slowly, still studying her finger. "When we started remote viewing, one of our first exercises was kind of like automatic writing, where we were told to let ourselves draw out ideograms, but that was done with me fully aware. This has never happened before. Wish I was holding a pen."

"Then you would have punctured your thigh," Alex said quietly. "You were using quite a bit of force."

"But what was I writing?" She frowned, trying to remember. "I can't remember a thing. That's never happened before either. I wasn't actually asleep, I don't think."

"This might be a side effect of the serum," Alex said. "Make a note of it and report it to Dr. Kirkland. He's trying to find the right dosage for each individual."

"To do what?" She turned her gaze to the man sitting across from her.

"To make sure you don't OD." He arched a brow at her. "It *is* a drug in you, you know. Haven't you considered that you can overdose on it? They think they can control the cause and effect through dosage, but this serum doesn't stay the same in every individual."

"So some would need more for it to take effect," Helen finished for him, nodding as she added, "and for some, it would be way too much."

She thought of Armando Chang's fascination with illusion. Was that part of the effect of SYMBIOS 2 on him? She had to have that chat with him when she returned to Center.

But what was she writing? She had drifted off—if

that was what one would call what happened—while memorizing the layout of Deutsche International. Whatever she was writing—did it have to do with the blueprint of the place? She wracked her brain, trying to remember. She had been tracing the elevator in the layout and had used what she could remember from the RV session earlier, focusing on the details. If she had somehow gone into remote viewing mode, she hadn't been aware of it and for the first time, couldn't recall anything. Besides, where was the downtime, that feeling of numbness?

She shook her head. The serum might be taking care of the downtime fatigue right now. No time to worry about it.

"We're almost at zero hour. How are you?" Alex interrupted her thoughts.

Helen glanced up. "I'm fine. I feel fine." Alex's eyes narrowed a fraction, but he didn't say anything. She cocked her head, a smile touching her lips. "Worried about me, Agent Diamond?"

Alex Diamond leaned back and closed his eyes again. "Try not to jab yourself before we get there."

There was just something about him that tempted her to bait him. Maybe it was his lack of reaction to anything.

"I bet you would be more worried had it been T. who had the serum in her and she started doing weird stuff," Helen said slyly.

"Yes," he said, calm as could be, eyes still closed.

Helen stared at him, then laughed. She was beginning to like the guy.

Twelve

He had a little bit of time before operations got under way. Of course his thoughts revolved around Elena Rostova. When he had flipped through the dictionary this morning, the word that jumped out at him was *revelation*. He didn't like surprises. Now was not the time for them, and he had experienced several today.

She was on her own. He had to let her do her job.

Nonetheless, he...worried because the serum was inside her and it was something he couldn't control. He almost laughed aloud. Worry wasn't an emotion that he experienced a lot, especially when it came to an operative and his or her job. He cared about the men and women who worked with him, but the risks and the sacrifices were not his problem; they were theirs. Surprise number one. He was worried about her.

It was eye-opening to him that he wanted to make sure she was all right, that she was drinking and eating even if she didn't feel normal hunger or thirst, that she understood that she was not only what she felt. But he was her monitor and part of his job was to not interfere with the experiment.

As usual, he was going to break the rules. That wasn't the surprise. The revelation playing on his mind was the knowledge that he hadn't wanted her to take the risk at all in that last moment. The urge to yank that needle out of her arm lasted only a quick second and dissipated as he watched her behaving normally, but that second was enough to give him pause.

He had several rules that were important to him. Do not mix sexual chemistry with personal emotion in a seduction. It would be unhealthy. Creating a sexual bond outside the parameters of a relationship—imprinting need and feeding it—was only possible if the operative remained somewhat detached. To be crude, don't mix business with pleasure.

Yet, when he saw Elena naked, he never denied the pleasure she gave him. Oh, at first it was pure male curiosity, but voyeurism was never much of a turn-on for him, since he'd spied on targets in all kinds of situations through the years. He'd liked what he'd seen. Since revelation was the keynote today, he might as well admit now that it'd grown into something else. Watching her had become a possessive habit.

He smiled at the term. He was sure Kirkland had thought so a couple of times even though the man hadn't voiced any disapproval. Kirkland would probably have said the same thing: don't mix business with pleasure.

Admittedly, sexual imprintment had everything to do with pleasure. And therein lay the danger for any operative. One emotional misstep, and the bond could turn around and make one the victim.

He didn't need all that sexual heat building from being in virtual reality with Elena Rostova to prove that he was very attracted to not just the operative, but also the woman. Her determination to succeed was very intriguing to a man like him. Her fearlessness and willingness to take on everything he threw at her, as well as her sexual response to him, were incredibly seductive.

He'd kept pushing her, making sure he was in charge, and the more he took, the more he found himself wanting because her capitulation was exciting to him. Not much of a revelation *there*. Seducing a dangerous woman was a lot like hunting a wild beast; the danger lay in being turned from hunter to hunted.

Usually, being a man, he could compartmentalize his emotions and the sexual act. And being who he was, he liked to break down each feeling until it was just a chemical explanation, like the stimulated release of vasopressin and oxytocin in the brain, the two hormones that were important in producing orgasm.

Sexual bonding was all about control, and giving in to emotions would only lead to loss of it. In the early days, he'd pushed himself to the point where he could recite prime numbers during orgasm.

His lips twisted at the memory. It'd been a while.

The irony of the situation didn't escape him. She'd just taken the serum that repressed pain and need, and he was contemplating taking off her clothes and making her need him. It was probably the last emotion she would be having right now.

But whether she felt it or not didn't matter because she *did* need him. He had accepted the responsibility to be her anchor, and that meant, even if she disagreed, making sure she stayed safe. He would need to monitor her even more closely now, even though he wouldn't interfere.

She would be overdoing it on her first time. Water. Lots of it. He frowned. He couldn't believe he'd forgotten to make sure she knew that before taking the serum. The brain wave oscillator wasn't helping, what with its unintended effect of giving him a dose of her emotional state when they were in sync. Feeling everything the seduced was going through was, in fact, seducing him. And how was it going to be when he had her in his arms in real life, undressing her for himself, giving himself the pleasure of touching her real-life body instead of watching her on a screen or playing with the virtual Helen? She would be the naked one for him to peruse and manipulate, just as she enjoyed doing that to his avatar right now. And how far would he dare to push the bond he'd already established?

It could go deeper. She hadn't been told about getting a personal trigger from him precisely because he knew she would prepare herself for it and fight him. It was only natural for the fiercely independent woman in her to resist, even if the operative part might be willing.

The brain wave synchronization enabled the deep immersion process and that was a success. He was now able to experience remote viewing in virtual reality. The months of training with her in CAVE had meant to stimulate her awareness of him as a man, and her freedom to create the likeness of his avatar was the beginning of the bonding process, allowing her to respond to him mentally and physically. Sexual chemistry, the release of vasopressin and oxytocin—it was in her medical charts. However, he didn't need the monitoring devices to tell him that *that* was a success.

"Minus thirty, over," T.'s voice came through his earpiece.

Thirty minutes to zero hour. T. had been one busy lady.

"Everything's set here," he said. "Unless there are any last-minute complications, we'll commence while you're in meeting, over."

"Just keep me informed. If I don't answer, it means I'm in the middle of conversation."

He smiled. "You're just trying to avoid coming out to meet me," he mocked. "What's the matter, *darling,* you afraid?"

There was a pause. "I'm doing my job keeping a few dozen lobbyists and the head honchos of Deutsche International interested in important political issues," T. said lightly, "while your group of shady characters interrupts our meeting. Does that sound like I'm afraid?"

"Testy." He couldn't help baiting her. "And what if the head honcho decides to meet with Alexander Barinsky? What are you going to do, T.?"

"I would be in deep shock," T. shot back dryly. "The top lobbyist for world weapons control being photographed talking to the notorious arms dealer Alexander Barinsky in a public forum? No, I don't think so. You'll all be escorted to his private office upstairs to wait for him."

"You have the timing all figured out, haven't you?" he said, lowering his voice. "One day, T., your time will run out."

"Melodrama doesn't suit you…Hades. Why don't you worry about some other female operative? The one who's depending on your success in getting the schematics from the system, for instance. Isn't timing more your problem than mine? I'll check in again minus ten minutes."

She cut off before he could reply and he couldn't help smiling. Very few people saw the nervous side of Tess Montgomery, and she was nervous indeed. She didn't want the chance of bumping into his group at all and he knew why. That woman was on the run.

She was right, though. Timing was going to be crucial where Helen was concerned. He pressed the key on the pad connecting him back to Command.

"How long will it take once the schematics are transferred, De Clerq? Over."

"It shouldn't take long to shuffle the images in the memory so they'll think they're seeing different angles with different people. It's uploading the virus that will take time. How long can you stay in their control room without being caught? Over."

"Small time window," he replied. "Once the feed is through, have the computer run a quick search for one or both of the Cummings, over."

"Will do, over."

Technology was a handy asset for high-tech covert work. With the virus in place, the building security would see random sequences of past images from their computer memory while the real feed was forwarded to his laptop and sent back to COMCEN via satellite. That way, COMCEN would be controlling the feed and blocking images of their operatives prowling around the place.

The distraction created by his group entering the

building would help him locate one or both the Cummings. Everyone's attention would be focused on the commotion, with Deutsche security busily trying to figure out what to do with Alexander Barinsky et al., without causing a publicity furor. Also, the security would be stretched thin, with the VIPs walking in and out.

The Cummings would be in the building somewhere, probably restricted areas. He could ask Elena to remote view, locate them that way, but she had a more important task. It was bad to depend on only one resource for any mission, anyway. He would track his target down the simple human way—by hacking into their security system and looking at their venue cameras.

"From past surveillance, we know they usually have three people working surveillance in that control room but our Intel is four months old. Things could change, but Guzman's still chief of security. T. has already fed him those pills. Be careful," De Clerq said. "The probability of your being seen entering is fifty-fifty, according to the computer. Over."

Every operation scenario was always run through the COMCEN computer program, jokingly called the Magic Eight Ball by the operatives. Barring a few miscalculations, it was accurate in zooming in on success rates of different missions. The miscalculations were usually human factors for which computer programs didn't have value, such as an operative not following procedure, as he tended to do. He didn't have a problem with the program itself; it was remarkably useful, but he didn't believe in predictability either.

It had amused him, though, to know that after comparing its pre-operation calculations and the post-operation debriefings, the computer was smart enough to create a new value—"predictable and unpredictable human dimension" values, the Eight Ball called it, in its mathematical summations—for factoring probabilities. Whether it understood or not, the damn program had somehow gotten a sense of humor and sarcasm.

"Maybe I could borrow Harry Potter's invisible cloak," he suggested. "Give that to Eight Ball to chew on. I'm sure it'll up the success probability exponentially, over."

From the other end, De Clerq gave a bark of amusement. "There's enough illusion shit the commandos and Helen are doing to confuse Eight Ball without bringing in your magic show, over."

True. He wondered how the COMCEN programmers explained to their program the remote viewing part for its calculations. What name would Eight Ball give this new value? One thing about working at CCC, there was always something new happening there.

And Elena Rostova was something new in his life. He hoped to buy extra time for her to locate the SEED. They could only use the distraction for so long before the Deutsche operatives figured out something else was happening.

When the mission was over, she would be back at COMCEN. How long would her downtime last when it hit her? He wanted her back in VR as soon as possible. When one's mind was at its limit that was the best time to push further. He wanted to cement that bond as deep as possible before she found a way to remove it.

Anticipation was like foreplay. There would come a time when it wouldn't be in virtual reality when he put his hand between Elena's legs. And there would be no more clothing. He wanted her naked under him, without the restriction of medical devices and drugs, without the thought of getting her to think of him while she remote viewed.

Revelation. And surprise number two. He wanted her to be just herself, the way she'd been at the swimming pool, before she'd realized she was being watched. That sheer delight when she jumped into the water. That unbridled sensuality as she kicked those naked limbs around. He wanted that for himself. He'd push inside her as she wrapped her long legs around him and he would ride her long and hard. He knew the dangerous point would come when he would get the chance to see whether the sexual bond could be triggered outside virtual reality.

They might want to use Elena in their incessant experiments on the mind, but he wanted her body and soul. For him. Not for them. She was Hell to them, but she would always be Elena to him.

No, the surprise was not about wanting her. He'd wanted her from the beginning. But now he wanted more than that, and sooner than he'd planned. It was testing his control. How long before he broke the other rule, of not sexually taking her in virtual reality? It was damn tempting, especially when he had all the controls on his side. And the knowledge that he'd succeeded in planting the trigger in her head.

He nodded his head in slight acknowledgment at the challenge ahead of him. It wasn't time. Even after this operation was finished, there were still further sessions in RV. He curbed another need to laugh. At this rate, when he had her naked under him, he'd probably not last very long. Maybe he'd need to whip out the prime numbers game again after all.

"Minus ten minutes, over," T. interrupted his reverie.

"On it, over." He clicked on the different channels so every operative would hear him. "I'll give the signal after I'm done with the schematic transfer in their security room, over."

He took in a deep breath and released it. Time to shut off all thought and focus on the mission. Compartmentalizing came easy, like a switch. He mentally ran through what he had to accomplish.

Set up the laptop. Wait for distraction. When the time came, find Guzman vomiting in the bathroom. He'd seen T.'s pills at work before; nasty stuff. Make Guzman call in through his radio to let him into their surveillance room. Target Guzman and get his fingerprint and security card. Decode.

They would believe him when he brought the message from the head of security. Insert disk to show them photos of faces to look for. Insert virus flashdrive. Upload initiated via his computer. De Clerq and Eight Ball would know immediately and take over. They would let him know when they found out the Cummings' location.

He could not worry about how Elena was doing at her end. She had her task to do and he had his.

Besides, he'd put a locator on her. He activated his mic. "Keep me updated on Helen once she disappears from my view."

Thirteen

From the briefing, Helen knew there was a big gathering of lobbyists at the institute, brought together by the prospect of a key U.N. relief fund that had just been made available. She had to smile at that because T.—Tess Montgomery—was so very good at making things like that happen. As expected, Alexander Barinsky's appearance caused a small ruckus among those who knew who he was.

Helen almost laughed out loud at how polite the security was in front of the media and their cameras. One of the men approached them, his face a mask as he courteously asked Alex to leave after the usual questions about appointments and availability.

"Herr Guzman, I know you understand what it is I do and that I would not come here without an important reason," Alex had said, in a Russian accent. "Please pass this message now. Tell Dr. Weber that Alexander Barinsky is here to have half his money returned on the sale of the SEED key because it appears that Mr. and

Mrs. Cummings sold half the key to me and half to Dr. Weber's foundation. Nonetheless, your key is useless without half of the codes." He paused, cocking his head slightly before adding softly, "If I leave now, you'll find that I will be less likely to negotiate another time. Tell him I also know the Cummings are here, and that I did not come alone. Surely, Dr. Weber doesn't want any violence happening today, not with so many important people around?"

The message did the job. They were escorted to wait in Dr. Weber's office. As they followed, Helen was listening to De Clerq executing point through her earpiece, reporting on which part of the operation was "green," meaning "on target." Somewhere, other commandos were doing their thing. T. would have her hands full by now handling the U.N. VIPs. The security detail should be concentrating on the big event right now.

"Video link's up. What's their security up to?" she heard De Clerq ask.

"A few have been sent to walk the target point perimeter. I assume they're taking Alex's threat seriously."

"Good. Keep an eye on them. Comm's green, by the way. We've tapped into their radio feed, too. We're monitoring all communication."

"What's the status on the SEED?" a voice asked.

"Status is green, over," De Clerq replied.

Helen cocked her head. That had sounded like Flyboy although she wasn't a hundred percent sure.

"Checkpoint Two is green," another voice chimed in.

Their escort let them pass the secretary's area and go into the office. Once they were in there, Alex turned suddenly and quietly rendered the man unconscious.

Helen watched as they efficiently tied up the man. They were all business as one commando set a laptop on the table and another connected a device to it. It was an interceptor program, used to check for listening devices. He nodded when it showed that the room was clean.

Everyone had completed their task. Now it was her turn. She turned to Alex. "Are you sure the elevator we want is on this floor we're going to?"

Alex nodded. "Our Intel comes from someone who has been in this office. This access elevator has one button, fits your description. It makes sense that Weber has the access from his office to this underground floor."

"Okay. What if there are cameras in the elevator?" She had been sure there was some kind of electronic surveillance when she remote viewed. "How are we going to bypass that?"

"The cameras will be taken care of, don't worry. The source said the elevator is in a closet."

The other two commandos with them were already walking around, opening doors.

"This source," Helen said, "is he a mole in their organization?"

"No," Alex said, pointing his guys at the doors off to the right of the main desk area. "He's one of us. Remember, this place is just a dummy corporation. They deal with lots of unsavory characters on the side."

"Infiltration?" Helen asked, checking behind some curtains for hidden openings.

"Yes."

"One of us, meaning one of the commandos?" She gave an exaggerated sigh when Alex didn't answer. Getting him to elaborate on anything was like pulling teeth. Or, hitting one's head repeatedly against a brick wall. Poor T. She pulled open the innocuous-looking doors of what looked like a supply closet, except that there wasn't any room for supplies. She turned, jerking her thumb towards a set of elevator doors. "Bingo!"

One of the men came forward, pulling out a small electronic component the size of a BlackBerry PDA from the inside of his jacket. Helen watched as he attached it to the security slot. A series of numbers started rapidly going through sequences searching for the correct pass code to activate the elevator.

"De Clerq, green status," Alex reported softly. "Is it uploading at your end? Over."

Helen could hear De Clerq's reply through her earpiece. "Yes, the computer's working on it already. All status green. The meeting's started so Weber's out of the way for the moment."

"What about surveillance?" Alex asked.

"Except for your task, it's all green. Pass code intercepted. Elevator doors will open on your say-so."

"Let me check on status." Alex glanced at his watch, then after a minute, instructed, "Right…now."

"Ten-four. The elevator doors should be opening at your end."

They were sliding apart silently. Helen studied the rich wood paneling from where she was. She remembered the smooth feel of the grain under her hands. So strange to actually see the real thing now, like walking in a dream.

"It's all yours, Hell," Alex said. "Get the key you said is down there. We'll be waiting up here. Just give the green light when you're back up here. We'll open the doors then."

Helen nodded. Alex and his men were going to stay here in case any of Weber's guards appeared. It was bound to happen if the unconscious security man who'd accompanied them didn't check in with them soon. She knew she didn't have that much time. She unzipped her pants, stepping out of them to reveal the black bodysuit she was wearing underneath. Shrugging out of her jacket, she adjusted the belt she'd pulled up to hide the bulkiness of some of the tools on it. She stepped inside the small elevator and turned to face the watchful eyes of the men on the other side.

"Good luck," Alex said.

His eyes, Helen noted, were that pale blue that reminded her of the quartz crystals in her apartment. Realization flashed suddenly in her mind that this man would much prefer to be the one going down in the elevator, that he wasn't used to having a supporting role.

"Close, Sesame," she replied. The door closed. Alone. Or was she? She looked up above and saw the surveillance camera and said aloud, "I hope you guys know about the microeye in here."

"Taken care of, Hell," De Clerq said in her earpiece. "They're getting a different feed."

"Okay," she said, and pressed the only button on the panel. "Here we go."

The elevator started moving. Strange how the feeling was so familiar, as if she'd done this journey before. It was small, like a service elevator, without the shiny frills of modern décor. She fingered the button on the panel lightly. An image of a long corridor flashed in her mind. She tilted her head, trying to follow her vision. Blinking lights. File cabinets.

The trip down took longer than she thought it would, grinding to a halt slowly. The doors slid open silently.

"Our video feed shows there's no one there, Hell. You're clear," De Clerq told her.

Helen wasn't taking any chances. If they could steal and manipulate video feeds so easily, so could the other side. She peered out and looked to the left and right quickly. Nothing. She stepped out.

"I'm in," she said.

"We don't have any feed that shows any activity described in your remote viewing session—nothing that would indicate the key."

"It's here," she said.

She didn't know how she knew. She just did. Maybe it was because the surroundings looked like what she'd seen during her RV session. This was the first time she was at the target location she'd been told to remote view. In her beginning CIA training sessions, an outbounder—an agent at the target area—would call in to confirm her observations, and in those later ones when she and the other candidates were given targets without a point of reference, such as a walk around what was an off-limit nuclear site in a foreign country, nothing could be confirmed firsthand.

There was an awareness in her that she was doing something entirely new in RV—checking up on her own vision and accomplishing the mission herself. She noted, with an objective calmness that was unfamiliar, that she should be excited that she'd been right so far. Yet she wasn't.

Target objective not in hand yet, Helen. She had to get that electronic key to prove to those big shots waiting back home that she was right.

The corridor was brightly lit. She turned to the left of the elevator. "Can you see me?" she asked softly.

"Yes."

"So if I open a door and pop inside, and if you see me on your screen, that's not the room." The one she wanted was obviously not even privy to the surveillance room.

"That would seem so."

"Just give me an affirmative if you see my image."

"Gotcha. Our computer has correlated each monitored room to their building schematics. The first three rooms are empty and not the one you described. Are you going inside them?"

Helen pulled out the small handgun and attached a silencer to its nose. "No." She knew what she saw and she was sticking to it. She walked past the first three rooms and turned the corner. "I see two doors to the left."

"There's only one monitored room."

"First one or second?"

"First."

"Going into the second room. If there's someone there, I hope they're friendly."

She pulled on the handle and swung the door open, pointing her weapon straight ahead. Two people turned. One of them stood up at the sight of her, reaching inside his jacket.

"*Was—*"

"*Scheiss—*"

Helen never missed this close. She shot the one who'd stood and pulled a gun on her, hearing the muffled thud of the bullet hitting him in the chest as he crumbled to the floor even as she swerved and pointed her weapon at the other man who was staring at her with wide, afraid eyes. She glanced around quickly. Yeah, this was the room—same shelves, same desk, everything looked the way she had seen it. There were some things she hadn't been able to discern in remote viewing, especially the exact arrangement and size of the room. The desk she'd seen was to the left; during her RV session, it felt as if it was in the center. That was to be expected since her focus was on the missing electronic key which was still attached to the some kind of device on the same desk.

She walked into the room and kicked the door shut with her foot. She kept her weapon on the man and waited till he raised his hands in surrender before speaking. "I see my target, Center. And I have one hostile down, another one being obedient for now."

"Where's the key?" De Clerq asked.

"It's on the table, hooked up to a decoder, perhaps? I don't know. How should I retrieve it?" She watched as her captive listened to her conversation and addressed him, *"Sprechen Sie Englisch?"*

The man nodded but didn't say anything. Helen kept her weapon on him as she made her way toward the desk.

"Cancel him," a voice suddenly said in her earpiece.

"What?" she asked, stopping at the desk. The side of the device had blinking numbers.

"Cancel him. You need your attention on the device and we don't want any witnesses."

"Who is this?" Helen asked.

"Hell?" De Clerq's voice came back on.

"Didn't you hear that?"

"Hear what?"

"You didn't hear another voice coming into our conversation, giving me instructions," Helen stated.

"No."

She frowned. "Is there an override feature with the devices we use to communicate? For example, if I want to talk to you alone."

"Of course. We all can communicate privately or to different sectors." There was a pause. "You're saying you've just gotten instructions from someone else other than Command?"

She looked at the man sitting there. In all her years as an operative, she'd never killed in cold blood before. She had shot back in self-defense or in the middle of a shootout, but this was different.

"I can't do it," she said.

"Do what, Hell?"

"Someone told me to cancel the remaining hostile. I've never shot at an unarmed man on purpose."

There was a pause. "I see," De Clerq said. "The suggestion was a wise one. You're looking at the enemy and given the chance, he'll kill you."

"I know that but I'd much prefer it if I kill him while he's actually trying to kill me," Helen said dryly. "Then I'd have a reason to take his head off. But for some stupid reason, I can't pull the trigger when he has his arms up in the air and he's smart enough to keep on doing it, too, since he told me he could speak English."

"Then you do what you have to do. We don't have much time. It's your call but you're going to be debriefed about it. Did the person talking to you say it's an order?"

"No, he didn't. And do you know who would give me orders besides you?"

"Since he spoke to you on private link, no, I don't know."

If De Clerq had a clue, he wasn't sharing it. "Are you sure?" Helen pressed. "Make a guess."

"Any member of the team could have suggested that, Hell," De Clerq told her. She couldn't tell from his quiet tone whether he was trying to be ambivalent or not. "And I agree with him. But it's still your call. Time's running. Get the key and get out of there ASAP."

A man's life was in her hands. She had never been put in this situation before and she didn't like it. It was different when she was fighting for her life. This was—she looked straight into the eyes of the man in the chair—someone who was looking at her with fear and hope. A long time ago, when she was caught stealing food, she had been the one looking at her would-be killer with the same fear and hope; he had let her go. She couldn't pull the trigger.

"Please don't kill me," he begged in accented English.

She approached the man. "If you want to live, put your hands very slowly behind your back," she ordered, pulling out the thin rope from her side pouch. He did so obediently. Quickly stepping behind him, she looped his neck. He jerked in surprise. She tugged in warning before adding in German, "Just in case you think about surprising me while I'm securing you, this cord is made of a material that would cut through your skin. *Verstehen Sie?*"

He nodded to show that he understood her and sat very still. She quickly stretched the rope downward and looped both his hands together, then putting the weapon down within easy reach, she pulled, tied a knot, and relooped it around the back steel support of the chair. Then she did the same thing with his feet. She taped his mouth.

That done, she went back to the desk. She turned the laptop around so she could keep an eye on the man as well.

"I'm removing the key from the device, HQ. That will interrupt whatever program that's running on the laptop," she said.

"Download the information into the flashdrive then destroy the laptop, over," De Clerq instructed.

"Done," she said, after several minutes.

She took out a microdigital camera and panned the room as she recorded it. She wanted Hades to see how accurate they had both been. She headed for the door and gave the man a last glance.

"I'd rather not say *wiedersehen,* if you don't mind," she told him then exited.

"Not a good move, Elena," a voice told her.

That got her attention all right. "Where are you?" she demanded as she ran down the corridor, retracing her steps back to the elevator.

Silence.

The elevator was still open. She checked her watch. Not that much time had passed. She got inside and pressed the button. Once she had the key, she was to return to her group, give it to Alex, and they would then head back down. Alex would somehow pass the key to their insider so that if they were stopped and searched, they wouldn't have anything on them.

"Helen?" De Clerq interrupted her thoughts.

Helen caught a note of urgency in his voice. "Yeah?"

"Our feed is showing a male speaking urgently on a mobile and running into one of the offices on the twelfth floor. There's an elevator behind a set of closet doors. We're assuming this is the same elevator you're on."

That made sense. It would be a pain to have to go all the way up to the boss's office if someone were needed on the ground floor.

"Wait, another one's just appeared. Weapon drawn. Two hostiles, repeat, two hostiles heading your way."

The guys running didn't bode well.

"What do you want me to do?" she asked calmly. There was no way to stop the moving elevator. "Take him out?"

"Not if he has his mobile on. We don't want each floor blocked off. We're monitoring the other feeds right now. So far, none of the other security seems to be aware that anything's wrong."

There wasn't any time to debate about this. "I'm climbing up into the elevator shaft," Helen announced, pulling out her rappel shot. "If you don't hear anything, it means I'm busy."

There was silence from De Clerq's end. She could see them all at CCC exchanging doubtful glances. The decision had been instinctive, and at moments like this, she usually followed her instinct rather than question it.

The webbing from the rappel-shot was made to hold triple her weight. She aimed at the top corner of the elevator and pulled the trigger. A "twap" resounded in the enclosed space as the prong pierced the metal. She pulled and flipped at the same time, using her feet to kick on parts of the ceiling panel as she "ran" across it,

Gennita Low

looking for the escape hatch used by repair technicians. At the third kick, a part of the panel gave way. She landed on her feet and pulled on the webbing again, this time running up the sides of the elevator and using her speed to give her enough momentum to let go of the rope so she could shove aside the open hatch. She pushed up quickly, popping the panel to the side as she hung on, half in and out of the elevator car. It didn't take her long to pull herself into the space above.

Air rushed like a miniature wind tunnel as the elevator continued moving upward. Helen ignored the lurching motion, the cracks of light flickering from between cinder blocks giving her an idea how fast the car was moving. The reverberation of speeding air and moving cables humming together distracted her for a second. Still on her knees, she pressed the trigger that would release the prong from the wall and felt the webbing snap back into the rappel-shot. She moved the paneling back into place even as the elevator was slowing down. That had the same effect of a train shuttle coming to a stop, and she had to hang on to an illuminated box attached to the top of the elevator car to keep her balance. Someone who had been there before her must have spilled some kind of oil; she could smell it and her shoes had no traction as she slid sideways, barely missing the cable.

"That wouldn't have felt good," she breathed out, more to herself than anyone.

"We have that on video here. Pretty nifty move, Agent Roston," De Clerq came in. "The door is opening. Our hostiles are looking into the elevator, weapons drawn."

Helen rose up on her knees, looking down at the panel, prepared for anything.

"First hostile's talking into his unit, shaking his head at his partner, looking around," De Clerq informed her. "He's definitely looking for an intruder. Someone must have called him from his post. The other's turning around and running off."

Knowing that De Clerq's end probably couldn't hear what was being said, Helen put her ear against the loosened panel, trying to catch all the words. The elevator started moving and the whistle of rushing wind cut off some of his words. They were going back down. The German was speaking fast and furiously.

"...no one here. No one's answering me on my mobile. Something's wrong...coming down to untie you now... Peter's alerting security about upstairs now. I heard over the walkie-talkie...visitors. Hang on, I have to call individual numbers—"

Shit. Her decision— Helen didn't allow herself to think. She couldn't afford to make another tactical mistake and let this man get more help. It might already be too late, what with the other hostile running off upstairs.

Unsteady from the moving elevator, she cocked her weapon then pushed the panel aside, lurching through the opening and popping a shot to the right. She guessed wrong. Her target was standing against the back of the elevator, not the front. He glanced up and dropped his communication unit, surprised but prepared, his hand holding his weapon already up and firing.

A shot grazed Hell's arm as she pulled back quickly. Another bullet whizzed past her and from the corner of her eye she could see sparks flying off the steel cable. As long as the stupid car was moving, she couldn't keep her balance.

That illuminated control box she had been hanging on to. That must be the override control panel of some sort.

She fired a few shots down through the opening to keep the man from picking up his communications unit. A stream of curses in German floated up. Good, she hoped he was hit, too. She turned her attention to the box. It had three buttons, all lit up. More shots from below. She threw herself to the side. Which one? Which one? She pressed the middle one.

The steel cables screeched at the sudden reversal, jerking her body violently. She rolled over the opening, curling her body to avoid the cable. One of her legs fell through. She could hear the man inside the elevator crashing into the wall as the car jerked and swayed for a few seconds as it readjusted. And started going back up. She must have pressed the up button.

She felt her foot being grabbed. She kicked out and leaned forward, pressing the top button this time. The elevator stopped suddenly. Her attacker now had both his hands on her dangling leg. Lying on her front, her other leg was trapped. He pulled on her leg viciously.

Helen could feel perspiration dripping down her face as she grabbed the cable with both her hands so she could twist her body sideways to allow her other leg space. If she let the bastard pull her through the opening with her body jammed so awkwardly, he would pull her leg out of its socket.

"Hmmph!" she growled, grimly gripping on and twisting, and squeezing her leg through the opening so she was no longer doing a split. A part of her registered the pain as the panel scraped the sides of her thighs. She let go.

The man below grunted as she slammed on top of him, using the wall to brace her weight. She used his initial surprise of finding his opponent a woman, grabbing him by the neck and jamming her fingers into the flesh hard so he would loosen his hold on her trapped leg. He grunted in pain.

"Scheiss!"

He freed one hand and yanked her head back by her hair. Ignoring her own pain, she turned her head the opposite way and smashed her elbow into his nose. This time he howled as he let go. Both his hands went up to protect his face.

Helen landed in a heap at his feet. She registered with slight surprise that the elevator was moving again, but there was no time to think about it as her opponent was reaching down for her again. Rage in his eyes. Blood dripping like a faucet from his nose. A string of German curses coming from his lips.

"Sorry, I don't like what you're calling me," she said to him and kicked at his balls.

He tried to jump out of the way but she made enough contact to cause him to howl some more. He dove on top of her and brought up a fist. She turned, saw his fallen weapon, brought it up and pulled the trigger. The shot reverberated in the small space as the bullet hit its mark. The man's fist lowered as he slowly toppled over.

Helen rolled over to avoid the dead weight, twisting to face the elevator doors. She had no idea whether she had been going up or down this time. She aimed, her finger on the trigger. The doors slid open. There was no one there.

"It's okay," a voice greeted her. "Status green."

It was the COMCEN password. She took her finger from the trigger but still didn't lower the weapon. She didn't recognize the voice.

A pair of boots came within sight. Her gaze followed the blue jeans upward, taking in the denim jacket, the arms with the hidden hands shoved inside the pockets, up to the owner's tanned face. A pair of silver eyes coolly looked down at her. His boot moved and kicked the body half on top of her aside.

"You made a mess," the stranger said.

Fourteen

Helen didn't need any of her unusual abilities to tell her the man standing in front of her was dangerous. Even looking up from where she was, his power unnerved her, as if he was standing too close for comfort. Something dark and ruthless lurked behind those silver eyes gazing down at her so dispassionately, taking in the whole scene in the elevator. She didn't particularly care for the way he just stood there watching her either. She felt like some new trainee being judged incompetent at handling a simple job.

"Need help getting up?" the stranger asked.

His voice was low, like a man who knew people would listen to him. Slightly husky, like he didn't talk much. Not that he was offering her any help either, because his hands were still in his pockets. One dark brow lifted, waiting for her answer.

Helen's eyes narrowed. She didn't need any help, especially from him. Moving her limbs tentatively, she stretched her right leg. No pain. She pushed herself to a crouch. He still just stood there, watching her as she tried to stand up and lost her balance.

She frowned, looking down at her right leg. She had felt a twinge and then it had given out, but there had been no pain. She tried getting up again, this time slowly and carefully, her eyes grimly on those jeans-clad legs as she straightened to her full height. Damn, she was hoping he would be shorter but no such luck. Finally she looked up, expecting to see scorn in his eyes.

There was none. Those silver eyes, though—they were damn compelling.

Danger.

Her whole being lit up like a thousand lightbulbs and she fought the urge to take a step back. Not liking how he was making her feel, she casually looked down at her hands. Blood. And grime from…? She frowned. The oily stuff she had felt while she was rolling around on top of the elevator.

Oh well. Then all her clothes were covered with the stuff. She looked back at the man as she wiped her hands nonchalantly down the side of her bodysuit. Fashionably spy-black to hide blood and grime, of course.

So, he wanted her to talk first? Maybe he was just speechless from admiration. "Did De Clerq send you?" she asked politely, taking a moment again to reexamine her hands, as if having a dead man at her feet was an everyday thing.

De Clerq was strangely silent in her earpiece. Maybe they were all speechless with admiration at what she'd done.

He didn't respond immediately as his gaze slid down

the length of her and back. It was irritating her. His dark brown hair was combed back neatly, reminding her that hers was probably hell to look at. A dark lock curled over his forehead. She quickly took in the masculine features—nothing soft, from the look in those strange eyes that glittered back at her to the uncompromising set of those lips. He looked too damn comfortable in his faded jacket. His weathered jeans fitted him too damn well. So casual. So ordinary. And everything about him sang danger.

It was her turn to arch an eyebrow. What? Were they going to just stand here?

"Do you still have the SEED?" he asked.

"Yes."

"Number One is going to set the stage upstairs to provide distraction. He'll demand to see Weber immediately and cause enough trouble to get more security going upstairs. Weber is still occupied. It's evening and most of the floors are empty, so you won't have trouble moving from floor to floor using the stairwell." He pointed to the direction she had to take, then looked down at her legs. "Are you injured?"

Helen straightened even more. She recalled her leg being twisted around like a limb in a wrestling match while her upper body was trapped above the elevator.

"Nothing I can't handle," she replied smoothly. After all, she didn't feel any pain. "What floor am I on again?"

"Twelfth. Can you make it?"

"If I don't, will you carry me?" she retorted. She gave him a cursory up and down glance. "Might dirty that nice clean outfit."

He moved for the first time. Just one step. And she

didn't like that she had to tilt her head up to look at him. She took in a breath. A heady sensation rushed through her. Gads, the man even smelled of danger. Either that or rocking around in the elevator had made her light-headed.

"Supersoldier-spy," he said softly, and there was *no* mistaking the mockery in that husky voice. "Surely twelve flights of steps is nothing to you, injured or not."

A challenge was a challenge. "What are you going to do? Stand here to time me?"

His speed took her by surprise. One moment she was inside the elevator with him. The next she found herself being lifted by the waist, shifted, and set back on her feet. It was so fast, she didn't have time to retaliate.

"I'm taking the elevator down of course," he told her as he took a step back.

She stared at him as he leaned forward to press the button.

"Down?" she echoed. "Why? I have the key card. There's nothing down there."

His eyes glittered back at her as the doors began to slide. "You have unfinished business," he said, and the doors shut.

Helen stared at the closed doors for a second. She remembered the man she'd tied in the vault. "De Clerq," she said sharply. "Who...was...that?"

"Number Nine," De Clerq told her.

One of the commandos. Figured. "Tell me he isn't going down to the vault," she said. She was mad at herself, for what her one mistake had caused her. "He doesn't have to do this."

"He finishes the operation. Now get the hell out of

the building. Security's already alerted about trouble on the top floor. Leave it to the others to get the rest of the operation. We need you back in the van pronto, with the key card."

She had no choice. The electronic card was more important than her pride. She turned in the direction he had pointed and started to...limp. She looked down in surprise. The serum was definitely blocking any pain.

She followed the signs to the exit doors. Right. Twelve flights of stairs. She could do it. She pushed them open. The body of a man slumped against the railing. No blood. But the angle of his head told her he was dead. She remembered De Clerq telling her that there were two men outside the elevator, with one running off, presumably to get more help. This must be him.

There was no doubt in her mind whom the unfortunate man had bumped into. Mr. I-am-a-god-in-jeans. She started limping down the stairs, then decided to take two at a time. No way was she going to let any injury cause any more delays in this mission.

"Agent 51, can you hear me?"

One needed quiet when one was remote viewing. It was hard enough to do it in a van full of electronic equipment that disturbed his senses. Didn't his monitor understand that he needed a modicum of silence? Some kind of white noise filter would be helpful.

But no, time and again they interrupted him with loud discussions about what was going on. He was pulled back in each time, catching drifts of conversation about what was happening inside Deutsche International.

Rage and frustration coursed through him. He

couldn't savor those delicious emotions in the energy spectrum. They were still going way too fast. And the fucking guys were constantly interrupting. This last time almost made him yell at them. Having a hard-on for so long with no relief was painful. Didn't they fucking know that? He needed to find a way to slow the images down…get some relief…so he could… More snippets of conversation cut through his focus.

"What the hell is going on at that place? The list HQ faxed me has some big-time names on it."

"I suspect COS Command Center has something to do with it. Security overload is perfect for a heist, isn't it?"

"Yeah, but they're taking a chance with so many people on alert in there."

Shut up! Shut the fuck up. But if he said what was on his mind, they would get mad and might not use him anymore. He had to be good, bide his time with this thing. Double dosage. He mustn't be greedy. He had plenty recorded from the earlier session and he could spend all of tonight rewinding and rewinding and re-winding…

"Agent 51, you've been quiet for a while now."

"They always look like they've fallen asleep when they're doing this. How do you tell the difference?"

"As long as he answers when I talk to him."

He'd better say something then. "I can hear you." Maybe he could be tactful with his request. It was too late anyway. Opening his eyes, he added, "But you need to speak softer. I can't sense very well when there's so much noise around me. You pulled my whole consciousness back here and I'll need ten minutes to get back into RV mode."

His monitor studied him for a moment, then nodded. "You're right. I apologize for the interruption. Are you sure the key's still there?"

He knew it was still in the building. As for the location of that room he saw…he hadn't been able to pinpoint it exactly. "I'm sure it's there," he answered truthfully, mentally crossing his fingers that they wouldn't push him for the location. He elaborated more, hoping it would satisfy them that he knew what he was talking about. "I see the same long dark shaft. Same enclosed tunnel and space. I sense the point of entry to that place in a very high-up location."

"So the key's still up at Weber's office somewhere then?"

"I don't know who Weber is but yes, the key is around there," he hedged.

"You'd better be right, 51," his monitor warned. "Now, what could we do to help you get back into RV mode? The drug's still good, right? You're feeling the beginnings of downtime, right?"

"Oh no, I'm okay, sir," he said, "but I need to go to take a piss, splash some water on my face."

"We don't have the time for that," the other man said impatiently. "I thought you psychics could control things like that."

"I'm not a psychic, sir," he told them, feeling somewhat indignant. What, did they think he was just someone they picked up from the Yellow Pages? "I was being trained in surveillance when I was reassigned by the director. I don't have any psychic abilities at all. We're specially trained for—"

"Oh, cut the crap. Just get back into whatever you

want to call it. You're a trained professional, right? You can suck in that piss for a while longer. Go on, 51, show us your tricks."

He didn't care whether this guy was one of his monitors or not. His attitude was pissing him off. A monitor was supposed to be the guiding hand, a person he could trust to help him if he encountered problems while remote viewing, and this man just wanted to use him.

Fine. He had been desperate to help because he wanted that drug so much, but now that he had some, he felt he was in control again. He could play them the way they played him; he could withhold information from them until absolutely necessary. Why not? The idea was brilliant! That way, he could get more of the serum because they would want him to help them.

Ignoring his pressing hard-on, he took in a deep breath and focused inward. He'd just have to figure a way to get off while he was in the ether.

Switch to Channel Three. Set programming time. Set channel.

Timer on. Record.

"I'm ready," he said.

"We'll talk quietly, 51, promise," the first agent, the one who seemed to be more understanding, said. "What do you see?"

Hot damn. The key's coordinates weren't the same. It was being moved! "I'm zooming in," he said. "Many people milling around the ground floor. I have to concentrate on which ones are your targets. Give me a few minutes."

"Good. We know they have operatives watching on the perimeters. We're keeping our eyes on them. We need to know which exit point they're taking so we can mount a surprise attack of our own."

"Okay," he said. *Change channel. Change channel.*

He was back in that vaultlike place where the electronic key exchanged hands. Except that this time, the two men who were working on them were dead. He didn't move nearer. He could feel emptiness in them—no energy. One was lying on the floor. The other was sitting down, hands tied, a piece of tape hanging off the side of his mouth.

He hovered closer to the one in the chair. This one was recently dead, the last one to go. There was still a little energy left but he was careful not to go too near and touch it. Out of curiosity, he had done it once before. He shuddered at the memory. No, that kind of energy wasn't beautiful.

However, this man was probably the last to see what had happened to the electronic key and he needed to touch something close to him that he'd used prior to death. The chair? No, too close.

The blinking light from the intercom on the desk. Someone was trying to contact him and from the looks of it, he had probably been trying to be rescued... hmm...when he was interrupted by his killer. Well, too late for him. The last thing he touched was probably the button answering the intercom. Where was it?

He hovered closer, warily, making sure he didn't get too close. He saw the electronic pad dangling by its wires on the side of the desk toward the dead man. Slowly, carefully, he reached out and touched each of the buttons on it.

He withdrew his hand quickly. Death energy. Yeah, the man was talking into the intercom when he was interrupted. But he didn't understand German, so he had no idea what the words yelling in his mind were about. And he didn't particularly care. He'd caught the image of a hand pulling the key out of the decoding device.

Record. Where was it? He saw stairs. Someone was moving it up…no, down a long flight of steps. Many, many flights. A stairwell. He would go there.

Change channel.

Monotonously running down flight after flight of stairs freed Helen's mind to quickly review what had taken place. She was totally focused on the exercise at hand, very aware of each turn of the stairway, yet a part of her appeared to be observing herself. The more she hurried, the more cut-off that part seemed to be.

She found herself thinking calmly, as if she was not running at all. It had to do with the serum, of course. She was injured. The drug was somehow kicking in.

The serum had an unusual dichotomy. On one hand, it impeded sensation. Helen couldn't feel any pain, even though she knew, from the way her right leg wasn't properly supporting her weight, that she was hurting. On the other hand, it didn't totally block out all emotions. Her usual warped sense of humor was still there. Also, she had reacted to Number Nine's presence quite strongly.

He had pissed her off, standing there like that, not doing a damn thing to help her. Not that she needed his help. It was those eyes looking at her with disdain, like he knew she would be a problem. And then to find out he was going back down for "unfinished" business— that irked her the most, that he'd been sent to do something she hadn't been capable of doing.

It was her fault that the operation had gone somewhat chaotic. If she had cancelled that man in the vault, there wouldn't have been any alert about what was happening and she wouldn't have had to fight with that operative in the elevator, and this Number Nine fellow wouldn't have had to move from whatever position he was in so he could save her ass.

She supposed she had to thank him for that. The idea of saying that to his face filled her with dismay. Maybe she could send him a postcard.

Dear Number Nine, thank you for saving my ass.

Helen chuckled quietly as she jumped down the last few steps. She didn't even know his name.

"Are you all right, Hell?" De Clerq asked.

They were probably wondering why she was laughing when she was supposed to be urgently running down the stairs. "I'm almost down at the ground floor," she told him. "Then I'll look for the emergency exit that was on the blueprint we were looking at in the plane, over."

"Copy that. How's the leg?"

She almost stopped in surprise. How did he know? "Did Number Nine tell you about my leg?" she asked.

"Affirmative. He said you might need help if you were required to jump into the van, over."

Need help to jump—Helen felt like turning around and running back upstairs to find the man. "Please tell him that I rolled down the last ten flights of stairs," she retorted, trying to keep the edge of anger from her voice. "I could probably roll myself into the van, thank you very much."

"He was just reporting in on your condition when Dr. Kirkland asked."

"Dr. K. could just have asked me," Helen pointed out.

"I'm doing good. Serum working like the eighth wonder. No pain."

And let out an involuntary gasp as she tried not to fall down the stairs.

"What is it, Hell?" De Clerq demanded.

"I don't…know," she managed. Her heart was beating erratically and she could barely think clearly. "Danger. I just sense danger."

"Is someone in the stairwell after you?"

"No." She gasped again, her breathing uneven. "No one. I can't explain this, De Clerq."

She felt the hair on the back of her neck standing. Her "warning" sense had never been so alarming before. Goose pimples. Heart pumping as if she were in fear, but she wasn't feeling scared at all.

"You're nearly there, Hell. Come on, you can do it. The exit isn't too far," De Clerq urged.

Helen stumbled down, trying to concentrate while trying to control her breathing. One of her eyelids fluttered uncontrollably. What the hell was happening to her?

Shit! Pause! Pause!

The images running in his head were muddled, crisscrossed with lines. His eyes hurt.

"Agent 51, what's wrong? Your hands are covering your eyes and you're moaning."

"Pain." He had changed channels and had appeared on what was a stairwell. He had felt the electronic key and had zapped down that flight of stairs in his phantom body. Then he'd slammed into—something hard. But that was impossible. "I can't see!"

"What do you mean you can't see? What are you doing, 51?" his monitor demanded. "We need you to focus. Are you with the key?"

He could feel all the precious recorded images melting inside him. No!

Pause! Pause!

He had to fight through this, get back his sight, so he could get out of here. His head pounded. He could hear his monitor talking about him.

"He's shaking like a leaf. It's the serum."

"Fuck! We're so damn close, we can't lose the key now! What do we do?"

"Another shot will kill him. Agent 51, listen to my voice. Focus on my voice. Focus. Change channel. Change channel and come back. Do you hear me?"

He heard the guiding voice in the chaotic darkness and focused on it like a man drowning. "Yes," he said obediently.

"Go to the closest exit and tell me where you are then come back."

He let his senses reach out to see which direction to go. Down. The vice around his head tightened and he screamed. He had to go down! But that thing was down there, too.

Change channel. Change... He screamed again at the pain in his head and he felt himself tumbling like a drunk acrobat. Down, down, down, somersaulting through the ether.

There was a glimpse…he could see something.

"What do you see, Agent 51?"

"The sign…says…" He tried to pronounce the German, panting the words out. *"Westlicher Ausgang."*

"Good. Now come back."

He gratefully did so, opening his eyes, and looking around at the interior of the van. His monitors weren't paying attention to him anymore as one shouted to the driver. The pain was receding, but he was still shaking from whatever it was that had attacked him. He looked down. He'd wet his pants. For the first time ever, he was afraid.

Helen forced herself to go even faster. She could do this. She had trained for this for two years and her body could take the punishment. All the while, her whole insides felt like a giant fist clenching tighter and tighter. It wasn't painful—just tremendously uncomfortable— and it played havoc with her ability to think at all.

She had no idea what was happening, just that something was crying out to her to move quickly, that something was wrong. Instinct, latent sixth sense, whatever. *Get out! Get out!*

She saw the exit and breathed a sigh of relief. Her eye had stopped doing that weird fluttering, thank goodness. For a moment there, she'd thought she was having a seizure of some kind.

She opened the door. At the same time, the awful squeezing sensation inside her stopped suddenly. She saw the CCC disguised vehicle she had arrived in heading down the alley toward her. The side doors opened and one of the operatives she had seen on the plane appeared.

The squeal of tires to the right. She turned. A dark brown truck, looking like it was a UPS truck or something, had just turned the corner. It could be making a delivery, except that it was speeding straight at her.

Everything went slow-motion in her head. She leapt into action, heading toward her agency's vehicle, which was slowing down.

A man from the speeding truck hung out of the passenger window. She gasped as she felt the shot hit her side. She fell on her knees and did a body roll, then got up immediately. The operative from her agency had jumped out and was running in her direction, shooting at the van behind her.

"Hurry!" he yelled, his hand reaching out.

Helen's legs felt like lead and she couldn't seem to move any faster. The slow motion was real, she realized suddenly. Her movements were slowing down, as if... she had been drugged.

With the last of her energy, she flung herself toward her rescuer.

"Can't...move...fast," she gasped out as she grabbed him.

She wasn't sure he heard her as he turned and calmly fired his weapon at the oncoming van, causing it to swerve, before turning to her. Then he half-dragged, half-carried her toward their waiting vehicle.

They launched themselves through the open doorway, hitting the floor, and Helen's partner immediately climbed on top of her.

"Hey!" But her protest was muffled by the carpeting.

Helen heard the squeal of wheels as their van gathered speed. More shots, some of which hit the side of the vehicle with metallic thuds. She realized that the man on her was protecting her. There was the slam of doors and her body was no longer trapped. She lifted her head.

"Status, status, dammit!" De Clerq's urgent voice piped up.

Helen frowned. That didn't come from the earpiece. She then realized that it must be coming from the van radio.

"We've got her with us. A truck is right behind our vehicle. Better alert Number One and Number Nine at ground zero. I shot a GPS tag at it, so let's hope it's attached. The shots we exchanged are going to get Deutsche's security operatives swarming around the scene," the man beside her reported. He belly-crawled to the back of the van and peeked out of the back window. "Tell Number Nine I'm not in the building to help with retrieval. Question—shall we let that van follow us all the way or do we find a way to retrieve them for questioning, too? Over."

"Copy on Hell's status. Copy on alert to Number One and Number Nine. Our men around the perimeter are reporting high activity. Keep driving while I communicate with the others, over."

"Copy."

"Who are they?" Hell asked.

"No idea," the man said.

"Umm, I think I was shot with some kind of drug. I can't move very well."

The man turned to her again. He checked her body, turning her on her back, lifting her arms and finally pulling something out of her side. "Tranq," he muttered. He studied her. "You should be out like a light by now."

"Yeah, well, supersoldier-spy and all that," she quipped, with a weak grin. "Like the Energizer Bunny, I just keep going and going."

"No pain?" he asked her.

"Nope." She closed her eyes. "But your mentioning that I should be out like a light is making me feel weaker."

"Of course," he muttered. "Psychological."

"Dr. Kirkland's going to have a hell of a time when I get back," she said with a smile. "The serum's a success, though."

"Hmm," the man said. "They didn't want to kill you. They fired real shots at me, but not you."

"Probably wanted to capture me," she suggested, opening her eyes. "They know about the key, then."

He nodded. "I think it's a good assumption that their plan was to get either you or the key, or both."

"Thanks for coming to my aid," she said. "What's your name again?"

He paused, then replied, "Heath." Abruptly, he stood up and said, "Why are we slowing down?"

"The vehicle behind us just turned left, sir."

Heath looked back briefly. "Guess they're giving up for now. Helen, you still have the item, right?"

"As far as I know," she said. "There's a small pocket inside my suit."

He came to kneel down by her again. "Which side?"

She sighed. "I suppose you want to put your hand in my clothes."

"Just to make sure it's there. You were in some kind of trouble before you came out of the building."

"There was no one with me," Helen said. But how could she explain what had happened in there? She shrugged. "The drug was probably bothering me. Right side."

She watched as he pulled down the zipper of her

bodysuit. He adjusted his position so he could slide his hand inside. Their eyes met.

"You know, Heath, I usually don't let my men touch me there on the first date."

A glimmer of amusement touched his lips. "Your men?" he asked, raising his brows. He moved his hand and she felt him nudging the card against her chest. He continued holding her gaze as he pulled her pants back out, then added softly, "There's touching, and there's touching."

Helen blinked and studied him for a second. Built like an athlete. Nice square jaw. His eyes reminded her of her favorite dog, Mimo, whose angelic eyes hid an imp that would rip apart a whole trash bag to go after the bone in there and then look at her with those heart-breaking hazel eyes when she got home. Mimo always got what she wanted from any man, woman or child by just looking at them, whether it was a gruff pat from the surly neighbor or a child to share his ice cream cone. Mimo was evil like that. And she had adored her.

"De Clerq, status has turned green," Heath said, as he stood up. "Our pursuers tranqued Helen, so there was another agenda. I'd make a list of those people who would know about our Hell and RV program. Give me status of others, over."

"Number One is on his way to airstrip. Number Nine retrieved just one target. The others escaped and there wasn't time to run after him. Number Five's waiting at airstrip. We want to know Helen's status. As for the list, do you know the names that are going to be on it? Some of them are major players in the agencies, over."

"Not my problem," Heath said, looking down at

Helen. "Helen can't walk just yet, but she can talk. She might need to be carried. Maybe Number Five will make himself useful today. He hadn't done much."

Helen grinned. Number Five was Flyboy. Good to know these guys had a sense of camaraderie. From De Clerq's report, she was getting a fair idea of what the rest of the "team" was doing. She had done her task and they were doing theirs. She frowned. Except for Number Nine. He didn't retrieve somebody—who? One of two. The Cummings. Her frown deepened. Her fault, maybe. She'd caused him to lose time.

"Actually, Number Five has taken off to collect some satellite pictures of your chase. Your GPS dart hit its mark. Good work. You, too, Hell. We might get some more useful info about the people that attacked you, Hell, over."

"Good," she said. "I'd like to know that myself. Especially if it's one of our agencies causing the trouble. What's next on the agenda?"

"We all get home and you get to show off to the big brass what you've retrieved for them."

"Okay, but will I ever know what the hell this operation's about, besides getting a stupid decoder key?" she asked. "The mission is over so giving me details won't interfere with my RV sessions."

"We'll discuss that during debriefing."

"Heath, will you be there?" she asked.

His gaze roved over her prone body. "I have another task to do," he said, before turning his attention back to the front.

Too many details destroyed objectivity in remote viewing because then the viewer would be creating the reality rather than collecting information. Once a session was over, the rest of the details would be provided, mostly to satisfy human curiosity. Sometimes, during her CIA sessions, they would just give her the percentage of success, without much else to tell her whether she "saw" the right target, or not.

She hoped CCC wouldn't do that. She lay there, staring at Heath's back. He was never there in the meetings. Was he her monitor?

Fifteen

The briefing had been short, to the point, and fortunately, no one questioned her abilities. All they had to do was take a look at her, of course.

"How are you really feeling?"

Helen turned. Dr. Kirkland had refrained from asking more than the standard questions during the meeting with the top agency executives. She had limped in on her own two feet and had shown them the electronic card. She wasn't required to give a detailed account of how she got to it; that was irrelevant because the point was to prove that TIRVVR worked. And with the targeted object in her hand, none of the big brass argued. Thus the meeting was short and focused mainly on her success.

After it was over, everyone was dismissed for rest and in her case, medical care. De Clerq was going to review the stolen satellite feed they had directed to the Center before debriefing. She'd learned that the trojan their insider had planted in Deutsche International's security system had a timer and would self-destruct once the mission was completed. That way, nobody could put a trace on them.

All in all, a pretty successful operation. She didn't feel particularly elated, but that wasn't what Dr. Kirkland wanted to know about anyway.

"I still don't feel tired," she told him, "although logic tells me that I should be dead on my feet from exhaustion. I'm not walking very well either."

"Yes, I've been told to look at that knee. You probably twisted it in the fight. Let's get you to the medical room and we'll have a complete checkup without interruptions."

To be honest, she didn't want to be stripped and prodded, but of course this was the best time for that because it would give the doctor information he needed for his study. It was strange. She wanted to…prowl.

She had to smile at the thought. At the moment, the prowling would look a lot more like limping. She looked down at her injured knee, trying to feel the pain. It would probably worsen her injury, too.

"All right." She allowed herself to be placed in a wheelchair again. She turned to De Clerq as Derek wheeled her off. "When will we all get together for a post-mission meeting?"

"Usually when most of the operatives are back," De Clerq answered. "If there is a long time in between operatives' return, we get together for a mini-update. We'll make sure you're kept in the loop. Rest up before debriefing, Hell."

She nodded, not bothering to tell him that she couldn't rest. When they were out in the hallway, she asked casually, "So who's back from operations and who's not, Dr. K.?"

"As far as I know, Heath's back. He was the one in the van with you. Alex, Sullivan and Shahrukh are all accounted for. Flyboy, T., and Jed are still out."

Helen hid a smile. She knew there were seven of the commandos left after the big incident that took two of them out. Add in Armando, and she had all their names now. Now all she had to do was find the time to study their files.

She wished she had shown more interest in doing so after she'd been told she'd "won" the coveted new job and would be finishing her training at Command Center, but she hadn't thought about it. She had been out of the field for two years, so on her days off, it had been great to finally find some time to relax a little bit and catch up with her GEM sisters. The GEM structure had also changed after the merger with the highly-secretive Covert Subversive Command Center and she was more interested in that than in the individual players. After all, she had trained and competed with military types before, so these COS commandos couldn't be much different.

Wrong. She should have paid attention to her instinct. She had gotten to know Flyboy and even though he appeared "normal," she had felt a subtle shift of difference in him now and then. And Armando Chang was definitely a study all by himself. Speaking of which—

"Where was Armando?" she asked, in the same casual tone. "I don't think I saw him at all."

"He didn't go on this operation," Dr. Kirkland told her. They entered the elevator that would take her to the medical sector. "I imagine he's in his quarters."

She remembered the mention of Flyboy going off for satellite pictures of vehicles. That left Jed McNeil, Number Nine. She frowned. God-in-jeans, she'd called him. Irritating god-in-jeans, she amended. He had to "retrieve," Heath had told her during the ride. She recalled Heath talking to De Clerq about telling Jed that he couldn't be there for backup or something. So was Jed still out there searching for a lost target? Was it her fault?

She didn't like the idea of her mistake causing extra work. When she was done with Dr. Kirkland, she would go search out Heath and ask him herself whether it was her fault, and if so, what exactly was Jed doing right now?

At the medical room, two nurses helped her undress. She eyed the pile of dust-smeared clothes ruefully as she thought about the wild ride on top of the elevator. The black hid the stains well, but they were probably ruined by whatever oily stuff had been coating the surface of the elevator.

"Your vitals are fine. Your leg looks better than I thought but will likely swell up more tomorrow. You'll probably need some painkillers then, too. I'll also schedule an MRI."

Good to know she hadn't made her injury more serious. "What would cause the odd muscle flutters, though, Doc?" she asked. She recalled the nausea, the feeling of being tightly squeezed, as if something was invading her being. She hadn't been able to see where she was going, and usually, she would have reacted to the loss of control. Yet, she'd been able to maintain her focus. The serum must have helped her overcome the initial fear. *Or Hades' training had prepared you for that.* She chose not to dwell on that particular subject right now. "I know it's probably my body reacting to the drug but if it keeps happening, how do we stop it?"

"We're going to do a few more tests. I'm afraid you'll have to go to the bathroom with a cup," Dr. Kirkland said.

Helen smiled, amused. "You think I'd cheat with a few sides of caffeine, Doc?" she teased. "Maybe put more stimulants in my body just for the hell of it?"

Dr. Kirkland shook his head. He stretched her leg out to the side and gestured to Derek for a towel to wipe off some of the grimy stains that had soaked through her pants. "No, but it's my job as a doctor and a scientist to eliminate every possible reason that could have worked against the serum before working on its effects on you. So far, you have shown some of the textbook symptoms of SYMBIOS 2 effects."

"The ability to withstand pain, less need of sleep, with my mental faculties still intact, yeah," Helen interrupted. "What else is missing?"

"The pain is there, it's just that the nerve center in your brain is desensitized to it," Dr. Kirkland explained. "Depending on where the pain is, or the injury, the part of your brain that controls that area is sending electrical and biosignals to that part of your body. As we've explained, we don't know exactly how pain suppressants like aspirin work, except that they do. The body just understands where to send that particular drug."

"So you're saying you don't know, other than my leg injury, exactly what other parts of me the serum might be affecting. You can't tell, even with tests? Oh, wait a minute, I *am* the test."

Helen winked at Derek. She enjoyed teasing Dr. K.

and the other scientists because they never had any solid answers about anything.

"Anything that affects and tricks the brain is dangerous, Helen," Dr. Kirkland cautioned quietly, his forehead creasing in a small frown. "We have to get to the bottom of this strange episode, especially if it happens again."

"I know," she said meekly. "Anything you say, Doc."

The doctor shook his head. "You're so like him. Both of you don't seem concerned about the changes to your bodies."

That got her attention. She knew who the "him" was in reference to.

"And what are his changes?" She waggled her finger. "Come on, Dr. Kirkland, give me something here. What's affecting the great secret monitor?"

Everything was like a piece of the puzzle and she pounced on all the information hungrily and eagerly. She wanted as many pieces as possible so she could form the picture.

Dr. Kirkland studied her for a moment, as if weighing whether he should say any more. He finished bandaging her leg and cut the access cloth.

"I've noticed recently that both your REM cycles begin and end together once or twice in a night. Do you have lucid dreams, Helen?" he asked.

REM. Rapid eye movement was the state of sleep in which the person was actively dreaming. "I have dreams now and then." Helen shrugged, keeping her expression bland, but her heart was thumping from this new piece of information. "Nothing unusual that I can think of."

"Pay more attention and see whether you can re-

member them. It would be interesting to compare notes
with his dreams."

"Does he tell you what his dreams are about?" she
asked curiously.

"It isn't part of the experiment, so there aren't any
notes taken. I've told him about the possibility of
putting his dreams on record."

She didn't like this idea at all. Her dreams were
private, too private to share.

Dr. Kirkland gave her an amused smile. "He had the
same exact expression you have on your face right
now." He tilted his head to one side. "When you agreed
to have all this done to you, didn't you expect there to
be drastic changes to your body as well as your mind?
Doesn't seeing Armando Chang's behavior give you
clues to possible side effects of the serum?"

"I've gone through workshops about all the possible effects, Dr. Kirkland," Helen replied. "Did you
imagine that I wasn't prepared for the risks? Although,
I must admit, it'd be cool to be able to do magic shows
like Armando."

As a way to distract him from talking more about
lucid dreaming, she opted to lighten the mood of the
conversation. Admittedly, she hadn't really thought
about the risks much in the beginning of the training.
Each program had been so challenging and knowing
that she had competition had made her focus solely on
winning. In her mind then, the serum and all its risks
were only for the winner and she hadn't won yet.

"Remember, Armando isn't doing remote viewing
and doesn't have the downtime a remote viewer undergoes after a session, so you're actually more tired than

our past testers of the serum, Hell, both mentally and physically," Dr. Kirkland warned. "When you come out of your state, you might need more rest than you thought. Or, something."

"Or, something…?" Helen dragged the word out, giving the doctor a questioning look. She had thought about that, too, but she wasn't one to keep worrying about something over which she had no control. If she was going to do this, she had to just do it. "What do you think is going to happen to me when I come out of my 'state,' as you called it?"

She stood up, testing her weight on her feet. Maybe a small niggle of discomfort? She couldn't tell.

"Pain would be the fairly obvious consequence. Your leg is going to be hurting. A lot. And don't be shy about telling me how much it is when you feel it, Hell. I have to know."

"Have I ever been shy about anything, Doc?" Helen smiled. "I promise I won't hide the pain."

"You might not be able to."

"Okay, then you don't have to worry about me lying to you about feeling pain, then," she said. "What else?"

"Maybe sensitivity to light. Your body lacks sleep. Your thinking might be affected. You haven't eaten much so you'll definitely be hungry. Your brain and body might compensate for your lack of sleep by producing different levels of hormones. With Armando, he definitely sees 'things' after using the serum. He also likes to sit in the dark, says the light bothers him."

Besides looking for Heath to ask him about the "retrieval," she also definitely needed to talk to Armando.

She could do this before the serum wore off. She had a feeling she would be sleeping like a log, after.

"All right," Helen said. "I'll get hold of you when things go crazy, Doc. Can I go now? Is it okay to walk on my own? Not too much, of course."

"Yes, but be careful. Take these painkillers. Get hold of me if there's any problem."

"All right. Umm, can someone give me some clothes to wear? And can I have my boots back?"

Once she was alone, she pulled out the electronic comm card from the side slit in her boots. It was Armando Chang's. She slid the card through the security slot in the communications channel and punched in her own security code. Armando would know it was from her and that she was calling from inside Center.

He came on after the third buzz. "Well, well, well, if it isn't the Princess of Darkness calling me," he drawled. "And how was the experience?"

"You're suddenly right to the point, Chang," Helen commented. "What, no roundabout chitchat about illusions and pain?"

"But you're calling me precisely to talk about that, aren't you?" he mocked. "I don't like being predictable."

He was far too perceptive. Of course he'd known she would call him with questions afterwards. "You gave me your card," she reminded him. "I take that as an offer to answer my questions."

"Everything has a price, Miss Roston," he said. "Are you ready for yours?"

"You're pissing me off, Chang," Hell warned. "Are you going to help me or not?"

"You're feeling anger? Cool. The serum's wearing

off a bit. The drug takes the edge off emotions like anger and pain, as you know." He affected a heavy accent, very similar to Dr. Kasparov's during their first meeting. "It increases your pain threshold by producing analgesia that blocks your pain receptors. It's anti-anxiety. It acts on the limbic system, thalamus and hypothalamus of the CNS to produce hypnotic effects. It also blocks serotonin and motor neurons. So, tell me, how's your limbic system and hypothalamus doing, Hell?"

She laughed. She liked his sarcasm. "They seem fine. At least, I think so."

"Then why do you need me, if you're fine?"

Hell looked at the clock on the wall. "I don't know how much time I have before I conk out from lack of sleep. When did it happen to you? I'd also rather see you in person to talk about this. I'm not comfortable with talking over the comm system."

"These walls have ears," Armando acknowledged softly.

"So you can whisper into mine," she retorted.

"I love an innovative woman. Where would you like to meet?"

"Any suggestion?"

"Room 18."

She tried to remember what that was. "The interrogation observation room? Why?"

"Because there are no cameras there."

"I don't have the clearance."

"Silly child. Do you need one with me?"

"All right. When? Now, I hope."

"Would I keep the princess waiting? Of course not.

I wouldn't miss this for the world. Here's a special code, when you're asked by the gatekeeper."

He gave it to her before clicking off, leaving Helen to stare down at the intercom speaker. That man was too damn cryptic. He had something up his sleeve. Dammit, now he had her using clichés, too.

She went to the computer panel in the wall and used her security code to access the COMCEN map. She typed in Room 18 and studied the directions that came up on the screen.

She had never been to the interrogation sector before. That hadn't been part of her training, not yet anyway. Interrogation was something behind-the-scenes that all Intel agencies tended to hide from even their own.

As a contract agent, this part of the shadowy world of cloak and daggers hadn't really concerned her before. She had been trained by GEM to resist certain interrogation techniques, but had been fortunate so far. She had been in danger a few times more than she'd cared for, but had never been forced to give information.

By the time she reached the level where Room 18 was located, she was definitely feeling more than a niggle of pain. She smothered a yawn. That was the first indication her body was coming back to normal. Which was good, wasn't it? She felt the bottle of painkillers Dr. Kirkland had given her in her pocket.

At the buzz and command of the electronic voice, she keyed in the code Armando Chang had given her. The doors slid open. Armando was standing there waiting, leaning against the wall, arms and legs lazily crossed, scruffy black T-shirt untucked from his black jeans.

"You look tired already," he said, his eyes keenly

studying her face as he straightened from his lazy stance. "It's almost here."

"What's almost here?" she asked.

"The reckoning."

Helen rolled her eyes. "Oh, please. You don't let up with the act, do you?"

"And the act is?" he asked as he turned to walk down the corridor. "How's the leg?"

"The leg's fine." Helen followed. "I meant the vampire act. The reckoning. You make me sound like I'm going to undergo a gothic horror change any minute now and will turn into the undead."

Armando slid an amused glance in her direction. A small smile played on his lips. "That's why I like you, Helen. You're funny and scary at the same time."

"*I* am funny and scary? Haha. Have you looked in the mirror lately?" Hell mocked back.

"Oh yes. Mirror, mirror on the wall, I say, and you know what? It answers back sometimes."

She darted a quick look back at him. Sometimes, she wasn't sure whether he was serious or not. "And what does it say?" she asked casually.

"Here's Room 18."

Armando pressed some buttons and the door unlocked with a click. It was dark inside. The only source of light was from the two-way mirror, coming through from the other side of the observation room. Helen stared at the scene for a long moment.

"That's Heath with one of the Cummings," she said.

"The female half. Caught by our Number Nine. Unfortunately, her husband escaped and we want him here, too."

There was no sound coming in from the other side,

even though Heath was speaking. He looked different, somehow, from when she'd met him in the truck. Then he turned and looked in their direction for a second. Helen blinked. His eyes—they were so cold compared to that melting puppy-dog gaze to which she'd been introduced earlier.

"Want to turn up the volume?" Armando asked.

She would love to hear what was being said but that wasn't why she was here. Armando first. Then, if there was time, Heath. And Jed—she wanted to know whether her mistake had cost him his target.

She shook her head. "I'm feeling more tired by the minute. I want to talk to you first, Chang. And please be as pithy as you can because I really, really don't want to fall asleep at your most interesting revelations."

She pulled out the bottle in her pocket and poured out two capsules. She popped them into her mouth.

Armando chuckled. "There's a certain irony here, I think, to be interrogated at the interrogation sector. There's a water fountain to your left."

"No doubt you're doing this on purpose to amuse yourself," Helen noted, as she went to get herself a drink.

"That, too, but I was serious about the cameras. You don't want your downtime to be recorded by the COMCEN cameras, do you? It'll be studied by every medical intern in the facility."

"What, they've never seen a woman fall asleep before? Or are you suggesting I'm really going to change into a vampire of sorts?" Helen joked, wiping her mouth with the back of her hand. There was a short silence. She sniffed and added, "Come on, Chang. I need info here. What happens next?"

He sighed. "It's almost here," he whispered. "Just don't fight it when it comes and it'll be less so."

"When what comes, and less what?" she asked impatiently.

"I don't know for you. Besides the pain and sleepiness, I mean," Armando said. "The drug inhibits and when it stops inhibiting, your brain tries to double everything it thinks your body is missing. There's a chemistry imbalance and wham! You're in a lot of trouble."

Helen frowned. She turned and watched Heath touch the face of the woman he was interviewing. "Is he trying to seduce her?" she asked. "I don't think that'll work when the woman is worried about her husband, you know."

Armando glanced at the couple for a few moments. "All information has a price. All traitors have a price. She might give her body up for freedom. And if she does, what else would she give up? Maybe the possible location of her husband?"

"And that's what Heath does? He seduces prisoners?" Helen asked slowly.

"Not necessarily. He likes to play with their minds. Everything's an illusion, as usual."

She was mesmerized by Heath's hands. They were massaging the woman's head now. Boy, that would feel good on her at this moment; she was beginning to have a slight tension headache. What was he saying to her? His hand went lower and unzipped the back of the woman's dress. Because the woman's back was toward her, Hell couldn't see her expression—what was she thinking? She wasn't fighting him. If it were her, she'd be kicking Heath's ass. But those hands. He was massaging the back of the woman's neck now. That *would* feel so good. She thought about Hades massaging her neck in a similar way when she was tense. That led her to thinking about Hades' hands, which wasn't good, because that further led her to think about what Hades' hand had done to her...

"Helen," Armando's voice cut in. "Look at me."

She did, startled that she had forgotten he was there. "What?"

"How long has it been since you had sex?"

"What?" she asked again, not sure why he was bringing that up.

"Because what Heath's doing to that woman is turning you on plenty, so much so you have the horniest look on your face. I know when a woman's longing for some pleasure."

"What?" She felt stupid but that was all she could say at the moment. "What are you talking about?"

"Answer me first, how long since you had sex? Because if it's been a while, your body chemistry is just about to overcompensate your needs. Let me demonstrate." Armando moved closer. He reached out in the semidarkness and trailed a hand up Helen's thigh. At the small gasp she let out, he nodded. "You see? You're sensitive to my touch." He came even closer and added, "That's your reckoning, my dear, which is a lot better than mine."

"I...don't know...what you're talking...about," Helen said obstinately. But she suddenly felt flushed with fever.

"I'll prove it to you," Armando said, and kissed her.

Helen burst into flame. Or at least, that was how it felt. Every sense zeroed in on the touch of his lips moving against hers. It was as if she had been cold for a very long time and had now found a source of heat.

She opened her mouth and kissed him back. His tongue danced with hers sensuously and he moved even closer, his hands on her hips, pulling her hard against his body. She twined her arms around his neck, dug her fingers in that long hair, desperately pulling him even nearer. The heat surrounded her, softening the edge of the tension headache, and she gave in to the tactile pleasure of his caresses for a few minutes.

It didn't feel right—wanting a man so desperately so suddenly—but she found she had no control at all. She wanted the kiss to go on; she wanted to feel him hard against her. She wanted that heat that was spreading like slow hot lava inside her, moving downward, following his hands as they squeezed her buttocks lightly, as they moved down some more to part her legs. Everywhere he touched, the heat stayed and grew.

Armando broke off the kiss. "I want you," he said thickly, "but is this what you want?"

All Helen wanted was his lips back where they were. "I feel hot all over. Kiss me some more," she demanded.

He sighed. "I was right, wasn't I? You haven't had sex in a long time." His slow sinuous caresses stopped, even though he still held her against his body. She could feel him hard and hot against her lower stomach. "We could continue, Hell. I'd be too happy to oblige you, but you might not be a happy camper when it's over, especially if you have a boyfriend."

"Why?" She could barely think, even though logic was telling her that she shouldn't be feeling like this so suddenly. All she wanted—she struggled with the urge to reach down to touch him—was to find out whether that part burning against her was really that sizzling hot. "Armando, how do I stop this?"

"I don't know. When your body decides it's back in balance, I guess."

"What do you do when it happens to you?" She pulled away from him and his hands dropped, freeing her. She wrapped her arms around herself, the loss of heat almost unbearable. She had expected pain, but this—she was totally flummoxed. "Is that why you don't tell the medics what's happening to you? That you get to feel like this, that all you want to do is…is…"

Helen waved her hand impatiently. Saying it crudely was too close to the truth. He was right. She would really be mad at herself if she let this control her.

Armando shook his head. "I told you, the serum is different for everyone. I don't go through what you're experiencing, Hell. I have…normal male needs. I suffer from…" He shook his head again. "Regardless, it's pretty obvious what you suffer from. Like I said, I'm happy to oblige."

"No, thanks," Helen said, licking her lips, desperately trying to ignore how sensitive they felt. "I think I'd better cut this meeting short before I—"

She glanced over at the two-way mirror and was surprised to see the room on the other side empty. Had she been so lost in one kiss that she didn't see two people leaving a room? That shocked her, that she could be distracted so easily.

"When did they leave?" she wondered aloud.

"Five or ten minutes after we started," Armando replied. He hadn't attempted to come closer to her again. "You weren't paying attention. I like that. And if you don't leave very soon, I'm going to have to seduce you. Then Alice in Wonderland is going to be all grown up by the time I'm done with you."

"Armando, you're a jerk. A really sexy jerk at the moment but still a jerk," Helen told him.

"And turning you on, nonetheless. What a pity about honor and all that. I really need to learn to overcome that problem." He sighed again. "Better go, Hell. We'll talk again when you've slept this off."

Sleep this off? He had to be kidding, right? Sleep was the furthest thing from her mind right now. "Okay, since you won't tell me what your reckoning, or whatever that term you used, is, at least tell me how you deal with it. Besides going to Dr. Kirkland. I really don't feel like telling him I'm in this state."

"Kiss me and I'll tell you what I do."

He truly was a bastard. "You're trying to make me lose control," she accused. "I thought you were being honorable."

"It's good to know the new anointed toy has weaknesses," Armando whispered. He took a few steps toward her. "Besides, I'm constantly fighting this honor thing. Most inconvenient. One kiss and I'll tell you my secret."

"Tell me now and I'll kiss you," Helen said. Never trust jerks. "That way, I'll know you've kept the bargain."

"Okay, I'll play along. My secret is simple." His hands came up and trapped her face between them. He kissed her softly once, his tongue tracing a fiery path from her lips to her neck. Helen bit her lips to stop the moan that threatened to escape, as she fought to pay attention to his words. He was speaking deliberately softly, playing with her senses. He bit her earlobe as he whispered, "It's illusion, remember? When I feel my pain, I go back to the source of my illusion. Where's yours, Helen? Where do you go where you can sort of disappear for a while, where you can get your satisfaction by tricking your brain?"

The CAVE. She had to go to the CAVE and...

"Are you him?" she asked, closing her eyes, wanting the heat to go on.

"I can be him if you want me to." His lips were close to hers again and tempting, very tempting.

She shook her head. Hades would have had her stripped naked here by now without any qualms. He had no honor. Armando Chang wasn't Hades.

This time Armando's kiss was firmer, more demanding. She couldn't help herself. She kissed him back. Each stroke of his tongue sent trills of pleasure down her spine. She didn't object when he pulled her closer again, his hands roaming her back freely, pulling her shirt out of her pants.

Okay, so the man had limited honor. For some reason, he'd changed his mind and was now intending to continue with his earlier seduction. His hands touched her bare skin and she almost screamed at the heat enveloping her. Hands—Hades touching her—now is *not* the time to think about Hades' hands, girl. It was too late. Heat and desire, all mixed up with the memory of Hades' hands in her pants, giving her what she needed. She wanted to take her clothes off. She had to leave before...

The sound of the door opening interrupted her wildly careening thoughts. The light came on. Releasing her lips, Armando lifted his head.

"Ah, I wondered how long it'd take before you decided enough was enough," he said mildly. Helen peered dazedly around Armando. Jed—Number Nine—stood at the doorway. She put a hand to her back and pulled her shirt down. That man seemed bent on appearing when she wasn't looking her best.

"What are you doing, Armando?" Jed asked quietly.

Armando's hands dropped to his sides. "Pretending to be the Prince of Darkness," he glibly replied. "Showing Agent Roston here a thing or two. Making you appear. I've been very busy, as you can tell."

"Don't you have somewhere to go, Agent Roston?" Jed asked politely. "I need to talk to Armando privately."

She would have stayed if she hadn't felt that any moment now she would lose control of her legs and she would end up in a pile at this man's feet again. That was all she needed.

"I was just going," she informed him and disentangled herself from Armando. Limping past, she couldn't resist bringing up the same subject from their last meeting. "Want to time me to my next destination?"

Jed's silver gaze stabbed hers. "It's easy to find you," he said, looking back at Armando, who had flopped down lazily onto one of the seats, "when you're so easily distracted."

Ouch. Hell glanced back. Armando smiled and shrugged. Had he really been trying to distract her? From what? She looked back at Jed. Or whom? At the moment, she was too muddled to try to figure this out. She had better go before she decided to do what was an inexplicable temptation at the moment. She wanted to walk over to Jed and mess up that perfectly combed hair and twist that errant lock across his forehead around her finger. She had to clench her hand to stop herself.

"Still distracted, aren't you?"

Helen blinked. "About what?"

"How long has it been since you slept, Miss Roston?" Jed asked softly. "Forty-eight, fifty-some hours? Your mind is showing signs of exhaustion and your body is catching up. I suggest you return to your quarters and get Dr. Kirkland to help you to get ready for bed, like a good little girl."

"Oh, she's ready to go to bed," Armando said.

Helen ignored Armando's chuckle. "The operation is finished and I can do what I like," she told him. Good little girl? Who did he think he was? Had it really been that long since she had slept?

"Then do it, so the rest of us can finish our jobs."

She stared defiantly at those silver eyes. "I'm sorry you weren't able to apprehend both the targets. I'll help you find the missing man."

"I don't need you to do my job. And now, if you'll excuse us?" He addressed Armando, "You didn't interrupt Number Eight like you were cued to do."

"I was…distracted. Can you send me to bed now, too?" Armando asked, amusement in his voice.

Jed turned and looked pointedly at Helen. Okay, she got the message. This was man-to-man private. She left the room and closed the door, wondering why she felt so prickly toward this one commando. After all, he'd shown up at the right time twice already. Both times, it seemed, she'd delayed his royal highness from some important task.

She shouldn't have mentioned about having finished her mission. After all, that gave him the opening to remind her that he still had his to do, and she was partially to blame for that. Okay, more than partially. If she hadn't made him lose time going back down the elevator, he could have had both the Cummings in custody by now.

Instead, only the woman was caught and now they had to interrogate her to find out where her husband could be hiding. A whole lot of work lay ahead for other people and it made Helen feel bad that she was to blame.

She had to get these overwhelming sensations under control somehow before she got back to work. Sleep. She knew she would just be lying in bed if she went to her quarters. The idea of having Dr. Kirkland and staff touching her right now made her want to puke. No, she had to tire herself out, get her mind off sex, then head to the CAVE. Armando said he tricked his mind into believing he was back in balance. She had to find out how he did it.

First…she thought of it a moment, then nodded. Yeah, she would go swimming. A couple of long and slow laps alone would take the edge off. Maybe she would sit in the hot tub for a few minutes and relax. Her injured leg would probably thank her for it.

The silent vibration of her cell phone interrupted her thoughts. She checked her message. Dr. Kirkland wanted to know whether she was okay and to make sure she got to bed soon.

Helen smiled. She hadn't had so many men wanting her in bed in a while. Her smile disappeared. Wasn't that the reason for her current dilemma? According to Armando, her body was overcompensating. All last year, she'd ignored her emotional and physical needs while in training. She had a healthy sex drive normally but she hadn't… She frowned. When was the last time…? She sighed. Pathetic. She could just imagine Dr. Kirkland's face if she text-messaged him: Super-soldier-spy needs sex for food.

Sixteen

He put down his dictionary. He'd forgotten one thing about dangerous women. They hated not being in control. And when they felt their control being threatened, they tended to be extremely obstinate. Their independence both irritated and amused him. It also had the perverse effect of turning him on.

Sleep-deprived. Nursing a leg injury. One could say Elena Rostova had had a pretty active day, from elevator-surfing, to hand-to-hand combat, to running down twelve flights of steps, to being chased by several unknown assailants and being shot with a tranquilizer.

Most of the operatives from the mission were already asleep or relaxing somewhere. None of them had had the same strenuous two days she had had. And what was she doing? She was going to take a swim.

She was being extremely obstinate about something. The look of defiance on her face told him that she suspected that he would be watching her sooner or later.

Of course he would, especially once he'd checked her sleeping quarters and found no one there.

He'd wondered how long the serum would stay in her system. In his opinion, a little too long. She should be in bed, exhausted. But there she was, larger than life on the screen, peeling off her clothes carelessly. His eyes narrowed slightly as he caught the brief wince of pain crossing her face as she pulled her pants off.

She was starting to come down. He buzzed Dr. Kirkland's line.

"Has she called you yet?" he asked.

"No, but I just text-messaged her and she sent back that she'd just taken the painkillers but was feeling fine."

"Does she even know what time of day it is?"

"I don't think her body will care, especially if she continues to fight sleep."

"She has a high tolerance for pain, then," he remarked, returning his attention to Helen. "When you talked to her, was she emotionally stable?"

"Yes, normal. Why?"

"She wasn't acting sensitive to light?"

"No, nothing similar to Armando's symptoms at all. Not yet, anyway."

"I'll call you back, Doc. Get some rest. Some of us should."

He leaned back and sipped on his drink as he watched the screen thoughtfully. She obviously didn't want to return to her quarters. Why? Was it because she didn't want Dr. Kirkland to examine her? But she wasn't hiding the pain, so what was it she didn't want Dr. Kirkland to know?

Her body gleamed in the soft light reflected by the pool. She didn't dive in, like she usually did, but sat at the tiled edge and draped her long legs over the shallow end. He watched the water slowly covering her body as she lowered herself in, lapping up her thighs, hips, narrow waist, to just below her breasts. Her eyes were closed as she stood there, not moving deeper.

He waited, his eyes feasting on her naked breasts, so white against the dark water. She was beautiful, like a water nymph, and he didn't bother to curb the desire rising hard in him. She slowly sank deeper and her long sigh sounded lush, sensuous, even through the speakers, reaching out in a secret caress. He took another sip of water. Elena Rostova might not know who he was, but she knew how to get to him.

He should be irritated. The initial plan was to let her rest, with him sleeping the same hours, letting their brain waves get in sync, and waking her up very early tomorrow and getting in another VR session. She would be rested but not a hundred percent, and still edgy from the serum in her system. The second time would be tougher because she would be prepared, so he had to initiate the attack while she was still tired. He would push her until she gave in.

He needed sleep himself. But he couldn't till she went to bed, too, not if he wanted to prepare for the next VR session.

She sighed again, a catlike purr that had nothing to do with exhaustion. His eyes narrowed slightly as he studied her. She sounded like a woman being pleasured. She wasn't swimming, just bobbing up and down in the water. Every time she pushed off the floor of the pool, her breasts teased him, wet and perky, and then they would disappear as her weight brought her back underwater, and she repeated this with her eyes closed, as if that were the most pleasurable thing to do.

His attention was riveted to her face, her sighs, her tantalizing breasts. She had never done this before. The sight made him want to join her in the pool. Naked. With her back against the wall, so he could push inside her hard. With her purrs against his ear as he molded those soft breasts in his hands.

As if she saw his fantasy in her mind, her hands reached up and massaged her nipples. Her low hum of pleasure zapped like an electric rod through him. The woman wasn't sleepy. Or tired. She was turned on.

She began swimming leisurely. Back and forth. Breaststroke, then backstroke, then breaststroke again. After the third lap, she suddenly stopped. She slapped the water hard with the palm of her hand.

"Dammit, dammit!" she murmured. "I'm too tired to swim any faster."

He cocked his head. Why was she avoiding sleep then? He watched as she pulled herself out of the pool and without picking up the towel nearby, she walked over to the hot tub.

"Very hot water," she said as she slipped in slowly, like she was in some pain with that leg.

She turned on the jets. She propped the injured leg against the jet and groaned.

Ah, that felt good to her. Her body was coming back to normal and she was, for some reason, fighting it and yet enjoying it at the same time. He had to get her alone so he could find out why for himself.

* * *

It wasn't going away. She could feel exhaustion knocking at her consciousness, and still she couldn't relax.

She must be going nuts. She was fantasizing about a virtual reality man. He wasn't real, girl. Stop thinking about him. But it was tough not to in her strangely sensitized state. Every small sensation ran across her skin like a rush of heat and air. Every movement made her squirm, left her a little breathless.

It reminded her too much of how she felt when Hades had touched her during the RV session. The more she thought of it, the more her gut tightened, as if her mind was deliberately feeding off her own feelings.

Her reaction to Armando's kiss had frightened her a little. That strange heat had charged through her system, overwhelmed her with a need for...

She shook her head. For sex? She shook her head again. She didn't want Armando, not in her head. His kiss and touch had somehow evoked the same intense desire she'd felt with Hades. But that was Hades manipulating her with pleasure. So what was manipulating her now?

Helen sighed. She couldn't even explain it to herself, so how was she going to do that with Dr. Kirkland? This Jacuzzi was perfect—she didn't have to move too much, and that racing currentlike feeling inside her had slowed down to a manageable crawl.

She could sleep here. And wake up a prune.

The jet of water hitting the side of her calf felt wonderful, in a pleasure-pain sort of way. The whirling hot water was a different kind of pleasure—slow and lulling, giving her body a gentle all-over massage. But it wasn't enough. She was still edgy inside. She knew the moment she stopped the whirlpool, that sensation would return.

"Mind if I join you?" A voice mixed in with the noise from the hot tub jets.

Helen opened her eyes. It was Heath, in swimming trunks. Didn't these commandos go to sleep? And why did they all have to look so damn good? In her current state, that was so not helping.

She shrugged. What could she say? Go away, I don't want anyone near me? Besides, the guy had saved her life today. Or yesterday. She frowned; she couldn't tell anymore.

Heath lowered himself into the tub. "Usually this place is empty when I come here," he said.

"I don't even know what time it is," Helen told him. "So am I interrupting your swim time?"

Those brown eyes, she noted, were back to that melt-me expression again, but she couldn't help remembering the other look she had seen recently, the one he'd used on the prisoner. Layers, these guys all had layers.

"No," he said. His eyes traveled to the water swirling around her shoulders. "You shouldn't be here."

"Why? Is there a schedule that marks this place closed at this hour?" she asked with a smile. "Besides, I just told you I don't even know the time."

His smile was slow, his teeth very white in the shadows. "You shouldn't be here naked then," he amended.

There was that. "You see, we could ignore that part and just have a nice conversation about what time it is," she mocked, "but no, you have to say the obvious.

Besides, if you were a gentleman, you wouldn't have joined me. You would have said, 'I'll come back later.'"

Helen leaned back against her tub, trying to be comfortable again. Maybe if she kept talking, she would distract herself. "Tell me, Heath, do you come here for your downtime after work? You were working, weren't you? Or you would be off resting with all the others."

"There's work and there's work," he said, his eyes steady.

"Just like there's touching and there's touching?" she asked, arching her eyebrows, reminding him of their earlier banter. "You sure have a way with words."

He leaned back, too, and surveyed her lazily for a few moments. The spray from the moving water had dampened his hair into dark tendrils. A thin gold chain with a small pendant gleamed against his wet chest. The pendant had an unusual shape and color, but she couldn't really make out what it looked like.

"We could talk, but what are you going to do when you have to leave?" he asked.

She looked at him seriously. "What if you have to leave first?"

His lips curved again. "I'm a very patient man."

"And do you always get what you want?" she asked lightly. Heath was here for something. She would bet her next chocolate milkshake on it.

"Most of the time."

"Even if you have to kill to get it?" she asked.

Distraction in the midst of attraction. It was something she had never done before. Most of the time, when she had to distract a target, it had been during an operation, or she was being polite to unwanted interest, or she had to be creative to get out of trouble. This time, she was doing it to distract herself.

"Sometimes." His tone of voice didn't change. "You had a long day and then some, even by COS standards. Why aren't you in bed, Helen?"

"You know, men have been asking me about that all night," she quipped.

"The last time I saw you, you'd been tranqued. And your leg was injured. The serum should be about out of your system by now, yet you don't act like you're in real pain. Either you have miraculous healing powers or you're on some kind of drugs."

"I took some painkillers," Helen admitted, "and it could be why I can't sleep just yet. And what's your excuse for not being in bed?"

"You should have come to me. I'm very good at taking pain away," he said, then gave her that sexy smile again. "I'm trained in pressure points."

Pressure points. And he avoided giving an answer to her question very nicely. "Do you use that in your job a lot, this talent with pressure points?" she asked.

"When I have to."

"Like tonight?" she asked. "I saw you from the observation room."

"I know."

"Do you use it during interrogation?" She searched his expression. That smile was gone and his eyes had the same flat look she had seen previously. "It's not just for taking away pain, is it? You can give pain by pressing on the right pressure points. I've seen it done before."

He was silent as he continued watching her. He raised

one hand and pressed the button on the side of the tub. The rushing jets stopped and the noise fizzled into a tense silence as the water around their bodies slowed its movement. The bubbles were slowly disappearing and it wouldn't be long before he could see through the water.

"Coward," she mocked softly. "You don't like my question so you're now trying to punish me by embarrassing me."

Heath leaned forward, his gaze hooded. "Affirmative," he said.

He moved a little closer toward her and she felt his hand on her leg. "Heath," she warned, not sure where this was leading to. An image of a hand slipping into her pants floated in her head... Helen pushed the thought firmly away.

"Relax," Heath murmured. "I'm just going to check your leg. Trust me, if I were planning to do more, I would have come in here naked."

His hands lifted her leg above the water. He touched the bruise that ran down the side of her thigh to her calf and gave a soft whistle. "Are you sure you don't feel more than a little pain?"

Helen closed her eyes. There was pain when she had to move the leg. But the moment things were still around her, like now, no noisy water, no jets massaging her legs, no movement... She shivered as his fingers trailed the side of her leg. It was starting again.

"Are you cold?" he asked.

She shook her head, not opening her eyes. She bit her lower lip as he applied some pressure with his forefingers under her knee. He moved closer, bending her leg higher as he pressed harder.

"It's beginning to hurt," she told him, opening her eyes.

He was watching her face. "There are many pressure points by the sciatic nerve that runs down your leg. There's one, high up your thigh. If you apply pressure on it, your limb will go numb a while, long enough for someone to give your leg a deep massage. The whirlpool jets did an okay job, but it's not going deep enough."

"Okay," she said.

"Then maybe you can go to sleep," he said, matter-of-factly, like a doctor to a patient. "You shouldn't let pain take away your sleep."

"Okay," she said again. If he thought it was the pain, let him. "As long as it's not more drugs. I'm getting a little tired of drugs right now."

"Understandable," he said. "Tell Dr. Kirkland you need a physical therapist who knows more than regular shiatsu."

"At this hour? We're not living in a five-star hotel, you know," Helen said wryly. She regarded him for a second. His appearance here was too coincidental. Had he sought her out or had someone sent him? "We're being watched, is that it? That's why you aren't doing it yourself."

Heath looked at her coolly. "This is COMCEN. There's always a possibility that someone's watching," he said, with a shrug. "But that's not it. You don't want me to touch you right now, Helen. I can feel your tension in your leg. I can't fix it if your muscles fight me."

She wasn't fighting him; she was fighting herself. A part of her felt dangerously close to coming apart, and she wasn't sure what it was yet, only that it made her feel vulnerable and that she didn't like the feeling.

It was as if a curtain was in front of her and if she peered behind it, all she would find was impenetrable darkness. It made her edgy, unsure of herself. All she could think of was Hades. She wanted his touch. The memory of how he'd pleasured her tightened her body even more.

Nuts. Bonkers. She wanted something that was all in her head.

"I can't relax for some reason," Helen said. That was putting it mildly, but she felt compelled to give an explanation. The man was, after all, trying to help her. "Sorry. It could be because I'm naked and you're not, but I'm not bashful, so that's not the real reason either."

Heath smiled again, and this time it was a wicked grin, as if a very naughty thought had crossed his mind. "I know the reason why," he said as his hands continued kneading her sore leg. "I have all the proof right here under my fingertips and it has nothing to do with your leg."

Helen had to smile back. The man was sexy as all get-out when he smiled like that. And he had very talented hands. "People read minds and you read nerves and muscles?" she teased.

He nodded. "They don't lie. You're tensing even more the deeper I massage. Plus, it's just going to tighten up again once you get out of the whirlpool. No more swimming tonight or you'll cramp up. I can feel it knotting under my fingers. See?" He stopped. His gaze was hooded, contemplative. "Helen? Try not to hold your breath like that or you'll pass out."

Helen ejected the air from her lungs. He knew. He didn't say it, but he knew that it had nothing to do with the pain in her leg. It had everything to do with the vibration of the water as his hands moved up and down her leg, each small lap hitting her skin sensuously, over and over, until she could barely breathe. She had to tighten her insides just to keep from groaning out loud. A massage? Relaxation was far, far away. Not even in the same zip code.

"Someone told me you're Number Eight in the commando hierarchy," Helen said. "Tell me, Heath, is this part of your job, giving a prognosis for your target?"

"Flyboy's right. Very little gets past you."

Actually, it just occurred to her that every one of the commandos she'd gotten to know had, in a way, been evaluating her. "Let me guess. Flyboy's a pre-serum assessment. Armando fancies himself as my warning or something. Alex Diamond's an observer. I'm too tired to go on." Helen gave a shrug and drawled, "Save me some energy, sweetheart. You tell me."

Heath's chest shook with silent laughter. She watched as the rivulets of water formed by the heated water trickled slowly down his damp skin. She quickly looked up and saw that he was watching her.

"Following your line of thought, I must be the post-serum assessment," he said, chuckling softly. "Maybe there's some truth in that. We're all curious about the newest member and making our own judgments of your…skills."

"Fair enough." She herself was curious about them all. "So tell me your assessment."

His hand on her knee started kneading again. "I know enough about drugs and their effects on the body and mind," he said, his voice so low she had to lean forward a little to catch his words. "Add a bit of knowledge about nerves and muscle control, and a target can be rendered very cooperative within minutes, don't you agree?"

They stared at each other as his hand continued its rhythmic massage. Every few moments Helen felt his finger or thumb pressing a spot by the right side of her thigh. She didn't stop him.

"This serum's effect on you," he continued, not taking his eyes off her, "is of interest to me. I'd like to try SYMBIOS 2 one day and see what it does. Unlike Armando, who's sensitive to light whenever he uses it, you're extremely sensitive to touch. I can tell that you're growing tired, both from exhaustion and from fighting whatever it is that you're fighting. My assessment? You're either going to go crazy like Armando when he can't sleep, or you'll find a way out of it. Whatever the problem is, let somebody know while you're experiencing it."

"Why?" She preferred to tell them later, when she didn't feel like this. Yes, it was obstinate of her, but right now she didn't particularly give a fig.

His hands moved a few inches higher. Something dark slipped into his eyes, changing his expression. "It's coming to a point where you can't control it. Your muscles are clenching so tightly you can't even relax. What is it, Helen? What do you want? Tell me."

His voice and his eyes were mesmerizing. His hand underwater was hypnotic. It made her want to confide, tell him her secrets. Helen pulled away. These COS commandos were dangerous, she reminded herself. Trained to seduce and trained to kill. None of them, it appeared, had a line they wouldn't cross. And they were all testing to see how far she would go with them.

"An interesting debriefing session," a voice interrupted. They both turned and looked up. T. walked in, towel in hand. "Derek said I might find you here, Hell."

Heath stretched out his arms over the sides of the tub. "Excellent timing," he remarked in a dry voice.

Seventeen

Note to self. When in trouble, ask self WWTD—what would T. do?

Because T. had just walked in there and gotten her operative literally out of hot water. Heath had just sat there in quiet mockery, nodding now and then at T.'s questions, as she handed Helen the towel. T. had then moved to his side.

"I heard that Julie Cummings likes whips and chains," T. had murmured.

That one sentence had succeeded in Heath taking his eyes off Helen and turning his head to stare up at T.

"Is that right?" he asked, in a rhetorical way.

"Whips, chains, and just enough pain," T. had continued, leaning a bit closer. "I made a bet with Jed that you wouldn't be able to handle her, that he'd have to take over and find out her husband's location himself."

"Is that so?" he'd asked softly.

T. had smiled bewitchingly. "Yes, that's so."

Helen had watched them as she secured her towel.

T. was her mentor and obviously knew how to handle these commandos. Second note to self. Learn from the best.

Not long after, T. was helping her into the elevator to her quarters.

Third note to self. Never get into the spa tub naked at this hour of the night. Or day. What the hell time was it?

Helen gave a mental sigh of frustration. She was limping more now. She supposed she was in for a lecture from both T. and Dr. Kirkland.

T. glanced at her. "Overkill has always been my favorite nickname for you," she remarked. "Or maybe it's Hellbent."

"Please, I really don't want to have a tongue-lashing right now," Hell said, as she gingerly stepped into the elevator.

She could feel T.'s probing gaze on her, taking in her condition, analyzing, making conclusions. She knew there was concern in there, too, but T. was, first and foremost, her chief. Their friendship was second.

"I should be saying, 'What were you thinking?' But I think that's the problem here. You aren't your usual self, not without sleep, not with you dealing with remote-viewing downtime as well as exhaustion."

"And you're going to ask next, 'Why aren't you in bed?'" Helen joked. Everyone was asking her that, so she might as well do it for them. "I'm trying to get there, T. I can't sleep right now."

"So you'd rather hang around and let each of them test you?"

"Why are they testing me?" Hell leaned against the elevator wall for support. She was feeling both hot and cold at the same time and had to work at concentrating on T.'s words instead of the sensations.

"Because they are predators, darling, and predators can smell a good hunt. They're also all males and you were in their domain yesterday and left your mark everywhere. And, now, you're at your most vulnerable, and each of them thinks he can get you before the other one does."

Helen stared at T. for a moment. "You worked with them for two years. Pretty closely. Did they do that to you?"

T. shook her head. "I came in at their most vulnerable, after a few of their own were killed, and both our agencies were scrambling a bit. Different circumstances, Hell. I'm not one of them, but you're going to be part of their team. I never used this serum. Some of them have and they know some things they can't or won't share with me. Obviously you're having certain effects from it or you wouldn't be stupid enough to be in the same room with Number Eight while he's in interrogation mode." The "pling" of the elevator announced their arrival at Helen's floor. T. offered Helen her shoulder. "Need help?"

Helen noticed that T. didn't attempt to touch her. She placed a hand on her chief's shoulder for support. She suddenly realized that touching didn't make her feel; it was being touched that was causing the problems. T. seemed to understand that.

"Thank you," Helen said, and she didn't mean just for the offer of support.

"You're welcome."

"That doesn't mean I couldn't have handled Heath," Helen said as they walked slowly.

"Of course," T. said with a small smile. "Now tell me why you think you can't sleep when you look like you're falling over from exhaustion."

"Actually, I've only been feeling the exhaustion the last fifteen minutes. Before that, the pain and tiredness were barely there. I was hoping the swimming would accelerate it and maybe it did, but the other stuff hadn't gone away."

"What other stuff?"

Helen told her about the strange sensations, how she had been overwhelmed by them, and how she had to really focus on conversation or physical activity to take the edge off. T. listened silently, not asking questions, as she continued to try to explain what was happening, including what Armando had told her.

They reached Helen's quarters and Helen keyed in the access codes. The grayness of the surroundings was, for once, comforting. The color had been found to be suitable for remote-viewing activity because it behaved like white noise to the senses, cutting out mental interference. Whether it was true or a bunch of BS, it was working for Helen just enough that she felt some control returning. Just a little bit.

"They're going to wake up Dr. Kirkland now that you're back in quarters," T. said. "When he calls, let him know I'm here supervising you and that it won't be necessary for him or his assistants to help you. They can monitor your vitals and do all that brain wave entrainment stuff from their control room."

Oh, good. Helen nodded. That had been partly the reason for not going to bed sooner. She hadn't wanted anyone to touch her. Even in her strange mood, she'd been aware that physical contact was setting her off. T. was obviously coming to that conclusion too.

"This thing that Armando said was part of the after-effects—the reckoning—I'm thinking that he's telling the truth," T. said. "I know he's cryptic. He's like that, even before I brought him in for training."

"You brought him into CCC?" Helen asked, surprised. She pulled out a large T-shirt to sleep in from the chest of drawers by her bed.

"Yes. He isn't a full commando yet, but he's as bad as they are. But the cryptic talk, he did that before the drugs. He was, in another life, one of the many young siblings under the Triad brothers, and they all tended to learn to talk in double meanings, mostly because of the power struggles within their crime and cultural framework."

The communication module buzzed, interrupting T. It was Dr. Kirkland, his voice scratchy from sleep. Poor man. Helen felt bad that he'd had to be woken up several times because of her. She told him that T. was there to help her with setting up for sleep, and that there wasn't any need for him or Derek to come by. He agreed and told her to note down the time she activated the brain entrainment machine, just to double check with their records and reading tomorrow, and after asking her how her leg was, he bade her good-night.

"Go on, T., hearing about Armando's background helps me understand." And concentrate on getting ready, instead of getting distracted by the way her T-shirt had slid over her skin and the softness of the blanket on the bed as she busied herself turning it over. "That cart next to you with all the gadgets goes to the right side of my bed, by the way."

"Read the files tomorrow," T. told her. She pushed the cart Helen had indicated and watched as Helen poured herself a glass of water from the jug on the nightstand. "Back to what Armando told you about the body chemistry compensating once the serum is gone from the body. I think he might have your problem in a nutshell."

Helen took a long sip of water. She was thirsty suddenly. She took another gulp. Yeah, she was definitely winding down.

"If it's true, then now what?" She finished her drink and set the glass down for another refill. "I'm getting tired. Very quickly."

"Maybe it'll go away after you sleep."

On cue, Helen yawned. Maybe she could finally sleep after all. "I hope so."

"We'll talk more about this tomorrow when you can think more clearly. Perhaps comparing your vital stats pre- and post-operation will provide Dr. Kirkland with a clue. Do you want me to talk to him for you?"

Helen looked up in surprise. She hadn't seen T. so protective in ages. Of course, it'd been two years since she had actually been around T. during an operation. Her chief was probably worried that her being out of the field for so long had made her a wimp.

"No, I'll do that," Helen said. "I just didn't feel like being handled by anyone tonight, but once this condition goes away, it'll be okay. I'm really fine."

T. studied her for a moment. "Ready for bed, then? Tell me what I have to do with these things," she said, gesturing to the equipment on the tray.

"Look scary, don't they?" Helen asked, with a small

grin. "I put on these tabs on my pulse points. That's the ear plugs for the brain entrainment machine. As soon as I'm ready, that's the switch and once it's powered, it'll transmit information to their control room. I need you to record down the first reading so they can pinpoint where to start their comparison from their charts."

T. handed her the tab transmitters and watched her fix them on different parts of her body. "Before I go, I want back the ring I gave you," she said.

Aha. Now she knew why T. had been looking for her. She pulled off the ring and handed it to T. "Are you going to tell me why you gave it to me in the first place?" she asked casually.

T. pocketed the ring. "After your rest. I would tell you tonight, but you'll be asleep by the time I'm done. You truly look like hell now."

"Thanks." She'd probably feel like hell when she woke up, too. If she weren't getting so tired, she'd laugh at her own pun. "If you talk to my monitor before I do, tell him the RV session details were exact as we saw them. I've made a recording with the microdigital. Give it to him."

"Okay."

Helen smiled sleepily. "Gotcha. You do talk to him. In fact, he probably sent you here tonight. Everyone's been trying to get me to—" she yawned loudly "—bed. He was probably tired of being kept waiting. Men are so impatient."

T. smiled back. She turned the switch on and after a minute, wrote down all the readings on the chart. She turned back to Helen. "Good night."

Helen nodded. After T. had turned off the lights and

left, she kicked off the sheet. The feel of it was distracting. Concentrate on the sound waves. Sleep. She found herself drifting off. Her T-shirt was so damn bothersome. She thought about removing it. She lifted a hand tiredly, tugging at the material. It brushed across her nipples. She moaned softly as she fell asleep.

He walked into the water, determined to get to her. She was naked, her breasts bobbing in and out as she bounced up and down. Her eyes were closed as he approached her, walking deeper and deeper in the water.

Just when he reached her, her eyes opened. Pretty hazel eyes, the kind that changed colors depending on her mood. Right now, they reflected back the green of the water, mysterious and tempting.

He wanted her a lot closer. He grasped her by the waist and easily lifted her high enough so he could examine those beautiful breasts at eye level. So beautiful. He had wanted to have those nipples in his mouth the first time she'd stripped naked. He leaned in and took one of them delicately between his teeth. His tongue flicked at it gently. And just like that he was hard as a rock.

She moaned and squirmed closer against him, burying his face into her softness as he moved toward the shallow end of the pool. He wanted to bury something else. A lot deeper. Impatiently, he pushed her against the cool tiles of the swimming pool wall, still holding her by the waist. Her thighs parted willingly, wrapping themselves around his torso.

His palms slid over her wet bare thighs, his thumbs forming an inverted V right above her clitoris. She sighed and shivered, waiting.

He gently sucked at the nipple in his mouth. So delicious. He slid his thumbs lower and parted her lips below, readying her. Hot. He could feel the surge of deep need pushing up, insisting—demanding—to be inside her now. She moaned again as his thumbs ruthlessly readied her, using her slick wetness to torment and pleasure.

"Yesssss…" she gasped as he lowered her back into the water, pushing his erection intimately against her heat. He positioned them both so he could enter, and as he pushed her relentlessly down on his erection, his thumb added a touch of pressure on her sensitive nub. She moaned throatily into his ear as she slid lower, as he went deeper inside her. He shuddered at the feel of her softness, and pushed her down harder.

"Hades!" she gasped.

He opened his eyes. Darkness. His breathing was erratic. Sweet Jesus. He kicked the sheet off his body. The cool air hit the heat between his legs. He reached down and fisted his penis, painfully hard and erect.

He was so damn close to coming he actually felt light-headed from the need to finish off. He squeezed the head of his penis, willing the fierce raging need down. Not working.

The urgency to finish off where his erotic dream had ended fought his usual ironclad will. He hadn't had that kind of dream about a specific woman in a long time. Helen's naked body in the water was imprinted in his brain tonight. The way she had fingered her nipples and moaned. That was why he dreamed about it. He'd wanted to do exactly what he had dreamed—suck on the nipples, play with her pussy till she moaned like that for him.

He felt his erection harden again, lengthening, and pleasure shot through him as he lazily slid his hand down, his eyes half closing as he thought about Helen's breasts and being inside her, and up again, in long measured strokes, the way he'd wanted to move inside her. She had felt so…damn…good. His eyes closed as he concentrated on his surging pleasure. If he were really inside her now, he would grind against her hard. Like this. And like this. He would bury himself so deep inside her, she'd moan his name out.

"Hades!"

He stopped, his desire raging at the second interruption. *That* wasn't his fantasy. That— he turned his head to look at the monitor by his bed—came from Helen's quarters.

Hades. That was what had woken him up from his dreams. She'd called out the name by which she knew him. Of course he wouldn't have addressed his own self as Hades. She had called him in her sleep.

He frowned. She'd called him in *his* dream? He reached out, turning the knobs by the monitor. The microeye in Helen's quarters was equipped with night-vision sensors; he activated it so he could zoom in on her sleeping figure.

She was tossing around, still asleep, moaning softly. She was pulling at her shirt, as if she was trying to take it off, except that she wasn't sitting up.

He glanced at the wavelength reading of her state of sleep showing on top of the screen. REM. She was dreaming. They had both been dreaming. He frowned. He reached up and touched the tabs attached to his forehead. Was she dreaming his dream? And he'd somehow woken up and she hadn't. Impossible.

Was she really having an erotic dream, too? Or, did she somehow invade his own dream? His other hand was still around his hard-on. His gaze went back to the monitor. The image was shadowy but he could see her hand moving over her breasts. What if he— He slowly pulled on his erection, easily building his need back up stroke by stroke. This time he was more calculating, envisioning Elena's wet breasts in his mouth again, and her long, long legs wrapped around his waist as he took her, playing with his own pleasure until dots of light obscured his sight of the monitor. And still he wouldn't let himself come as he continued watching Helen in her sleep.

She was moving even more agitatedly now, kicking away the sheet covering her legs. Was she dreaming that she was in that swimming pool, with him inside her? The hungry heat between his own legs was demanding release. He squeezed the head again, giving in to the torturous feeling of elusive pleasure, fighting the urgency to finish off. His whole body seized up with sensation, his thigh muscles tightening. Need and desire roared through him and he let it, not moving his hand.

A high-pitched whine came from the monitor. It was Elena. "No…!" she murmured, her voice a little desperate, as if it was she who wasn't allowed to reach the peak, too.

He'd known about her sensitive condition as the serum's hold on her body slowly dissipated, had wanted to test her tomorrow during a RV session. It had made sense—her body chemistry was overcompensating.

And still he didn't want to believe it was possible. He waited a moment, taking control of his breathing. He looked at the monitor again. Brain wave scan verging between REM and theta. Theta was the state desired for remote viewing. A glance at Elena's shadowy form showed her lying on her back, very still, her hand still grasping her T-shirt.

He noticed, for the first time, that she wasn't wearing any underwear. His whole attention zoomed in on to that part of her as he slowly masturbated. Deliberately, slowly, like the way he liked sex. No underwear. His hand tightened. He'd seen her naked before but he'd never had the leisure of her lying still for his examination. She was always moving around and he had been more captivated by her saucy sexuality.

Her hand started that impatient pulling again, as his own pleasure grew and he edged closer to orgasm. Testing his theory was going to kill him. He hadn't played with himself like this since he was in training.

His gaze fixed on Helen's moving legs. Part them. With his own legs. Put this inside her. His back arched as he stopped himself from coming. On the screen, Helen's soft screech reverberated in his head, testing his usual control. The sound was sexual, emitted by a woman in the throes of desire. His orgasm hovered over him like a demanding sergeant and his whole body sagged from the need to obey the order to continue. But his will was stronger.

He peeled off the tabs connected to the machine that was meant to regulate their sleep patterns. He wasn't sure how it'd happened, but somehow, he and Helen had connected on an even deeper level than intended.

He waited, but she wasn't getting out of REM and her discomfort was obvious. At this rate, she wouldn't be able to remote view tomorrow, and he needed her to find Cummings for him before the latter reached Russia. If Cummings got to Russia, he'd disappear.

Never refuse what the gods offered. He wanted her. Now. And he was tired of jerking off when it came to Elena Rostova.

He sat up in bed, leaned over, made some adjustments to Helen's brain entrainment readings, and shut off the controls to the monitor with a password. There was no other microeye in her quarters but the one he'd put there himself. He could go there now. No one would disturb them once he'd keyed in his access code. They knew better.

Helen heard herself moaning before she came awake. The sound wave from the brain entrainment machine seemed louder. An intense need filled her as she battered through sleep and sensation. Her back arched up as another frisson of pleasure rocketed through her, making her gasp.

Frustration ate at her as she realized that she was cheated out of finishing her dream. She had been with a man but she couldn't remember his face, just that he was naked in water, and he had been making love to her. She remembered his mouth on her breast—his teeth— and she shivered from the memory.

The pleasure was unbelievably intimate. She had never had a wet dream before, and this one had left a raging need in her loins. She moved restlessly, half asleep and trying to chase after the lost dream.

At first she thought she'd fallen back to sleep. A hand gently grasped her by the jaw, firmly squeezing her mouth open. Something dropped in. Bitter. Familiar.

Suddenly fully awake, Helen's eyes flew wide open, her hands automatically flying up to grab the one holding her face. Big mistake. Her attacker put his weight on top of her upper body, trapping her hands. His hand clamped over her mouth and nose as she struggled.

She knew what the taste meant. She'd taken the pill several times before. She tried to kick and gasped out when pain shot up her right leg. She jerked her face violently, trying to free one of her hands.

A hand reached down between her legs. She hadn't bothered with underwear tonight. Not that it would have stopped him. It wouldn't take him long to find out that she was already in a state of arousal. Her struggles froze as her sensitivity betrayed her, and pleasure started to build. She whimpered deep in her throat, caught between anger and desire.

Her attacker leaned even more on top of her, playing with her with that one hand and deliberately forcing her breath out with his weight, he used his other hand to block her nostrils at the same time. She swallowed air, along with the melting pill. Damn, damn, damn, damn...her curses were muffled. He mocked her by biting her on the neck, silently telling her that he was in charge. She raged at herself before she went out like a light.

When she opened her eyes again, it was still very dark, and he was no longer on top of her. He was sitting by her, all shadow. He was massaging her bad leg, slowly kneading the area that was injured. It was a good kind of pain, mingled with that edgy pleasure that her sensitivity had given her for hours. She inhaled sharply as the back of his hand touched her intimately as he continued massaging. *That* was no accident. She was sure of it.

Not that she could do anything. She couldn't move. And she knew who it was sitting beside her. The back of his hand caressed her again, leisurely.

"Hades, you bastard," she breathed out. She didn't need to ask him why he was here in her room. She fought back a shudder as she felt another intimate touch. All the while, he kept working on the tight muscles of her thigh, as if he really was there to massage her sore leg.

"At your service," he acknowledged. His voice came over the sound waves projected through her earplugs, just like Dr. Kirkland sometimes communicated with her when she was getting ready for bed, except it had been altered electronically. "I heard you calling my name."

That was in her dream. Wasn't it? "Turn the light on," she ordered, straining desperately to see through the darkness.

"You can't have it all your way now, can you?" he mocked knowingly. "What if I don't have brown eyes and a big cock?"

She wanted to hear his real voice, not this soft electronically-modulated tone that was mixing with the sound waves. Of course that was why he'd given her the pill. He hadn't wanted her to know how he looked or sounded. *But he was here in person.* Her heart thudded loudly as she stared up at him hungrily.

"I'll be able to move again soon enough to do it myself," she told him.

"No," he told her. His voice was soft. "Not tonight. Not with the dose I gave you."

Helen shivered at the implication. He ran his thumbs

up and down the side of her thighs with firm pressure. Oh, Lord, that felt so good. She had known that she needed it but knew she wouldn't be able to handle some stranger touching her in her condition.

And he isn't a stranger? Her mind mocked her even as she succumbed to the magic of his care. It was different. It was Hades. Her argument had the big holes of a slice of Swiss cheese, but she didn't care. She knew those hands.

"Why are you here?" she finally had to ask, wondering whether she could actually still be dreaming, caught as she was between the pleasure still riding her and the pain in her leg.

"You woke me up with your dream."

Helen's eyes widened. "What do you mean?" she asked slowly. Was he saying that he was dreaming about—

"I was inside you and enjoying myself when you woke me up," he told her, confirming her suspicions, leaning so close now that she caught a whiff of his male scent and a hint of cologne. "You called my name, so here I am. I always finish what I start, especially when it comes to pleasuring a woman."

He stopped, and one hand moved up and cupped her intimately. Helen tried to stop the small gasp of pleasure from escaping her lips but to no avail. Her skin was still so sensitive that being touched right now was akin to torture.

His hand felt like a brand, his fingers marking her.

"Don't—" she managed to groan out, even as her body eagerly responded to the feel of his fingers. "I...it's too much."

She vaguely wondered whether he knew how she

was right now. If he was Heath—she tried to focus on the shadow, tried to remember what Heath looked like.

Hades' other hand gently pulled her right leg outwards, giving him more access, ignoring her growl of outrage. "You enjoyed this during our VR session. We're even doing this in our dreams now. Don't you enjoy the real thing?"

Too much. The knowledge that she was lying there with her legs parted and not wearing underwear filled her with hot anticipation. What was he doing? All thoughts fled as he skillfully brought the smoldering embers of frustration to a fiery burn. All thoughts, all logic, everything went out the window. She sighed as fingers parted her, just like in her dream.

But this is real, Helen. This is real. It was too late. His finger stroked her where she wanted and her need for release felt so swollen that she thought she would burst. Her eyes closed from the sheer sensual pleasure swirling through her being.

"You do like it," he whispered and after a few more strokes, he paused.

"No, don't stop," Helen breathed out quickly, so close again that she didn't care she sounded desperate.

"It has to be my way," he said. "Right now, I'm just giving you a taste while I work on your injury. A deep massage will help you walk without crutches tomorrow. You need to lie very still while I do it."

As if she could move if she'd wanted! He'd given her no choice in that matter. But there wasn't any time to argue with him. To demonstrate his promise, he started pleasuring her again, using her slick wetness to make his point. And slowing down at the wrong moment.

"Bastard," Helen panted out. "I'm going to kick your ass for this."

"Not tonight," he said. "Tonight, you're in a highly-aroused state with an injured leg. Advantage, mine."

The way he said *mine* should have pissed her off. Instead it excited her. He excited her, this shadow who knew her body so well.

She could fight him, too, if only she could think straight. The sound of a cap coming off distracted her thoughts. She heard the squish. Liquid. Lotion? He lathered her with it from thigh to calf and gave her leg a vigorous rubdown. Whatever the lotion was, it heated up and penetrated like those stinky sports gels, except without the smell, and she could feel her muscles relaxing even more.

His palm stroked up her thigh. Her heart raced as she suddenly realized his intention.

"No!"

He didn't pay any attention, rubbing her between the legs with the remaining lotion in his hand. She felt his fingers parting her, touching her already sensitive clitoris, and all around it.

"Oh…" she moaned, losing focus on the heat in her leg as another part of her started to tingle. Heat. Oh, my God, the heat. It rivaled the glow raging in her lower belly. She felt tormented inside and outside.

He stopped touching her there and went back to concentrating on just her leg. A nice, slow, deep massage, while in another part of her, the heat turned into a pulsing yearning. Helen wanted to scream. She wanted his hands higher, back where it was deliciously on fire. But he ignored her for what seemed like hours.

She heard herself panting. The tingle had grown into a roaring fire of need. He ignored her, totally absorbed in ministering to her leg.

Please. Higher, please. She wasn't going to beg. She wasn't going to let him know she was unbearably excited by being in his control.

She gritted her teeth as the heat teased her like an invisible hand. The yearning was unbearably erotic, driving her crazy, making her weak with desire. Her whole body grew tired of fighting the strange and wonderful sensations that had been attacking her all night. She desperately wanted to give in to them.

And still he ignored her. He was an excellent masseur. An arrogant, manipulating bastard, but an excellent masseur nonetheless. She couldn't stand it any longer.

"You could try…" lost in sensation, she was unable to form a coherent sentence "…asking. Apparently you don't know how to do that."

He paused from his massage of her leg. "Yes."

"Hades!"

He had inserted a finger inside her. He wasn't waiting for an answer.

"I'm asking. Say yes, Elena."

His way of asking was unfair and unethical. She must have mumbled those words; she wasn't sure. The pulsing heat caused by the lotion, his slow and knowing hand, every fiber in her was shouting yes. She was drowning, her mind steeped in pleasure, and not caring to come up for air.

"Be persuasive, Elena. Innovative negotiation, as all GEM operatives know," he mocked her. "Sometimes, no words are needed, sweetheart."

To make his point, he scooted lower in her bed and leaned down. Helen could only watch helplessly as his head dipped in slow motion, as if giving her a chance to stop him. She couldn't. She wanted him. Too late. His mouth made contact where his hand had been, his tongue taking over what his fingers had been doing.

Helen squeezed her eyes shut. Too much. No, it was just right. It was very obvious that he knew how to please a woman. He kissed her like a lover who knew his partner's body too well, nibbling the sensitive flesh and rolling his tongue lazily across her nub. Over and over. He was thorough as he built the pleasure to a feverish pitch, guiding her to that edge of madness.

Biting down on her lower lip, she let out a long mewing groan throatily as an orgasm crashed through her like rolling thunder. Her body had wanted this for so long that it was determined to keep the orgasm going for as long as it could, fighting her need for control, sweeping her and holding her in a haze of pleasure until she thought she would die from not breathing.

"Is that a yes?" His husky voice finally penetrated her senses, a soft hush over the monotone of the sound wave from the brain entrainment machine.

She was still trying to catch her breath, her body giving small spasms as the pleasure lingered. And lingered. She was still hot, the heat building up again. She made another sound of rage when he blew on her softly.

"No answer?" he mocked. "But I have all night to persuade you. More?"

More meant more lotion. His hands were all over her, traveling slickly up her belly, under her T-shirt to her torso, till he cupped both her breasts possessively. He played with her nipples as his mouth went back to pleasuring her. The lotion took effect almost immediately, overwhelming her until all she could feel was the heat, his hands and his mouth.

By the time he'd stopped, she was weak from pleasure and desire, and still she remained unsatiated, as her body ached for more. She wanted more.

He slid up her body. She heard a sharp tear and registered vaguely that he was destroying her favorite old T-shirt. His mouth caught her right nipple, pulled on it with his teeth. Just like in the dream. Oh, God. Only the heat was doubling the pleasure. And also the hunger.

"Please," she gasped out, no longer caring about pride.

He slid up higher. "Is that a yes?"

She would think of revenge another time. Right now, there was another urgent need, one that had nothing to do with maiming or kicking or any of the horrible, painful things she'd thought of doing to his body.

"Yes," she panted out. "Yes, yes, yes. Happy now?"

"Only if you are, sweet Elena. No more negotiations and no more words."

And with that his legs parted hers even more and he reached down. She felt him nudging her. Probing. Invasive. Oh. Oh.

"Ohhhh…"

She had never felt like this before. Her heightened state of sensitivity, along with the heat from the lotion, and the inexorable friction of flesh against flesh, brought on another instant orgasm as he pushed inside her. For a long moment he lay on top, chest to chest, stomach to stomach, his breath warm on the side of her face, flexing inside her, evidently enjoying her body's internal rhythmic response.

"I like the real thing better," he finally said, and started moving.

She moaned as he pulled out, desperate to circle her arms around his waist and pull him back. Every stroke was agonizing delight. It was as if he was driving heat into her and it was spreading like wildfire. Uncontrollable. Burning down every one of her mental defenses and barriers.

He laced his hands with hers and she felt her arms moving outward and upward till they were over her head. At the same time he pushed deep inside her. His mouth bit her neck, sucking gently at another sensitive spot.

Spread-eagled, vulnerable, and she didn't care. She cried out again when he pulled out.

"Shhh. We have a few hours, Elena. Patience."

His promise didn't sound comforting at all.

Eighteen

He smiled in the dark. He would have to report to the agency that their new topical analgesic with their experimental bio-DMSO had been a resounding success. DMSO, an antioxidant, had the ability to penetrate nerve fibers and administer a drug deeply into an inflammation, but although tasteless, it had a telltale smell. Not this version. This one, as far as he could tell, was doing just fine.

Just as fine as the moaning woman under him. He liked the sound of her calling his name. She had a sexy way of hiccupping. And he wanted to taste her again.

That was what had been missing from all these months of watching her. Her taste, the sound of her real voice, her scent—these tactile things were not the same in virtual reality. Now he couldn't get enough of tasting her.

And she needed the topical analgesic for her injury. It relaxed the nerves and he could work on her soreness. Only he'd crossed the line again, administering it somewhere else. It worked very well there, too.

Holding still inside her, he enjoyed the feel of her multiple orgasms, teasing and squeezing him. She was slick and wet from pleasure. Judging from how sensitive she still was, keeping her there for a while would be easy enough.

He carefully pulled her body till her legs dangled off the bed. "This is going to hurt a little, sweetheart. But it'll only be for a moment. Just tell me when it starts hurting."

He spread her thighs. Wider. He stopped when she winced. He used his knee to keep her that way as he rubbed the lotion up and down the inside of her right thigh, and then, what was left on his hands, *there*.

"Hades—" She was silent for a few moments, her breathing quickening. "What is that you have?"

"It's good for inflammation," he told her truthfully.

"*You're* the inflammation," she muttered. "Oh…"

"Because I want to distract you while I do this," he said, beginning to massage her injured leg again. Also, because he liked to hear her moan and hiccup. "Have to keep you relaxed while the agent delivers the steroid so you'll heal quicker, love, and stop any internal bleeding."

"Oh, stop sounding like you're giving me a damn lecture, Hades. You aren't my doctor and…and…" Her voice became breathless.

"You mean, your doctor doesn't do this to you?" he asked helpfully, leaning forward and probing her wet slit with the head of his penis. He smiled slyly at the sound of her hiccup. At the same time, he extended her injured leg up higher, testing it. She didn't seem to feel any discomfort from that as he buried his length inside her.

He closed his eyes, enjoying the feel of her as he moved in her shallowly. Her heat beat at him, tempting him to go faster. But he didn't know when he would be able to do this again and he meant to enjoy her.

He supposed it would be all right to reveal his identity to her soon. After all, she had passed the test given by the department heads. Once this operation was wrapped up, with the SEED *and* both the Cummings in custody, all operations would be for COMCEN and not to prove to some funding committee. Then, he could introduce himself to Elena in person.

He extended her injured leg even farther, until her toes tickled his jawline. It allowed him to push in even deeper. The soft moan coming from her lips didn't sound like her leg was giving her any pain at the moment.

Or maybe he wouldn't tell her after all. He remained in that position, not moving, as he ran his knuckles up and down her thigh, feeling and searching. Satisfied that there were no more knots of tension that might block the medication from working its way into the injured tissues, he then turned his full attention to the owner of the leg.

"I'm done with your injury, miss," he mocked her, knowing it would infuriate her to point out her helplessness. "Is there any other place where you need my attention?"

"You can…go to hell," she told him.

He laughed. "But I'm in hell," he told her, smiling. "You mean, you want me out of hell."

"Stop teasing me, Hades," she said, her voice low and smoky. "Either move or take it out. Something. You're…I can't take this anymore."

A voice like that could make a man come. Maybe it was good that he didn't hear her real voice that much. But having had her, it would be hard to not come back and taste her again. Either way, he meant to have his fill tonight.

Silently, he answered her plea. Her breathing became small gasps as his thrusts grew longer and harder. Faster. He felt his blood heating up, rushing through him as he sank deeper and deeper. All her heat absorbing all of his, taking his passion inside her and giving him hers.

Afterwards, he laid his face against her heaving breasts, breathing in her scent. His tongue darted out, lazily licking one of those mounds. Sweet and spicy Elena. He was not ready to leave her.

"I still can't move," she said and he smiled at the satiated drawl.

"That's because this session isn't over yet," he told her, kissing his way down her flat stomach. Sweet. Spicy. Tangy.

He cupped the sexy cheeks of her ass and concentrated on taking care of business. He smiled wickedly as the woman in his care hiccupped his name and called him all sorts of other names. He ignored them and her expletives became moans.

He could come to enjoy doing this a lot.

Soft and warm. Pleasant. Helen stretched, turning over with a soft, satiated hum. She burrowed deeper into her pillow.

She wanted to sleep the day away. What a wonderful night of... She came fully awake.

"Fuck!" she cursed out loud as she scrambled to a sitting position, looking around wildly.

Of course she was alone. It had been a dream. Her freaking weird mood yesterday had caused—she caught sight of her torn T-shirt lying on the floor.

"Fuck!" she said again. She looked under the covers, then flopped onto her back, staring up at the ceiling.

She didn't know what to think. Last night. Oh, my. Last night.

Hades had been here and he had—she closed her eyes at the thought of everything he'd done to her last night. And she was shocked at herself. She had liked the things he'd done. More than liked.

She should be mad. The man had taken advantage of her. She had been fighting that sensitivity all those hours and he'd appeared and… Her face burned from the memory of how intimate they had been.

She looked up and caught sight of the red blinking light of the camera. Her chin automatically went up. Was he watching? Of course he was.

"Pervert," she called out, trying to summon up some anger. She couldn't. Apparently, total relaxation wasn't conducive to anger. She sighed reluctantly. And a good night of hot, mind-blowing sex with a faceless man.

She rubbed her eyes with the heel of her hands, wondering how she was going to face a debriefing session today with these memories playing havoc with her mind. What was wrong with her? The thought of someone drugging her like that and doing the things he did should put her in a rage. But she had wanted Hades, had—she growled in disgust—begged for him to continue. Had said yes, yes, yes.

She looked at the blinking camera again. "It was under duress," she yelled out. She wouldn't have said yes if he hadn't… That brought back another host of memories of what he had actually done to make her say "yes, yes, yes," and she didn't want to go there.

Touching her ears, she realized that her earbuds weren't in. She turned. They were by the brain entrainment machine, which was off. She frowned. She really had fallen asleep like a log.

Determinedly, she slid out of bed, not caring that she was naked. He'd obviously seen her like that before, so why was she blushing like a virgin, dammit? *Because he'd touched and kissed her everywhere last night. Because she couldn't forget where his mouth and hands had been.*

She was not going to let him have the satisfaction of seeing how much she remembered. She halted midway to the restroom and looked down curiously at her leg. She had been walking very quickly; she wasn't limping or feeling any pain. There was a huge bruise starting to show up the whole side of her leg but—she turned it one way, then another—only slight discomfort. No pain.

In the bathroom, she looked at her reflection and made a face. She touched her neck and shivered at the memory of teeth biting her. The sensitivity—it was still there, but not edgy like before.

She quickly washed up and pulled a towel around her before stepping back into the room. Someone would be coming up here to check on her soon and she had a feeling the room would betray the previous night's activities. She groaned. She hadn't been exactly quiet during the whole thing either. God.

Her bed looked innocent enough, one indentation on the pillow, the sheets a little rumpled. Easy to explain.

She hadn't been able to move, that's why! She could feel her cheeks heating up again as she stared at the bed, as she pictured herself lying there in the dark. Helpless. Totally in his power. He had applied something on her, turning everything into a world of ⌐ ısations—the heat, the soft caresses, his tongue. Oh, my God, his tongue. Had she really lain there for hours and let him explore her so intimately like that?

She closed her eyes, remembering too clearly how it had been. All night. She hadn't gotten enough after the first time, and he had been willing to give her what she'd wanted over and over again. He had made love to her with his mouth till she had finally fallen asleep from exhaustion and satiation. Her last thought had been that she didn't mind not being able to move if he'd keep doing that forever.

Helen shook her head. She had lust in her brain. And she'd better get herself back under control because there was a full day ahead.

The intercom's buzz brought her back to reality. She crossed the room to answer it. It was Dr. Kirkland, of course. She'd better screw her head back on tightly because today was debriefing day. She sighed. Great choice of word, Helen.

An hour and forty-five minutes later, with a big breakfast in her, she felt almost back to normal. Dr. Kirkland had examined her injury, touching her bruise and the surrounding area, gently probing. It still felt slightly prickly to have someone touching but at least that strange traveling electrical tingling wasn't happening. She even felt comfortable enough to discuss it with Dr. Kirkland. He listened to her description quietly.

"It's still present, sort of," she told him when he asked whether the sensation was gone. "It's never happened before when I remote viewed so, yeah, I'd say it has to do with the serum."

Of course he knew about her visitor. Figured. He had to be told since he was her doctor. She commended herself for looking nonchalant when he brought the subject up.

"I would have recommended trying the dimethyl sufoxide substitute today if you were unable to walk."

Helen looked Dr. Kirkland squarely in the eye, as if nothing out of the ordinary happened. "My monitor introduced whatever it was to me."

She didn't mention the dark. Or the other parts of the introduction. She didn't think her monitor would supply those details as well. She knew him that well, at least.

"It's a compound that we've been working on that emulates the properties of a commercial solvent."

"I've heard of DMSO," she told him, surprised that she could even recall any of the conversation from the previous night. "I have a friend who was a weight lifter and he told me about its use, especially for painful injured tissues."

Dr. Kirkland nodded. "Oh yes, it was quite popular among weight lifters for a while. They're always the first to try out controversial products." He picked up his chart. "So, no need for any painkillers today and we'll monitor your leg carefully. I've reviewed the tape of what that man in the elevator did. You were lucky he didn't pull it in the other direction or you'd have a broken leg today instead."

Helen cocked her head. "But I'd have been able to walk on it, probably." She laughed at the doctor's expression. "I wouldn't have known, Doc. I didn't feel anything at that point."

"That's the very real danger of the serum," he said. "I'm going to double-check on the dosage and compare it with the other testee's body weight. There must be an answer to your problem."

Hell chose not to go into that particular subject again. "In an operation where I may have been alone and needed to get out of Dodge, perhaps it could save me from being caught," she said instead, giving him a wry smile. "Pain can be an impediment to saving my own life."

Dr. Kirkland smiled back. "You two are getting too in sync. Your monitor said those exact words to me last night." He checked his wristwatch. "This morning, I mean."

"And one of these days, you'll slip up and say his name and I'll know his identity," Helen said lightly. "Right, Doc?"

"You know the protocol to a successful experiment, Hell," he said, as he squiggled onto her medical chart. "There are different parts, some of which are meant to ensure that the testee isn't skewing the results by giving expected answers."

"Doc, I've already passed the remote viewing with flying colors. They have the key to prove it," she pointed out.

"Maybe there are other tests," Dr. Kirkland said. "You can bring this up with your monitor in the next VR session."

Seeing Hades so soon? Even in VR? She gulped. "When?"

Thank goodness Dr. Kirkland didn't see her reaction. "After debriefing and a break. He wants another remote viewing session done today."

"Well, that explains the absence of coffee at breakfast," Helen said, as nonchalantly as she could manage.

Nineteen

Helen mentally repeated their names. Alex Diamond, Shahrukh Kingsley (oh, fitting name for Big Swimming Guy), Michael Hunter—a shock to hear Flyboy's real name—and he winked at her, with that smile that had probably generated a few thousand female sighs, Jack Sullivan, Armando Chang, looking half-asleep, Heath Cliffe (she arched her eyebrows slightly at his name, too, his brown eyes lighting up with amusement when she gave him a bland stare as his gaze traveled down to her leg), and Jed McNeil—is the man attached to that denim jacket?

They were the official COS commandos. She knew four of the original were killed in action during that mission a few years back, and only two of those positions had been filled—Jack Sullivan and Armando. They were finally formally introduced to her as a group, a sign that she was now part of the team. Right? She wasn't sure,

Then there was Drew De Clerq, the team coordinator. She found out that he was just acting operations chief in the mission she had been on. Operations chief was actually Alex Diamond's title. How interesting. When GEM and COMCEN formed a merger, T., her operations chief, had comanaged Alex's job with different commandos when he went missing.

At the moment, her chief, taking a seat across from her, was studiously avoiding looking at Alex Diamond throughout the introductions. Or at least, it seemed that way to Helen. She wanted to laugh. Those two reminded her of two lions in a mating ritual. It took the beasts forever to get together but when they did—

She hid a smile.

"Any questions about who is who, Hell?" De Clerq asked.

Yeah, which one of you came to my room last night? Helen shook her head. *Don't go there now.* "No, I'm very happy to make your acquaintance," she drawled out in a Southern accent. "I've heard so much but never seen all of you together."

It was true. For a team, these men didn't seem to hang out together much. They liked their space too much, she figured. All wild beasts chained together by...by what? She wasn't sure yet, but she was going to find out one of these days.

"How are you feeling?" Alex asked. "I read in the initial report that you've been attacked by several hostiles. And shot at."

"Tranqued, actually," Heath interrupted, "and she kept running."

"So whoever that was waiting outside wasn't there to kill her," chimed in Shahrukh.

Helen took a good look at Shahrukh. Big Swimming Guy. This was the first time she'd seen him this close-up. Dressed in a light orange cotton Indian shirt with elaborate Eastern embroidery, he was the most exotic-looking man she'd met, with his longish wavy locks of black hair and fierce deep-set black eyes. As usual, an image of him wearing some kind of medieval leather armor and swinging a big broadsword floated into her mind. He spoke with a slight accent that she couldn't place. Maybe Turkish, with that name.

"Then it's someone who knows about our Hell," Flyboy said.

Helen looked from one man to the other. Our Hell? She caught T.'s amused gaze. She really had to ask her chief how she'd dealt working with these beasts on her own all these years.

"It's also someone who wants to stop our Hell," Jed said.

Did she imagine it or was there just a slight note of mockery in that man's small emphasis of *our?* She was finding it difficult to keep her mind from wondering about each of these men because of last night. Well, she was human. Of course she was going to think about that!

However, she was also the newest "member" here. She had to at least give the impression that she could keep up with the boys without staring at each of them and trying to see them naked. She stared down at her notepad. Now why did she think of that? It immediately put her mind to feverish work. Not good, especially when—

"What's your take on this, Agent Roston?" Jed asked.

Especially when she was expected to speak on serious matters. "Maybe they were testing me, too," she muttered.

"And who are these 'they' that you have in mind?"

Helen glanced up at Jed McNeil sharply. Those weird silver eyes could be so unnerving to look at, especially if they looked back as if they knew exactly what she was thinking at that moment.

"These people appear to know about me, so I'm going to assume that they know about the experiment. If it's not an insider, or someone who has somehow gotten leaked information, then it's the other agencies," she said.

"Oh great, you have to bring up all the agencies. That really narrows it down," Jack Sullivan spoke up for the first time.

Helen shrugged. She had never talked to Sullivan, so she couldn't tell whether he was being sarcastic. He looked the most normal of the whole group, actually. Not that average meant ugly or anything, not with that square jaw, boy-next-door attractiveness, and football-star build. He just looked like a regular American boy, with his backward cap and wrinkled flannel shirt.

"Just throwing out possibilities," she said.

"We can narrow it down to agencies which have similar remote viewing programs," T. said quietly. "I have something that's of interest to Hell and Dr. Kirkland."

Helen turned to her chief as the latter pulled out sheets of paper and passed them around. She frowned as she read the page given to her. She looked up when she was done. It was about the ring T. had taken back from her.

"The ring? An…energy alarm?" she asked.

T. nodded. "At GEM, we have info that years ago the

CIA created energy alarms at some point during their remote-viewing program when they were fully funded that could detect the presence of remote viewers who might be spying on their meetings. I suppose they were paranoid after their own CIA-trained operatives were successful in penetrating other agencies. Intel has also shown that this paranoia was also present in other countries. We have quite a lot of information on the old KGB programs. They were also experimenting with high-tech energy deflectors. I'm sure Dr. Kasparov is familiar with early versions of it, if we ask him."

"So according to your chart here, the ring you gave me was responsible for that seizure or whatever it was that happened in the stairwell?" Helen scratched the side of her forehead. Her head was actually aching a little from the memory of it. "It's not the serum, then. But why didn't you tell me?"

T. shook her head. "First, you shouldn't have felt anything, Hell. It's not an alarm system to warn the remote viewer. When the CIA had it installed in their secret rooms, it acted as a deflector. They'd tested it with their own remote viewers at that time. None were able to get enough information about the meeting when it was happening or 'see' the room the usual remote-viewing way, according to the papers, and none reported any seizures or reaction like the one you had. This test was repeated several times through the years, and other than a good success rate of blocking out unwanted entities in their meetings, there were no reports of it being a health hazard to the CIA viewers."

"Okay, my RV classes must have forgotten to warn me about energy alarms," Helen said. "You're telling me that these things can stop me, too, and yet they didn't try this on us when we were training?"

"No, she didn't say that," Alex Diamond cut in. "Tasha's only affirming the fact that the CIA had a good success rate of blocking out unwanted entities in their meetings at that time."

Her chief's blink of surprise didn't escape Helen's notice. Why did Alex still refer to her as Tasha, when she was Tess now? Tasha was just one of T.'s many personas.

"So what's wrong with my logic that it can stop me, too?" Helen countered.

"Because the CIA never established the fact that they'd stopped any other remote viewers except their own," Alex said. "If they did, Tasha would have said so in this report, isn't that right, T.?"

Ooooh. Back to T.

T. smiled. Helen noticed she didn't even glance in Alex's direction. "That's right," she agreed. "With new technology, we've managed to create a miniature version and we were charting Helen's and her monitor's surroundings just to test how sensitive it is, and whether it works."

"Apparently it does," Alex said, "and apparently, according to the activity in the chart here, the same time Hell had that attack, we can establish a new fact, that there are remote viewers who sense it differently."

"No, it establishes that something set off GEM's version of the energy alarm and when that happened, it triggered some kind of reaction in Agent Roston," T. said.

"Would that something be another entity, let's say, and can GEM's people establish that there was another remote viewer in the area and somehow that bothered Agent Roston?" Alex asked, in a very polite voice.

"I'm taking care of it," T. replied, and for the first time, she looked at Alex.

"You didn't bring this up last night when we were being updated about what happened to Helen in the stairwell."

Helen's own tension meter went up about ten notches watching those two eye each other. She could safely rule out Alex Diamond as the person in her room last night, that was for sure.

"I wasn't sure since we haven't run tests on the ring yet," T. said, her beautiful eyes narrowing slightly.

"I meant the fact that GEM has this kind of device in its possession and that you have given one to one of our operatives to wear. I thought GEM was our partner?"

Helen's gaze quickly swept around the table once, gauging the other commandos' reactions. They seemed to be sitting back and watching, enjoying it as much as she was. Obviously, like her, they'd never seen T. on the verge of losing a battle.

Her chief leaned back in her chair. "We aren't full partners in everything, Alex. I realize that the merger was done in your absence and you probably don't have the full details, but the written agreement is somewhere in this building, I'm sure. GEM has retained quite a bit of its independence, and—" she paused, before continuing softly "—will continue to do so with its operatives."

Whoa, T. had drawn first blood. No way were they arguing about her and GEM operatives. There was a wealth of hidden challenges in this exchange for an interested observer to mine and sieve. No one said a word during the small silence that followed.

"Nonetheless, Agent Roston is our operative, as per her contract, and your giving her that device meant you'd kept certain information to yourself that could have jeopardized our operation, and future missions as well. As a partner, it's your responsibility as co-operations chief to at least tell the operations chief on the COMCEN side about certain things that might affect the ongoing operation. I'll, of course, bring this up as a suggestion during the council meeting between our agencies, but I think this is an issue we could easily solve during our own personal time."

Helen bit her lower lip. T. sharing information with Alex Diamond would mean meeting or talking with the man a lot more, and from all accounts, T. had been keeping her distance, in some case, even keeping several continents between herself and Alex Diamond.

She had to give it to Alex Diamond, though. She'd never seen a man able to keep T. on her toes. She wanted to snicker at the "personal" time comment. She wasn't going to sit by and not help out her chief, though. After all, T. had shown up to help her last night. She cleared her throat, tapping the tip of her pen on the paper in front of her, as if to make a point.

"The device, as explained here, wasn't supposed to have an effect on me but on interfering entities," Helen said. "I see it as protection gear, something like a bulletproof vest, except it was made for a remote viewer. So do you boys report on every piece of protection gear on you during an operation? I'm sure, if the device had worked normally, without my strange experience in the stairwell, this chart would have read the same. T. would have brought back the same results and none of you would care because there wouldn't have been any proof that it actually happened. So my having this reaction at the same time as shown on this chart shows that it was actually I who was interfering with the overall mission, and T. wouldn't have known that in the first place."

There was a chuckle from the end of the table. It was Flyboy. He was scratching his nose, probably hiding a grin. "What I want to know is, when are we going to be issued our very own magic decoder ring?" he queried, tongue-in-cheek.

Jack Sullivan snorted. "Rings are for sissies," he drawled. "Why don't you tell us what you've found out tracking the satellite, Flyboy, so I can get out of here and take a shower? It's gotten mighty stuffy and I'm running behind with...operation duties."

"If you'd start your day earlier, you'd have all that done already," Shahrukh said.

"Oh yeah, some of us just love the crack of dawn like you do, right, Armando?"

"Early bird catches the worm," Armando said, twiddling his pen between his fingers like a majorette's baton, "but better late than never."

"Just love a dude," Jack said blandly, "who can speak from both sides of his mouth. Let's hear the satellite findings, Flyboy."

Helen loved the exchange. It showed they were a lot more relaxed with each other than they pretended to be. She glanced over at T. Her chief was also smiling at the talking men. Helen looked back at Alex, who was studying her chief with brooding eyes. He hadn't said anything else after her own comment. It appeared that he wasn't that concerned with her "device" jeopardizing the operation after all. More likely, he just wanted to rile a reaction from T.

"Satellite tracked that van to a fake identity, of course. But it has CIA marks all over it. Easy to track when they had the vehicle delivered to a well-known CIA landing strip, you know. Why they would take the time to give a fake identity and not even bother to at least mask their entry points…"

Listening, but a little distracted by what she'd found out, Helen looked down at her ringless finger. Energy alarm. Did she somehow sense its warning through her "danger" sense? And somehow, it was amplified to the point that it affected her. Something *did* happen at that moment and it wasn't because of the serum.

The idea of another remote viewer in her vicinity had occurred to her before, and had been the subject of discussion during training. From Q and A sessions, she'd learned that it took a very high-level remote viewer to see different forms of energy, such as another remote viewer, and it took a lot of energy for one remote viewer to even communicate with another. That was why RV was a solo thing, with many remote viewers working the same event on their own, in separate modules. Too much energy working together destroyed their concentration as well as objectivity. She let go of the idea and returned her attention to the commandos.

"I'm going to call our liaison, Steve McMillan, for information from his CIA contacts at TIARA. He'll get us the names of the people who requested the use of the plane at that time."

"Do you suspect rogues or was it a sanctioned CIA operation?"

"Too early to tell. But either way, we have to deal with it. We can't have them interfering, especially with something like this. None of the big brass are going to take it seriously when the departments are fighting over remote viewers. No VIP's going to want to be arguing over that on record."

Helen frowned. The other possibility of actually being spied upon by a remote viewer from the CIA was disconcerting. It was no fun being on the other end of the game. They had trained her, so why were they after her now?

There was so much she still had to learn about her newly-acquired skill. There was so much more she didn't know. Her CIA monitor had told her that practice and time would help her achieve higher levels, even without a personal trainer. But she had Hades as her monitor now, and she had a feeling that he knew a lot more than he was telling her.

"Actually, let me talk to Nikki Harden and set up a meeting with her husband, Rick, from TIARA." Jed McNeil spoke for the first time since the meeting started. "I don't want Steve McMillan reporting back to Admiral Madison about this yet."

Helen looked at him. Nikki Harden was a retired GEM operative, a legend among her sisters because of her background. On her return from her training hiatus, she'd learned that Nikki had gotten married recently, but the details were lost among a hundred other pieces of news she had to absorb.

"I'll let her know so she expects your call, Jed," T. said. "You know she doesn't like to be surprised."

Jed's lips curled up at the corners. "Just because Diamond's spoiling your fun, you don't have to spoil mine, too."

"Darling, you're having entirely too much of that lately. Now that we've established that our attackers were actually one of our own agencies and not a foreign entity, what's our next course of action?"

"We divide into two groups. One takes care of finding out the CIA culprit. The other takes care of our current operation, which is still ongoing, by the way. We need the other half of the Cummings. He isn't to be allowed to escape or he might barter for his wife's release with his information. Heath, you've interviewed the woman, what's your take on this?"

Because it was still ongoing, Helen refrained from asking questions about the electronic key she'd retrieved. If the powers-that-be decided to test her again, she didn't want any chance of them saying that her RV was contaminated by information.

Besides, it was more interesting watching the COS commandos. Her training had isolated her for two years. She'd forgotten how much prep there was in between operations. She was also a GEM operative, essentially trained to work alone, so working with a group of men was something new. However, she hadn't been away from the field so long that she couldn't sense that these were all dangerous men. They were sitting here listening to one of their own calmly dissecting the psyche of their prisoner. "Interview," they called it. "Interrogate," T. had said last night.

She felt a small shiver running down her back at the thought of Heath Cliffe in a room alone with the woman she saw. She'd spent last night with one of them, had practically enjoyed relinquishing control to him, and for the first time, she understood a little of these men's training. It wasn't all physical strength and macho stuff like the guys against whom she'd been pitted. These men were—she searched for a word—untamed. Working outside the boundaries, and given the freedom to live in the shadows like they do, would be bound to unleash a certain wildness in a man.

Yet, studying them, she saw that they were bound to some kind of duty, or at least, they appeared to be bound by responsibility because if they weren't, they wouldn't be here. She wondered about each of these men's backgrounds—who they were and what brought them here to black operations. The more she learned about them, the more this world of shadows fit them well. Each of these men, sitting here looking so civilized around a table, was not quite tamed. The few times she'd been alone with one of them had shown her one thing. They disregarded rules and ethics when it fit their purpose, and their agenda, she realized, was never black and white. Not Armando's. Not Heath's. Not even Diamond's. And definitely not whoever Hades was.

At that precise moment, Flyboy caught her eye and signaled to her that he'd call her later. He gave her another one of his devastating smiles. When exactly had he returned from his satellite tracking? Surely it hadn't taken that long once he found out that the CIA used one of their own secret landing strips? She smiled back sweetly. They were her wild beasts and she would learn to train them.

CIA secret medical facility

The voices were faint but he heard them. They were discussing their next step. It always paid to pretend not to be aware of everything.

"They'll track back to our department but I think we're safe for now. They're going to think it's the RV department anyway."

"I can't believe she's that good. She's just achieved Level Two, according to the reports."

"Yes, but don't forget it's her physical training that's gotten her out of this. She beat out the rest of the candidates, you know, so she's got to be damn good."

"What we need is to find one of these candidates and get him to kill her for us. We can't afford this. She's a threat to our network in the CIA, even more so than the fucking admiral's internal investigations and committee overviews."

"We need to lay low for a while. We have our own remote viewer, hell, a whole hospital of them, if we need more. We have our own serum. We have what we need to counter any of their moves, if they're going to use her to spy on our activities. Don't worry. We've been around for over a decade. No one's going to dig us out that easily. Meanwhile, we have to hide him. He's still useful. Did pretty good back there."

"Yes, but look at him staring into space like a madman. Not going to last, man."

"Like I said, the facility has plenty of candidates."

He was afraid. Mad. Not that kind of mad. He wasn't a lunatic, no matter what those fuckers think. He was pissed-off mad.

All his beautiful collection of images…gone. They were gone! Ever since his remote viewing self had bumped into that woman in the stairs, ever since that awful experience—whatever it was—he hadn't been able to rewind. Empty. Like a blank tape. There wasn't one image left. Empty. That other viewer had sucked it out of him somehow.

It had been what had kept him going all these months when they'd abandoned him in this stupid hospital, the images and all those feelings he'd collected from the people from whom he'd taken them. The memories of their sex lives—how he loved the glow of their lust rushing in him. And he had collected some really sexy ones this last time too, especially from that woman everyone was after, the one who had a husband. She was mighty fine and what a hot lusty kinky babe. Always wanting sex, that one…oh the lost images! He could remember them, but who the fuck cared about memories when he couldn't rewind and taste the energy?

That woman he'd bumped into—he had to somehow find that woman and get it back. It had to be inside her still and she was probably enjoying his collection. Somehow, she'd stolen it from him. He'd heard his monitors talking about her, that she could remote view and then physically lead a team into action without her needing any downtime, so that meant she was on the serum, too, only something better. Something way stronger because she had fucking stolen his images without being in remote-viewing mode! How the fuck did she do that?

Empty. He wanted to howl, but he had to somehow behave normally after this downtime. He was just doubly depressed, that was all. He was going to convince them to give him the serum again, so he could collect some images. Then maybe he could get two doses, like before, and explore that power again. Only he had to be very careful not to let any of these fuckers know.

When he was stronger, he'd think of this woman. Find her. Take back what was his.

Twenty

Theta wavelength. First the white light. Then he appeared. A moment later, the scene appeared. He had recreated her quarters and was lounging in his perfect naked state on her bed. Bastard.

Could one blush in virtual reality? Of course, the more she thought about it, the more heated her face became.

"What's this all about, Hades?" Helen asked. She was never going to look at her bed the same again.

"A little teasing," he said, that Southern drawl she'd requested totally unsuitable now for some reason. *"Afraid?"*

"I'm not afraid of an avatar," she sniffed.

He patted the space by his side. *"Exactly. How are you walking? Are you feeling better?"* he asked solicitously, as if nothing had happened between them.

Helen glared at him. She walked up to the bed, hands on hips. *"You crossed the line last night. There was no reason for you to come into my room and...and..."*

She paused. She almost said "make love to me." That

wasn't right; she didn't even know who he was. But for some reason, she couldn't say "have sex with me" or cruder still, "fuck me." It was all her fault. How the hell did one talk to a totally naked avatar hunk that one had created out of fantasy? This was ridiculous. He had manipulated her from day one and she was blindsided by herself! It made her even madder thinking about it.

"And?" he prompted.

She was just going to have to be smarter. Think of a way out of this.

"And take advantage of me," she told him. *"I wasn't in any state to say no to you, you knew that."*

"If I hadn't known that you're attracted to me and would have wanted me before your condition, I wouldn't have come to you, Elena," he said.

"That's not fair either!" she yelled. She leaned over him, wanting to wring his neck. *"You read my mind or sensed my feelings or whatever it is that we share here in VR. Those were my thoughts and you weren't supposed to see or feel them, dammit!"*

"Those were my dreams you were invading," he pointed out quietly. *"You weren't supposed to see or feel them either."*

Helen opened her mouth, then shut it. He got her there. She sat down. *"Are you really having wet dreams about me?"*

He smiled. *"We were both very wet in that dream."*

"How did you know I was having it, too?"

His brown eyes searched hers for a moment. *"If I told you that every time I touched myself you moaned out my name, would you believe me?"*

"No, I wouldn't," Helen said. She looked at the part

of him that he could only have been touching. It was still gloriously big. She really, really had to do something about that because after last night...looking at it made her hot all over. *"You...oh man, I can't believe I'm asking this, you were...I mean..."* She coughed, trying not to think about his hand around that part. *"Never mind. I don't want to know."*

"But it affected you and you were already in a very aroused state, which is another thing we have to discuss." He shifted slightly, turning toward her. *"I don't think it's the ring that caused your problem. It had to be a combination of things. Why do you think the serum affected you that way?"*

"I don't know," she said, and added reluctantly, *"Armando Chang suggested it might be because I hadn't had sex for a long time."*

"And with the serum's dissipation, the body and brain overcompensated," Hades murmured. *"How long is a long time?"*

Helen pursed her lips. *"I'm not going to tell you anything about my sex life,"* she told him. *"And you can stop looking at me like that."*

"Like what?"

Like he was going to make love to her all over again on the bed. She had never been so aware of a man in her life. She wanted to turn and touch him the way he had touched her. She wanted to use her mouth.

"I would like that very much," he told her.

She gritted her teeth and growled. *"You see? You weren't supposed to know what I'm thinking!"*

"Actually, it's more an impression. I told you, I can't read your mind. But your feelings come through very

clearly to me." His hand reached out for her fisted one and gently uncurled her fingers. *"It's going to be all right."*

"Easy for you to say," she said. He wasn't the one thinking lustful thoughts about a make-believe persona. *"You aren't suffering from chemical overcompensation."*

"But as your monitor, I do somewhat feel it, especially when you're thinking about it." His brown eyes narrowed thoughtfully. *"It's still there. It feels similar to the surge of adrenaline after doing something dangerous and exciting."*

He tugged her closer and his hand slowly caressed her arm, his thumb drawing circles, sending little tendrils of pleasure up and down her spine. It wasn't as bad as yesterday and for some reason, she didn't mind that he was doing it to her. Yesterday, she hadn't wanted anyone touching her at all.

His eyes closed and he added, *"No wonder you didn't want anyone to touch you. Even at this mild stage, I can feel it. It feels like a man would feel when he gets aroused. And it being ten times worse yesterday, I'd say it probably felt like my avatar with a hard-on all day, with no release in sight."*

Helen watched him lying on "her" bed. It occurred to her that he had deliberately chosen this scene to make her uncomfortable enough so that he could "read" her feelings. He had guessed that she wouldn't tell him, so he'd set out to find out his own way. The mind behind the avatar was calculating and devious and he knew her too well.

"Yeah, well, now I know what it feels like to walk around with a big dick," she said sarcastically. *"Happy now?"*

He laughed and pulled her on top of him. *"I'm happier if you feel the dick inside you actually,"* he said with an evil gleam in his eye. *"It seems that you still need more therapy. Maybe I'll come by again tonight."*

"I won't be surprised a second time," she warned.

"Maybe you'll take the pill willingly," he teased.

"Maybe pigs could fly. You're just afraid that if I touch you, I'll know exactly who you are."

She liked being on top of him, except this wasn't real. Her brain was telling her that but her body didn't seem to care one bit. He felt real, almost as real as last night.

"Of course," he acknowledged, *"but I also liked having you totally helpless. It's exciting."*

"That's because you're also a controlling bastard. You're probably into dominant and submissive sex games." Her eyes narrowed. Didn't T. hint last night that Heath liked that kind of thing? *"Are you?"*

His lips quirked. *"You'll just have to find out."*

"We can't do this all the time," she said. *"I'm not going to let it happen."*

"But if I was really a dominant, you'd have no say in the matter, would you?" he asked, amused. *"I'll just take you where I want, however I please."*

It was just a stupid conversation in virtual reality but his words sounded like a promise. She should be pissed off with him but how do you get angry at something that was making you excited?

"Besides," he added, *"we can't have you walking around feeling agitated and craving sex, can we? There are at least seven men out there who are too willing to*

*take you to bed, Elena, if you ask them. Do you really
want to do that because you suspect one of them is
me?"*

*"Of course not! And I'm not walking around craving
sex either! This thing's going to go away and I'll be fine
when it's over. You're crazy if you think I was going to
have sex with any guy just because I'm feeling this
way."*

*"But temptation can grow and yesterday, without
control or understanding of why you felt the way you
did, who knows? If I were walking around with a hard-
on all day, I'd look for a woman."*

"But not just any woman, I hope?" She was going
to put a fist in his nice flat stomach any moment now.

He smiled. *"No, not just any woman. Just as you didn't
go for just any man. You fought it. I can feel you still
fighting it, but it's not going away because it isn't a rash,
sweetheart. It isn't something a pill can fix. And if that's
the side effect from the serum each time you use it…"*

Helen stared at him, speechless for a few seconds.
"No," she finally said. *"If the overcompensating theory
is true, then at some point, I'd have had enough sex that
I…uh…stop smiling like that!"*

He had cleverly manipulated the conversation again.
If it was true, then she was going to need to have sex to
offset this…effect…her body was creating, and he was
pointing out that she could either go out and find herself
a lover or just have him. The idea of going out to find
a lover just because she needed to have sex was totally
out of the question. Tasteless. So like a man. Ugh.

"It wouldn't be just sex with me," he said softly. *"We
aren't strangers. In fact, you have access to me that few*

*people do. And when this need of yours is over, you won't
have to say any awkward goodbye to your lover because
I'm just an avatar in a program. You just have to make
sure you have enough sex from then on, of course."*

Helen began to laugh helplessly. *"This is the most
ridiculous proposition I've ever had in my life."* Virtual
reality was going to drive her into the nuthouse. A naked
man she'd created in a program was telling her how to
run her love life. *"You're just very lucky it wasn't a lack
of PMS my body's overcompensating or you're going
to have the biggest bitch walking around in virtual
reality."*

Her dream avatar actually shuddered. *"Thank the
gods for blessing me with your problem, then,"* he said.

Without warning, he twisted her onto her back. She
looked up at him in surprise. Surely not here. Not now—

*"Your quarters are all gray. Perfect for a remote
viewing session. I need you to find Mr. Cummings. I
know it's difficult to locate a person, but perhaps you
can describe the surroundings like before and I can
recognize the place."*

Helen gasped as she felt his legs spreading hers apart.
She felt heated flesh against hers and looked down. She
was naked! How was that possible?

"It's my virtual reality, too," he murmured, *"and I
know how you feel under me now. I know how you taste.
What it's like to be inside you. How your breast really
feels in my hand."*

She hadn't thought of it that way. It had always been
her virtual reality. He had allowed her to control that for
long enough that she hadn't thought about what he
could do to her, that she was his avatar here.

"Wait..." she said.

But he was familiar with her body, and he knew that she was still sensitive. Worse, he knew how she liked to be touched and he was doing it all over again, his fingers readying her as his head dipped down to nibble the side of her breast. His tongue traced a sensuous pattern up the slope before leisurely licking her nipple.

Even worse, this time she could move, and she didn't push him away or beat him to a pulp. Instead, she did what she wanted to do last night. She ran her hands through his hair, pulling his head closer.

He kissed his way up her neck as his fingers searched for a more intimate part of her, found it, and began a rhythmic caress that had her squirming.

He kissed her earlobe, bit it, and whispered, *"Checkered flag, sweet Elena. I promise to finish this when you get back."*

"You...are...such a bas...tard," she managed to gasp out. He had set off her remote view trigger code.

She opened her eyes. She was in her race car, going into the ether. The feel of him, the thought of him, the need for him. It was his link into her consciousness and he'd deliberately set it all up. She could feel him with her as she zoomed into the ether. She had been sexually imprinted and there was nothing she could do about it. She was virtually his.

Helen looked around her apartment restlessly. She had a few days off. She should be taking advantage of the free time to do the stuff she enjoyed, like gardening and reading. Marlena, one of her GEM sisters, was in town and called to ask whether she wanted to go out shopping and do some catching-up.

Helen would love a girls' day out; Marlena was great company and had tons to tell her. The fact that Nikki was pregnant, for one. Helen made a note to buy something for the baby shower. Marlena also commiserated with her about working in a team, especially with that team.

"Alex Diamond's a horrible man. Manipulative and ruthless," she sniffed over the phone.

Helen smiled. Alex Diamond? Horrible? That meant Marlena had had a run-in of sorts with the man and had lost. One had to read between the lines with M. "What about the others? Tell me what you know."

"I haven't dealt with too many of them, just mostly a few minutes here and there. Ask T. and Vivi about Armando Chang. They're sort of buddies with him. Shahrukh is a good guy, if there's such a thing when it comes to these commandos. He's always polite to me, anyway. Flyboy's a flirt, but you'd know that by now. Heath...well...hmm, Heath. Let's just say Stash doesn't like Heath because Heath always stands too close to me."

Helen had yet to meet Stash, the man who had snared her friend. She had to admit that she was curious about him, too. Finding out that M. was married had shocked her. Marlena was about as elusive as T. when it came to relationships. "When will I get to meet this Stash? I'm sorry I missed your wedding. I have a gift and I feel bad that I can't see you today to give it to you."

"Helen, drop whatever it is you're doing and come with me. There's nothing like shopping to soothe the soul," Marlena had advised. "A beautiful outfit, the right pair of shoes, the finest underwear, and you'll forget about those damn commandos at COMCEN."

She'd taken a rain check, using her RV downtime as an excuse. "I'm still dealing with the serum in my system. Let me sleep it off. In a couple of days, M.?"

But she couldn't sleep. That edgy feeling was teasing her like an itch; the more she ignored it, the more it bothered her. Yeah, she'd better stay at home until it went away.

However, the only way to get rid of it, it seemed, was giving in to it, and she was definitely not going to call Dr. Kirkland to tell Hades that her problem was still a problem.

She shook her head. It was good to have a few days to herself, get her head screwed back on, and figure out how to beat this thing. Armando's explanation made sense, but she had a feeling that there was more going on than just her body chemistry overcompensating. She couldn't rid herself of the nagging feeling that it had to do with her weird experience in the stairwell.

According to the chart, there was a spike in the energy reading from the ring T.'d given her at about the same moment she went blind. No, she didn't actually go blind; it was sort of—Helen frowned, trying to recall the sensation—like rain water splattering on glasses, except more gooey. She shuddered. Yeah, gooey was the right word there. Something sticky and alien colliding into, then slithering, inside her.

Helen sat up, eyes widening. If the energy alarm really somehow blocked a remote viewer from sensing certain things, then that meant a remote viewer in that area couldn't have seen her. Could it be that his or her "shadow" form had unwittingly crashed through her as he or she ran down the stairwell?

Helen pinched the bridge of her nose. She was giving herself a headache with this. But if it was true, how did that cause her to feel like she did now? The idea was too far-fetched, but everything in TIVRRV was far-fetched, so what was one more theory?

She shivered again at the thought of that odd invasive sensation. She didn't like that feeling at all. It was as if her whole warning system was screaming danger...as if there was an intruder.

An intruder. Inside her. Helen bit her lip. Did he or she leave something behind? Was that why she didn't feel like herself?

She walked around her living room, trying to shake off the restlessness. Her mind kept wandering back to Hades. His touch. His dreams of her that invaded her own. His manipulation of her.

Sitting down at her laptop, she activated the program that had created her avatar. This had been the beginning of his manipulation of her, dammit. She had taken the bait like a hungry fish.

She studied the avatar, the tall and blond creation with the chocolate eyes. She made a face at the obvious and then grinned at the thought of making it tiny and ineffective. But that was part of NOPAIN, manipulating the subject to participate, even in anger or retaliation. If she continued playing with the avatar's sexuality, even in fun, she was just continuing her own sexual imprint by him.

But she couldn't help herself. Avoiding the lower

part of the body, she jerked the wireless mouse back and forth, playing with the avatar's facial features. Changing the hairstyle shorter.

Helen closed her eyes. Dark hair. That fit that personality. Eyes? Dark? Black? Leaner body?

His hands. She didn't want to think of his hands, but that was what connected her to him physically. She could remember his touch—every intimate detail. He had very powerful hands; he'd shifted her body on her bed effortlessly. And talented lips and tongue. She remembered those too well.

Helen licked her lips, feeling flushed as she remembered her pleasure from that night. God, she wanted his hands on her again, virtual or not. But he was...

Water. She smelt the sea. And then she saw a man lying there. Dying. She was sure he was dying. A man turned toward her. Her vision got cloudy and she blinked hard, trying to focus. Must. Try. To. See. She took a step forward. Hard to breathe, as if the air was very thick here.

Okay, calm down, Helen. Step back. Step away. Oh, my God.

At the last second, Helen turned and ran. She felt herself sinking, falling into oblivion. But not before she told herself to remember what she saw.

Faded blue jeans.

Silver eyes.

Oh, my God. Not. Him.

The sizzling sequel to *Virtually His*
by acclaimed author

GENNITA LOW

Elite operative Helen "Hell" Roston is mastering a cutting-edge
form of espionage that combines virtual reality with
mind synchronization. Her highly skilled trainer, Jed McNeil,
guides her through dangerous missions for COS Command.

But McNeil is the last man Hell wants inside her mind
and in control of her body. He may be an experienced agent
but he's still a rival, and Hell can't quite trust him completely....

VIRTUALLY HERS

"[Low's] hard-edged, gritty and romantic books
are genuine thrill rides."
—*Romantic Times BOOKreviews* on
The Hunter (starred review)

Available the first week of August 2007
wherever paperbacks are sold!

New York Times bestselling author

SUZANNE FORSTER

Alison Fairmont Villard wakes in a hospital bed with a
face she doesn't recognize and a husband she doesn't
know. Andrew Villard, a self-made millionaire, has a bright
future but a shadowy past. When he tells Alison the details
of their life together, she has no choice but to believe
him—and to accept the shocking proposal he offers.

When the veil of amnesia lifts, it's too late. Alison is caught
in a web of her own making....

The Arrangement

"Strongly recommended."
—*The Mystery Reader* on
The Lonely Girls Club (starred review)

*Available the first week of May 2007
wherever paperbacks are sold!*

MIRA®

nocturne™

IT'S TIME TO DISCOVER
THE RAINTREE TRILOGY...

There have always been those among us
who are more than human...

Don't miss the dramatic first book by
New York Times bestselling author

LINDA
HOWARD

RAINTREE:
Inferno

On sale May.

Raintree: Haunted by Linda Winstead Jones
Available June.

Raintree: Sanctuary by Beverly Barton
Available July.

REQUEST YOUR FREE BOOKS!

2 FREE NOVELS
FROM THE ROMANCE/SUSPENSE
COLLECTION PLUS 2 FREE GIFTS!

YES! Please send me 2 FREE novels from the Romance/Suspense Collection and my 2 FREE gifts. After receiving them, if I don't wish to receive any more books, I can return the shipping statement marked "cancel." If I don't cancel, I will receive 4 brand-new novels every month and be billed just $5.49 per book in the U.S., or $5.99 per book in Canada, plus 25¢ shipping and handling per book plus applicable taxes, if any*. That's a savings of at least 20% off the cover price! I understand that accepting the 2 free books and gifts places me under no obligation to buy anything. I can always return a shipment and cancel at any time. Even if I never buy another book from the Reader Service, the two free books and gifts are mine to keep forever.

185 MDN EF5Y 385 MDN EF6C

Name	(PLEASE PRINT)	
Address		Apt. #
City	State/Prov.	Zip/Postal Code

Signature (if under 18, a parent or guardian must sign)

Mail to **The Reader Service:**
IN U.S.A.: P.O. Box 1867, Buffalo, NY 14240-1867
IN CANADA: P.O. Box 609, Fort Erie, Ontario L2A 5X3

Not valid to current subscribers to the Romance Collection,
the Suspense Collection or the Romance/Suspense Collection.

Want to try two free books from another line?
Call 1-800-873-8635 or visit www.morefreebooks.com.

* Terms and prices subject to change without notice. NY residents add applicable sales tax. Canadian residents will be charged applicable provincial taxes and GST. This offer is limited to one order per household. All orders subject to approval. Credit or debit balances in a customer's account(s) may be offset by any other outstanding balance owed by or to the customer. Please allow 4 to 6 weeks for delivery.

Your Privacy: Harlequin is committed to protecting your privacy. Our Privacy Policy is available online at www.eHarlequin.com or upon request from the Reader Service. From time to time we make our lists of customers available to reputable firms who may have a product or service of interest to you. If you would prefer we not share your name and address, please check here. ☐

BOB07